Kiss me hello

GRACE BURROWES

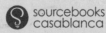

sourcebooks
casablanca

Copyright © 2015 by Grace Burrowes
Cover and internal design © 2015 by Sourcebooks, Inc.
Cover design by Dawn Adams
Cover photo © Philip Lee Harvey/Corbis

Published by Sourcebooks Casablanca, an imprint of Sourcebooks, Inc.
P.O. Box 4410, Naperville, Illinois 60567-4410
(630) 961-3900
Fax: (630) 961-2168
www.sourcebooks.com

Printed and bound in Canada.
MBP 10 9 8 7 6 5 4 3 2 1

To the children.

Chapter 1

COMPARED TO MACKENZIE KNIGHTLEY, THE NEW GIRL was small, scared, and lacked both weapons and defenses. Mac held out a hand to her in a reassuring gesture, but she turned her face away.

An eloquent rejection.

"What's her name?" Mac asked the groom, who watched from across the barn aisle.

"Luna, short for Lunatic. She doesn't strike any of us as therapeutic riding material, but Adelia will have her occasional stray."

Mac suspected Adelia had had his brother James a time or two, when James had been a different kind of stray. Adelia apparently bore James no grudge for wandering away, as strays were wont to do.

"Luna." Mac said the name softly, and saw no reaction in the mare's eyes. She looked at him steadily now, her expression showing wary resignation.

Another person, another disappointment. Mac knew the sentiment firsthand. He took a step closer. Luna raised her head a couple of inches, the better to keep him in focus.

"Has she been vetted?" Mac asked.

"What would be the point?"

Neils Haddonfield was the head groom at the Damson County Therapeutic Riding Association's barn—the barn manager, really. He was big, blond, and quiet, gentle as a lamb with the children and the horses, and hell in a muck truck with whiny parents.

"Let's see if we can make her more comfortable." Mac took the final step toward the mare and ran a hand down her neck. She gave no sign she felt the caress, so Mac went on a hunt for her sweet spots.

Females were females after all, and some things held true across species.

When his fingers dug into the coarse hair over her withers, she gave a little invisible shudder, one Mac understood, because his hand was listening for it. He settled in, gently, firmly, and the mare's head dropped a few inches. He added a second hand on the other side of her withers, and she braced her misshapen front feet wider.

"She likes that," Neils said, frowning.

"You give her any bute?" Mac asked as he moved his hands a few inches up her neck.

"A couple grams after breakfast."

The medication was helping her stand on the rubber brick surface of the barn aisle. Left to her own devices, she might well be lying flat out in the weak spring sunshine just to get off her neglected feet.

"We could put her in the stocks," Neils said. "Get it over with more quickly."

"And give her a horror of the stocks, me, and anybody who helped put her into them. I'm only making a start on those feet today. Getting her reliably sound will take months, if it can be accomplished at all. Can you take over on this side of her neck?"

Neils moved, taking up the slow massaging scratch Mac had started. The mare's expression registered the shift, but she didn't raise her head.

Mac pulled his wheeled toolbox over and ran a hand down one of the mare's legs. She stood for it, though she had to know what came next.

When he lifted her left foreleg, she let out a sigh, because shifting hundreds of pounds of body weight to the three hooves remaining on the ground had to be painful. The phenolbutazone would help, but it wouldn't eliminate the discomfort entirely.

Working quickly, he nipped off as much of the mare's overgrown toe as he dared, then set the foot gently back down. He stepped away, signaling to the horse she could take a moment to recover, while Neils kept up the scratching.

"Good girl," Mac said, extending his hand to her nose again. "You're a stoic, little Luna, and you have more in common with the riders here than you think. Give it time, and we'll find you someplace to call home."

He worked around the horse quickly but quietly, spending a few minutes on each hoof, rather than finishing one before moving on to another. She seemed to understand his method and appreciate it. By the time he ran his hand down her leg to file the final hoof into shape, she'd already shifted her weight in anticipation.

"She's sensible," Neils said, patting the shaggy neck. "Who would have thought? But then, they're all sensible for you, MacKenzie."

"One beast to another," Mac said, using his foot to nudge the wheeled toolbox away from the horse. "Do we know anything about this one besides that she's been badly neglected?"

"Adelia thinks she might have seen her a few years

ago on the Howard County circuit, and the arthritis in the feet suggests she might have been worked too long and hard over fences, but that's only a hunch."

"What are you feeding her?"

They went on, as only two horsemen can, over every detail of the mare's care. What she ought to be fed, with whom she might be safely turned out, how soon. Whether grass was a good idea, because spring grass could pack a nutritional wallop.

"I'd hand graze her," Mac said, eyeing the mare. "She needs every chance we can give her to associate people with good things. To horses, new grass is the mother of all good things."

Adelia Scoffield sauntered up in riding jeans, chaps, and a short-sleeved T-shirt, though the day was cool. She'd been on one horse after another since Mac had pulled up a couple of hours ago, and her exertions showed in the dark sweaty curls at her temples.

"Have you two listed all the reasons why Luna is a bad idea?" she asked.

"Shame on you, Adelia." Neils passed the lead rope to Mac. "You will catch your death, running around like that." He shrugged out of his jacket and draped it over Adelia's shoulders. Adelia gave the lapel a little sniff, something Luna would have understood, had she not been so nervous.

"We were admiring your new addition," Mac said. "I've done what I can for her feet, but it's a slow process. She was leery, but she gave me the benefit of the doubt."

"Poor thing." Adelia held out her hand to the mare, who took two steps back. Mac moved with the horse to avoid a situation where the mare hit the end of the lead rope and started making the bad decisions common to anxious horses.

"Easy," Mac crooned, his hand going to the mare's withers. "It's just the boss coming to see if Neils and I are behaving. She's good people, if you overlook her tendency to pick up hopeless cases like Neils."

"You're just jealous," Adelia said. "I came to see if Neils can go on a mission of mercy for me." When Adelia made no move to come closer, the mare relaxed marginally beside Mac.

"Neils and mercy don't strike me as the most compatible combination," Mac said, petting the horse slowly.

"We got a call from Sid Lindstrom." Adelia took another surreptitious whiff of the coat. "Sid's the foster parent of one of our new riders, and says there are two behemoth horses on their new property, horses that weren't there on the day of closing."

"Behemoth horses aren't suitable for therapeutic programs," Neils began, hands going to his hips. "You can't—"

"I wasn't going to," Adelia said gently. Something passed between the small dark-haired woman and the big blond man that suggested to Mac they were a couple, if the routine with the jacket hadn't confirmed the notion already.

He liked both of them, and respected what they were doing with the therapeutic riding program, though the idea that everybody but MacKenzie Knightley had somebody with whom they could exchange silent looks and warm jackets was tiresome.

"I *said* we could take over some pony chow, and send somebody to check on the situation," Adelia went on.

"They could be stray pensioners who broke out of the neighbor's paddock this morning, but it's spring, Neils. What if somebody's stallion got loose, and the other horse is a mare in season who's eloped with him? That's not a safe situation for greenhorns to manage, and these people know very little about horses."

"Because their foster kid rides in our program, we're going to start making house calls?" Neils tried to glower as he put the question to his boss, but the guy was whupped. He stood only a couple of inches shorter than Mac's six foot four, but Neils had become a whupped puppy the first time Adelia had turned her big brown eyes on him.

"One barn call," Adelia said. "If they can afford a four-hundred-acre farm free and clear, then they are potential sponsors for the therapeutic riding program." She reached out to the mare again, but the horse came out of the daze induced by Mac's petting and scratching, and backed up again.

"Somebody's a little shy," Adelia said, dropping her hand. "Will you go, Neils?"

"What's the address?"

She told him, and Mac's hand went still on the horse's neck.

"I'll go," Mac said. The mare shrugged, a perfectly normal horsey reminder to resume his scratching.

"You will?" Adelia's expression was curious, while Neils looked relieved.

"It's on my way home, and Luna was my last customer here this morning. It's Saturday, and I have the time."

"My thanks." When Neils reached for Luna's lead rope, the little horse did not flinch or take a step back.

Mac gathered up his tools and loaded his farrier's truck—not to be confused with his everyday truck. He took a minute to watch a therapeutic riding session getting started in the small indoor arena. A kid with no feeling below her thighs was settling onto the back of a therapy pony, the girl's expression rapt, while the horse stood stock-still and awaited his burden.

The girl had earned this moment, learning parts of the horse, names of the tack and equipment, and doing what she could from her wheelchair to contribute to the care of the horses. Mac had watched week by week as she'd progressed toward this day.

Her name was Lindy, and Mac stood silently at a distance as she sat her mount. A special moment.

Mac turned away, climbed into his truck, and drove off. Once en route, he checked his messages to see if any of his paying clients had gotten locked up Friday night—an attorney who specialized in criminal defense often racked up messages over the weekend—but, oh happy day, his mailbox was empty.

Which left him free to wonder why Luna was uncomfortable around women, or whether she'd merely been reacting to MacKenzie Knightley's own unease with the fairer sex.

He pulled up the lane of the address Adelia had given him, which was, indeed, a four-hundred-acre farm. Four hundred three and a quarter acres, to be exact.

Fences were starting to sag, and boards had warped their nails out of the posts. A spring growth of weeds had yet to be whacked down from the driveway's center, and the most recent crop of winter potholes hadn't yet been filled in with gravel. The white paint on the north side of the loafing shed was peeling, and the stone barn itself needed some pointing and parging near the foundation.

All in all, a damned depressing sight for a man who'd had as happy a childhood on a farm as a boy could.

Which was to say, very happy.

"Hello, the house!" Mac called.

No response, which wasn't a good sign. Farms were busy places, full of activity. Even if humans weren't in evidence, then the dogs, cats, and chickens usually were. But this farm had no dogs, no sheep, no cows, no visible animal life of any species.

"Over here!"

The shout came from the far side of the hill, where the land rolled down to a draw that Mac would bet still sported a pond and a fine fishing stream, but the tone of voice had been tense, frightened maybe.

He didn't run. If a horse were cast against a fence, or two horses were taking a dislike to each other, then tearing onto the scene wouldn't help.

"Coming," he yelled back. "Coming over the hill." He rummaged in his truck, extracting two lead ropes and two worn leather halters, as well as a half-empty box of sugar cubes.

When he crested the hill, the sight that met his eyes was so unexpected he stopped in his tracks, and had to remind himself to resume breathing.

~~~

They were not horses, they were equine barges, munching grass and twitching their tails in a slow progress across the field where Sid had discovered them. They shifted along, first one foot, a pause to munch grass, then the other foot, all with the ominous inexorability of equine glaciers, leaving Sid to wonder how in the hell anybody controlled them.

If anybody could control them.

What would it feel like if one of those massive horse feet descended on a human toe? How many hours would elapse before the beast would deign to shuffle its foot off the bloody remains, to lip grass on some other blighted part of the earth?

How did animals that large mate, for God's sake? Surely the earth would shake, and the female's back would break, and giving birth to even the smallest member of the species would be excruciating.

This litany of horror was interrupted by a shout from back over the rise in the direction of the house and barn. The voice was mature male, which meant it wasn't Luis.

Help, then, from the therapeutic riding program.

"Over here!" Sid yelled back.

The animals twitched their ears, which had Sid grabbing for the only weapon the house had had to offer, useless though it likely was. Something as big as these horses could run over anything in its path and not notice an obstacle as insignificant as a human.

"You planning on sweeping them out of your pasture?"

A man stood a few feet away, a man built on the same scale as the damned horses, but leaner—meaner?

"Hello, mister. I'm Sidonie Lindstrom," she said, clambering down off the granite outcropping she'd been perched on. "You're from the therapeutic riding place?"

"I'm their farrier." His voice was peat smoke and island single malt, and his eyes were sky blue beneath long, dark lashes. Which was of absolutely no moment, and neither was the arrestingly masculine cast of his features.

"What's a farrier?" Sid asked.

"Horseshoer." He wasn't smiling, but something in his blue eyes suggested she amused him.

"Blacksmith? Like Vulcan or Saturn?"

"Close enough. You say you didn't notice these two were on the property when you took possession?"

"I didn't say." Sid took a minute to study her guest— she supposed he was a guest of some sort—while his gaze went to the two big red horses yards away. Enormous, huge, *flatulent* horses.

"Do they do that a lot?" she asked, wincing as a sulfurous breeze came to her nose. God above, was this how the cavalry mowed down its enemies?

"When they're on good grass, yes." Absolutely deadpan. "Daisy!"

The nearest beast lifted its great head and eyed the man.

"You two are acquainted?"

"There aren't many pairs like this around anymore," he replied. "Buttercup!" The second animal lifted its head, and worse, shuffled a foot in the direction of the humans.

"What are you doing, mister?" Sid scrambled up on the rocks, shamelessly using the blacksmith's meaty shoulder for leverage.

"You're afraid of them?" he asked, not budging an inch.

"Anybody in their right damned mind would be afraid of them," Sid shot back. "They could sit on you and not even notice."

"They'd notice. They notice a single fly landing on

them. They'd notice even a little thing like you. Come here, ladies." He took a box of sugar cubes from his jacket pocket and shook it, which caused both animals to incrementally speed up in their approach. They were walking, but walking quickly, and Sid could swear she felt seismic vibrations.

"You're supposed to help here, you know, not provoke them." Her voice didn't shake, but her body was beginning to send out the flight-or-flight-or-*flight!* signals.

She'd gotten mighty good at the flight response.

"Calm down," Mr. Sugar Cubes said. "If you're upset, they'll pick up on it."

"Smart ladies, then, because I'm beyond upset. These are not fixtures, and they should not convey with the property. A washing machine or a dryer I could overlook, but these—crap on a croissant, they could bite you, mister."

He was holding out his hand—and a sizable paw it was too—with one sugar cube balanced on his palm. The first horse to reach him stuck out its big nose and wiggled its horsey lips over his hand, and then the sugar cube was gone.

"You too, Buttercup." He put a second sugar cube on his hand, and the other horse repeated the disappearing act. "Good girls." He moved to stand between the horses, letting one sniff his pocket while he scratched the neck of the other. "You need some good tucker, ladies, and your feet are a disgrace. But, my, it is good to see you."

Red hair was falling like a fine blizzard from where he scratched the horse's shoulders, and the mare was craning her neck as the man talked and scratched some more.

"Not to interrupt your class reunion, but what am I supposed to do with your girlfriends?" Sid asked.

"They aren't mine, though they might well be yours. Come meet them."

He turned, and in a lithe, one-armed move, scooped Sid from the safety of her rocky perch and set her on her feet between him and the horses.

"Mister, if you ever handle me like that again—"

"You'll do what?"

"You won't like where it hurts. How do you tell them apart?"

They were peering at her, the big, hairy pair of them, probably thinking of having a Sidonie Salad, and Sid took a step back, only to bump into a hard wall of muscular male chest.

"Look at their faces," he said. "Buttercup has a blaze, and Daisy has a snip and a star."

Sid was pressed so tightly against him she could *feel* him speak. She could also feel he wasn't in the least tense or worried, which suggested the man was in want of brains.

What he called faces were noses about a yard long, with big, pointed hairy ears at one end, nostrils and teeth at the other, and eyes high up in between. Still, those eyes were regarding Sid with something like intelligence, with a patient curiosity, like old people or small children viewed newcomers.

"How do you know them?" she asked, hands at her sides.

"Thirteen years ago, they were the state champs. They're elderly now, for their breed, and it looks to me like they wintered none too well. You going to pet them or stare them into submission?"

"*Pet...!?*"

Before she could rephrase what had come out as only a squeak, Vulcan had taken her hand in his much larger one and laid it on the neck of the nearest horse.

"Scratch. They thrive on a little special treatment, same as the rest of us."

Sid had no choice but to oblige him, because his hand covered hers as it rested on the horse's neck. Over the scent of horse and chilly spring day, Sid got a whiff of cloves and cinnamon underlaid with notes that suggested not a bakery, but a faraway meadow where the sunshine fell differently and clothes would be superfluous.

The hand that wasn't covering Sid's rested on her shoulder, preventing her from ducking and running.

"Talk to them," he said. "They're working draft animals, and they're used to people communicating with them."

"What do I say?"

"Introduce yourself. Compliment them, welcome them. The words don't matter so much as the tone of the voice." He seemed serious, and the horse was lowering its head closer to the ground the longer Sid scratched her neck.

"Like that, don't you, girl? I'm Sid, and don't get too comfortable here, because I am no kind of farmer, and neither is Luis."

The horse let loose another sibilant, odoriferous fart.

"Pleased to meet you too. There, I talked to her, and she responded. Can I call the SPCA now?"

"No, you may not. Daisy will get jealous if you neglect her."

"And bitch slap me with her tail?"

"At least."

Sid could see that happening, so she dropped her hand, then held it out to the other horse.

"You too? I'm changing your names to Subzero and Kenmore, because you're the size of industrial freezers." The horse sighed as Sid began scratching the second hairy neck, and Sid hid a smile. "Where's your dignity, horse? There's a man present, of sorts."

"You want me to leave?"

"Yes, particularly if you're going to take these two with you."

"Smaller draft horses than these won't fit in a conventional horse trailer. The halters I brought with me won't fit them either, though I'll be happy to clear out if you're—"

"No! That's not what I—" Sid fell silent. What did she expect him to do, if he wasn't going to take the horses with him? "Will the SPCA come get them, or animal control?"

"You want them put down?" he asked.

That deep voice held a chill, one that had Sid twisting around to peer at him over her shoulder. "Put down to what?"

"Euthanized, put to sleep. Killed for your convenience."

His tone was positively arctic, though he was standing so close to Sid she could feel his body heat through her clothes.

"Don't be an ass. They've wandered off from somebody's property. They're merely strays, and need to be taken home."

"I'm not so sure of that, but let's find them somewhere to put up overnight, and we can argue the details where Daisy and Buttercup can't hear us. Come along."

He took Sid by the wrist, and began leading her away from the horses.

Sid trundled along with him—beside him seemed the safest place to be—but glanced warily over her shoulder.

"We're being followed."

He dropped her wrist and turned so quickly Sid barely had time to step back.

"Scat!" He waved his hands and charged at the nearest horse, who shied and then stood her ground a few feet off. "Scram, Daisy! Shoo!"

The horse stood very tall, then lowered her head, and ponderously scampered a few feet before standing very tall again. The second horse gave a big shrug of her neck and hopped sideways.

"You get them all wound up," Sid said, edging toward the gate, "I am burying you where you fall, mister, and the grave will be shallow, because there's a lot of you to bury."

"They want to play. Head for the barn. This won't take long."

Sid did not need to be told twice. She shamelessly hustled for the gate, stopping to watch what happened in the field behind her only when she'd climbed to the highest fence board.

A two-ton version of tag-you're-it seemed to be going on, with the horses galumphing up to the man, then veering away only to stop, wheel, and charge him again. He dodged easily, and swatted at them on the neck and shoulders and rump when they went by. When they were a few steps past him, the horses would kick up their back legs or buck, and by God, the ground did shake.

The guy was grinning now, his face transformed

from forbiddingly handsome to stunningly attractive. He called to each horse, good-naturedly taunting first one then the other, until by some unspoken consent, both mares approached him with their heads down.

Sid couldn't hear what he said to them, but she saw the way he touched them, the way he fiddled with those big ears, and gave each horse one last scratch. The mares watched him walk back toward the barn, and Sid could have sworn their expressions were forlorn.

"You're old friends with them," she said as he climbed over the fence. She tried to turn on the top board, only to find herself plucked straight up into the air, then set gently on her feet. "For the love of meadow muffins, mister, are you trying to get your face slapped?"

His lips quirked, but he did not smile. "No."

"What am I supposed to do about your lady friends?"

"Nothing for right now. Who's the kid?"

"What kid?" Sid followed the blacksmith's gaze to the front porch of their new house. Their new old house.

"The kid who's going to tear me into little bitty pieces if you don't let him know I'm your new best friend."

"Never had a best friend before," Sid said, but the man had a point. Luis was looking daggers at the blacksmith, the boy's shirt luffing against his skinny body, showing tension in every bone and sinew. "Come on, I'll introduce you. Or I would if you'd told me your name."

"Everybody calls me Mac."

She eyed him up and down as they started for the house. "Like the truck? Don't they have a plant around here somewhere?"

"Hagerstown, but it's Volvo now, and no, not like the truck. Like MacKenzie."

"Pleased to meet you, Mr. MacKenzie. I'd be more pleased if you'd take those free-to-good-homes along with you."

"No, it's MacKenzie, as in MacKenzie Knightley. I'm fairly certain the horses are yours."

"You've said that twice now, and while I'm a woman slow to anger"—he snorted beside her—"it's only fair to warn you the notion of me owning those mastodons will sour my mood considerably. Luis!" Sid's voice caught the boy as he was slouching away from the porch post to duck into the house. "He's shy."

"Right."

"He is, and you'd be too if you'd been in eight foster homes in less than three years. Be nice, Mr. Knightley."

"Or you'll beat me up?"

"I'll tell your horses on you, and they will be very disappointed in you."

They reached the porch, and Luis was back to holding up a porch post, his hands tucked into his armpits, because at almost sixteen, he was too macho to wear a damned jacket.

"Luis, this is Mac. He's come to tell us what to do with the horses."

"Luis." Mac surprised her by holding out one of those big hands, and Sid said a quick prayer her son would not embarrass her. "Pleased to meet you."

Her foster son, but that was splitting hairs.

Luis looked at Mac's hand, which the man continued to hold out, while his gaze held the boy's. Slowly, Luis offered his hand.

"MacKenzie Knightley. My friends call me Mac."

"Luis Martineau."

"You know anything about horses, Luis?"

"Only what I've learned from Neils and Adelia," Luis said. "Horses are to be respected."

The slight emphasis on the last word had Sid's heart catching. Luis had taken to his riding lessons like nothing else she'd thrown at him, likely because of the people as much as the horses.

"They are to be respected," Mac said, "and cared for. Those two mares are in the beginning stages of neglect, and somebody will have to look after them."

Sid took up a lean on another porch post. "I wish you all the luck in the world with that, Mr. Knightley, because that somebody will not be me or Luis. Now, having settled that, may I offer you a cup of coffee?"

"I'm a tea drinker, actually."

"You're in luck," she said, heading for the door. "The only room we've unpacked is the kitchen, and the only thing we've stocked is the fridge."

Chapter 2

MAC DID NOT WATCH SID LINDSTROM'S SAUCY LITTLE butt disappear through the door before him, mostly because the kid would take it amiss.

But it was an effort not to. A surprising, intriguing, vaguely resented effort.

Mac's two younger brothers, Trent and James, shared the mistaken belief that Mac was indifferent to women. Or maybe they thought he preferred men, though that was patently not true.

Eighty percent of Mac's criminal clients were men, and of the remaining twenty, women were much more likely to write bad checks than blow someone away in a drug deal gone bad.

Mac liked women, often admired them for their courage, stamina, and grace under pressure, and was as prone to appreciating their physical attributes as the next man—perhaps more prone, given that his appreciation was invariably silent.

He'd grown used to looking and not touching, and with Sid Lindstrom, the unprecedented urge to touch, to taste, to gather her scent and learn the feel and sound and details of her, was interesting.

Though if she'd take on two tons of stray horse with a broom, a mere man had best watch himself around her.

"What kind of tea?" she asked him, opening a cupboard. Just for the pleasure of sniffing the flowery scent of her hair, he stood right behind her.

"This'll do." He reached over her shoulder and plucked a box of generic, bagged decaf.

"And you no doubt take it plain. Luis, are you joining us?"

The boy's dark gaze went from Mac to Sid, back to Mac. He scrubbed a hand through unruly dark red hair, then shook his head.

"I'll finish setting up my room."

"Let me know if you need any help. I'll be making the pizza run around four o'clock."

Luis ghosted out of the kitchen. Maybe he'd learned to move quietly in his eight different foster homes, or maybe he'd learned it on the street.

"He must like you," Sid said, putting a fancy stainless steel teakettle on the stove.

"How on earth would you conclude that? I thought he was trying to visually slice my throat." Mac opened another cupboard and found some mugs decorated in bright paisley rainbows.

"He would not have left you alone with me if he'd been the least bit worried. Spoons are in the drawer."

Mac took out one spoon and dropped it into the smaller of the two mugs. Outside, sitting on her rock, his first impression of Sidonie had been of isolation and stillness.

And he'd been surprised—he hadn't been expecting *Sid* Lindstrom to sport a lovely set of female curves, big green eyes, and a wide, full mouth. Her hair was blond with hints of auburn, and was tucked into a braid that hung down the inside of her jacket.

How long was that braid, and what would it look like loose against the naked skin of her back?

"Are you smiling at that mug?" She stood, arms crossed, by the stove. "I have to ask, because you seem so disinclined to the expression generally."

"What will you do with those horses?"

She blinked at his deflection of the question—he *had* been smiling—shrugged out of her jacket, and hung it on a peg beside the door.

"I don't know the first thing about horses." She took the steaming kettle off the stove. "Don't know the first thing about farms, except you can sell them for a lot of money. The horses need a new home in any case, because I'm only out here to catch my breath. Damson Valley is supposed to be pretty, safe, friendly, and cheap. I don't intend to be here for long."

Well, of course she didn't. The first woman Mac had noticed in any significant sense, and she wouldn't let the grass grow under her feet. Probably for the best, even if that fat braid did hang right down to the top of her fanny.

"A pair like that can't go just anywhere. Draft animals are literally a breed apart from the typical pleasure horse, or even the typical show horse."

"They're bigger, that's for damned sure. You going to stand there or be sociable and join me at the table?" She didn't wait for him to answer, but took both mugs to the table.

Mac moved instinctively to hold her chair, but this resulted in a little wrestling match over the chair.

"Mr. Knightley, what do you think you're doing?" She didn't take her hand off the back of the chair, her expression puzzled.

"Holding your chair for you."

"*Suitez-vous*, Vulcan." She tucked her butt into the chair. "Get the milk, would you?"

He stole another whiff of her hair first, but was pleased to see she drank whole milk, not skim, not that pansy-ass two percent. Worst of all in his estimation were those who drank one percent—a token gesture of fat to prove how gastronomically brave they were, maybe, or how sophisticated. If he ever caught his brothers—

"What did that milk jug do to deserve such a thunderous expression?" She took the gallon jug from him.

"Looking for the expiration date. You can never be too careful."

He hung his jacket over hers, same peg.

"How are draft horses different, and why can't I run an ad, free to good home? Put 'em on Craigslist under Equine Dirigibles?" She poured milk into her tea, then capped the jug and set it on the table. "And for pity's sake, sit. Unless you're metabolically incapable of sitting? My brother Tony certainly was."

She pursed her lips, then took a sip of her tea.

Was. Mac heard the past tense. A guy who'd lost both parents in early adulthood couldn't miss that particular use of it.

"Draft horses are different from other breeds in several regards," Mac said, taking the chair next to hers. "Conventional tack won't fit them, conventional trailers won't haul them, conventional feeding protocols won't keep them fit, conventional fencing won't keep them safe."

"So they're a lot of trouble. Lovely."

"Luis isn't a lot of trouble?"

He'd made her smile. The lady apparently enjoyed verbal sparring, as would any self-respecting lawyer.

"Point taken, but Luis and I chose each other. I am certain Thing One and Thing Two were not here when we did the walk through before settlement."

"If they were on the far side of the pond, particularly if they were having a prone nap, you wouldn't have seen them over the lip of the pond."

"How do you know this property so well?"

Even a lawyer might not have known to lob that verbal grenade.

"I'm from around here," Mac said, not examining the motives behind his prevarication. "My brothers and I own a business in town, and we all live a few miles from here in one direction or another."

"Are they blacksmiths too?"

"It's not that kind of business. If you're simply going to sell this place, why take up residence here?"

Some sort of thumpa-thumpa rock music started up on the floor above. Sid's gaze drifted to the ceiling, and Mac saw for the first time what had been lurking behind the offhand, dukes-up manner. She was worried and sad. Then too, she'd used the past tense regarding her brother.

The loss of a brother…

"You moved out here for the boy?" he asked, mostly to cut off such bleak thoughts.

"You ever lived in Baltimore or DC?" she shot back.

"I went to school at the University of Maryland, so I've spent plenty of time in DC and Baltimore both."

"Probably not the parts of town where Luis grew up. It's a damned swamp. Just running to the corner store for an overpriced loaf of white bread, a kid has a thousand opportunities to go astray or be the victim of somebody gone astray. The compulsory school day is a gauntlet you and I cannot imagine. Weekends are just as bad."

"You lived in those neighborhoods?"

She set her rainbow mug down on the table and cradled it between her two hands. Pretty hands, plain nails, clean and blunt. *No rings*.

"That's the thing about cities. You think they're large, sprawling, and complicated, but when trouble wants to find a kid, trouble is just a few bus stops away. I'm pretty sure Luis wasn't a gang member, but he was the next thing."

Not good, but understandable. A gang was a family, of sorts. "You said he's been in foster care for three years? He would have had to have been a child…"

"Not by urban standards. He was the man of the house, with two younger sisters and a mama to look after. He was doing a fine job too."

So proud of the kid. "By selling drugs, muling them, maybe by selling himself outside the gay bars?"

She hunched forward, as if the temperature in the kitchen had just dropped twenty degrees.

"We have crime out here too, Sidonie Lindstrom, and we have children. My sister-in-law Hannah grew up in foster care, and some of the things she suffered in the care of the state would break your heart."

"You have kids?"

The question took him aback. He needed to ogle less and pay attention more. "I do not."

"Luis isn't my first foster kid, but I was warned. The other foster parents all said there are kids that get to you. You love them all, or you try to, but a lot of foster kids are simply putting in time while their parents get their act together."

Mac waited and waited while a clock over the sink ticked softly.

"I want to adopt him," Sid went on. "Summer's coming, and summer is another swamp. With all the budget cutbacks, summer school slots are getting harder to come by, and Luis gets great grades. He's smart. So smart, in some ways, and yet such an idiot. This place seemed safe, seemed like what I was supposed to do next, because nothing and nobody means more to me than that kid."

Adopt. A difficult, complicated word.

"Farms can be great places for kids." Mac sounded like an ad from the county extension office, but it was the best he could do. "On a farm, anybody can make a meaningful contribution, no matter how young or old, and a kid with an ounce of imagination will never be bored on a farm."

"You were raised on a farm?"

"I...was."

"Then you know what to do with those horses. Why don't you take them?"

"I don't have the right fencing." *Fortunately*.

"Why can't I run an ad?"

"Horse slaughter in the United States is subject to periodic bans, but anybody can buy a horse at auction and take him to the boats in Baltimore."

"Boats?" She hiked her foot up onto the chair. She was that petite, that limber.

"The horse walks on under his own steam on this end, but by the time the boat docks in Europe, he's packaged in cellophane and ready for human consumption, and the entire operation is outside the purview of any U.S. humane organization, or any regulatory body, to ensure the horse, who is not regarded here as a food source, is safe to eat."

"Daisy and Buttercup…?"

"Are nice, big animals. At sixty cents a pound live weight, they'd bring a fair price."

Her hand went to her stomach, and Mac did not feel the least guilty. "Luis would put me on the boat with them if I let that happen to Daisy and Buttercup."

Good man, Luis. "They're happy here, and they'd give Luis something to do."

"Like what?"

"They probably shouldn't be at grass twenty-four-seven. When spring really gets under way, that can lead to grass colic, so somebody should bring them in at night and turn them out each morning. When it gets hotter, you reverse that schedule, so they don't have to deal with the worst heat outside, but can loaf in the barn where it's cooler. They'll need fresh water every time they're brought in. Someone should groom them from time to time to make sure they aren't sporting any scurf or scratches, and when the flies get bad, they'll need—"

Sid held up a slim, freckled hand. "Stop. You make it sound like they're a full-time job."

"They're a commitment. As to that, the four-board fence you have should probably be reinforced with a strand of electric, but I can get that done in a day or two, if the boy will help."

"What will that do to my electric bill?"

Not a no. Daisy and Buttercup were counting on Mac being able to dodge Sidonie Lindstrom's no.

"Won't cost you anything. We'll run the fence off a solar cell."

"Which will cost me how much to purchase?"

She'd crossed her arms and sat back against her chair to glare at him as she fired off her questions.

"Not one damned cent. My brothers and I have all the material on hand. We each own some land, and Trent has a growing herd of horses. Consider it a housewarming present."

"Do you always offer your presents with such pugnacity?"

"Yes."

This did not have the intimidating effect Mac intended. Sid's lips quirked, and then that wide, wicked mouth of hers blossomed into a soft, sweet smile.

"I'm not very good at presents either," she said, patting his hand. She rose and took their mugs to the sink, affording Mac a much-needed moment to absorb that smile while she rinsed out their dishes.

Sidonie Lindstrom went from tough, hard-nosed, and combative to alluring, in the space of a single smile. Mac had been expecting a nice, rousing little argument—the lady seemed to enjoy a spat—and instead she'd given him a benediction in the form of her smile.

"You'll need some tack too," he said, studying the molding over the door. Either water was getting in through some crack, or the staining had been a half-assed job. "I'll put the word out and see if we can come up with some halters at least. Their feet need a good trim, and you'll want the vet out for spring shots, and they probably need their teeth floated too."

"Now we're talking money," she said, her frown back in place as she turned and leaned against the sink.

"Money's a problem?" People who bought big farms generally had at least big borrowing capability.

Her gaze went back to the ceiling. The next floor up boasted at least five bedrooms, one of which was directly above the kitchen. The music had been turned down, though the bass still vibrated gently through the kitchen.

"Money is a problem, and it isn't," Sid said. "At the moment, we're cash poor, though I don't anticipate that will be the case in a few months."

Because she was going to flip the place. Mac didn't like that idea at all.

"The vet and the dentist will leave you a bill. Most of them will work with you if net thirty's not an option. I can look after the trimming and show Luis what to look for."

"Why?"

Her smile was nowhere in evidence, but Mac understood the compelling urge to look gift horses in the mouth.

"We're neighbors. I don't know what that means where you come from, but out here, it means we help each other when the need arises. Whoever told you Damson Valley is a friendly place was telling the God's honest truth."

Though Mac himself wasn't much given to friendliness—usually.

"Fine, then how can I help you?"

He wasn't expecting that. Her question earned his respect—a little more of his respect.

"I'll think about it."

"Don't think too long." She pulled a towel from the handle of the refrigerator—more bright colors, chickens and flowers this time—and dried their mugs.

"Because you're selling this place?" He rose and studied the line of her back, trying not to be mesmerized by the way that thick coppery-blond braid kept brushing the top of her backside over faded, comfortably worn jeans.

"Because I do not like to be beholden to anybody, Mr. Knightley. What do I owe you for coming by here today?" She kept her back to him, and Mac had the sense she was steeling herself for the answer.

Cash poor, indeed.

"A couple slices of pizza will do. Maybe three, provided nobody orders any anchovies. But first, Luis and I will have to get some stalls cleaned out in the barn and scare up something to use as halters. We'll need buckets and bedding too."

She dried the second mug and set it up in the cupboard, then turned back around. "Luis can be difficult."

"Then we should get along, because I can be outright impossible."

"Yes." The smile bloomed again, that blessed, beautiful, soul-warming smile. "I can see this about you, MacKenzie Knightley. Outright impossible."

Damned if she wasn't giving him the impression she liked that just fine.

———~~~———

Sid sent Luis grumbling out to the barn. From the looks of his room, he'd been napping, not setting his personal space to rights.

To have both males out of the house was a relief. Men had a noisy, biological presence, and not the kind of noise Sid enjoyed. The noise she liked was suburban or urban. Varied, impersonal, too complicated to attribute to any one person or source.

"You miss it too, don't you?" she asked a fat, long-haired marmalade cat reclining on Luis's bed.

The beast squeezed its eyes shut in answer, and began to rumble when Sid scratched its neck. What if horses could purr? The racket from those two red monsters would resemble jet engines. Sid scooped up the cat and went to the window, the better to watch Luis shuffling across the yard to the barn.

He hadn't wanted to move out here either, but where else were they to go?

For the thousand millionth time, the thought "if Tony hadn't died" tried to take root in Sid's mind, a useless, stupid thought. She pushed it aside, and brought the cat with her down the hall to her bedroom.

Sid hadn't chosen the largest bedroom in the house, but rather, had taken the one at the back, with a high ceiling, a private balcony, and a view out over the fields and pastures that comprised her property.

"I will learn to appreciate it," she informed the cat. "I may not like it, but for now, it's home." She put the cat down on her bed, a big fluffy four-poster that went well with the room, and sat beside him.

To close her eyes would feel heavenly. To enjoy for a moment the quiet of the house without male feet—teenage or otherwise—stomping through it, to know somebody else had an eye on Luis for even a little while.

Sid lay down, the cat curling up against her side, and let herself drift.

———~~~———

"How long you been taking lessons with Adelia?"

Mac posed what he hoped was a neutral question. With teenagers, anything, *anything* could become grist for the drama mill. He recalled his younger brothers' adolescent moodiness as if it were yesterday, and gave thanks they'd all weathered those storms without irreparable injury.

"I've been taking lessons for a few weeks. Before we moved here, Sid brought me out on weekends once she signed me up with them."

Nothing more, no polite overtures, no small talk. Maybe they'd get along after all.

"You muck your horse's stall at the riding school?"

"And scrub the water buckets, groom my horse, throw hay, and clean my tack."

"Then you're just the man these ponies have been looking for." Mac walked into the barn's understory. The good news was the structure was built of chestnut beams and fieldstone and likely to last forever with minor maintenance.

The bad news was the minor maintenance probably hadn't been done for ten years. Cobwebs hung everywhere, dust accumulated in sedimentary layers on every surface, and little light came through windows larded with fly specking and dirt.

"Water's back here," Mac said, going to the sidewall of the barn. The frost-free spigot was barely discernible in the gloom, a bucket festooned with cobwebs still hanging from the hook. "Say a prayer it works."

He spoke in Spanish, a little to keep Luis's attention, a little to practice. A criminal defense attorney with some bilingual ability had an advantage, both in garnering business and in earning trust with Hispanic clients. Then too, Spanish was easy and pretty.

"People who live beyond civilization's borders can't be expected to speak civilized languages."

Mac looked up from the rusty water gushing into the old bucket, because Luis had spoken in the soft, lilting French of the islands.

"People who are new to a territory ought to do more listening than judging," Mac replied in the same language, and he went on in French, because the look on Luis's face was positively comical. "I dated a girl from Toronto in high school, and she helped me with what I'd learned in class. I also spent a couple summers crewing on a sailboat in the Caribbean. Dump this, would you? I'll find us some brushes and rags."

Luis took the bucket without another word and disappeared out into the sunshine.

Mac rummaged in the old dairy, which had been made over into a tack room of sorts, and came up with more buckets, muck forks, old toweling, and a bucket brush.

"Let's focus on the run-in stall," he said—in English—when Luis came back. "The rest of this barn needs a crew and some serious cleaning equipment."

"May we speak French?" Luis asked, using what was apparently his native language. "I seldom hear it, and I don't want—I prefer it."

Luis didn't want to forget his mother tongue, and Social Services had not thought to place him with a family who spoke it—if they'd had one to offer him.

"If you're not too proud to ask," Mac said, "I'm not too proud to stumble around, provided you correct my errors."

A glint came into Luis's eyes, humor perhaps, or guile. "I will correct you."

"I will correct you as well." Mac tossed an old towel at him. "Refill the bucket and start on those windows. You'll need the brush too."

"While you do what?"

"Muck the hell out of the run-in."

They worked mostly in silence, which was fine with Mac. Luis worked hard, like a person his age could, with single-minded determination to do the job right. The windows didn't exactly sparkle when he was done—the old single-pane glass needed newspaper and vinegar for a real shine—but they let in light.

"It looks better," Luis said. "But that's only one corner of the barn."

"It's a start. We'd better knock off now, or the feed store will close before we can get to it."

Uneasiness crossed the kid's features before his expression went blank. "Sidonie will prefer I remain here."

"Then she can come with me, or you both can, or I'll leave you directions to the feed store so you know where it is." Getting into a truck with a strange man was apparently on Luis's don't-even list. Mac did not speculate about why. "We'll need to clean up some before we're seen in public, in any case, but, Luis?"

The boy stopped a few steps up the barn aisle.

"You put up the muck forks and buckets and so forth every time, because if a horse gets loose, he can tangle himself up in them, destroy them, or do harm to himself."

Luis retrieved the muck fork from where he'd propped it near the water spigot. Mac gathered up the rest of the forks, buckets, towels, and brushes and followed Luis back to the dairy/tack room.

"How do you know the horses?" Luis asked as they turned for the house. "Sid says you know their names."

"Buttercup has the blaze. Daisy has the star and the snip. I grew up around here, and those two were the state champs at one point."

"They're champions?"

"They were, years ago. Does Sid speak French?"

"She tries, but she is too proud. She has to be the mother."

This last was said with a sweet smile as they walked back to the house. When this boy filled out, he would turn heads and break hearts—provided he stayed out of jail.

"Lost my dad when I was not much older than you are now," Mac said. "A mother is a fine thing to have."

Luis's head came up. "My *mother*'s in jail. Twenty years for CDS distribution, and a lot of other bullshit."

"You ever get to see her?" *Controlled Dangerous Substances, a.k.a. street drugs.*

"She's in Jessup."

Not an answer. Jessup was a lot closer to Baltimore, though, and moving out here would make visits to the prison harder to arrange.

"I've visited Jessup. The facilities aren't bad, for a jail."

Luis snorted and preceded Mac into the kitchen.

Mac tried to picture his own late mother in jail. A criminal defense attorney saw people go to jail almost daily. Bad people, good people, some of them even innocent good people.

But his own mother?

He followed Luis into the house and wondered what would make a woman like Sidonie Lindstrom—a pretty, unmarried city girl who probably read more magazines than books and loved the smell of car exhaust—take on the challenge of a kid like Luis.

Chapter 3

SID WAS DREAMING OF AN EXPEDITION TO WHITE FLINT Mall down in the thriving suburb of Rockville. To the bargain rack at Lord and Taylor, where the slickest Little Black Dress hung in just her size. Finished silk, a plunging neckline, the hemline at exactly mid-thigh, with floral aubergine embroidery on the hem and neckline. Modest, but with the potential to tease, particularly when matched with onyx and gold jewelry, and three-inch spikes. The dress would *feel* lovely against her skin, and make her want to move around in it simply for the caress of the fabric on her bare—

Something—the cat's tail?—brushed her nose.

"Wakey, wakey, princess."

That gravelly baritone had no place in either Sid's dreams or her realities. She opened her eyes.

MacKenzie Knightley sat on the white frothy duvet covering her bed, perfectly at ease for all his size and dark coloring.

"I was resting my eyes."

"Right." He dropped her braid and stood, without cracking a smile—without needing to crack a smile; his amusement was that evident. "You've been resting your eyes for a while now, I'm guessing."

"Why would you guess that?" Sid bounced and slogged her way to the edge of the bed. Big beds were for sleeping in, not for making dignified exits from.

"I'd guess that, because you've got a crease on your cheek from the pillows, and because I stood in that doorway there"—he pointed ten feet across the room—"and for about five straight minutes, I politely suggested you wake up."

Sid made it to the edge of the bed, but her brain was having trouble waking up along with her body.

"Where's Luis?" she asked.

"Braiding some baling twine halters to use until we can scare up the real deal. I suggested he and I make an excursion to the feed store and pick up the pizza so you could sleep, but he was reluctant to leave you here alone."

"Pizza." Sid's mind latched onto the image of a big, piping hot, loaded deep-dish with a mug of cold root beer to go with it. "I suppose we can't get anything delivered here?"

"You suppose right," Mac said. "I'll leave you to get yourself in order while I round up Luis."

He headed for the stairs, giving Sid a chance to appreciate his departing side. Lithe, like a big cat, and quiet, but not as incongruous in her bedroom as he should have been. The high ceilings, the solid stone construction of the house, the old oaks in the yard, and the open fields beyond suited him.

Maybe she could sell the place to him, except a horseshoer—she forgot the other word he'd used—probably couldn't afford this much land.

Sid stopped dead in front of her cheval mirror.

"God in heaven." She had a crease on her cheek, her hair was a wreck, and her clothes looked like they'd never gotten acquainted with the dryer's wrinkle-guard feature.

MacKenzie Knightley had seen her like this.

Apparently, country boys didn't scare easily. Sid set to work with her brush, changed into fresh jeans that fit a little more snugly, and a green silk blouse that complemented her eyes. Brown suede half boots and a denim jacket with green and brown beading on the hems completed the picture.

"You'll do," she informed her image. When she sauntered into the kitchen, Luis and MacKenzie were sitting at the table, working lengths of some hairy-looking twine.

"You've taken up macramé, Luis?" She tousled his hair, because they had company, and Luis wouldn't give her sass for it.

"Making halters for the horses. I'm supposed to bring them in at night and turn them out in the morning until the hot weather comes."

"They might be gone by hot weather," Sid said, going to the fridge.

Luis set the twine on the table and stood. "Gone where?"

"I'm not sure, but we know next to nothing about caring for livestock, Luis. You know this place isn't long-term for us."

"But you told Social Services—"

"Luis Martineau, what I tell that bunch of officious bi—biddies, or your good-for-nothing lawyer, has nothing to do with reality, any more than they're really concerned with your best interests. Now what do you want on your pizza?"

She felt MacKenzie Knightley watching them, but what did a horseshoer know about the red tape, posturing, and endless regulations that went along with being a foster parent? What did he know about Luis's family, much less Sid's own situation?

And as far as Sid was concerned, "good-for-nothing lawyer" was a redundant term.

"You know how I like my pizza," Luis said, "and I don't see why we have to sell the horses when we just moved here."

Sid was about to tell him that wasn't his decision, but something in his eyes promised her a knock-down, drag-out, steel cage bout of pouting and sulking if she pulled rank on him in front of their guest.

"We'll talk about it later," Sid said.

"I'll be the one taking care of them," Luis said. "If they're no inconvenience to you, I don't see why you have to get rid of them."

Damnably logical, until one of the mastodons stepped on his foot, and Child Protective Services was out here, sniffing around and muttering about lack of supervision.

"They're not foster children, Luis, and playing the guilt card this early in an argument is a low shot, and bad strategy."

"They aren't foster children," Luis said, his chin coming up. "They don't have a lawyer. Nobody is required to report when those horses are abandoned or treated badly. Nobody owes them food or shelter. They have nobody and nothing, no rights."

"I hate to interrupt," Knightley said, getting to his feet, "but the feed store isn't open all night. We can continue this over pizza, can't we?"

"Yes," Sid said, grudgingly grateful to him for intervening. "As long as you're willing to look after the

horses, Luis, we can take our time about finding them
another home."

"I'd leave it there," Knightley said to Luis. "You're
too much of a gentleman to fight dirty in front of me,
and Sidonie's too stubborn to back down while I'm here.
You'll make more progress without a peanut gallery."

"She is stubborn," Luis said, the corners of his mouth
trying to turn up.

"And you." Knightley took Sid's purse down from a
hook near the door and passed it to her. "Don't needle
him over dinner. Let him spend a few days scrubbing
water buckets, trudging in and out from the pasture in
the pouring-down rain and wind and mud, spooning
honey before and after school every day, and see if his
position doesn't shift closer to center."

The prospect of Luis seeing reason all on his own
cheered Sid, as did the idea that they were only a few
miles—only!—from some place that served pizza and
Greek fare Knightley swore was worth the drive.

"You two coming with me, or are we going to cara-
van?" Knightley asked.

His face gave away nothing, not eagerness for their company, not distress at having to share his vehicle. Nothing.

"We'll follow you," Sid said.

"Then we'll find the pizza place by way of the feed
store. You should have a couple bags of senior feed on
hand for your ponies, and probably pick up some joint
supplement for them as well."

He climbed into his truck—a big blue thing that
looked like it could pull house trailers—and fired it up.

"Diesel," Luis said, which was proof positive guys
had different genes.

Sid fished in her purse for the car keys. "You can tell that from listening to it?"

"You can't?"

"You want to drive?" Sid asked, rather than admit her ignorance. Knightley's wheels sounded like a truck. Like a big powerful truck.

She tossed Luis the keys and buckled in. Fortunately, Knightley drove below the posted speed, no doubt making allowances for the fact that they were following. In the waning light, the countryside was pretty enough, with a few fields already bright green, and others not yet planted.

"Do you know what the green stuff is?" Sid asked.

"Winter wheat. There's fields of it near the high school."

Where they'd registered him on Friday, because the Department of Social Services frowned on foster children having any time off from school, even when those children pulled straight A's in merit classes. Sid had pushed it, giving Luis three days off before enrolling him, hoping social workers out here in the country were a more reasonable breed.

Maybe pigs could fly in this fresh rural air too.

"Feed store," Luis said, dutifully putting on his turn signal and following Knightley into the parking lot of a building sporting a "Damson County Farmers' Co-op" sign over a front-facing loading dock. "You coming in?"

"Sure, unless you're paying for this pony chow?"

"I would, if that would make a difference."

Sid got out and studied Luis over the roof of the car. "You just met these horses, Luis, right?"

He jammed his hands in his pockets, a young man trying to figure out how not to get in trouble for telling the truth, because he would assuredly get in trouble if he lied.

"I saw their tracks in the pasture the day we moved in, and I knew the tracks couldn't have been there from last year. Mac's waiting for us."

Tracks. Oh, right. Little dude from way downtown saw horse tracks. Like she would believe that.

"You knew the horses were there, and you said nothing. This is not good, Luis."

"They were abandoned," Luis said again. "Left to starve or die. They don't deserve that, Sid. They were state champions, and nobody cares what happened to them."

Spare me from crusading adolescents. "We don't know what their story is, but we'll talk more about this later."

Knightley started walking toward Sid's little Mustang convertible as if he'd heard his cue. "You might consider getting something with four-wheel drive," he said. "Winters can be tricky out here."

"This thing's paid off," Sid said, patting the candy-apple-red hood. "Car payments can be tricky too. Where's the horse food aisle?"

"It doesn't work like that," Knightley said. "Come on inside, and I'll show you the ropes."

He held the door for her—for a farm boy, he had polished manners—and explained that they ordered the feed at the counter, and the nice man would put it in Sid's car for them. This was good, because the feed came in fifty-pound bags, which meant hefting it out of her car's trunk would be a job she and Luis shared.

Fifty dollars later, they had two bags of horse feed and some fancy fairy dust with joint supplement in it for horses. Luis was listening raptly as Knightley explained the ins and outs of feeding draft horses, as opposed to the school horses Luis had met thus far.

"Are we going to stand here all night," Sid asked, "or take pity on a starving woman?"

The man and the boy turned to look at her at the same moment, their expressions showing the same consternation.

"Pizza," she said, enunciating carefully. "Gyros, cheesecake. Nu-tri-tion, such as it can be found out here in the provinces. Ringing any bells?"

"Sid gets cranky when her blood sugar's low," Luis said. "And she's tired."

"I never would have guessed." Knightley turned to open his truck door—his unlocked truck door. "The restaurant is right down this road about two miles on the left. You can't miss it."

"We'll meet you there." Sid hopped into her car and started the engine, lest Luis get Knightley going on some other No Girls Allowed topic. That had happened occasionally with Tony, but not often. Luis had kept his distance from Tony, and Sid hadn't really known what to do about it.

But then, Tony hadn't been trying to be any kind of role model for Luis. He'd regarded the foster children as Sid's "little experiment." They came and went, and if Sid wanted to send them birthday and Christmas cards, or go to their graduations, that was her decision.

When she'd told him Luis was different, Luis was a keeper, he'd scoffed.

"They're all different to you, Sid. You'd keep every one of them if you could get away with it."

Damn him, even if he was dead, he'd been right.

———

Mac had made a horrendous mistake, one evident before
the food had been brought to the table. Aspidistra's was
getting crowded, because Saturday night was an eat-out
night in the local surrounds, and the options were few
unless driving forty minutes to Frederick or Hagerstown
held some appeal.

Mac lived about four miles away, and the folks
politely noticing MacKenzie Knightley sitting down to
a public meal with a female-who-wore-no-ring were his
neighbors. He'd taken the waitress, Marcella Ebersole,
to the junior prom almost twenty years and many dress
sizes ago, and had his hand as far up her skirts as nature
and the backseat of a restored Super Beetle would allow.

He'd also defended Marcella's son on shoplifting
charges last year and gotten the kid probation before
judgment, thus preserving the boy's shot at some college scholarships.

Two booths down, Mrs. Fletcher, Mac's old youth
choir director, sat with her husband of five decades,
beaming at the man, though in her words, he couldn't
carry a tune in a bucket.

At the bar, Mac's nemesis from middle school
wrestling tournaments, Joey Hinlicky Jr., sat nursing a
longneck. Joey was referred to as Deuce now, because
his son sported the same moniker, as well as his dad's
penchant for mischief.

And damned if Joe hadn't winked at Mac before the
pizza was even out of the oven.

Marcella had smirked at him.

Mrs. Fletcher had smiled.

What the hell had he been thinking?

Mac returned the smiles, nods, and winks with as much civility as he was capable of, which only seemed to amuse the idiots and goons around him. Fortunately, he was with a woman and a boy who took their tucker seriously. Luis matched Mac slice for slice, and Sid held her own as well, even finishing Luis's piece of cheesecake.

"Never had key lime cheesecake before," Sid observed. "Is it a local delicacy?"

"I've never had a dessert from Vespa Boon's kitchen that wasn't delicious," Mac said. "Though I admit key lime cheesecake is new to me too. If nobody's ordering seconds though, I'll be on my way."

He started to get out his wallet, but Sid reached across the table to circle his wrist with her fingers.

In front of the whole goddamned restaurant, of course.

"Put that away, Mr. Knightley."

He wanted to, if for no other reason than to get her hands off of him, but she held fast, and her gaze bored into his.

"You came over to help with those horses then spent half your afternoon cleaning up our barn. You said you'd take a couple slices of pizza as your reward, and it's hardly a reward if you have to pay for it."

Mac *had* said that, so he sat back and stuffed his wallet in his pocket. Convicted by his own testimony.

"May I at least get the tip?"

"No, you may not."

He sat there feeling about two feet tall while Sid rummaged in a paisley green bag and came up with some sort of tie-dyed cloth billfold.

"Then you have my thanks," Mac said, because his mama had raised him right. "I enjoyed the food and the company."

Sid tossed a twenty and a ten onto the table. This wasn't an expensive place to eat—far from it—but letting a woman pay for his meal was...

"You're too much of a gentleman to argue with her in public," Luis said, getting to his feet, and now the kid was smirking too.

"I am." Mac rose and reached for Sid's jacket, which hung on the coat rack at the corner of their booth. He went on in French, though it was arguably rude. "See that you continue to set a good example for me, lest I forget my upbringing and embarrass us both."

"I don't embarrass easily," Luis said.

Sid watched this exchange but made no comment while Mac held out her jacket for her. She looked like she wanted to argue, or to snatch it from him, but Luis was grinning at them like one of the porpoises at the National Aquarium over in Baltimore. Sid turned her back and slipped her arms into the jacket, then flipped her braid out and draped it over her shoulder.

"Take me home, Luis." She tossed him the keys. "Maybe in the morning, those equine asteroids will have ridden their bicycles back to whatever planet they came from. Mr. Knightley, thank you for all your help."

She was dismissing him, and Mac felt more relief than was polite to be parting from her. People would talk, that was inevitable, but Mac had spent most of his adult life making sure they weren't talking about him.

But then—oh, ye gods and little fishes—Sidonie

Lindstrom made sure Mac was *all* that folks would talk about for at least the next three weeks.

She went up on her toes, put a hand on the back of his neck, and brushed a kiss to his cheek. To make matters infinitely worse, she hesitated for a moment, lingering near, her hand at his nape. She hovered long enough that Mac got a whiff of something fresh and flowery, a hint of lily of the valley over the clean scent of her shampoo. His hand was at her waist to steady her, though he'd not a clue how it ended up there.

"You're welcome," he managed.

Sid settled back down on her heels, her fingers brushing at the back of his neck before she withdrew her hand.

No doubt by the time church services were over tomorrow morning, Mac's friends and neighbors would have him married to Sid Lindstrom, living at the farm, and picking out names for their firstborn.

Then his brothers would start in on him, and his misery would be complete.

These thoughts preserved Mac from blushing, but only just.

"Shall we go?" he suggested, shrugging into his own jacket. "Do you know how to get home from here?"

"We'll manage," the Kissing Fiend assured him, "but I'll meet you fellows in the parking lot. I need to make a pit stop before we head back to the Ponderosa."

She sashayed off toward the ladies' room, leaving Mac to walk—not run—for the door, with Luis matching him step for step.

"Is everything around here so white-bread?" Luis asked as they gained the chilly night air.

"White-bread and then some. We have a liberal smat-
tering of Mennonite, and even some Amish."

"Like *Witness* and all that?"

"Daisy and Buttercup are genuine Amish plow
stock," Mac said, realizing too late he probably
shouldn't admit he knew their bloodlines. "But you'll
see some diversity at the high school, though it's all
recently acquired."

"It's bad enough being dark-skinned and red-haired in
the city. I'm going to be the freak of the universe out here."

"You'll be different, but then, being six-foot-four
before the end of my sophomore year made me different, and in my experience, that can be a good thing.
Does Sid always kiss strange men in public?"

"Sid's Sid." Luis's teeth gleamed in the darkness.
"But, yeah, she's a kisser. Took me a while to get used
to it, but it's kind of nice too. I figure it's her way of
telling the whole world I'm partly hers."

Mac considered that. Sure as shit, he was not anybody's, except perhaps his brothers'. "I'll hurt her feelings if I ask her not to do it again?"

Luis's smile disappeared. "I dunno, but it was just a
kiss. Big guy like you can't take a little smoocheroo?"

Mac let the conversation lapse because Sid was
churning across the parking lot in her fake cowgirl
boots, hugging her decorative denim jacket close against
the night breeze.

"Spring, my fat aunt Fanny," she said as she
approached them. "Luis, don't spare the horses, as it
were. Mr. Knightley, good night."

Mac found himself holding the car door open for
her. On the other side of the car, Luis stopped before

climbing in. "You said you could find us some real halters, didn't you?" he asked.

What was it with these people, that they memorized a man's every blessed word?

"I did say that. I'll make some calls when I get home tonight."

Luis wasn't buying that, the little twerp. "How do we call you if we have questions about the horses?"

"Luis," Sid broke in, "get in the car before I freeze to death."

Mac drew out one of his farrier's cards and tossed it onto the roof of the car. "Evenings and weekends are the best time to reach me. My thanks again for dinner." He closed the car door and turned his back on them both.

The kissing female, the smirking, brooding boy, the pair of them.

He climbed into his truck, cranked up the heat, slipped in a disc of Vera Winston playing late Brahms piano solos, and turned on the seat heater for good measure. Shoeing horses was hard on a man's back, and some days Mac was already half convinced he should put away his tools.

He'd always do his brother's horses, of course. James was the family mechanic—when he wasn't mooning after his piano teacher—and Mac was the family horseshoer. Trent's position was more subtle.

He was the family dad, the middle brother, the glue, the guy who checked on the fraternal chickens, making sure Mac wasn't too isolated, and James wasn't socially exhausting himself.

Though their roles had started to change with Trent's marriage to Hannah earlier in the year. Now James was showing signs of getting Vera Winston into double harness, and that would mean James had at least a stepdaughter to go with Trent and Hannah's pair of seven-year-olds.

Eight-year-olds, soon.

Mac stabbed at the CD controls, and swapped out Brahms for early Brubeck. Children had been abundantly in evidence at the restaurant—babies, toddlers, tweens, and teens. Children and doting parents, and even grandparents.

He switched the music to Mel Tormé, soothing, bluesy crooning that suited Mac's out-of-sorts frame of mind. His mood did not improve when he saw lights on at his house, and recalled James was bringing the everyday truck back from its visit to James's garage.

"Made yourself at home, I see," Mac observed as he walked into his own kitchen. James was at the table, doing the crossword puzzle in the local newspaper, while one of Mac's cats supervised as it sprawled over half the funnies. The kitchen light haloed James's blond hair. A loaf of homemade bread sat on the classifieds, amid a few crumbs, and a tub of homemade butter at James's elbow.

"The kettle should still be hot," James said, not looking up. "What's a three-letter word for difficulty or trouble?"

Sid. "Dunno. My truck's done?"

"Rub," James said, his pencil making neat strokes. "You're the Shakespeare nut. You should have known that one. Your truck's done, but I didn't check your spare."

"Why should you need to?"

"Because that model has been recalled. Road salt

corrodes the spare brace assembly. Take it to the dealer and get it checked, lest your spare go thumping down onto the tarmac without warning. I need four letters for a word that means—" James looked up, his gaze going to the clock. "Where have you been, Mac? I'm almost done with this puzzle, and it's the Saturday special."

Prevaricating was pointless. James had a social network that made the online utilities pale by comparison. By this time tomorrow, word of Mac's dinner out, and the way it had concluded, would be all over the valley.

"I had pizza with my last stop of the day," Mac said, hanging up his jacket. "Spent the first part of the day with the therapeutic riding ponies. Adelia sends her regards."

James stuck his pencil behind his ear. "She doing OK?"

"She and Neils are doing OK." Mac added water to the teakettle. James had never been the possessive sort, nor did he tolerate possessiveness in his female acquaintances.

"She deserves to be happy, and Neils is good people. I wasn't aware you were shoeing horses for anyone but the therapeutic riding program."

"And our brother, Mr. Many Ponies. These people were connected with the riding program." Mac put the kettle on the stove, turned on the burner, and wondered why James had hung out here on a Saturday night when he had his own place not two miles away.

"You ever talk to Hannah much about foster care?" Mac asked.

"Some."

"What does she say?"

He heard James's chair scraping back, and then his brother was standing beside him at the stove. "She says it was lonely, but not all of it was bad. Why?"

"No reason. You want some tea?"

"Sure."

James's tone was casual—James did a virtuosic job with casual—but Mac wasn't fooled. His youngest brother was studying him, and the guy was brilliant at most anything he turned his hand to, including needling his elders or chasing women.

Except until recently, the women had done the chasing, which was beyond brilliant. Now James was smitten with his Vera, though the course of true love had apparently hit bad footing.

"Cream is in the fridge," Mac reminded him.

"Why do you use cream? Clogging your arteries can't be good for an old man like you."

"You are six years my junior," Mac said, taking the boiling kettle off. "This means I can still whup your ass on my worst days. Get the agave nectar."

James rummaged in the cupboard for a squeeze bottle. "Did Trent turn you on to this stuff?"

"Other way around." Mac took the bottle from him. "I use cream because I enjoy its richness, most flavor compounds being fat soluble, and because dairy fat is good for you. I also use it because you don't need as much to get the same dairy impact as you would with milk, so you can have your tea hotter than if you'd dosed it with milk. Let's take this to the study."

"Why is everything an appellate argument with you?" James asked, trailing after Mac with his own tea.

"You asked me why I used cream. I answered. Did you know the home place has been flipped again?"

James closed the study door. "I knew it was for sale."

"That was my last call of the day." James would hear about this too, of course. Luis would go to school, he'd say something about the draft horses being on the property, and the whole story would eventually reach James's ears.

"That could not have been easy." James sprawled on one end of the couch. "The place doesn't look like anybody has kept it up in recent years."

"The property is still salvageable with hard work and hard cash." Mac took the rocking chair he'd built to suit his personal dimensions. James was also several inches over six feet, Trent about the same, but they both seemed to wear their height more easily than Mac did.

More gracefully.

"So who bought it?" James asked after a thoughtful sip of Earl Grey. "What kind of horses do they have?"

"A lady with a foster kid bought it, or came by it somehow, and they aren't horse people, James, but they have Daisy and Buttercup."

James, the true horseman in the family, came immediately alert. "Our Daisy and our Buttercup?"

"They aren't ours anymore, James, and haven't been for a long, long time."

———※———

"I'm telling you, Sid, he knew exactly where everything was." Luis sat on the kitchen counter, looking like a giant, adolescent, cookie-ingesting vulture.

When had he grown taller than Sid's own five foot seven inches, and where was he going to stop? And why didn't anybody warn a woman that old Formica never really came clean?

"So Knightley knows his way around a barn. He's a farm boy who shoes horses. Why wouldn't he?" A mighty big farm boy.

"You never believe me," Luis said, brushing crumbs from his lap onto the floor. "I'm telling you, Sid, he reached up into the rafters and found a hoof pick, like he'd hung it up on his personal nail just yesterday."

She scrubbed at a brown stain on the counter, knowing she'd get nowhere with it. "What's a hoof pick?"

"Like the thing in the nail file you use to clean under your fingernails, but for horses."

"Maybe you always hang those things from the rafters, and as tall as he is, he spotted it up there."

Which meant he'd probably seen the top of the fridge, which likely hadn't been scrubbed since the Flood.

"You couldn't see jack in that barn because the windows were all filthy," Luis insisted. "Knightley knows this place, and I'm thinking he knew the horses were here."

"So you've convicted him of abandoning and neglecting those equine asteroids, all without benefit of judge or jury?"

When had Sid appointed herself the guy's public defender? She gave up on the stain and wrung the hell out of the tired rag she'd been using.

"I'm raising questions." Luis's tone was maddeningly patient, but then, the defining joy of adolescence was to condescend to slow-witted adults. "Questions you ought to be raising."

To throw the rag or to be an adult? Sid ran the rag under the tap and wrung it out again.

"Weese, I am grateful that you're so protective of me, but I'm the mama. It's my job to protect you. What

I know about Knightley is he showed up here when we needed him, dealt with the horses, spent more time acquainting us with their preferred pony chow, and even joined us for a surprisingly good dinner at the local watering hole. His actions suggest he's a decent man, if a little low on charm."

Charm challenged, in fact.

"I didn't think you liked him," Luis said, taking still more cookies from the package.

Fortunately, Sid didn't particularly like peanut butter cookies, for that bunch was doomed to annihilation by morning.

"I don't know Mr. Knightley well enough to like him or dislike him," Sid said. "I was grateful he came when needed, and equally grateful that he rode off into the sunset. I'm about to do likewise, and you shouldn't be up too late either."

She wrung the rag out again, as hard as she could, and draped it over the spigot.

"I still have to set up my computer," Luis said around a mouthful of cookie. "How long before we have high speed out here?"

"Yeah. About the high speed."

Luis rolled up the package of cookies and slipped a rubber band around it.

"I'll get a job," he said. "I can pay for the horse food, and help out with the bills, and high speed really only makes a difference for graphics. You don't need it for email and social stuff."

Sid would rather he scolded her, even if she was the mama. Dial-up not two hours from the nation's capital was proof positive of parental incompetence.

"Weese, I am sorry. First thing Monday, I'll call the estate lawyers and harass the hell out of them. They said it could take a year, but it's been six months. Something has to break loose sometime soon."

Though every time Sid called them, they probably billed the estate for it.

"I'll get a job, Sid."

Six months was a long time to a teenager, particularly a disillusioned teenager who'd been let down enough for a long lifetime. Six months was a long time when bills were coming due too.

"So you get a job." Sid swiped the cookies and stashed them in a cupboard. "We only have one car between us, and you don't have your license yet. How will you get to and from this job? We've been over this and over this: your job now is to rack up as many advanced placement courses as you can, Weese. That's money in the bank; that's entrée; that's laps ahead of the pack."

Also time spent in the company of people his own age, something Luis didn't appear to care for.

"I can do both." He hopped down from the counter, lithe as a dancer. "You did."

"I do not recommend it," Sid shot back. "By the time Tony took me in, I was a wreck, and I had no friends, and you don't want to end up like that."

Luis gave her a long, sad perusal, then balled up the paper towel he'd been using as a napkin and, with the faultless grace of the natural athlete, lobbed it into the contractor bag pressed into service until they found their wastebaskets.

"I've got Mac's card," Luis said, leaping topics in

a display of teenaged tact. "He said he'd find us some halters for our horses."

"Ours for now," Sid said tiredly. "They're only our horses for now."

Chapter 4

UNTIL A FEW YEARS AGO, WHEN SOMEBODY LOCAL referred to "the Knightley boys," they meant Trent and Mac. Only within the past five years, with joint owner-ship of a law practice, had the duo become a trio.

And James, like most youngest siblings, figured he was more aware of this distinction than his brothers were. Underdogs watched overdogs much more closely than the converse, simply as a matter of survival.

"How are the mares?" James asked. "They have to be, what, seventeen years old?"

"Closer to twenty," Mac said, cradling his mug of tea in both hands. "They were the last pair Dad broke before he died."

The study became silent while each brother pushed back memories of a long-ago spring that had put an end to both of their childhoods.

"The mares are a little underweight, their feet are long, their teeth probably need some attention, but overall, they seemed hale." Mac had chosen a green-and-purple-paisley-patterned mug, probably locally made craftware he'd picked up at Boonesboro Days, or some festival over in Frederick.

"Will the new owners look after them?" James posed the question sincerely, but he was struck by Mac's pre-occupied expression.

"They'll tend to the mares to the best of their ability,

but they aren't horse people, and the lady of the house does not enjoy comfortable finances."

MacKenzie Knightley could use language delicately, for all he was frowning mightily. His surgical gift with language was part of what made him so effective before juries.

"You went to dinner with the people who have Daisy and Buttercup?"

Mac simply nodded, and James's curiosity spiked upward, while his own tea grew cold in its plain white mug. "When's the last time you went out to dinner with an adult female, Mac?"

"Be ten years this July third." He hadn't glanced at a clock or a calendar, hadn't hesitated.

"You know the exact date, like a drunk knows his sobriety date?"

Mac took a sip of tea in a manner another lawyer— say, James—would have called dilatory. "This wasn't a date. The foster kid was with us. We merely went out for pizza."

"You don't look like you *merely* went out for pizza, MacKenzie." He looked, to James's expert eye, like a guy who'd been coldcocked with the celestial two-by-four of love—or lust, or fascination, or whatever passed for attraction in the labyrinthine depths of Mac's brain.

"She kissed me, James."

What did a baby brother say to such a disclosure from an elder, and such a bewildered disclosure?

"You break your streak after *ten years* without a date, and all you can say is she kissed you?"

"Nothing will come of it." Mac set his teacup aside—on a coaster, of course. "Nothing *can* come of it, and I don't think she meant anything anyway."

"Was I adopted?" James took the last swallow of Mac's tea in hopes his brother would at least look at him.

The bewildered expression was replaced by vintage Scowling Oldest Brother. "For crap's sake, James. What kind of question is that? Seen yourself in the mirror lately?"

No, he hadn't, particularly. "I have blue eyes, wavy hair, and big feet, the same as you and Trent, but I have to wonder, Mac. Trent's excuse was his first wife broke his heart, and apparently his pecker too, because since Merle came along, he's been a born-again virgin, at least until Hannah got him sorted out. You don't have that excuse, and as far as I'm concerned, the proper use of a weekend for a single guy who closely resembles me is to get his ashes hauled by some fun-loving, easygoing female, or females, if you swing that way."

Which, of course, Mac didn't.

Mac wore the expression of a defense attorney patiently waiting for the prosecutor to finish bungling cross-examination. "Does this digression have a point, James?"

"You're unattached, solvent, good-looking, and of age," James said—or nearly shouted. "*Go play, Mac.* What are you waiting for? If you're gay, then for God's sake go find some like-minded mischief, just don't..."

"Don't what?" Mac was looking at him with Mac's version of a smile, which had more to do with the eyes, while his mouth was in its characteristic solemn line.

"Don't die of loneliness," James said, rising.

"Like you were dying of loneliness, bedding down with everything that crooked her brokenhearted little finger at you?"

The problem was, they hadn't beaten the shit out of

each other for fifteen years, and yet James paused on his way to the door, because the question was fair.

"I've wondered if you and I haven't been trying to solve the same problem from different directions, but if we have, then we're both wrong, Mac. A little flirting and flinging isn't going to hurt you, and it might be fun."

Might ease that loneliness James had so incautiously brought into the conversation.

Mac looked, if anything, puzzled by this pronouncement. James sat back down as a thought occurred to him.

"You aren't carrying a torch for someone, are you? Damn it, Mac, that would be just like you. True blue, unrequited bullshit, self-sacrificing, waste of a—" A very good man.

James fell silent, but Mac's reply still took a couple of heartbeats to materialize.

"I'm not carrying any torches, not that it's any of your business. Isn't it past your bedtime, James?"

"It's always bedtime somewhere," James said, getting back to his feet. Mac's hesitation had been telling. He wasn't carrying a torch, exactly, but something lay behind Mac's monastic existence. Maybe Trent could shed some light on it, assuming he could disentangle himself from his new wife long enough to consider the matter.

Mac stood and took his mug back from James's hands. "Does it mean anything when a woman kisses you in public?"

Such a casual question. "No, MacKenzie, it usually doesn't mean anything, except perhaps that she likes you, is interested in you, wants to have her wicked way with you, and considers you worth pursuing."

"God, let's hope not."

—∿—

The practice of criminal defense law was in some ways easy. The object of the game was clear: get the client acquitted, if at all possible. If that wasn't possible, then get him or her the lightest consequences the circumstances allowed.

The lines were bright: evidence was admissible or inadmissible. A case was decided by a judge or by a jury. A verdict was guilty or innocent. A charge was prosecuted or dropped.

And yet, Mac had long since realized that being immersed in these bright lines and clear distinctions was poor preparation for dealing with the messy reality of life's conflicted emotions.

Such as liking a woman but being uncomfortable with the liking.

Or finding a woman attractive but dreading the consequences of acting on the attraction.

James saw more than most, particularly where his family was concerned. James had picked up immediately on the seriousness of the situation between Trent and Hannah. James was the uncle their nieces confided things in more easily.

That hurt, but it was the way things had to be if Mac was to keep his sanity.

Mac had very nearly confided to James what exactly could keep a man home every Saturday night for ten years. James might not understand, but he would not judge.

Lawyers got the knack of not judging, because they saw all too often the hopeless corners life painted their clients into.

And sometimes, the lawyers got painted into some of those same corners.

———*\/\/*———

"You got a minute?" James spoke quietly, appearing unannounced in Trent's office. While that wasn't particularly unusual, Trenton Knightley's little brother seldom appeared bothered by much of anything.

James looked more than a tad bothered now.

"My next appointment isn't until this afternoon," Trent said as James closed the door. "Is this a discussion we should take out to lunch with us?" Trent ran a hand through his hair, the hair he'd been intending to have trimmed over the lunch hour.

"Is your hair getting longer?"

"No, James. Of all the Homo sapiens sucking air on this planet, I'm the only one whose hair doesn't grow." Trent tucked the financial disclosure he'd been studying back into the fat blue divorce file from whence it sprang. "Hannah likes my hair long."

Only an older brother would notice James's mental wince. "Lunch with you would be a novel treat, even if your wife is turning you into a barbarian."

A happy barbarian. "We could grab Mac and make it a threesome."

"No, we could not. He has juvenile delinquency court today and never makes it free by lunchtime. Where's Han?"

"Facilitating a four-way negotiation for Aaron Glover. What are you in the mood for?" If James needed to take something off-site, then Trent would keep the questions general until they were at least out of the building.

James and Hannah, and Mac too, for that matter, had

been whispering in corners a great deal lately, and while Trent trusted his wife and his brothers with his life, the sense of being kept in the dark was not comfortable.

"Protein," James said. "I'm usually in the mood for protein."

Big old sloppy burgers, then, such as a man could enjoy in the company of another man and not feel guilty. They were finishing up their meal before James set the baseball and office talk aside.

James aimed a check-please-honey smile at the waitress, then turned a serious gaze on Trent. "May I ask you a question?"

"Anything." Trent saw the surprise that response gave his younger brother, but did James think Trent would start listing topics that were suddenly out of bounds now that Trent was married?

Wasn't going to happen.

James opened a paper napkin to its modest, square dimensions. "Did Mac ever date?"

Huh? "Mac doesn't date, and until lately, you did almost nothing but date, to use a euphemism."

The napkin was clean—James was nothing if not fastidious—and James began to fold it back up.

"I ran around. Not the same thing. Mac's a good-looking son of a bitch, well heeled, has the same manners Mom taught us, and is surprisingly well read. Why isn't he sporting a trail of interested ladies?"

"Because he's Mac." And women were not hounds, to go baying after anything that smelled like a rabbit. But that wasn't really an answer, was it?

"When did he post the No Trespassing signs, Trent? Did he date in high school?"

"Yes," Trent said, thinking back. "Mac was reserved, but never wanted for female companionship. We often double-dated at the football games, and he was halfway serious about a couple of young ladies toward his senior year. He applied to some Canadian colleges too, on the strength of one young lady's appeal."

The napkin folding absorbed James's attention, or perhaps James's nimble fingers distracted Trent's focus—James had started taking piano lessons again, of all things.

"What happened to Mac after high school?" James asked.

James was gathering data, conducting pretrial discovery. Not exactly cross-examining, but maybe taking a deposition. Fishing in the waters of family history.

"His girlfriend ended up going to Europe for the summer, I think, and staying, and Mac figured he'd save money by starting college in-state. Then Dad died."

And life stopped, and for James, things had gone downhill from there, something Trent and Mac had only recently become aware of.

"Did Mac date after Dad died?"

"Not at first."

None of them had done anything in the first year after their father's unexpected death, except reel with grief and try to cope.

More paper folding. As an uncle, James had developed a knack for things that would entertain two little girls—card tricks, sleight of hand, silly jokes.

"When you were both at the University of Maryland, did Mac date then?"

"Why are you suddenly interested in Mac's social life, James?"

James aimed a blue-eyed stare at Trent. "Why are you content to let our brother live in isolation from everybody except us and his clients? He's not a bad guy, Trent, just a little shy."

"Shy? MacKenzie Knightley is shy? Have you run that theory past the prosecutors he opposes regularly? Mac's about as shy in the courtroom as a chain saw."

"Life is not a courtroom, and you didn't spend a week looking after Merle and Grace with him when you and Hannah recently honeymooned. He is putty in their hands, and yet he left them to me at every opportunity."

"They're little girls, James. Most grown men with any sense would dodge them when they gang up and start giggling."

Because next came the princess movies.

"Would not. Something's going on with Mac, Trent, and not something happy."

"What about you and Vera?" Vera being James's piano teacher at least, and perhaps something far more.

"There is no me and Vera, and don't try to change the subject."

Trent considered himself determined, when the need arose, or tenacious, but James and Mac could be sulking-mule stubborn.

"To answer your question, yes, Mac dated as an undergraduate, and was pretty serious about a woman named Linda, but she ditched him. He had another semi-serious thing going with a first-year law student whose name I forget, but that didn't go anywhere either. Why isn't there a you and Vera?"

James stopped fiddling with the hapless napkin. "Anybody ever tell you you're stubborn?"

Trent smiled, because no friendship came close to the friendship he could enjoy with his brothers at certain moments.

"Never one time. You?"

A smile spread over James's handsome features, one full of pride, humor, and mischief.

"Never. Now, listen up. I called Adelia to get the facts, which could have been damned delicate if Neils had picked up the call. Seems Mac was doing his regular impersonation of a farrier for the therapeutic riding horses, and one of their clients called in to say they'd found some stray horses in a back pasture."

"Stray horses? How likely is that?"

"Very likely, if it's the back paddock at the home place, Trent, and the stray horses were Daisy and Buttercup."

"Well, damn." Guilt rose up along with memories. When their father had died, James had been only thirteen. Trent and Mac had spent the summer on the farm, dealing with the logistical wreckage of a life cut short, and then they'd both gone back to college.

Leaving James to deal with their mother, the farm, and his own adolescent grief.

James had coped, until their mother had died of ovarian cancer the year James had finished high school.

"Were the horses on the property when we sold it?" Trent asked, and how had Trent not known one way or another?

"They were there, weed whacking between planting and harvest on a field board lease. Their new owner was supposed to come fetch them before we closed on the sale of the farm, but I never... It was a detail. I figured the people who bought us out wouldn't just let a pair of

one-ton animals wander around indefinitely, and who
knows if the horses have been there this whole time, or
only recently been returned to that back pasture."

The waitress came around with the bill, which James
took care of, and Trent didn't bother to argue, lest the
waitress have that much longer to flirt—pointlessly—
with James.

When the waitress sashayed away—and James
didn't even bother to watch—Trent picked up the reins
of the conversation.

"What did Mac have to say about this situation?"

"Said the mares are managing, though they need
some care. He also said the people who bought the place
aren't horse people."

The self-preservation instincts of a man who'd
recently added two females to his household kicked in.

"I don't have space left for two more horses," Trent
said, "much less two draft animals. You?"

"No fencing, though Inskip might let me board them
with his cows."

"Not a good plan." Because if there was one thing
worse than a loose horse, it was a loose draft horse—or
two loose draft horses. "What do Daisy and Buttercup
have to do with Mac's nonexistent love life?"

James added a few little tucks and folds to his napkin.
"Mac went out to dinner with the lady who owns the
place and her foster kid. She kissed Mac right there in
the restaurant, with everybody, including Vespa Boon
herself, looking on."

Little brothers must tattle, but Trent sensed no glee
in James's disclosure. "I've seen Mac's clients sometimes kiss him in the courtroom, when he gets them

acquitted against the odds, or keeps them out of jail on subsequent offenses."

"Life is not a courtroom," James said again. "A client kissing you or me or even Mac is not the same as this woman, who'd just met him, pulling a public stunt like that with Mac."

"Maybe not." Trent took the last sip of his water. "But it's Mac's business. You wouldn't like it if he told you you're a damned fool for letting Vera go, and ought to get on your horse and win her back, would you?"

James passed over the napkin, which had been transformed into an origami swan, complete with beak, tail, and majestic wings.

"He already has."

——~~——

Everything about living in the country was different, and from Sid's perspective, mostly not in a good way.

Traipsing the length of the muddy, rutted driveway—nobody spoke sidewalk in these here bucolic parts—to catch the bus would wreck Luis's designer sneakers in no time.

Getting to sleep without the monotonous swish and whump of traffic six floors down was impossible. The night sounds were isolated and natural—barking dogs, crowing roosters, and even the occasional hooting owl—none of which was in the least comforting.

Sid had the sense if she screamed, no one on two feet would hear her, and the cows and horses wouldn't care.

And she wanted to scream—she wanted badly to scream.

Social Services would make an unannounced home

visit any day, and the house was barely put to rights. When the case had been transferred up to Damson County from Baltimore, Sid had been warned the rules might change.

This far from the city, caseloads were probably more manageable, and rules more strictly enforced. The new caseworker wouldn't be as sensitive about Tony's death and its impact on Sid. The local Department of Social Services might also not be as understanding about the cultural challenges facing a kid whose mixed heritage had been unusual, even in the metropolitan area.

"I hate it here," Sid informed her oldest cat, Bojangles. He was big, black, and long-haired, a perfect ornament to an apartment decorated in Eclectic Self-Expression, but no kind of farm cat. "Your turncoat brothers are probably all out gorging on mice until they're the size of those idiot horses. It's down to you and me, Bo."

Bo yawned.

"Thank you for sharing."

Sid went back to hanging up clothes, clothes she'd probably not wear out here in the land of blue jeans and Timbos. Carhartt outerwear was popular too—so flattering to the figure.

"I'm home!"

The kitchen door banged as Luis announced himself, and Sid glanced at the vintage Garfield clock on her nightstand in consternation. Another day shot—completely shot—and still the house gave new meaning to the term "suitcase bomb."

"Up here, Weese!"

He appeared in the doorway a moment later, his hair sticking out in all directions, his expression amused.

"You're trying to do housework again, Sid. I've warned you about this."

"Putting clothes away is not housework. It's unavoidable drudgery, unless I'm to live out of boxes until we move again. How was school?"

"Same, same. My trig teacher is cute."

"You made it a point to tell her that?"

"Cute, as in, gray hair, nerves of steel, twinkling blue eyes. I think she likes me. Said her grandson has red hair, and he's brilliant. She's about this high." He held his hand out at the height of his own shoulder. "You hungry?"

He didn't mention any cute girls, which was a good thing—probably. "Starved, now that you're asking."

Sid followed Luis down to the kitchen, which at least bore a semblance of functionality.

"Why do you suppose we always come and go through the kitchen door, rather than the front door?" she mused.

"The house was designed so the kitchen is closer to the barns and buildings," Luis said. "The house wants us to come and go this way. Did you use up the last of the raspberry jam?"

The kitchen door was thus closer to the mud—or something worse than mud. "I might have. We should still have some apricot."

Luis made a face, because apricot preserves had been classified in one of their frequent squabbles as girl food.

"You've finished your first week here, Luis. Can you dance to it?"

He was quiet as he assembled a triple-decker PBJ, then stepped away from the counter so Sid could get to work on fixing her own smaller sandwich.

"It's not as bad as I thought it would be. The usual gang of idiots is missing the worst tier at the bottom. They talk about some of the kids being in gangs, or dealing, or into the cult-worship bullshit, but I get the sense it's ninety-nine percent talk, which is a relief."

Luis wasn't stupid. Not by any means. "They're all junior plow jockeys and bake-sale queens?"

"The whole spectrum is present—the jocks, the nerds, the preppies, the hoods, the lost—but the middle rungs are wider in each group, I guess. The feel of the school is still like a school, not like a juvie hall without uniforms. What's for dinner?"

"This is our house. A PBJ *is* dinner."

"It's Friday, and even in our house, we're allowed to celebrate the weekend." Luis screwed the lid back onto the apricot jam, then did the same with the peanut butter, and put them away when Sid had finished making her sandwich. "I could go for a piece of that lime cheesecake."

Sid stared at the sandwich she'd made: peanut butter and apricot jam on stale whole wheat, and one slice was the heel, dammit.

"If we got a dog," she said, "I could feed him this sandwich, and he'd think it was the greatest treat he'd had all week."

"If we got a dog, you'd have to make sure it had all its shots, or DSS would impound him or some shit."

The mood in the kitchen went from end-of-week relaxed to sullen-anxious-teenager in a blink.

"They haven't called, Luis. I left the worker a message on Monday, according to Hoyle, and there hasn't been a call back."

"Call them again. We're supposed to go to a review hearing within thirty days of moving out here, and it's been ten days already."

Technically, the workday wasn't over for fifteen more minutes. Sid passed Luis her sandwich, and while he watched, dialed the number for DSS again. She got voice mail—she always got voice mail—but left the prescribed message and the house number for a return call.

"Satisfied?" she said, hanging up.

"I will be satisfied when they close my case and leave me in peace."

"There are two ways through that door, Luis. You can turn eighteen, which is more than two years off, or you can let me adopt you. I support either outcome, you know that."

He glared at the half of Sid's sandwich he hadn't eaten. "Do we have to talk about this now?"

"We have to talk about it sometime," she said gently. "You won't go to counseling, and letting you drift along in foster care for another two years makes the state look bad come federal funding time."

"As if I give a rat's crap how the state looks."

"As long as your case is open, Luis, they can come along and move you back to a group home. Bad grades, hooking school, a fender bender, a dirty urine, anything, and they can take you from me, and me from you. Your lawyer made that plain enough."

Such a helpful little SOB, that lawyer. Somewhere along the line he'd confused pontificating with zealous advocacy.

"My lawyer, the social worker, the judge." Luis scrubbed his hand through his hair, and gave her a look from old, sad eyes. "I'll bring in the ponies, and then maybe you'll be willing to spring for cheesecake."

He banged out of the kitchen, taking another bite of sandwich as he went, leaving a ringing silence behind.

Why in the ever-loving hell had Sid started that riff about Luis being moved? He'd come home in a decent mood, his impression of the school surprisingly positive after the first week, and she had to go pissing on his parade with that talk about...

The phone rang, interrupting her self-castigation.

"Sid Lindstrom."

"Hello, Mrs. Lindstrom, I'm Amy Snyder, the caseworker assigned to Luis Martineau. How are you?"

"Unpacking," Sid said, not correcting the social worker's choice of title, "but getting there. What can I do for you, Ms. Snyder?"

"Call me Amy. I wanted to touch base with you, see how you're settling in, and let you know I'll stop out next week some time during business hours to introduce myself to you and Luis. May I say hello to him now?"

"He's out with the livestock. If you like, I can have him call you back in a few minutes."

A slight pause, suggesting Sid had either given the wrong answer, or the woman was typing in her contact note as they spoke.

"I'll talk to him when I make my home visit. Do you have any questions about moving out here? You have Luis enrolled in school?"

"I have. I did want to ask when the review hearing is. I understand we're supposed to attend one in the next few weeks, and Luis is already anxious about it."

Another pause while the worker probably looked at the court order from Baltimore.

"I'll put one in the works when I come in on Monday,

and the court will send out the hearing notice. Luis is encouraged to come because the judge is supposed to see the kids in the courtroom regularly."

"Luis knows the drill. We'll look forward to meeting you in person next week."

They hung up, and in the pit of Sid's stomach, in the place that never forgot she'd already lost a brother, and Luis wasn't hers to keep yet, unease germinated and tried to set down roots.

"Heaven help me, lime cheesecake sounds like just the antidote."

———~~~———

What was a kid supposed to do with his weekends in the country?

Sid put the question to herself as she climbed out of bed early Saturday morning—bedroom curtains weren't in the budget yet, and the sun apparently rose earlier out here than it did in the city. She made pancakes, breakfast being her fave meal of the day, and sat down to consider which room she might focus on putting to rights.

All of them, none of them. A straight week of laundry, unpacking, washing glassware, dusting corners, and trying to domesticate left her without motivation.

"You cooked." Luis scrubbed his hand over his eyes as he came down the kitchen steps. Even the guy's sweats were nudging into high-water territory.

"Alert the media. I left your plate in the microwave. Coffee's hot."

Luis got to bottom of the steps and stretched. "I think I'll have tea."

"When did you become a tea drinker?" And when had he developed such defined biceps?

"I've always liked it. My mom used to fix us tea without the tea. Mostly hot milk and sugar. Where's the syrup?"

"Hell if I know," Sid said, though maple syrup doubtless lurked in the cupboards somewhere. "You'll have to rough it with butter and sugar."

"I like butter and sugar. You heard back from Dewey, Cheatham, and Howe about the estate yet?"

It all comes, said Rabbit, from watching Rocky and Bullwinkle *reruns.* "I called Mr. Granger twice, and haven't heard back, natch. What will you do with your day?"

"Mac said he'd bring over some halters and show me a few things about handling the horses."

"Mac?" Sid knew damned good and well which Mac.

"I called him this week and reminded him. Making do with braided baling twine isn't going to cut it if my girls have a frisky day."

"Your girls?" Sid barely resisted the urge to cross her arms.

"We've gone through the first bag of feed." Luis put the kettle on the burner and turned the heat on high. "Probably not a good idea to run out."

"Weese…"

"I got a lead on a job," he said, getting down a mug and tossing in a tea bag. "There's a guy over the hill — Hiram Inskip — who farms a lot of our land, and he might need some help."

"I recall the name. What do you know about farming?"

"I know you get to drive tractors and use a lot of equipment. I'm good at engines."

He was genius with engines, but big engines ate boys' fingers for dinner. "You're fifteen. Child labor isn't legal, and machines are dangerous."

"I will be sixteen before school's out, Sid, and we need the money."

"Water's boiling." She took a sip of her coffee rather than argue. They did need the money. When she'd taken a break from the house chores yesterday, she'd reread the addendum to the contract of sale Tony had signed for the farm.

Or she'd tried to read it. Goddamn lawyers spoke in demon tongues and wrote in them too. Heretofore, wherefore, notwithstanding, except on the condition, insofar as, bullshit-of-the-first-part language.

From what she'd been able to discern, Tony had become absolute owner of the property, but he'd agreed to honor the leases and agreements made by the previous owners regarding use of the land. He was under no obligation to renew those leases, but he had to let them run their courses.

And this Inskip fellow was the guy responsible for leasing the land under cultivation. Another guy had the right to cut up the deadfall in the woods. There was some sort of rent owed by both, but not—had Abraham Lincoln himself drafted these contracts?—until crops had been sold in the fall.

If only Tony—

"You want some OJ?" Luis opened the fridge and stood eyeing the contents as only an adolescent who had never paid an electricity bill himself might do.

"Still working on my coffee, thanks. Did Knightley say when he's coming over?"

"This afternoon. He'll work at the riding school first,

and that reminds me. Now that we live out here, can I move my lessons to midweek? That's when the individual lessons are, and Adelia said I'm ready."

But the checkbook was not.

"We can talk to her about it when we see her tomorrow," Sid said. "You never did tell me what you'll do with your Saturday."

"I have some homework, and I'll make some more progress on the barn, maybe give the girls a grooming."

"They like that?"

"Didn't you used to like it when your mom brushed your hair?" He was regarding her with puzzlement, a boy with mostly good memories of a mother others would say did a bad job.

"She was usually in a hurry. Leave the dishes. I'll clean up after I get dressed."

She tousled Luis's hair as she went by, needing the touch. Luis loved his mother, loved his little sisters, even though it had been months since he'd seen them. That didn't threaten Sid, exactly, but she was aware she was a consolation prize in his mom sweepstakes.

"Weese, Mother's Day is coming up. You want to make a trip to Jessup?"

"Nah."

"She'd like to see you."

"That's not what her letters say, and she'd ask me about the girls."

Sid headed up the stairs. Luis's younger sisters were a sore point, to say the least. Maybe Ms. Call-me-Amy Snyder could do something about that, because Sid's efforts to arrange visits between Luis and his siblings had been a complete failure.

Chapter 5

MAC TRIED TO TELL HIMSELF HE WASN'T LOOKING FOR-ward to stopping by the home place again, wasn't pleased to have an excuse to see what Sid Lindstrom was doing with the house—with his old bedroom—or how the mares were faring in Luis's care.

But self-deception had never been his strong suit, and he finished with Adelia's school horses in record time. He also stopped by the Farmers' Co-op and picked up a couple more bags of senior feed, a pair of leather lead shanks, a horsey first aid kit, and a few other odds and ends.

All of which, he admitted to himself as he pulled into the driveway, constituted procrastination.

"Mac!"

Luis waved to him from the barn aisle, so Mac eased his truck into what had been the chicken yard.

"Hullo!" Luis waved a muck fork like it was a lightsaber. "I've been working on the barn." He had the diffident grin of a pleased adolescent, but he waited while Mac retrieved the halters and lead shanks from the backseat of the truck.

"Greetings yourself, Luis. Your halters and some decent leather leads. How are the ladies?"

"I think they've put on some weight, but, man, do they shed."

"They need to." Mac walked beside Luis into the barn. "Big animals like that don't dissipate heat as well as the little ones do. And, my heavens, you must have spent the whole week in here cleaning and mucking." The place looked worlds better, not a cobweb in sight. "Did you pressure wash these stones?"

"Scrubbed 'em," Luis said, eyes on the cobbled flooring. "My knees aged a decade. Come see the tack room."

He led the way to the old dairy, which was as spruce and tidy as the rest of the understory. What few pieces of grooming equipment the place still boasted were neatly stowed on hooks and in buckets. Two big metal garbage cans stood to one side of the door.

"I brought you a couple more bags of feed," Mac said. "A housewarming, or barnwarming for the ladies."

The kid's eyes shifted away, indicating gifts were a delicate issue with Luis's pride, or perhaps with his foster mom's.

"Thank you."

"There's something I haven't quite found a way to tell Sid." Mac studied the window, noting that even the corners were clean. "My dad is the guy who bred Daisy and Buttercup. I consider I owe them." He chanced a glance at Luis, then went back to a visual inventory of all the work the kid had done.

Luis left off working the buckles of one of the new halters, the stiffness of the leather making for a tough fit between straps and hardware.

"Owe them, how?"

"Draft horses have become something of a rarity. They take special care, and they can't exactly be passed around from one little girl to the next like a show pony. When you bring an animal like that into the world, you have to be prepared to take responsibility for it."

Luis held up the halter, probably inspecting it for a price, which he would not find. "You sold both mares, right?"

"We did, but I think it's like being a parent, Luis. Just because your darling girl marries the man of her dreams, she doesn't stop being your daughter."

"You have kids?"

The question, so prosaic, so commonplace, cut to the bone. *Again*.

"I do not, which is probably why finding Daisy and Buttercup here sits so poorly with me. If they've had to shift for themselves, it's my fault, and I'm in your debt."

As were Trent and James, though Mac hadn't put it to either brother in that light.

Luis opened one of the metal trash cans and peered inside as the rich scent of rice bran and molasses wafted across the tack room.

"Sid hasn't said anything about getting rid of the horses, but she isn't exactly running out to stock up on feed, either."

Could she even lift a feed bag by herself? "She needs to get to know them. I never met the lady who wasn't smitten by horses."

The lid went back on the trash can with a hollow clank. "Sid's not prone to being smitten. Not so it shows."

"You know her pretty well." Mac was not going to interrogate this kid, not about his foster mother, in any case.

"She knows me just as well." Luis's smile was bashful, but it made him look older. "I gave her hell and a half the first few months I was with her, but she hung on, and hung on, until one day, I realized it mattered to me whether I hurt her feelings."

What a hell of a thing, that a kid needed months to admit a capacity for empathy.

"Riding out the bucks is half of getting any relationship under way," Mac replied. "I'd say she loves you."

"She says it too." Luis's smile became rueful. "At the strangest times and places."

"Women."

They shared the kind of look Mac usually reserved for his brothers, and then a shout cut through the air.

"Weese! I'm back!"

"Groceries." Luis trotted off, male bonding clearly taking a backseat to foraging through shopping bags. He turned and took a few steps backward. "Come on, or she'll get the best stuff put away before you even know it's in the house. Dibs on the nachos."

Teenage boys would never change in some biological fundamentals, no matter what else did. Mac took one last glance around the barn, pleased in his bones to see it so improved.

He approached Sid's little red car as she hefted grocery bags out of the trunk.

"Let me help with those." He tried to scoop a bag out of her grip. She wrestled him for it but gave up eventually. "Pass me another."

"How will you get the kitchen door open, Mr. Knightley?"

"You'll hold it for me," he said, taking his burden up the porch steps. "Then you'll start putting this stuff away while I bring in the rest."

"But Luis…" She trailed after him and held the door open.

"Luis is inventorying the spoils." Mac leaned closer

to lower his voice. "Or doing some quality assurance on the nachos."

Luis sat on the counter, the nachos in hand, orange-crumb dust already accumulating on his fingers.

"I skipped lunch." Luis held out the bag. "Or I'm having nachos for lunch."

Mac stood just behind Sid, admiring the view, taking in her scent, willing to hold her groceries all day. From this angle, the blouse she'd tucked into her jeans allowed him a hint of a peek of cleavage, and while peeking might not be exactly gentlemanly, it wasn't illegal either.

"You should be ashamed, Luis, and get off the counter. We have company." Sid walked across the kitchen, sexy little cowgirl boot heels thumping, the fringe on her open jacket dancing with each step. She snatched the nachos out of his hand and smacked him with the bag.

"Don't hit me with the nachos," Luis wailed. "Not my nachos, Sid!" But he was grinning and dodging for the chips while Sid tried to land another swat.

"You see what I have to put up with, Mr. Knightley. Insubordination, disrespect, attitude. *Nacho hogging*."

Luis swiped the bag back and darted for the door, yelling over his shoulder, "Mine at last! Fly, my pretties! Fly!"

Mac set down the groceries he'd been holding, unable to suppress a smile. "He's a *Wizard of Oz* fan?"

"Old movies, old cartoons." Sid shrugged out of her jacket, hung it on a chair, and began peering into the bags on the counter. "Vintage TV was one thing he and Tony had in common." She stowed her plunder in the fridge: yogurt, a big brick of orange cheddar, a tub of sour cream, butter, a brand of ice cream Mac considered worth his own notice.

"You like your dairy."

"Love it." Her tone was flat as she kept stowing the goods.

"I'm sorry if bringing up your late brother is awkward."

She turned then, her expression puzzled. "Not bringing him up feels awkward, like he's not only dead but also somehow disgraced, though bringing him up doesn't help. I'm sorry." She turned her back to Mac again and began rummaging in the second bag. "You'll probably want to be going, now that you've brought Luis the what-do-you-call-'ems. And my thanks. I'm sure they'll be much appreciated."

Maybe it was her tone of voice, casual and offhand; maybe it was the way she tossed things into the cupboard, or the line of her spine under that silk blouse.

Mac crossed the kitchen to stand immediately behind her. "It's OK to cry, Sid."

She pokered right up, her back to his chest, a jar of raspberry jam in her hand.

"No, Mr. Knightley, it is not." She set the jar on the counter quite firmly, and kept her hand around it. "Not when I have a house to set to rights, groceries to put away, and a child to raise. Crying is for when you have nothing left to do and nobody to do it for. I've cried enough."

Have not.

What she wanted was an argument, a fight, a rousing battle to keep her together. Mac could understand better than she'd ever know, but he could not oblige.

"My dad died when I was little more than a kid myself, Sid. I can still, right this minute, feel the lump in my throat that took the better part of five years to ease. Just when I thought maybe I was regaining my balance, my mom was diagnosed with ovarian cancer."

Some of the starch went out of her. Her shoulders dropped, and she braced herself on the counter. Mac didn't step away.

"Luis doesn't know what to do with me when I mope."

She didn't know what to do with herself.

"When you grieve." Mac reached around her and put the jam up on the shelf next to a jar of apricot preserves. "It's called grieving, Sid."

She nodded, and only then did Mac move off, going to another grocery bag. "What was he like, your brother?"

"Tony was the best." She didn't march up to Mac and chase him off her groceries, so he put frozen vegetables into the freezer. Snow peas—she was a snow peas kind of lady. Knowing that about her pleased him.

"My brothers are the best too," he said. "Though sometimes they require pointed guidance."

"Tony didn't." She stared at a jar of guacamole dip. "He was the kind of guy anybody could talk to. That came in handy in his line of work."

"What did he do?" Snow peas and a cruciferous medley. Mac approved of both.

"He ran his own video production company. I was the second in command, the one who stepped and fetched and caught up all the loose ends. My title was head of HR, but I had my fingers into everything. We were quite successful, while Tony was well."

"He was ill?"

Mac purposely didn't look up from the grocery bag he'd nearly emptied. Going through Sid's provisions like this, putting them away with her was intimate. Almost as intimate as listening to her reluctant admissions of grief.

"Tony was ill." She sat at the table, her chin resting on her stacked fists. "I could tell you it was lymphoma, but it was AIDS. Damned, rotten, stupid AIDS. He always promised he was careful, but he was a guy. That was talk to placate the womenfolk, or maybe he only started being careful when I came to live with him."

Mac opened the guacamole dip, set it in front of her, found the backup bag of nachos, and put that at her elbow.

"You haven't had lunch yet. Eat."

She gave him a measuring look, then tore open the chips. "My brother died of AIDS. You may now start compulsively washing your hands or something."

Mac turned a chair around and straddled it. "It's an illness, not a curse from the angry gods of right-wing morality. What do you want to drink?"

She studied her chip now, one sporting a little dab of guacamole on a corner. "It's hard for me when people are nice, Mr. Knightley."

"Mac," he said, reaching into the bag. "It's hard for you when they're not nice, too, would be my guess. Stubborn people deal better with a little traction, a dash of sand in the gears."

She peered up at him through sad, shiny eyes. "You are an unlikely philosopher."

"I'm stubborn too." Mac patted Sid's hand and rose, going to the fridge. "I'm putting together a sandwich, and you're eating it." He set fixings on the counter: turkey, Swiss cheese, bread, mustard, a tomato, mayo, butter…

"What is it with men and food?" Sid bit off the corner of the nacho and considered the uneaten portion.

"It's life and food. The two are related, and you're alive, which is nothing to be ashamed of. What happened to the production company?"

"Tony's spouse, Thorvald, inherited Tony's share, though without Tony, it's just a lot of equipment, a leased studio, and a few contracts."

"You really know a guy named Thorvald?"

"He'd like you," Sid said, eyeing Mac as he fished a knife out of the silverware drawer. "He was a tramp, and I've wondered if he didn't kill Tony indirectly."

"AIDS killed Tony, and you are only torturing yourself by trying to read more into it than that. Mayonnaise or mustard?"

"Just mustard. How long ago did your dad die?"

"I was out of high school. Mom died about twelve years ago, but I still stumble, sometimes."

"Stumble?"

"She loved this…life. Loved each little crocus, each daffodil, each robin. She loved the way the light was so clear the sunset before the first frost. She loved the first snow. She simply *loved*, and when Dad died, she folded in on herself. I'll be walking along and identify a particular birdsong, and I think 'I'll tell Mom.' But it's a decade later, and I won't tell Mom ever again. I stumble."

"I stumble to my knees." Sid dipped a second nacho into the guacamole. "The people who ought to be tidying up Tony's estate don't seem to care whether we live or die while they twiddle their thumbs at an obscene hourly rate. I want the paperwork, the bullshit, to be over, you know?"

Mac passed her a turkey and Swiss on rye. "Probate is a detailed process, done right. How about milk with that?"

Sid crunched her nacho. "Moo juice is fine by me. Do you know about probate from your parents' deaths?"

"Mostly." Mac busied himself putting away the sandwich fixings. Trust and estate—stiffs and gifts—wasn't his legal area, but he owned part of a law practice that had a T&E department.

"I purely hate lawyers, Mr. Knightley. Hate them with a cold-blooded, unrelenting passion."

"A lot of people feel that way." *Until they were arrested, or were served with divorce papers, or found themselves permanently disabled by some incompetent doctor.* "There have been lawyers in my family since forever, and they can be useful people to have on your side."

"That's just it." Sid picked up her sandwich in two hands, rocking her hips from side to side in the chair, as if settling in for a tug of war. "The lawyers are never on your side. They may take your money, but they're on their own side, ultimately."

Now was not the time to argue—or to tell Sid he was a lawyer. "They can't break the law to please a client."

"And yet they drag their feet, prevaricate, don't return phone calls, all the while charging an hourly rate that would bankrupt The Donald in nothing flat."

Some lawyers did that, though it was hard to get away with in a small town. Word traveled quickly.

"You having trouble with a particular lawyer?"

"The lawyers handling Tony's estate, for starters. Seems they can pay the rent on the studio and give Thor free rein with the business decisions, but with

Tony's personal assets, they are as tightfisted as my Scottish granny."

"Who are they?"

Sid gave Mac the name of the firm.

"Over in Baltimore?"

"With offices in DC and Boston. This is a good sandwich."

Which brought up another touchy subject: "When was the last time you sat down to eat something with protein in it, Sidonie?"

"Pancakes have eggs in them, so this morning."

And she thought lawyers were bad. "You going to let Luis get away with having nachos for lunch?"

"I didn't see you chasing after him to retrieve the contraband." She took another bite of her sandwich, chewing like a squirrel. "He's fast, and getting bigger by the day."

"Boys will do that, but we're discussing proper nutrition." Mac opened a few cupboards, found what he was looking for, and turned a burner on. "You don't have much here in the way of fresh produce, Sid. Veggies are good for growing boys."

And grieving ladies. Mac kept that thought to himself.

"You have a point," Sid conceded. "But somebody would have to cook the fresh veggies."

"You cook the frozen ones," he said, pouring milk into a saucepan. "Fresh ones aren't that different. Do I take it that some of your financial worries would be alleviated if Tony's estate were disbursed?"

Sid glared at the remaining two-thirds of her sandwich, which was answer enough.

"Tony was a fricking financial genius. He bought this farm on a whim, to flip it in a few years, or so he said.

Tony could spot a deal." She chewed more slowly. "Yes, I am shamelessly sitting on my rosy ass, at least for now, when I ought to be out finding work. Except I want to be here for Luis, and we just moved here, and there isn't much call for a video production infield utility gofer out here in God's country."

"File for unemployment. It's income, and if you worked, you earned it."

"I worked up until a year ago, when Tony started having bad spells. I'm not sure I still qualify for unemployment. What are you doing there, Knightley? Making free with my comestibles?"

"Here." Mac put a steaming mug of hot chocolate in front of her. "You said you'd drink milk. This is milk."

"You made me *hot chocolate*?"

"It's comfort food and good for you."

Sid's brows knitted, and she traced a finger around the rim of the mug. "I don't have any of the mix. How did you do this?"

"You have bitter cocoa, sugar, vanilla, salt, and milk."

Sid took a sip, then a second sip. "Yours is better than the instant kind. More chocolate." She swiped at her top lip with her tongue.

"You want another sandwich?" Or maybe Mac would scrub the cobblestones Luis had already wrecked his knees scrubbing.

"I want you to sit and stop pillaging in my kitchen. How did you learn to make this?"

"My mother believed her sons should know their way around the kitchen, particularly when she had no daughters to assist her. You done with the nachos?"

"Knightley, *sit*."

Mac sat, which was a bad idea. He had a front-row seat when Sid once again licked that little chocolate-milk mustache off her lips.

"Who's your lawyer?" he asked, needing to see her dander up again. Sid hated lawyers, which he tried to regard as a good thing.

"I don't have a lawyer, nor do I want one."

She was enjoying the hot chocolate, though. Mac couldn't help but notice that.

"You should have one, because the estate lawyers don't represent you. They don't have your best interests at heart. They won't hop to it just because you say so." They'd go merrily billing away, in fact, not exactly milking the estate, but doing a thorough job of administering it.

Sid saluted with her mug. "That is the damned truth. How do I afford a lawyer when the estate people won't turn loose of the first nickel? What you call your basic conundrum, there."

"It's your lawyer's job to get the nickels turned loose," Mac said, "particularly if Tony set up some sort of trust with you as beneficiary."

"Weese got the trust from a life insurance policy. I get a wad of cash, I think."

She thought. Six months into probate, and she hadn't seen a preliminary accounting, nor apparently even had a peek at the will or the trust documents.

Not good.

"How about I have my lawyer make a few calls?" Mac asked, putting the lid back on the guacamole dip.

"No thank you. Lawyers who make calls are lawyers who send out bills. Did you make any more of this stuff?" She nodded at her mug.

Sid would let him fix her another hot chocolate, but not arrange free legal help. Usually, people were pestering Mac to take their cases, to "look over" the charging documents, or "talk to the cops" for them. His clients often wanted something for nothing and were happy to get it.

"I can make you more, Sidonie."

"How about you show me how?"

Mac did, standing next to Sid at the stove, leaving her to stir the milk with the wooden spoon while he put away the nachos and dip and wiped off the table.

"What do you suppose Luis is up to?" he asked when she'd poured the hot chocolate into two mugs.

"Damned if I know. He's in love with those horses, though, and that's going to be a problem."

"How?"

"We cannot afford them."

A money problem, Mac could solve. A problem with Sid's pride, only Sid could solve.

"What if the owner paid you to board them here," Mac suggested. "Paid you what they're costing you, plus something for their care?"

"That would be Luis's idea of a prayer answered. He seems to spend more time out at that barn with each day."

Whatever that quote was, about the outside of a horse being good for the inside of a man, it went double for kids, probably quadruple for foster kids.

"Have you seen what he's done there?" Mac asked.

"I have not," Sid said, passing him his hot chocolate. "I figure he'll let me into the secret clubhouse when he wants me to see it."

"Take a look. He's working miracles. Now, about the horses."

"And their imaginary owner, who has not, in the two weeks since we closed on this place, so much as picked up the phone to ask after his fair damsels. I asked the real estate agent to call the previous owner, but even his agent can't find him. I don't suppose you know who this paragon of pet-owning responsibility would be?"

Mac took a fortifying sip of his hot chocolate. "In a sense, I think that would be me."

———

And here I was beginning to like him—or his hot chocolate.

"Mr. Knightley, I do not appreciate prevarication, mendacity, or manipulation," Sid said. "Why would you leave your horses here, come on the scene as if you knew nothing, and now offer me some sort of confession?"

"I can explain."

The road to hell should be paved with those three words. "You can keep your explanations," Sid said. "I cannot abide people who trade in falsehoods. Ask Luis—on your way out the door."

Sid had also respected this guy, respected his generosity and competence, his willingness to deal with Luis—but when had her judgment regarding guys ever been trustworthy?

"You asked me a question, Sidonie, at least let me answer it." Mac sat back in his chair, reminding Sid she couldn't bodily toss him anywhere.

"So answer, then beat it. Take the mastodons with you." At least Sid had his hot chocolate recipe to keep.

"I didn't leave them here. I never had title to them, and if you can't listen with an open mind, why should I bother? I can walk out that door, and there isn't a judge or a jury on this earth that would hold me responsible for those horses. I hold myself responsible. Why don't you run your ad on Craigslist, and explain to Luis why his horses ended up in a freezer headed for Belgium?"

MacKenzie Knightley wasn't the kind of guy whose fuse burned down quickly and loudly. His arguments were soft, reasonable, and nasty.

"You said they were yours. Now they're Luis's?"

He had blue eyes, and they reflected a world of frustration. A guy this size, this frustrated, whom Sid didn't know well at all, ought to be intimidating.

And he was, but not scary. MacKenzie Knightley was formidable, but she would have bet her leather bomber jacket he was honorable. Surely any guy who scolded her about protein and grief while he made her sandwiches and hot chocolate had to have some honor?

"My father bred that pair," he said, staring at his mug. "They were the last pair out of his own mares, and he was looking very much forward to seeing what they could do. We broke them to drive, to the plow, and even to ride, and they were smart about it. Full of common sense, like the best ones are. I competed them at the state fair and did well."

"Which is how you knew them at sight?" More than a decade later, he knew them at sight.

"Yes. But we sold them when we sold the farm after my mother died, and the new owners were supposed to come pick them up after we'd closed with the farm's buyers. Not everyone has a stock trailer that can handle such a big pair of animals, so we thought nothing of it. James was the only one living here, and when he moved out, the horses were contentedly enjoying pasture board. I don't think it occurred to him—to any of us—to follow up."

"Who's James?" Sid asked.

"My baby brother. Six years younger. Wonderful guy."

"Are you telling me those horses have been lounging here for the past ten or twelve years unattended? I do not believe that."

"I don't know."

Sid saw no guile, no deception in Mac's eyes. What she saw surprised her: he truly did feel responsible, wretchedly so.

"They're enormous horses, Knightley. Somebody would have noticed them." Though she'd been on the property for a week before she'd caught sight of them—and she didn't have a job in DC or Baltimore that kept her away for most of the day.

He rose and took his mug to the sink, and he didn't stop there. He scrubbed his mug out with soap and hot water, then put it in the drain rack.

"It's possible they were someplace else for years at a time," he said, "but came back here to board, because the property can accommodate them. Their feet have been tended to occasionally, so they weren't feral."

One-ton feral horses. Sid abruptly missed the blandishments of the city all over again.

"They need bigger pastures than other horses?"

"Not that so much as they need stronger fencing, bigger stalls, higher ceilings, and very stout gates. A couple tons of horse regularly scratching on a fence post will soon have it on the ground."

Sid was by no means as sturdy as a fence post and neither was Luis. "You're sure this is your Daisy and your Buttercup?"

"I'd bet my farrier's tools on it, and those belonged to my dad."

Which, Sid supposed, was comparable to a solemn vow for MacKenzie Knightley.

"Why didn't you come right out and tell me what was going on?" Sid asked. "I cannot stand lying. Will not stand it."

Now his gaze slid away, but Sid let the question hang. No matter how much she liked Mac's hot chocolate, or Luis liked his horses, the man would deal honestly with her or not deal with her at all.

"You've put together that I was raised on this farm?"

Well, hell. "No, I did not. This is where you grew up?"

"My mom died in the bedroom where Luis is sleeping now. She wanted it that way, and hospice and James and Trent and I made it possible. The memories are mixed, but mostly good. They're just not all happy."

How could a man have good memories of the very house where his mom had died?

"So you didn't tell me you grew up here, didn't tell me those used to be your horses, and I have to wonder what else you're not telling me."

Sid was abruptly having to take slow, deep breaths, because the thought of three boys losing their mother—not to a few years in jail, but for forever—made her chest ache.

"Would you like to tell me about the day Tony died?" Mac didn't raise his voice, didn't put any particular inflection in the question at all, and his salvo landed directly on target as a result.

"I would not. So you were minding your business, and then last Saturday, you got the wind taken out of your sails." A relief to think Mac's deception was a symptom of simple human bewilderment—a not entirely convincing relief.

"Yes." He leaned back against the sink, looking incongruously domestic, a linen towel listing Scottish swear words over his shoulder. "The wind taken out of my sails, to see the place had been sold again, to see Daisy and Buttercup, to feel like we'd—like *I* had let them down by losing track of them. I'm not stupid, but I need time to figure out the things most other people take right in stride. Compared to my brothers, I'm slow."

Damn him for being able to put that into words, for being brave enough.

"But you can cut right through situations that would stop everybody else," Sid finished for him, because that was the other half of the syllogism of life at the social margins.

"Pretty much." Mac studied her, and must have seen the relenting in her eyes. "Truce?" He held out a big, callused, competent hand.

Sid didn't want to touch him, because if she did, all her mad would evaporate, and she might even feel some compassion for him.

Some liking. For him, his hot chocolate, his lectures on proper nutrition, and for the grieving boy he'd been.

He closed the distance for her, taking her hand and giving it a firm shake. "You'll let me pay their board?"

Well. *End of sharing time.*

"How much?"

He named a figure, no hesitation, and the amount was enough to make Sid wish he had eight other horses lurking on the back forty.

"I'll ask Adelia if that's a fair price," she said. "Luis has a lesson tomorrow, and she and Neils can tell me whether to agree to this."

"I understand. They might also be willing to have Luis do some weekend work for them, and reduce or eliminate the price of his lessons accordingly."

Of course, Sid had to look the gift horse in the mouth. "Why would they do that?"

"Because I'll tell them he works his butt off for the right motivation, and they always need help on weekends."

The slight undertone of regret was gone from his voice, and Sid was relieved to hear it go. Whatever the motivation, she did not like to see MacKenzie Knightley at a loss.

"Luis is already thinking of asking the tenant farmer if he has any work for a teenage boy this summer," Sid said.

"You mean the guy who farms your land?"

"His name is Hiram Inskip, and Luis says he lives over that way." Sid gestured with her chin. "Who names a kid Hiram on purpose?"

"I know him. He's my brother James's neighbor, and getting on. He also farms James's land, and his own boys are grown and gone."

"Is there anybody you don't know in this valley?" Sid got up to take her mug to the sink as a funny look crossed Mac's features, a little amused, a little exasperated.

"I don't know the new people." He shifted a couple of feet to the left, while Sid turned on the spigot. "With the exception of present company."

Mac was close enough that she caught a whiff of cinnamon and clove from him again, and had to stop herself from leaning closer. Cinnamon, clove, and something else, something absurdly enticing on a guy who stood nearly six and a half feet, and wore work boots, faded jeans, and a flannel shirt.

Gay guys typically had the corner on the designer scents. Sid stopped that thought before it could wander any closer to admitting she missed her brother.

"You get the saddest look in your eyes sometimes." Knightley's voice was soft, while he reached over and turned off the water. "Let me know if you're keeping the horses. Otherwise, I'll be putting up a load of fencing on James's property."

"What about your own property?"

"I have some acreage, but James is a horseman. Speaking of horsemen, I thought I'd spend some time with Luis this afternoon. He might enjoy learning to drive a team."

Not subtle. "*If* I decide they can stay."

"Yes, ma'am. If you decide they can stay."

Mac's eyes weren't exactly dancing, but warmth lurked behind the solemn blue. Sid gave the spigot an extra twist and tried not to smile.

"I'll call you when I've spoken to Adelia and Neils," she said. "Luis apparently has your number."

Mac pulled out a worn wallet and extracted a card. "That's my cell. Feel free to use it."

"We're listed," Sid said, then regretted it. That was almost the same as giving him their phone number, and while it shouldn't mean anything, she hadn't given a man her number in ages, not for any reason.

"I'll be going." Mac slipped his wallet back into its pocket. "Call me if you need anything, Sidonie. Whether you keep the horses for me or not, we're still neighbors."

He left, not letting the screen door bang. Sid turned around and hiked herself up to sit on the counter, Luis-style.

Sidonie. She liked his hot chocolate, his cool blue eyes, and worst of all, she liked the sound of her name on his lips. Mac gave it just the slightest French inflection, like Luis had when he'd first been placed with her.

No, this was not good at all.

Chapter 6

HANNAH KNIGHTLEY WAS A HAPPY WOMAN. AT THE beginning of the year, she'd married a man she couldn't help but love—and desire. In Trent Knightley she'd found the man of her dreams as well as a father to her little girl, and gained a stepdaughter to love as well.

As if that weren't enough, Trent came with two brothers whom Hannah and Grace both adored.

Trent had the polish. He was good on his feet, smooth, subtle, effective, and efficient. In the courtroom, other people said he was damned good. To Hannah, his courtroom presence was sexy-good.

James had the charm. If he had to confront, in the courtroom or elsewhere, he was every bit as lethal as his brothers, but his preference was to flirt and cajole, to commiserate and tease and reason. With any luck, he was about to charm his Vera to the altar.

That left MacKenzie, who had the…fathomless blue eyes. Mac was still a puzzle to Hannah, but his ferocious loyalty to his brothers would have endeared him to her if his attentiveness to his nieces hadn't already.

And Mac was knocking on her office door, looking uncharacteristically hesitant.

She came around her desk. "To what do I owe the honor?"

"I never did take you to lunch when you signed on." Mac had his suits tailor-made for him by some little

Amish guy up in Pennsylvania, and bought his shoes, ties, and accessories on his occasional trips to New York. He never looked anything less than dressed to the teeth in the office, and he never seemed to appreciate what an impression he made.

"So we're going to lunch?" Hannah asked.

"Do you have time? I can ask another day if you and Trent have plans." Mac was staring out the window across the parking lot. Hannah had seen him in the same pose any number of times in James's or Trent's offices.

"I've been abandoned so Trent can meet with a client before a shelter care hearing this afternoon. We can play hooky as long as you want, but I warn you, I don't share my desserts."

"Nor do I." He smiled at her, a brief flash of teeth that reminded her of James more than Trent. "Where would you like to go?"

"Some place quiet."

He took her to the Knightley menfolk's favorite steak joint, which was subdued and not cheap. The food was excellent, and Mac proved to have more conversation than Hannah might have guessed.

He asked her about Grace and Merle's adjustment to a blended family situation, asked her how the horseback riding was coming since Trent had bought both Grace and Hannah their own mounts. He listened to her fret about the approach of summer, and the demands that would inevitably make for extra supervision of the girls. By the time Hannah's chocolate mousse was sitting in front of her, she still had no idea what Mac's true agenda might be.

"You're not having dessert?" she asked.

"James gave me one of Vera's recipes," Mac said, "and I've got a stash of brownies at home to show for it. May I ask you something?"

"I was wondering when you would."

"What was foster care like?"

Hannah's spoon clattered into the ceramic bowl holding her mousse.

"What was it like?" She studied Mac as she parroted the question, but the guy had a phenomenal poker face. "Why do you ask?"

He smoothed his hand over the tablecloth in front of him, turned his water goblet exactly three hundred and sixty degrees, then turned it back again, precisely to its starting point.

"You heard I got kissed?" he asked.

Kissing in the passive voice. Interesting. "I overheard James and Trent remarking on it. They clammed up when I walked into the room, though."

He looked relieved, then pained. "I took a horseshoeing client and her foster son out for pizza, or they took me. They might be boarding some horses for me."

"Daisy and Buttercup, the wayward draft mares. That part, Trent let me in on. What do you want to know, Mac? And, no, I will not repeat every word to Trent, though I won't lie to him if he asks me, either."

"No lying," he said, lining his water goblet up with the end of his knife. "I'm not even asking you to fudge, Hannah. Repeat every word to Trent, just tell me what it was like being raised in foster care."

Fudge. One of the best criminal defense attorneys in the state, and he used the verb *to fudge*.

Hannah had to think, to consider and discard words

and phrases, because nobody had asked this question before—not even her husband.

"Have you ever seen that Photoshop card of a fox trying to fit in with a bunch of sheep?" she asked. "You have to look twice to see what doesn't go, because the angle of his nose is exactly the same as the sheeps', the height of his head, the slope of his neck into his shoulders. He's a fox-shaped sheep, at first glance. It was like that. Always feeling like I had to fit in, always knowing I didn't."

Abruptly, Hannah had had enough mousse.

"What was the worst part of it?"

Mac's question suggested her brother-in-law had a degree of fortitude she hadn't appreciated. Answering was simple, also difficult.

"The hardest part was watching the little kids get adopted," Hannah said, "and being truly happy for them, but knowing I couldn't stay, I could not *accept* that I wasn't as lovable, as cute, as whatever they were that I wasn't. Then I convinced myself I didn't want to be adopted."

How painful the memory was, even half a life-time later.

"Why didn't you want to be adopted, Hannah?"

This mattered to him. For Mac to wade into such personal waters, this had to matter to him a lot. Hannah pushed the chocolate mousse to his side of the table.

"Because I'd lost faith by then, Mac. I could not stand to have my hopes raised one more time, then dashed by yet another family."

He ignored a perfectly luscious dessert. "So you hated your foster parents?"

"No, I did not hate them. Some of them I resented. Most of them I genuinely liked. It can't be easy, treating a kid who's essentially a stranger as if he's family, especially knowing all that kid wants is to get back to the family who abused or neglected him. I didn't consider the parenting angle of the equation until Grace came along, though."

"Would you ever consider doing foster care?"

"Trent and I have discussed it," she said, which might be a small violation of marital confidentiality. Very small. Trent and his brothers had few secrets from each other. "We have our hands full with the girls, and we'd like more children when the time is right. We didn't rule it out, though."

Mac said nothing, and Hannah saw wheels turning within wheels in his thoughtful expression.

"Was there something else you wanted to ask, Mac?"

"Yes. Were you ever in a single-parent foster home?"

"By default, twice. In one home, the foster dad died, in another, the couple split up. I ended up living with the wife in both cases."

"How was that?"

"They were nice ladies. They tried to make it a hen party, but finances eventually got the better of the situation, or emotions. In both cases it was the breadwinner who'd died or left the home. The state takes a dim view of adults supporting themselves on a foster care stipend that's supposed to be for the kid. The placements, as they say, disrupted."

Mac made a face, apparently not liking that euphemism any more than Hannah did. He picked up his spoon and rearranged the mousse into the center of the bowl.

"The laws have changed a lot since I was in foster care, Mac. There's a lot more emphasis now on getting kids into a permanent situation sooner, either back at home, or in an adoptive home, or with relatives, if necessary. In general, the system has improved. Are you thinking of becoming a foster parent?"

A wild guess, a hunch, but the way Mac's spoon paused amid the mousse suggested the idea had crossed his mind.

"With my schedule?" He sat back, leaving the spoon in the bowl. "Single parenting is hard. I saw that when my father died and Mom was left with James, who was a good kid, but all boy all the time. I'll be content to enjoy my nieces. A nephew or two wouldn't go amiss either though." He spoke contemplatively, as if he were already picking out the exact fishing hole he'd take his nephews to for the first outing.

"Not you too. James has been hinting, and Trent just smirks at him."

"Trent's obnoxiously happy these days." Mac's expression became more fierce. "I appreciate that, you know. He wasn't always such a cheerful guy."

"He had his brothers. He's told me how much he leaned on you and James, and how instrumental you were in helping him get custody of Merle."

Mac waved at the waiter. "He'd do the same for us. Do you want your mousse back?"

"All yours."

Mac polished it off in about two bites, not even attempting to make conversation while he did. When they were getting up to leave, he held Hannah's coat for her and ushered her through the doors, out into the spring day.

Mac paused as he opened the passenger side of his

truck, a big, no-nonsense rig that would ensure he never had trouble getting to court, no matter the weather.

"I'm sorry you had to go through all that not feeling appreciated, Hannah. Not feeling wanted."

Hannah hardly knew what to say as Mac's arms came around her. She'd danced with him at the Christmas party, and she knew he was as graceful in his long bones as Trent and James were, and she'd hugged Mac in passing, but she and Mac had never…embraced.

"You're ours now, you know." Mac's lips grazed her forehead, gentle as a breeze. "We look after what's ours, no matter what."

His arms slipped away, and he stepped back, waiting for Hannah to climb in. She was still smiling foolishly when he started up the engine and turned the truck for the office. James flirted, Trent had exchanged vows with her, but Mac…

Mac said the words, the simple, sweet words that took heart and courage and meant so much. And she hadn't even known she'd needed to hear them.

—◊◊◊—

"But, Mr. Mac, they wasn't my pants." The client looked hopeful, painfully so, expecting his lawyer to buy that ration of horseshit.

"Whose were they?" Mac asked, stifling the urge to glance at the desk clock sitting beside school pictures of Grace and Merle.

"There was this guy, name was Leroy. Ain't never seen him before, but he was over at Doobie's hanging, ya know?"

Another hopeful glance, while the client furrowed his

brow as if trying to recall details. "I think he was a friend of Shay's. You know Shay?"

"Street" names being what they were, Mac had to guess. "Charlemagne Harold?"

"Yeah, that Shay. You got him off that time on the B&E. Anyhow, there was this Leroy dude, and we were grillin' some steaks, and Shay and Little Alvie got to horsing around in the backyard—we was drinkin' beer, you know. It was Doobie's backyard, and it's a free country—and they got a little enthusiastic."

Mac did look at the clock. Wrigley Hanford St. Cloud—a.k.a. Wiggles, The Hand, and Cloudy—was a handsome, skinny, dark-haired bad liar who might have twenty years to his name. To blow a .24, he'd been soaking in his *beer* for days. And this little yard party had included OxyContin and a significant quantity of high quality weed.

"They got enthusiastic," Mac said, "about breaking the law."

"Nah, Mr. Mac. I'm telling you. They were just joking around, but they grabbed the ketchup and the mustard and shit and started squirting each other. Leroy got me with the mustard right on the…" Wiggles gestured toward his crotch. "So the dude says to me, 'Trade you pants.' We traded, and they were Leroy's pants I had on when I got arrested. Honest."

Such creativity would be wasted down at Roxbury. "Why is there no mention of Leroy in any of the co-defendants' statements?" Mac asked.

"I think he's from New York." A hint of honest—well, genuine—anxiety flitted across Wiggles's face.

"If Leroy is Doobie's out-of-town connection,

Wiggles, then why did Leroy have a script pad from the local free clinic in his pants pockets?"

"I dunno, Mr. Mac. Maybe he picked it up for Alvie's sister. Tina's real good at…" Now the client was looking anywhere but at Mac. "Maybe he got it for someone else."

Mac stood, feeling a need to put distance between himself and the mess that was Wrigley's life. Leroy's magic traveling pants had been a treasure trove of evidence: a pipe with THC residue in the bowl, a bottle of pills with no prescription label, a bag of excellent weed, rolling papers…

"You want to do some work for the narcotics task force, Wrigley?"

"No, sir." With an emphatic shake of the head.

"Could you piss clean now?"

"Yes, sir. I'm out on bail. I know better than to party when I got a court date."

"I need to talk to Alvie's sister," Mac said. "Why wasn't Leroy on the scene when the cops showed up?"

"Went right over the back fence as soon as Tina began screaming. Never saw a man move like that, but Alvie said Leroy's into martial arts or some shit."

This had an incongruous ring of truth. Mac had been to the scene, and there was, indeed, a back fence.

"Do you know where Leroy bought the pants?"

A long shot. Mac let the question hang in the air as hope dawned in Wrigley's eyes.

"Now that you mention it, Mr. Mac, fucker bought his pants in New York. Some little boutique in the Village, I think he said."

"Let's hope he didn't rip out the label. You were in

possession of the pants, though, so you were in possession of everything in them. That doesn't give me much to work with, Wrigley, but your record isn't that bad, and you don't have any violent offenses. You going to meetings?"

"Ninety in ninety. I know the drill, Mr. Mac."

Not that the twelve-step waltz had done a thing for the vast majority of Mac's clients. "You're in treatment?"

"I went to that place you sent me, and they're real nice. Alvie's been there too."

Rehab was often old home week by another name. Somebody needed to figure out why that was.

"You stay away from Alvie." Mac glared down at his client for emphasis. "You stay away from him, Tina, Shay, the whole crowd. They aren't your friends until I get you an acquittal or you do your time. We clear on that?"

"But Tina's…" Another sidling glance from the client and Mac wanted to howl.

"I do not care if she's doing you five times a day. I don't care if she's carrying your firstborn and only son. For the next six weeks, you don't know her, you don't see her, you don't, for God's sake, send her incriminating texts, and you don't dial her number on a cell phone the cops are panting to confiscate."

"Yes, Mr. Mac. Never saw the bitch before in my life."

Wiggles referred to the current love of his life as "the bitch." Delightful.

"Where are you staying?"

The client's gaze dropped to the floor.

"You can't stay with Tina either, Wrig. The task force is watching her place, and you tell anybody I said that, my ass is dead meat with the few cops who'll still talk to me. Got it?"

"Didn't hear nothing from nobody, Mr. Mac."

"High volume, short-stay foot traffic getting out of pimpmobiles with New York tags is not the kind of image you want your lady to have."

Another nod, but the guy's foot started going, a rapid jiggle that shook the change in his pocket. "We done here, Mr. Mac?"

"You filled out all the forms Sarah gave you?"

"She's the chick out front?"

"The very one." Not a bitch, but a chick.

"Yeah, we're good. She's nice." Nice in Wrigley's parlance probably referred to people to whom he would not sell drugs during daylight hours.

"Then we're done, but, Wrigley?"

The man was already on his feet, a hand on the doorknob.

"Court isn't for six weeks. They will be the longest, hardest six weeks of your life. Do not tell yourself you're going to the Division of Corrections, so why not enjoy yourself now. Do not tell yourself they won't be watching you, because you've already got a trial date. Do not tell yourself it's your last chance to give Tina the baby she says she wants. In short, don't bullshit yourself. If you honest-to-God behave for the next few weeks, use your head, and have a little luck, there's a chance I can keep you out of jail."

"I can do that, Mr. Mac. I can stay with my sister, and she don't fuck around."

"Stay with your sister, and if the deal stinks at the District Court level, then we'll pray a jury, and it will be more weeks of toeing the line. When's the last time you worked for a wage?"

"I always work. My brother-in-law lets me help out in his garage. I'm good with that shit."

Another ray of sunshine. "Then work your little back-side off. A job will keep you out of trouble and look better when you have to pay court costs and fines and supervision fees. I can't work miracles, Wrigley, but I can hold the state to the letter of the law."

"I'll be good, Mr. Mac, or my sister will be telling that judge to lock me up for a long time." He slipped through the door, a skinny, good-looking young man who wouldn't fare well at DOC. Not well at all.

Mac sat at his desk, denying the urge to knock off early for once, and go the hell home at a decent hour. He punched a number on speed dial, skipped through the voice menu at the State's Attorney's office, and waited until Julie Leonard picked up.

"Knightley here. How are you, Julie?"

"Mac. It's never a good thing when you call." A sincere compliment from a prosecutor. "Unless you want to do dinner?"

"I've heard Mr. Leonard is the jealous type, though the thought flatters." Julie was a good-looking redhead who took her job seriously. Mac liked her, and he respected her.

But on her end of the discussion, an interesting pause was in progress.

"Julie?"

"Mr. Leonard has run off with his dad's secretary. The gossip was all over the defense bar luncheon, Mac. I'm surprised you haven't heard."

Merle and Grace beamed at Mac from their matching frames on his desk. At least Julie wouldn't drag any children through this divorce, though she might not see it that way.

"I don't go to the defense bar luncheon regularly. I'm sorry. You doing OK?"

Stupid question. He could hear that she was pissed as hell.

"Yes, I'm doing OK, because what else is there to do? You go to court, prosecute your cases, and hope it blows over. This isn't why you called, though."

Legal gossip never "blew over." One of the joys of small town practice.

"I can keep my mouth shut, Julie. If you ever need to vent, I will respect your confidences, and for what it's worth, Harmon Anderson's secretary has an irritating laugh and doesn't know how to behave. You want me to say something to Trent?"

"How am I supposed to throw your guys in jail when you turn up sweet, MacKenzie? And why would I want your brother—? Oh."

Mac gave her a beat of silence for the gears to mesh in her nimble brain.

"We can work out something in the way of professional courtesy for the fee," Mac said. "I'm the managing partner. I can see to that much. Trent's good, Julie, and he's been through a fairly public divorce himself. Call him. If you don't want to work with Trent because you oppose me, I'll ask the assignment clerk to keep my clients off your dockets for the duration. In the alternative, Trent will steer you to the right member of the family law bar. Mr. Leonard won't know what hit him."

"Thanks." Her voice held a trace of incredulity, as if bad things had to keep happening to an otherwise nice lady.

"Now that we've solved your domestic troubles," Mac said, "I want to know if you've seen the evidence reports on the St. Cloud case."

"Hang on." Mac heard her shuffling files. "The trial's weeks away, but yes. Paraphernalia, prescription drugs, blew a .24. You want a suppression hearing?"

"He's of age, and they were on private property, so the blood alcohol is irrelevant," Mac said. "The paraphernalia bears none of his prints, and neither does the script bottle the script was found in. He has no violent offenses, and, Julie, I am going to tear your chain of custody apart."

"I liked you better when you turned up sweet."

"I like you fine," Mac said, sensing a weakening in the state's posture, "but you have better things to do than burden the taxpayers with St. Cloud's upkeep for the next six years."

Like getting on with a life outside the office.

What a notion.

—⁓—

Mac felt eyes on his back before he heard Sid's voice.

"Do you come here every Saturday?" she asked.

He carefully put down the hoof he'd been rasping and straightened. He didn't want to aggravate his back, and he didn't want to spook the horse—though Thomas was as close to bombproof as an equine could be.

"I work here at least every other Saturday, and sometimes more, depending on the needs of the clients. You never did call me."

She looked away, which gave Mac a chance to study her. Jeans, a man's V-neck T-shirt under a jacket that looked to be genuine leather, and where he expected to find her silly little fringed half boots, she sported a broken-in pair of running shoes.

Sidonie was tired. The lines around her eyes and a slight pallor suggested it; the grooves bracketing her mouth confirmed it. Another time, Mac would tell her not to wear sneakers in a horse barn.

"I'm about done with Thomas," Mac said. "Is Luis here for a lesson?"

"Adelia had a cancellation, so she asked him if he wanted to fill in, and that was that. Luis enjoys his lessons."

"Adelia and Neils have a good operation here. I'll put this guy up, and you can explain why you never let me know what you decided about the mares."

Sid let him get away with that taunt, which provoked an unwelcome spike of concern. Mac had not called her, had not called Luis, had not driven by the place on reconnaissance. Where women and self-discipline were concerned, he did not permit himself any slack.

In his actions. His imagination was another very lively thing entirely.

He put the gelding into a stall, pausing a moment to scratch the beast under the chin—Thomas did not stand on ceremony where his pleasures were concerned—then closed the stall door to find Sid eyeing the little horse from the aisle.

"He seems sweet."

"Therapy pony of the year. There are stories about him you would not believe."

"Try me."

"Hi, Mr. Mac!" Lindy rolled by slowly, the uneven barn floor making for difficult going.

"Hello, Lindy. You come to spoil your horse?"

"He's not legally mine," she said. "Except he's mine to love. Hello." The child directed the last greeting to Sid.

"Hello." Sid extended a hand. "My name's Sid."

"Lindy, and this is Thomas, and pretty soon, he's going to teach me to canter *all over* the ring."

"You tell Adelia to let me know when," Mac said, "I'll bring my video camera."

"Thanks, Mr. Mac!"

She turned her wheelchair to face the stall, and Mac took his box of sugar from his pocket. "Give him a couple for me."

She grinned up at him, took the sugar cubes, and began to talk to the horse in low, earnest tones.

"Come along." Mac took Sid by the elbow. "Thomas is having office hours."

"To have the kind of mobility the horse can give her must mean a lot to her."

"Means the world," Mac said. "Her grades are up, she's on less medication, and only seeing the therapist half as often—the typical response for kids in a good program. Shall we sit, or maybe you'd like to walk a fence with me?"

"Walk a fence?"

Sidonie excelled at patrolling borders. Walking the fence should appeal to her.

"It's spring, the freezing and thawing all winter can work on the posts. The animals reaching for spring grass can wiggle them some more. Boards get loose, nails

pop. Next thing you know, horses are out. Adelia and
Neils have a lot to do. If you and I are going to talk, we
can also be useful."

And have some privacy and fresh air.

"Lead on."

They walked in silence, with Mac purposely slowing
his steps, not to accommodate Sid—she was churning
along at a smart pace beside him—but because spring
seemed a benign reality just around the corner. Out of
the breeze, the sun brought a gentle warmth, the new
grass made for soft earth beneath the feet, and the light
had lost the thin, sharp quality of the winter months.

"You don't watch Luis's lessons?" Mac asked.

"I don't think he wants me to. He has every bit as
much pride as the next guy."

"He's a natural athlete. My brother James has the
same quality, Trent to a lesser extent."

She gave him a look he couldn't fathom. An up-and-
down, female perusal suggesting skepticism.

"You didn't call me, Sid. Was I supposed to call you? I
never did quite get the hang of reading the female mind."

"I'm sorry, and no, I don't expect—I don't want—
anybody to read my mind. I was busy getting the house
together because the social worker was supposed to come
out. They always tell you not to worry about the house-
keeping, but then they get out their little SmartPads and
start noting every wet dish towel and half-full trash can."

As if wet dish towels and half-full trash cans mattered
to a kid's well-being? "You're getting settled in?" Mac
stopped and leaned on the fence.

"I suppose. Yes. Well, not really. Luis is getting settled in, and that's good. I've started looking for work."

Mac faced the pasture, where several of the therapy ponies were nose down in the new grass. No flies yet, a horse's version of heaven on earth.

"You started looking for work because you don't want to board my horses," he guessed. "You'd rather bag groceries than accept money from me."

"It isn't you." She crossed her arms over the top board and propped a foot on the bottom one. "I need income, Mac, and, yes, I would rather not take your money. I'd rather have the option of not taking your money, to be more precise, but it seems at this point I don't have a choice."

He said nothing, being no stranger to the demands of pride.

"Luis wants us to keep them," she said. "But what if I can't keep Luis?"

"You haunt yourself with this?"

"Of course."

He hadn't expected her to make that admission. "You lost your brother, Sidonie. That doesn't mean you don't get to keep anybody else."

"What would you know about it?"

He heard the anger in her voice, heard the unbearable sadness behind it, and the bewilderment.

"When my father died, I was all too happy to scamper back to college a few months later. I couldn't stand to be home, couldn't stand the memories of my father sitting in the porch swing with my mother, complimenting her on her mashed potatoes, talking politics to his draft team, explaining lawn-mower engines to James. Dad was everywhere, and nowhere, and it tore at me. When you're making that transition from youth to adult, you desperately need for home to be the unchanging rock you assumed it was for your entire childhood."

None of this speech had been on Mac's agenda for the morning. He should have scheduled time with Thomas, but he went on speaking anyway.

"I realized eventually I had to be that rock for my family. That was how I'd get to keep a little of my dad for myself, by taking Trent in hand when he got to college, popping in at home every few weeks, and doing one hell of a job on the academics."

"Your point?"

"When you're grieving, it hurts to hold on, and it hurts to let go. Every day you have to renegotiate the balance between the two. All of your choices come at a cost, but you have to take on the choosing anyway." He'd never articulated that before, never acknowledged the effort wrapped up with the loss.

Sid expelled a sigh and dropped her head forward, so she was addressing the new, green earth.

"I'm tired and a little worried. We'll be OK once the estate is settled."

Which was likely months away. The bigger the estate, the more closely the probate court examined it.

"You're keeping those mares. I'll bring a check over midweek."

Mac's every instinct screamed at him that Sidonie needed holding and petting and comforting. She needed to lean, damn it, preferably on him, and she needed to cry, preferably on his broad shoulder. That much, Mac could give her, if she'd only reach for it.

Sid remained beside him, her foot propped on the fence, her gaze on the new grass.

She neither spoke nor moved for a long moment, and Mac had offered what practical help and comfort he could. He didn't know what else to do, so he walked away and left Sid the privacy she seemed to crave.

Chapter 7

FROM HER PERCH ON THE PORCH SWING, SID WATCHED the behemoths—be*she*moths?—munching their grass. She'd grown used to seeing them in their pasture, to seeing Luis leading them into and out of the barn. He talked to them, and they seemed to listen, some secret code emerging between young man and old horses.

A pair of one-ton hussies.

Sid sipped her tea, enjoying a break from sending out résumés. Damson County was far enough west and north that commutes to Baltimore or DC would be a pain in the behind, particularly if she was supposed to be home when Luis got off the bus. He was old enough to be home alone, but DSS frowned mightily on latch-key children.

Sid was tired simply from keeping house and sending out her paper. How on earth was she supposed to cope with a long commute?

A movement along the wall of the barn caught her eye. She set her teacup down and watched. The high weeds rustled, undulating with the passing of some animal traveling along the stone foundation.

All three of her cats were accounted for on the porch.

A rat?

A snake?

A stray cat?

Nothing good wiggled in the weeds like that, so Sid

fetched the broom from the kitchen and advanced slowly across the yard. An odd sound came from the weeds, an animal sound but not right.

From behind Sid, a low growl told her one of the cats had come to investigate.

"Bo, get back on the porch!" She waved the broom at him, but old alley cats didn't flinch at mere brooms. "Scat, you! This isn't some rat in a pizza box."

The rat, or whatever, made the noises again, and Bo hunkered, wiggling his back end down as if to pounce.

"No, drat you!" Sid pushed him two feet to the side with her broom, then wheeled to watch the clump of weeds where the noise came from. A dark brown nose poked out, weaving slightly, followed by dark button eyes.

"What the hell?"

Bo growled again, and Sid barely saw an orange blur detach itself from the porch swing and start slinking across the driveway.

"No, Harvard! You get back!"

She waved the broom at the second cat, and pivoted back to see something teetering out of the bushes.

A raccoon, an adorable if big raccoon. Enormous, really, and looking drunk, or like it had eaten something raccoons weren't supposed to eat.

"Oh, you poor thing."

She started to advance on the animal, only to hear a voice crack like a whip behind her.

"Sidonie, don't. Step back *now*." MacKenzie Knightley, and he was sighting down the barrel of a serious-looking gun.

"What the hell do you think you're doing!" Sid was nowhere near his line of fire, but waved her broom anyway when the gun discharged with a loud report, and the raccoon expired like a deflated balloon.

The silence in the wake of that shot felt *obscene*.

"Who the hell do you think you are?!" She flew at him, broom raised, prepared to deliver as many stout swats as it took to drive him from the property. "You don't come onto my land and kill an animal just because it needs help."

Mac set the gun against his truck—how had Sid not heard that vehicle lumbering up the drive?—and snatched the broom away from her.

"Bad idea, Knightley." She raised her hand to wallop him solidly across the cheek, a sick thrill coursing through her. In some terrible way, smacking him as hard as she could would feel *wonderful*.

Except the blow never landed. He imprisoned her wrist in an implacable grip and folded her arm down to her side.

"Calm down, Sidonie. Rabies is nothing to fool with."

"Tell the raccoon to calm down," Sid said through clenched teeth. She was trying to wrestle her hand free and trying to kick Mac when she got the inspiration to body slam him. She threw herself against him, her momentum having exactly no impact against his much larger frame, and that only made her more angry.

"You killed a helpless animal," she railed. "Hauled off and shot it, judge, jury, and executioner. You can't do that on my property. You can't just—"

He wrestled with her silently while she bellowed and raged, until some dim corner of Sid's mind realized she was pressed hard against Mac's chest, his arms were around her, and she was bawling like a distraught child.

"Sidonie, hush." He held her snugly, securely. "The

raccoon was ill, suffering, prey for anything healthier that came along. Living in misery. That animal would not have lived much longer, and every moment would have been agony."

"I know." She choked out the two words and buried her face against his shirt, all the fight and every ounce of dignity going out of her. "I hate you."

"Hate me all you want. All you need to."

Mac's hand stroked slowly over her hair, the same way he touched the horses. A soothing, reassuring touch that turned Sid's spine to mush.

"I really do hate you."

"Then you won't mind if I take a small liberty." He scooped her up behind the knees and hefted her against his chest. "You can hate me for this too."

"A goddamned caveman is loose in Damson County," Sid muttered, but she didn't put it past MacKenzie Knightley to drop her if she started struggling. In a few steps, he sat with her on the porch swing, taking the place immediately beside her.

He produced a hankie from some pocket and shrugged out of his jacket, wrapping it around Sid's shoulders and anchoring it with his arm.

"What kind of caveman goes around with a mono-grammed handkerchief?" Sid groused.

"One prepared for saber-toothed women who are too softhearted for their own good."

"I'm not softhearted." Sid blotted her tears and silently recited a lot of bad words no softhearted woman should know. Mac's jacket smelled like him—cinnamon and clove and meadows—and sitting beside him, his body heat was a palpable comfort.

"You will admit that raccoon was dangerous in the first place, Sidonie, and overdue for the Rainbow Pasture in the second?"

"The Rainbow Pasture?" She couldn't help but smile, his tone of voice was so stern and his euphemism so unexpected.

"That's what my nieces call heaven." He set the swing to rocking with the heel of one boot. "You looked tired to me on Saturday, Sidonie." His arm drew her closer, as if he expected her to wiggle away to disprove his words.

"I am tired, but I've been tired since…" She turned her face to his shoulder. *Since forever*.

"Since your brother died."

"The reasons to run you off the property just keep adding up, Knightley."

"You'll have me quaking in m'boots." His hand settled against the side of her head then slipped over her hair. "What did you have for lunch?"

"The help-wanted ads. They're enough to ruin anybody's appetite."

"Sid, you can't keep up with a teenager, much less a teenager and this property, without proper rest and nutrition. Stay here and do not fuss at me, or you'll meet the only caveman in Damson County with an entire lecture on women and their fool notions about how to look after themselves."

He got off the swing and disappeared into the kitchen, leaving Sid to admit she'd enjoyed his warmth, enjoyed the solid, muscular bulk of him, though she was also grateful to have a few minutes to herself. She snuggled into his jacket, suspecting MacKenzie Knightley was perceptive enough to leave her in peace on purpose.

When she woke up, Mac was scowling down at her. "You need a nap."

"I am not eight years old to need an afternoon nap. What did you cook?"

"Eight-year-olds are long past the nap stage. You have no red meat on the premises, so it's vegetable soup and grilled cheese sandwiches. Shall I carry you into the kitchen?"

"God, no." Sid swung her legs down and stood quickly, lest she be carried over the threshold of her own kitchen.

"Land sakes, woman." Mac had a hand under each of her elbows. "You need a keeper. When you're hypoglycemic, standing up too fast is a recipe for disaster." He steered her into the kitchen, managing to hold the door as he guided her by one arm. "My guess is you're anemic into the bargain if you're avoiding red meat. Eat up, or I'll fetch that broom you're so fond of and use it on your backside."

Sid sat. "You're kind of cute—in an overbearing way—when you're clucking and fussing."

"Fine," he said, taking the teakettle off the stove. "Call me names, but eat what's in front of you."

"I'll take some high-octane Darjeeling—two tea bags, please." She picked up a golden-brown, still-warm grilled cheese sandwich with the cheese threatening to ooze over the crusts. "And lots of sugar in it too."

"You will not. The last thing you need is a shot of caffeine at this point in the day to keep you up all night."

She wanted to argue with him, but he'd truly grilled the bread in butter and loaded on the cheese. "You put oregano in this?"

"A little of this and that." Mac set a steaming mug of herb tea at her elbow. "What time does Luis get here?"

"Another half hour. Shouldn't you be out wrestling horses somewhere?"

"My clients are all taken care of for the day."

"Then sit and stop glowering at me. You make a good grilled cheese."

He turned a chair around and straddled it. "Has the social worker been here yet?"

"She has not."

A little silence, while Sid savored hot food made by someone besides herself.

"What kind of job are you looking for?"

"Paying job, for starters." She glanced up from the sandwich she was bolting to see he was smiling at her.

God above, MacKenzie Knightley was a handsome man. His demeanor camouflaged it, but he had the kind of face that looked out from perfectly lighted ads in men's magazines. Strong, masculine bones, thick dark hair, dramatic eyebrows, and a pair of perfect, chiseled lips.

They looked sculpted, but they'd be soft, those lips.

"I know people," he said. "I can probably find you something that pays. Not a lot—salaries are less out here than in DC and Baltimore—but something. You'll need benefits too, health insurance at least."

"I don't want a job mucking stalls, Knightley. How many of these did you make?" She held out the remaining crust of her sandwich.

He got up and opened the oven, then put a second grilled cheese on her plate.

"You might as well eat the last one," Sid said. "But

you're not getting me a job. Bad enough you're paying us for mares that aren't yours, and then you have to see my annual meltdown, and feed me"—she took a sniff of gustatory heaven—"garlic salt, and pizza seasonings along with the oregano, right?"

"Maybe a dash. What kind of work do you enjoy, Sid?"

She gave up fencing with him—the food was too good for that—and talked about all the parts of managing a production crew she'd enjoyed. The stepping and fetching, the variety, the sense of being needed, the lack of time chained to a desk.

The freedom and the knowledge that she was helping to create something.

"Let me think about it," he said, rising. "If I make more for Luis, will it ruin his dinner?"

"Grilled cheese sandwiches will *be* his dinner." She picked up half of the second sandwich, though the food was making her drowsy. "We haven't fallen into a routine here yet, or not a good one. He comes home, grabs something to eat, then disappears into the barn or goes off into the fields. As it gets later, he hits the books. He's pretty self-sufficient."

Mac gave her a look over his shoulder from his post at the sink.

"You are not to do my dirty dishes, Knightley. I have a few scruples left."

"Eat your soup before it gets cold."

He was like those draft horses: too big, too solid, physically but also emotionally, to be bullied, intimidated, argued, or swayed off his chosen path.

For a few minutes earlier that afternoon, his solidness had been a blessed comfort. Sid finished her soup and her sandwich—every bite—then took her dishes to the sink for MacKenzie Knightley to wash.

———※———

Sidonie Lindstrom was working herself up to a swivet.

Mac put the last dish in the drain rack and forcibly turned his thoughts away from what might have happened if she'd come any closer to that miserable coon. The Maryland Department of Natural Resources considered every one of them rabid, and they were illegal as pets as a consequence.

She'd been determined to fix it, to help it.

Though she might have died in the process.

"I'm running a string of electric fencing around the mares' pasture," Mac said, knowing full well he had no right to be on Sid's property without her permission. "I picked up the supplies from my brothers, and Luis can lend a hand. He'll need to know how to fix it too."

Sid watched him drying his hands on a towel, and Mac would have given his last five retainers to know what was going through her head.

"You don't live here, Knightley. It's not your pasture to worry about."

"It's you and the mares I'm worried about." He tucked the towel over the handle of the refrigerator. "If the mares get loose and somebody's car hits them, you are liable for all the damage done to the car and the loss of human life. You'll also have to pay to have the horse's remains disposed of, because the authorities frown on burying horses in the backyard."

"And one good lawsuit can ruin your whole life." She saluted with her tea mug. "Fine, take liberties with my fences. You'll probably add to the property value, and Luis will like the idea of keeping his ladies safe."

Nobody would ever take liberties with Sid Lindstrom's fences again, though somebody had apparently tried.

"Every man worth the name needs to keep his ladies safe," Mac said. "Don't ridicule Luis for being honorable." What drivel was he spouting, when he should have been chasing Sid up the stairs—to take a nap?

She pushed her hair out of her eyes, much as Merle or Grace might do, though the gesture was weary.

"You're right, and I'm sorry. Tony was so much older than I. I don't have a sense for what a guy, fifteen going on sixteen, might want out of life."

"But you're determined to finish raising him?"

She took a sip of her tea. Stalling. Mac told his clients to ask for a cup of water when they were on the witness stand and cross-examination was getting too intense.

"I was sixteen when my mother died, and I was headed for foster care until Tony stepped up and announced he was ready, willing, and able to take in the half sister eighteen years his junior, a kid he barely knew, one he'd seen mostly at holidays and a few family gatherings, and not a very nice kid at that."

Mac resisted the urge to sit at the table. Sid would need space when she was parting with confidences, just as some of his clients needed him to move around the office, water his plants, and otherwise look preoccupied when they confessed their misdeeds—or made up their lies.

Sid had no plants, so he started putting away the dishes he'd washed.

"Most of us have trouble being consistently nice at sixteen, Sid."

Her dishes were pretty, something he hadn't noticed earlier, and the dishes, cups, and bowls all matched.

"Luis doesn't have trouble being nice. He's a solid-gold gentleman, MacKenzie. I don't know whether it's his culture, his upbringing, or his determination not to be the trash society sometimes tells him he'll become, but he's good to the bone."

"You ever tell him that?"

She fell silent, while Mac finished with the dishes.

"Mac's here!" Luis banged in the door, already swinging his backpack off his bony shoulder. "Are the horses OK?"

"They're fine," Mac said.

Sid got to her feet and hugged the boy.

"What's that for?" Luis asked.

"Because you're fine too." She messed his hair with one hand. "Mighty fine. You want a grilled cheese? MacKenzie's making his secret recipe."

"Sure, make it two. We're doing spring track in gym." He disappeared up the steps, and Mac started getting out all the sandwich fixings he'd just put away.

"Get over here," he said, "and I'll show you the secret recipe, or today's version. The result varies with the supplies on hand and my mood."

"A caveman of moods." Sid put her mug in the sink and stood right beside him, close enough that he could catch the clean scent of her shampoo.

"You should be going for whole, multigrain bread. More fiber, a bigger dose of phytochemicals, and less gluten."

"Another caveman lecture." She leaned her cheek

against his shoulder, and everything inside Mac turned up happy, savoring the contact she'd initiated. "I thought the average caveman only lived about thirty-five years."

"If he'd been relegated to eating the junk we eat, the race would have died out," Mac growled. The cheese slicer caught, and he about shredded the entire brick of cheddar on his next pass.

Sid was still leaning against him, her expression wistful, and twice in the past five minutes, she'd addressed him not as Mr. Knightley, or Knightley, but as MacKenzie.

When was the last time somebody had addressed him by the name his parents had given him? When was the last time Mac's insides had turned up happy, all at once, and all over the simple act of a lady leaning on his shoulder?

~~~

Sid sat on the porch swing, watching, while out in the pasture, Luis hefted a bag of plastic things that kept the electric fence wire from shorting out on the fence posts.

Insulators. Seemed there was science to everything, and as MacKenzie Knightley explained something to Luis, the boy leaned in, examining an object in Mac's hand. The horses had come to inspect, and stood a few yards off, lipping grass and occasionally looking up to see what Mac and Luis were up to.

The peace of the scene seeped into Sid's bones. A pretty day, warm in the sun, the green hills and fields coming to life all around, the beasts at pasture. She would not have chosen this variety of therapy, but the simple beauty of the surroundings put her tantrum over the raccoon in perspective.

The raccoon was not an adult human with AIDS. Not her brother, in any but the most metaphysical sense, and MacKenzie had done what Sid didn't know enough to do for the animal.

But God in heaven, what if she'd picked the raccoon up, with some vague notion of getting it to a vet, extended a hand for it to bite and scratch? Where would Luis be then?

MacKenzie Knightley had taken off his shirt. He slid an arm through a roll of wire, and hefted it up to his shoulder to walk along the fence line, playing out line as he moved.

Holy everlasting…*God*. Shoeing horses must put the muscles on a man like no gym routine ever could. He was male beauty on a grand scale, striding along in his jeans and boots, while his back, arms, and shoulders were a visual symphony of strength and competence.

Sid shamelessly ogled and wallowed in the sight of him. Had she ever seen a man who looked that genuinely good with his shirt off? Tony and Thor had had plenty of well-turned-out friends, guys who worked out regularly and took a lot of pride in their appearance and health. Tony had too, at least up until…

Seeing a guy that healthy restored some cheer to Sid. People died of AIDS and even worse ailments every day, but there were also guys—there was at least one guy— in blooming, natural good health.

And that guy was right here on her farm. Those arms had scooped her up as easily as if she were a sack of feed, had held her as securely as if she were precious to him.

The sound of wheels coming up the driveway cut off those oddly gratifying thoughts. A white compact with state plates made an awkward job of negotiating the bumps and ruts of the lane.

Mac and Luis looked up too, and Mac snagged his shirt off a fence post and shrugged back into it.

Social workers never did have much of a sense of timing.

A trim, petite young woman got out of the car, her hair cut in a no-nonsense bob, sensible shoes on her feet. Under a jacket, a denim jumper showed that made her look about fourteen years old. If she was trying to look nonthreatening, the electronic notepad she cradled against her left side ruined the effect completely.

"Mrs. Lindstrom? I'm Amy Snyder."

She stuck out a hand, and Sid shook it, noting from the corner of her eye that Mac and Luis were climbing over the fence.

"Nice to meet you, Amy. Luis is joining us. He'll be relieved you've come to visit."

"I didn't review his medical chart. Is he medicated for anxiety?"

The question took Sid aback, but she tried to hide her reaction. "He functions well, but he suffers the normal anxiety of a kid whose future is in the hands of strangers. Would you like a cup of tea?"

"No, thank you." Already the idiot woman was making a note on her pad.

"Hi, Luis!" She extended her hand again. "I'm Amy Snyder, your caseworker from Damson County DSS. How are you?"

"Hello." Luis took off a leather glove and shook

the lady's hand. "We were just stringing some electric fence for the horses. Do you know when my hearing will be?"

Ms. Snyder retrieved her hand, and eyed Mac up and down. "I don't believe I know this gentleman, though I have to say, you look familiar, sir."

"MacKenzie," he said, taking the proffered hand. "Nice to meet you. I'm a neighbor to Sid and Luis, and they're boarding my horses for me."

"Do you want to meet the horses?" Luis asked. Sid gave him points for patience, because Ms. Snyder hadn't answered his question about the hearing.

"Perhaps another time. If we might get the house tour out of the way, that would be helpful."

"I'll put away the fence tools," Mac said, nodding at the woman in parting.

"And, Luis," Ms. Snyder said, "I'll just take your picture out here where we have good light." She fished a camera out of her shoulder bag, and Luis stood, his expression impassive, while he was subjected to the regular indignity of having his picture taken by a complete stranger for the benefit of her "files."

"Kitchen's this way," Sid said, leading the way. She did not so much as glance at Luis, did not intrude even more on his limited privacy while they trooped into the house. He hated having his picture taken, hated it, and there was nothing Sid could do to prevent it.

"How's school going, Luis?" Ms. Snyder started on the usual litany: school, summer plans, physical health, mental health, social health. Luis had never laid eyes on the woman before in his life, and he was supposed to tell her who his girlfriend was so DSS could run a background check on the young lady's family.

Right.

"The house looks very spacious and well kept," Ms. Snyder—Amy—said when she'd stuck her nose into every room and closet. "Do you know how old it is?"

"Mac says it's on the battle maps at Antietam," Luis said. "It dates at least from the 1850s, or the old part does."

Interesting. Mac hadn't told Sid that tidbit.

"Old houses can require a lot of maintenance," Amy replied, making another damned infernal note. "I should look at the rest of the buildings."

So they strolled from one outbuilding to the other, with Sid learning from Luis which shed was the summer kitchen, which was the smokehouse, which was the hog house.

Damned if the woman didn't open every door, peer into every space, and come to an abrupt halt at the back of what turned out to be the hog house.

"I think I've seen enough." She closed a door, and hustled out of the cobwebs and gloom. When they got to the bright light of day, she was scribbling notes on her pad nineteen to the dozen. "I'll discuss this with my supervisor, and get back to you. We might have a problem."

When a social worker started with the "might have" and "possibly" and "potential" talk, they were setting up the bad news for painless delivery.

Painless to them. "What problem would that be?" Sid asked.

Call-me-Amy put her notebook to sleep. "Nothing major. The most common reason why a home is denied a foster care license is the physical facility. Doors that don't lock, windows that won't open, fire escapes that don't work, that sort of thing. When that's the case, the Department always gives the family a chance to rectify that situation first, and we put our request in writing so you know exactly why your license was revoked. If we have to revoke a license, the decision can be administratively appealed."

Sid heard footsteps behind her, but they were drowned out entirely by the roaring in her ears that started with the words, "exactly why your license was revoked."

"Perhaps you can be more specific, Amy," she managed. "What is the problem, and when will you and your supervisor make a determination about it?" Sid kept her voice calm, but beside her, Luis had gone tense.

"We can discuss this later, Mrs. Lindstrom. It might be nothing at all." A furtive glance at Luis, a warning glance.

"Tell us," Luis said. "The sooner you tell us, the sooner we can start fixing it."

The worker bit her lip and glanced around the farmstead. "This building has an outhouse at the back of it. That is clearly out of code. There are families in this county with no indoor plumbing, and the Department can't do anything about that, but we can't permit that sort of thing in foster homes. Any outhouse is just too unsanitary, particularly if your water comes from the property's well."

"Oh, for pity's sake..." Sid heard the incredulous note in her voice, but couldn't reel herself in. "Nobody has used the hog house, much less the two-seater in ages. You saw the dust."

"With all due respect, Mrs. Lindstrom, you've only recently moved here. You have no idea what the previous owners did on this property or with that, that *facility*. I'll discuss this with my supervisor, and you're within your rights to retain counsel. Luis, I'm sorry."

Somewhere in the past thirty seconds, a large hand had landed on Sid's shoulder. How could such a big man move so silently?

"The problem is the outhouse at the back of the hog house?" MacKenzie asked.

"This is a confidential discussion," the social worker said, slipping the notebook into a gray case labeled "State of Maryland." "I'll be in touch shortly."

"I'm waiving my confidentiality," Luis said, crossing his arms. "Call my lawyer if you need to hear it from him. You want his number? Mac's a friend."

Oh, Luis…

"That won't be necessary," MacKenzie said, his other hand landing on Luis's shoulder. "You need to tell the nice lady I was just asking about demolishing that entire building, including the outhouse. Builders in the city will pay good money for seasoned barn lumber. Then too, I've lived in the area all my life, Ms. Snyder, and I can attest as a neighbor that no part of this building has been put to its intended uses for at least thirty years."

The worker must have realized she'd been outflanked.

"I will bring this up with my supervisor tomorrow. The outhouse might not be unsanitary, but it's still unsafe, and if you're doing foster care on this property, small children have to be taken into account."

When Sid would have railed that she never accepted small children, Mac's hand gently squeezed her shoulder.

"Let us know what your supervisor has to say," Sid managed. "We'll fix it."

"And you never said when my hearing is," Luis added.

"I'll get back to you on that," the worker said. "We have foster care court mostly on Tuesdays in this county, so it will be a Tuesday."

Not another word was spoken until the little white car had bumped down the lane and then turned onto the road. They stood there, the three of them, Mac with an arm over Sid's and Luis's shoulders.

"Into the house, you two," he said, moving them along as he started walking. "We have a demolition to plan."

Chapter 8

"I'M NOT CALLING THAT WOMAN TO FIND OUT WHEN my hearing is," Luis said. "She should have at least known that before she came out here snooping and taking pictures."

"Do you know why she takes your picture?" Mac asked, filling the teakettle at the sink.

"Because she's a nosy twit," Luis said.

From the look on Sid's face, Mac gathered that was a polite version of her opinion on the matter.

"A few years ago, there was a family of children who got caught between the foster care systems of two neighboring states. The case was transferred from one jurisdiction to the other, but nobody followed up, and nobody picked up the ball. The children died in their second placement from the neglect of their court-ordered care providers. The details are hazy—maybe a worker fudged the files, saying he or she had gone to see the children, when in fact, they hadn't—but the reality is, the children died on the state's watch."

He put the kettle on the stove, giving Sid and Luis a chance to absorb his words.

"Taking your picture does several things," Mac said. "It assures the supervisors that you're alive, that the worker laid eyes on you, and that you are where you're supposed to be. It also lets the DSS know, from one worker to the next, what you look like, so nobody will trot out any old teenaged boy and say he's Luis Martineau when he isn't. Those pictures are for your safety. Who wants tea?"

"I do," Sid said. "Generic decaf will do. Luis?"

"Nah. How come none of my workers have explained this to me? They just whip out their cameras and snap away."

"Have you asked?" Mac put the question casually. Luis was bright; he didn't need to be hammered on cross-examination.

"I will," Luis said, grinning. "See if she even knows."

"Get-the-social-worker," Sid said, frowning. "We agreed we weren't going to play that game, Luis."

"You going to call your lawyer, Luis?" Mac asked, setting out two mugs. Mac considered letting them know that he himself was a lawyer, then discarded the idea on the basis of bad timing. More important issues were on the table, and he wanted to drop that detail on Sid when he had her to himself.

"I don't even know who my lawyer is." Luis scrubbed a hand over his eyes. "I was bluffing. You go to the hearing, and some dude comes bouncing up to you in a suit, talking fast, calling you Louis, and shuffling papers. That's your lawyer. I am not calling *her* to find out who my lawyer is."

"I can call her," Sid offered. "See what her supervisor said."

Her tone was preoccupied, worried, and Mac hated that.

Well, damn.

"Let her call you. I heard her say she would, and we have a hog house to dismantle." Mac took a seat at the table. He'd purposely taken the chair across from Sid, which left him beside Luis. Less chance he'd be tempted to touch her in front of the boy.

"What's involved in dismantling a hog house?" Sid wrapped her hands around the mug of tea as if they were cold, and she still had that distracted look in her eyes.

"It can't be that complicated," Mac said. "It's only a hog house."

"It involves heavy equipment," James said. "Hang on. I have to get rid of another call."

Mac hung on until James came back on the line.

"At least a dozer and a grader, if you want to do it right, and about eighteen guys swarming over the place with claw hammers and trucks, and making a racket. From what my clients tell me, about half a side of beef and a cold keg might be in order too, if you want a break on the price. It's one long, tiring day. Why not burn the damned thing down? Get the fire department to use it as a teaching exercise?"

"Because the owner needs to sell the weathered lumber," Mac said, kicking another rock out of the ruts in Sid's driveway. "DSS would likely say any open burning is contrary to their almighty code."

A silence, while James's legal brain added up the evidence and Mac mentally started on an estimate for grading and paving the lane.

"This is at the home place, isn't it, Mac? It's the foster mom with the teenage boy who rides at Adelia's."

"The very hog house where we dropped cherry bombs down the two-seater. The one where I caught you trying to smoke oregano in ninth grade because your buddies said it would get you high. The two-seater makes the hog house a public health hazard, according to Miss Amy Snyder."

Who would have thought a guy could get sentimental about a hog house, much less a two-seater privy?

"Never dated Amy Snyder. She's likely new."

"She's about twelve years old," Mac replied on a sigh. "They're all looking like children to me anymore, James. It's depressing." Such were the admissions a man could make on the phone to his baby brother when contemplating the demise of a perfectly good hog house.

"Let me call in a few favors, make some calls. I gather sooner is better than later?"

DSS could be one of those "snatch the kid now and ask questions later agencies," though Ms. Snyder wasn't about to make a move without consulting her superiors.

"This weekend would do nicely, and I'll spring for the keg and the steaks. You can bring the potato salad, and because they have children, we'll let Hannah and Trent get away with condiments and snacks."

"Alert the media: MacKenzie Knightley will openly condone the consumption of potato chips by somebody other than himself."

"Family meeting," James said, taking his sister-in-law's hand in his and towing her down the hallway toward his brother's office. "Is Trent in?"

"He should be." Hannah, bless her, fell in step beside him. "Is this a good family meeting or a hard one? Since when did we start having family meetings, much less on company time?"

"Since Mac has fallen ass over tin cups for the lady who bought the home place. Her and her foster kid." James paused to knock on Trent's half-open door. "Trent, I'm stealing your wife."

"Not again." Trent opened the door the rest of the way. "Mac has taken to swiping Hannah for lunch. Now you're absconding with her too. Maybe you should get wives of your own?"

James let that pass—the only woman he'd want for a wife didn't want him—and pulled Hannah into Trent's office, shutting the door behind them.

"I just got a call from Mac," James said. "He's organizing the demolition of the hog house at the home place, and doing it because Social Services is threatening to jerk the foster care license of the family living there. Seems the two-seater is a public health hazard or some such bull—baloney."

"It is a health hazard," Trent said, leaning against his desk and crossing his arms. "Or it would be, if anybody had ever used it. Why can't it just be filled in?"

"Mac wants to sell off the barn lumber," James explained, "which is a good idea. Interior contractors down the road will pay through the nose for it."

"For barn lumber?" Hannah asked. She crossed to her husband and straightened his tie, which sported Pooh, Tigger, and Eeyore on a blue silk background. James could almost hear his brother purring, which was…fine. It was *fine* that Trent and Hannah were so goddamned happy. *Fine* that they were comfortable letting James see how damned happy they were. Every time they were in each other's damned happy company.

Hannah had asked a question, something about…

"Weathered barn lumber is the latest craze in paneling the den," James said, "the rec room, the conservatory, and so forth in those McMansions sporting dens, rec rooms, and conservatories. There's only so much vintage barn lumber left these days. Selling it isn't a bad idea—mahogany's no less dear—but it's complicated."

"As hog houses go, ours was enormous," Trent said. "The building has to be forty feet long."

Forty by twenty-eight, give or take. "The point is *Mac*, not the damned hog house. When's the last time MacKenzie Knightley took an interest in something outside this law firm?"

"He shoes horses at the therapeutic riding place," Hannah said. "He does our horses."

"That's obligation, not an interest," James said. "This is the woman who kissed him in public. Maybe you haven't noticed, but our brother has been missing in action since lunch today."

"Mac's a big boy," Trent said, his expression considering. "He's overdue for some kissing."

Marriage made perfectly sensible people stupid. "First you tell me he hasn't dated since law school. Now you tell me he's overdue for some kissing. *Of course* he's overdue, but this will get complicated in a hurry, Trent."

"Why should it? Adults kiss all the time." Trent kissed his wife, who smiled up at him beneficently. "The lucky ones do, anyway."

Blessed baby Jesus.

"Have you considered who this kid's lawyer might be, Trent?" James fired the question with more intensity than he'd intended. "The boy's an out-of-county transfer, and I'm under the impression Legal Assistance dumps those on you."

Trent's expression sobered. "They invariably do."

Hannah looked from one brother to the other. "Uh-oh?"

"Right," James said. "Big flipping uh-oh."

"James just called back." Mac stuffed his phone back in its holster. "We're set for Saturday, assuming the weather cooperates."

"Just like that?" Sid hunched forward on the swing and braced her elbows on her knees. "You make a few phone calls, and, boom, we're good to go?"

"I make a few phone calls, James makes a few phone calls, his friends make a few phone calls, and yes, we're all set. You're all set." Thank God, fraternal loyalty, and good cell reception. "The timing is perfect, because the construction season is only now getting under way. Demand for your lumber should be high."

He shifted against the porch post he was leaning on, stifling the urge to sit on that swing with her. Luis was upstairs doing his homework, leaving Mac and his conscience—his *self-discipline*—without any reinforcements.

"Won't it be hard for you," Sid murmured, "to flatten a building that was here when you were a child? Didn't you name your 4-H pigs after Daisy Duke or something?"

"I told the social worker the truth," Mac replied. "We never raised hogs. My mother said the good Lord put bacon on sale at the grocery store for reasons. Dad said she'd get to naming the hogs, and it's never a good idea to name animals you're bound to butcher. We ran dairy cows, dairy goats, laying hens, and farmed hay and crops."

Sid fell silent, her expression hard to read in the gathering darkness. The temperature was dropping too, making Mac think again of wrapping his jacket around her shoulders.

"What is that bird?" she asked, head coming up. "I've heard it the past few nights because I'm sleeping with my window cracked for fresh air."

"It's not a bird, it's a tree frog. A chorus of tree frogs. They probably have some fancy name. I always knew them as peepers, and they sing in spring to attract their mates."

This year, they were right on schedule, a comfort to any man raised on a farm.

"That's sweet. Frogs in my trees, lonely frogs."

Horny frogs.

Mac pushed off the porch railing. "I'd best be going. If you want to know who Luis's lawyer is, call the courthouse with his case number. Have Luis call, on second thought. They might not give any information out to you over the phone."

"Then they probably won't give it out to him either," she said, rising. "The joys of foster parenting are without number."

She'd said it ironically, a little edge to her humor. "Every night I go to bed, MacKenzie, and I thank God for one more day when that kid didn't have to face turmoil and upheaval. I thank God he ate at my table, threw his wash into my machine, and didn't think twice about whether he'd still be here when the sun set again. He has taken months to reach this point, and I don't know what I'd do…"

Sid fell silent and crossed the porch.

"Thank you." She went up on her toes, and while panic welled in Mac's gut, pressed her mouth to his. "Thank you so much."

She subsided, leaning on his chest, while her scent hit Mac's nose, and pure animal lust went ricocheting in all the wrong places.

Step back.

Except the porch railing blocked that maneuver.

"You smell so good, MacKenzie," she said, sighing against his chest. "You taste good." She kissed him again, and in the half second when Mac might have asserted reason over instinct, her breasts pressed against his chest.

"Sidonie." He closed his eyes and heard the tiny peepers singing their hearts out in the chilly spring air. "I can't—"

She was a delicate kisser. Mac withstood the pleasure and pain of that as long as he could, letting her tongue feather across his lips, feeling her body tucking more closely against his. He slid a hand into her hair at her nape, and anchored her gently while his free arm wrapped around her.

To hold a woman, to have her close and warm and willing in his arms…

It had been so long, so wretchedly, desperately long. Years of telling himself nobody ever died of celibacy.

But he had died. Died a little every night, died of knowing he wasn't desired and couldn't reciprocate even if he had been. Died every time he heard his brother James casually picking up some eager female over the phone, died both times when he'd stood up at weddings with his brother Trent.

Mac came back to life as a blaze of lust ignited him from the inside, and what started out as a gentle kiss on Sidonie's part turned into a pillaging rampage on his. His grip on her became commanding, his mouth voracious. He rocked his body into hers, insisting that she feel his arousal as intensely as he did.

"MacKenzie." She pulled back, gaze searching his face. "God in heaven."

Then she was back like the second half of a hurricane, burrowing into him, her mouth open beneath his, her tongue questing for his while her arms lashed around his neck.

"Want," Sid growled, pushing against his erection. "God, how I want."

She got a hand between them, going for his belt buckle right there on the porch. Mac's heart leaped as another thought battered its way into his brain.

The kid was right upstairs.

Being found in flagrante delicto on the porch with the neighbor was as good a way to cost Sidonie her foster care license as decorating the property with derelict outhouses.

Mac lifted his head but held her to him tightly. "Sweetheart, whoa. Luis—"

"Right." She nodded, and Mac was pleased to hear her panting, to *feel* her panting against his chest. "Luis, but *God*, MacKenzie."

He ran a shaky hand over her hair. God, indeed. "It's been a while for me, Sid." Lame, but the truth. "I'm sorry if I got a little too—" What? Enthusiastic didn't begin to describe the end of a ten-year drought.

"It's been forever for me," she said, "but you..."
She pressed her forehead to his sternum. "You've been
saving up, or you're hiding your light under a basket. I
have never before in my life been kissed dizzy."

She was clinging to him, leaning on him to stay upright.

"I kissed you dizzy?"

She patted his chest, right over his heart. "It's like I
can feel the pull of the moon on the tides in your kisses.
See the stars, hear the angels singing. Crap."

"Crap?"

"Analogies and bodily urges are a disastrous combination. Hold me, MacKenzie."

Mac tucked his chin over Sid's crown and stroked
his hand along her back, learning the feel of her. She
seemed content to be held, and he was thrilled, beyond
thrilled, to hold her.

As his libido's clamoring subsided to a simmering
grumble, Mac realized something else: Sidonie Lindstrom
was a *foster parent*. She couldn't be as wedded to tradi-
tional ideas about family as the average female if she was
willing to go through hell to adopt one teenager.

Emily Dickinson's "thing with feathers" perched in
his soul took wing.

With Sidonie, for the first time in years, Mac
acknowledged that there could be *hope*. He gathered her
more tenderly into his embrace, pressed his lips to her
hair, and closed his eyes.

He swallowed hard, inventoried his courage, and
found it wasn't even a matter of courage. The sensation
was just there, in his body, his mind, his heart: *hope*.

"Here comes the entertainment."

Mac growled the words, but loudly enough that Sid could hear him. A black SUV was bumping up the lane, joining the line of pickups and vans in the barnyard. The guy who got out was tall, blue-eyed, blond, and Sid would have classified him as drop-dead gorgeous if she hadn't met his more rugged older brother first.

"You must be James," she said, walking forward to take a Dutch oven from his hands. "I'm Sid. Thanks for coming."

"Greetings, Sid." He flashed her a megawatt smile, and tipped his cowboy hat, for God's sake. Entertainment indeed. "That's the signature Knightley brothers' potato salad, which recipe has not been improved upon even by MacKenzie himself. Mac." James smiled up at his brother, who was glowering from the porch. "Things under control?"

"For now. Trent, Hannah, and the hooligans will be here any minute."

"I'll pay my respects to Daisy and Buttercup then. Sid, nice place you have here."

He winked at her and sauntered off with the gunslinger gait of a man who'd have good moves on the dance floor, and probably in a few other choice locations too.

"That boy needs a spanking," Sid said as Mac came to stand behind her. "Just on general principles, he needs regular spanking."

"Don't tell him that, or he'll be inviting you over to admire his toy collection."

"I didn't mean—"

Mac was smiling at his brother's retreating back.

"That was teasing, wasn't it, MacKenzie? You don't honestly think he'd be that gauche, that forward?"

"Not now. A couple years ago, James was in constant rut, but he seems to have settled down."

"Is there a woman involved?" Mac had never said much about his family, but they'd certainly stepped up for this demolition party.

"A good woman, thank God. She's making him work for it. Simple strategies are often the most effective with dumb animals. Best get that stuff in the fridge if we're not going to eat for another hour or so."

In addition to being a farrier—that was the word— Mac seemed to be something of a foodie, so Sid took his advice and headed for the kitchen.

As she turned to go, she could have sworn Mac patted her fanny.

She whipped around to take him to task, but he was walking away. From the back, he looked like the grown-up version of James, who was plenty on the tall side. It's just that Mac didn't need to swagger, while James needed to make that good woman see reason.

Sid realized she was comparing male tushes. *How lovely.*

She was still smirking when she took the potato salad into the kitchen, though she spared one particular porch post a glance as she went by. In the four days since Mac had kissed the living daylights out of her, she'd made sure to get all-weather cushions on the porch swing. She had plans for that swing.

When Mac had driven up this morning, she'd had a hard time not hyperventilating, she was that giddy to see him again, which was ridiculous. A woman who had long since celebrated her thirtieth birthday had no business—

No, she had *every* business. If he was the right guy, she had every business in the world ogling him, being giddy over him, and generally thanking God every waking minute that, contrary to established convictions, one man remained on the face of the planet about whom she could get stupid.

Wheels crunched on the driveway as she put the potato salad in the fridge and went back out on the porch. Another truck was pulling up, the kind with a backseat.

Yet another good-looking Knightley brother got out, this one sporting dark hair, about as much height as James boasted, and a quieter smile. An auburn-haired lady climbed out of the passenger's side, and two little girls soon emerged from the backseat.

"This is where Dad grew up?" one of them asked.

Both girls were dark-haired. One sported two braids, the other a single plait. The one with two braids took her mother's hand, as both mother and daughter peered around.

"He did, but first we should greet our hostess," the lady said. "Hi, you must be Sidonie, and I'm Hannah. This is Grace, and that's Merle."

"And I'm Trent." The guy stuck out his hand, and Sid was treated to a firm shake. "Can we bring in the loot, or have you set up tables somewhere else?"

"Tables are around back. James just got here and is flirting with Daisy and Buttercup."

Trent and Hannah exchanged a smile.

"He has a certain charm, our James," Hannah said. "Girls, best behavior. Stay away from the hog house where the crews are working, or you could get hurt. Let Uncle Mac and Uncle James know you're here."

They tore off, best behavior apparently encompassing a dead run toward the pasture.

"They're horse savvy," Trent said. "And uncle savvy. Do you need help with anything?"

"If she does"—Hannah linked her arm through her husband's—"I can assist. You get to pound nails, or pull them out, and say bad words as long as the girls are out of earshot."

"The keg's on the picnic table," Sid added. "Luis won't rat you out if he hears the occasional colorful expletive."

Trent saluted, blew his wife a kiss, and headed for the cacophony of hammer blows, shouts, and power drills at the hog house.

"Leaving us to set up lunch," Hannah said. "I'm happy to answer any questions you have about MacKenzie, except I'm relatively new to the family myself."

"No questions," Sid said as they retrieved bags of cups, napkins, and paper plates from the truck. "On second thought, what on earth do his brothers get that man for Christmas?"

—◦◦◦—

"As I see it, you have two problems." James reached out to the nearest mare, Daisy, and the horse obligingly sniffed him over.

"She remembers you," Mac said, pleased for James's sake.

"All the ladies remember me." James grinned, but Mac could spot the counterfeit humor in his youngest brother's smile.

"You have things patched up with Vera yet?" Mac asked.

"I do not." James scratched Daisy behind one big hairy ear. "I'm not used to doing the chasing, Mac, and I've bungled it. I'm even more clueless when it comes to patching up what I've put wrong. I'm off stride."

"I'm guessing Vera is a gal who appreciates the direct approach."

James looked intrigued. "Groveling?"

"Groveling is very direct, but far be it from me to offer advice for the lovelorn. What are my two problems?"

James dropped his hand, and the mare ambled off. "First, what the hell are you doing hanging around this place? The memories, at least the last ones, aren't good. Not for any of us."

No, they were not. But Mac had only recently come to understand that James had the worst memories of the three brothers. James had been left at home with their grieving mother while Trent and Mac had gone off to college, and his adolescence had turned into a quiet nightmare. That James had been able to tell Mac that much had put them on more equal footing and shifted their relationship closer to friends and brothers than merely brothers.

As if there was anything *mere* about being brothers.

"We've seen hard times here, true enough," Mac said. "I left before Dad died, and growing up here I was happy. Very happy."

The happiest he'd ever been. The realization sank in, bringing order to some little corner of the chaos that was his internal landscape.

"What's my second problem?" Mac asked.

"Have you considered that Trent may end up representing the boy?"

Crappity-crap-crap-crap. No, Mac had not.

"Trent will do a good job," Mac said. "Luis is a good kid. He shouldn't be hard to represent."

"Bullshit." James kept his voice down, but his posture radiated tension. "When you represent a kid in delinquency court, Mac, the job is clear-cut, easy. You're supposed to get the little hoodlum off, or at least keep him or her at home if you can, same as if they were adult criminals. The child welfare attorney has a different role."

"What do you mean? My knowledge of family law would fill a bottle cap."

Mac could admit that to James, because having complementary areas of expertise was one of the reasons their firm did well.

"Mine would fill two bottle caps," James replied. "But with a child welfare case, the attorney is supposed to advocate for what the kid wants, provided the child has considered judgment on the issue in question."

"What in the lawyering hell does that mean?"

"I'd ask Trent if you really want to know, but my take on it is that the attorney can decide the kid's reasons for his position—wanting to go home, to stay in foster care, to be placed with siblings, whatever—are unsound, and advocate not for what the kid wants, but for what is in the kid's best interests. It's slippery."

"Slippery isn't good," Mac said slowly. Slippery wasn't black and white, and Mac thrived on black and white. "Give me examples."

"Luis might want to be placed with his siblings, and that family might be willing to take him, but not adopt him.

Trent would have to weigh the sense in reuniting siblings with the disruption to Luis of changing schools and families again, and leaving a potential pre-adopt placement with Sid for one that doesn't offer permanence. It's tricky."

Tricky, slippery. Reasons why a rational man avoided family law like the plague.

Why, if that man were smart, he'd avoid entangling himself in Luis's situation like all the biblical plagues combined.

While Luis lived a reality he'd done little to create every hour of every day.

"I don't think it will come to that," Mac said. "Luis is levelheaded as teenagers go. He won't force Trent into that kind of corner."

"A levelheaded teenager is a contradiction in terms. I know. I was one."

James pushed away from the fence, leaving Mac to stare out over the greening pasture, seeing nothing. He was still there when Trent came up on his shoulder forty-five minutes later.

"Lunch is about to be served," Trent said. "James is manning the grill, which strikes me as disrespectful of the steaks when you're on hand to do it right."

"James takes his nutrition seriously. Though I think he's dropped some weight."

"Pining for Vera?"

"Growing up," Mac said. "And pining for Vera. My money's on James though. He gets what he goes after, usually."

"He's worried about you. The girls look good for being in their dotage." The mares were back at their grass, oblivious to guests or brewing legal storms.

Mac appreciated that Trent was easing up to whatever he wanted to discuss. That came with being a dad, a guy who liked the complications and unexpected twists of the typical family law case. James had competed on horseback over fences as a younger man. If Trent had taken the same path, he would have ridden broncs, and done so with the lithe elegance of the natural champion. Nothing unseated the guy. Nothing.

"Why is *James* worried about me?" Mac asked.

"You're falling in love."

Mac considered his conversation with James, and considered Trent's version of James's concerns. "Did I tell you what to do with Hannah?"

"Yes."

"I told you not to mix business and personal agendas, Trent. I never said you had to leave her alone."

"You told me not to get us sued and not to trifle with her. Same thing. It was good advice, and I followed it."

"You think I'll get us sued?"

"You're not denying the allegation," Trent said, his voice quite, quite casual.

"I wasn't aware the Annotated Code of Maryland now included an article on falling in love," Mac said, equally casually.

"It doesn't, but, Mac, have you considered that it isn't Sidonie you're attracted to, but the prospect of coming home that tugs at your heartstrings?"

"Yes, Trenton Edwards, I have considered that, and while I do not concede that I am falling in love with anybody, I have had at least two opportunities to buy this place in the last ten years. I also could have kept it in the family rather than sell it when Mom died."

"So three times, you've passed up an opportunity to call this place home again, but now I'm settled, and James will be soon. That puts things in a different light."

"You mean well," Mac said. His criminal clients often meant well too, and yet, they were convicted on the basis of what followed those good intentions. "I'm going to get me a steak. You coming?"

"Stubborn." Trent pushed off the fence. "So goddamned stubborn. Hannah will kill me if I let anything happen to you. Grace and Merle will dance on my bones."

"Nothing's going to happen to me." Mac biffed Trent on the arm. "It's good to know you'd notice if it did."

Chapter 9

"GOING TO GET HIS ASS HANDED TO HIM," JAMES SAID, but he kept his voice down because there were children on the property. One kid could overhear every swear word uttered on an entire four-hundred-acre farm. "You said it's already happened twice before, once in law school, once in college. A guy like Mac doesn't shrug off getting kicked to the curb."

"Correct me if I'm wrong"—Trent pulled up a cooler and hunkered beside James—"but isn't it you who's enjoying the view from the curb these days?"

"Yeah, but there's always room for one more. Mac stands too close to Sidonie, Trent. She's grieving, and he'll be her transition toy."

"Which role devastated you all fourteen hundred times you were dragged, beaten, and bullied into it, including, just possibly, the last time too?"

Older brothers should qualify as a biblical plague. "Eat your steak," James said around a mouthful of scrumptious potato salad. "I like Sid, but a broken-hearted woman is trouble."

"Now you know how Mac and I felt fourteen hundred times over watching you in action."

Well, hell. James washed his potato salad down with cold beer.

"You've met Luis?" Trent asked.

Merciful in victory, that was Trent. "Luis was helping

stack the lumber on the trucks. Seems like a hard worker. Needs some meat on his bones."

"Growth spurts are hell on a man's physique. He's been hitting the keg for his hydration though."

James stopped chewing and set his plate aside. "Not good. Where's Mac?"

"Took Merle and Grace to see the horses."

Whoever decided beer, potato salad, and a spring day edging toward warm was a good combination? "And there goes Luis around to the picnic table again."

"You get Mac." Trent shoveled another piece of steak into his mouth. "I'll keep an eye on the kid and ask Hannah to keep Sid busy in the kitchen."

"Don't get upset." James was shifting from foot to foot, a few feet away from Mac—outside swinging range— just as he'd learned to do when he was a kid and he'd done something stupid.

"What'd you do, James?" Mac asked. "If you hit on Sid, it's your own fault she smacked you."

"I didn't hit on Sid, though she's a perfectly lovely lady. Can you, uh, come around to the back of the house?"

"He means now, Uncle Mac," Grace offered from beside her uncle. "It's OK. Merle and I will run off our cake out in the pasture."

"Tell your mother where you're going first," Mac said. "Don't bother the horses, and stay away from the pond. Watch where you step too. You know what poison ivy looks like?"

"Yes, Uncle Mac," Merle piped up, taking her sister's hand. "And we won't poke at any snakes with sticks, and we won't get lost, and we won't play in the haymow without telling anybody. If we see a skunk, we'll run—quietly—the other way."

"How in the heck did we grow up here without regular trips to the emergency room?" Mac asked.

"There were a few, but you've got an emergency brewing in the backyard, bro," James said.

"You and your doomsaying. The sooner you and Vera talk things out, the happier this entire valley will be."

"Luis has been hitting the keg. Does the term minor in possession of alcohol ring any bells with you? Contributing to the condition of a minor? Underage drinking?"

"How about, the boy's mother will kill me?" Mac muttered, but he didn't take off at a run.

"That too, and then Social Services will start on her."

"Crap. Hadn't thought of that." Mac walked—quietly—toward the back of the house. "You know how much he's had?"

"Trent might, he's the dad at large."

"Yeah, but you were the delinquent."

"Never one time," James said. "If there's an expert on delinquency, it would be you."

Mac stopped short as they came around a corner of the summer kitchen. "Oh, Jesus." Trent was strolling with Luis toward the barn, an arm around the kid's shoulders. "Boy doesn't look too good."

"When did you set up that keg?"

"About nine this morning."

"Four hours of steady drinking," James said, "when he likely has no tolerance, and he can't weigh but about one twenty, one thirty wringing wet. I'll see if Hannah has aspirin and get some bottled water."

"Get him a clean shirt. He has Mom's old room—and bring some towels."

Mac followed Trent and his charge into the barn, saying prayers all the while that Hannah could keep Sid from getting curious.

"*Je suis...malade*." Luis grinned at his own savoir faire, then the corners of his mouth turned abruptly down. "*Pardon...*"

"You're *malade*, all right." Mac fetched a bucket out of the tack room.

"He's a bilingual drunk," Trent remarked. "That's pretty impressive."

"I got him a shirt," James said, coming up the aisle. "The ladies are dishing out dessert, so we're probably safe for a while. How you doing, sport?"

"*Malade. J'aime la bière.*"

"Yeah, *nous* all *aimons la bière*, until we're puking it up through our noses," Mac said. "When did you start drinking, Weese?"

"*Depuis mon cinquième anniversaire.*"

"He's been drinking since he was five years old?" James asked, shaking out the clean T-shirt. "I didn't try Dad's whiskey until I was six."

"You're not helping," Mac said, but James had been so sick and so brave when his older brothers had found him with a bottle of Jim Beam.

"Weese, you have to do two things before we sneak you up to your room for a nap," Mac said.

"I can doo anny-ting," Luis said, sweeping his arms open dramatically. "Anny-ting for you, *cher*."

"A singing, bilingual drunk," Trent muttered. "This just gets better and better."

"Go ahead and laugh," Mac said. "When he starts puking, we'll aim him in your direction."

Luis's arms collapsed to his side. "*Je*...don't feel so good."

"Here we go." Mac produced a bucket, and between him and Trent, they got Luis on his knees before it. "Take shallow breaths, kid. Pant if it helps, but you'll probably do yourself the most good if you just hurl."

"Best thing," James said, reaching over to pat Luis's shoulder. "Get it over with. It's just us guys, and we've all been exactly where you are. Just let 'er rip, toss those old cookies, pray to the five-gallon—"

"James." Trent used his most quelling, stern-dad voice. "You're going to make *me* sick."

"*Mon Dieu…*"

All three men were silent as Luis heaved twice, then gave up the beer his system hadn't yet processed.

"Glad that's over," James said, squatting beside the patient. "Here, drink this."

"No drinking," Luis said, sitting back on his heels and bracing his hands on his thighs. "Never again, the drinking."

"It's water." Mac took the bottle from James's hand and twisted off the cap. "Just rinse out your mouth, then take a few sips to see if your stomach is open for business."

"My stomach, she has died to death forever. I hate beer."

"A poetic, bilingual, singing drunk."

"Your stomach, she will appreciate the water." Mac brought the bottle to Luis's lips. "Little sips, fella."

Luis wrapped his hand around Mac's and took a couple of swallows.

"See how that sits," Mac suggested.

The bilingual, now-silent drunk opened his eyes and stared at the bucket.

"Look at me." James moved the bucket and gently turned Luis's face by the chin. "How you doing?"

Trent took the bucket Somewhere Else while James and Mac got Luis's arms free of his shirt.

"You're making progress," Mac said. "Worst part is over, for now. Gimme…that's it." Luis's head emerged from the T-shirt. "You think you're done being sick?"

"I will never be sick again, no more, *jamais*. I hate beer."

"Sure you do, sweetheart," James said. "On three?"

Mac nodded, and on three, they levered Luis, without his shirt, to his feet.

"We're going for a little walk," James said. "Right outside into the fresh air, around back where nobody will see, and then we're going to stick your aching, stupid head right under the pump. Won't that be fun?"

"Don't tease him," Mac said from Luis's other side. "Though you do seem to have a certain way with a drunk."

"Misery recognizes misery."

"Les Miz…" Luis muttered, his voice dropping away to hum a few bars of the main theme. He stumbled, Mac and James caught him, and Trent opened the barn doors to let them out into the spring sunshine.

"Hurts," Luis said, turning his face into Mac's shoulder. "*Le sol…*"

"Hurts my soul too," Mac said. "But James is right. You'll feel better soon."

Trent worked the handle of a squeaky pump, and Luis

stood dazedly while the first few rusty quarts gushed into the trough below the pump.

"Surprised that thing still works." James was holding Luis up on one side, Mac on the other. "Did we all sober up here at one time or another?"

"Not often," Mac said. "Daddy caught me sneaking in one night. Never said a word about drinking, but at breakfast the next morning, I got an oblique lecture about setting a good example. Luis, you ready?"

"I got the same lecture," Trent said.

"I got the one about how my older brothers would be so disappointed," James added. "Here we go."

At the last possible second, Luis realized what his fate would be, and he gave a token struggle but then submitted to his baptism stoically.

"Towel?" Mac held out a hand a few cold, wet moments later. Trent shoved a clean towel into it.

"I do eet." Luis snatched the towel away and scrubbed at his face and scalp. When he emerged from the towel, his dark red hair was sticking up in all directions, and his eyes were more focused. "I will get even, you," he said, glaring at Mac.

"You will get sober. Sober enough to drink at least a quart of water, take four aspirin, and get yourself upstairs to sleep off your idiocy."

"Four is a lot." James held the water bottle out to Luis. "Start with two. See if they stay down. We aren't all built on the dimensions of Sister Mary MacKenzie here."

"I get even for leaving the beer out for me."

A little silence, while the three brothers exchanged looks.

"Are you an alcoholic?" Trent asked. The question was without inflection, almost bored.

"I am not." Luis took the water bottle and studied it. "But if I were?"

"Then we'd get you the help you need." Mac draped the towel over Luis's shoulders. "So you'd better be telling us the truth. If you have a drinking problem, you need to tell us now. Every kid I know experiments with forbidden fruit, and most come through it older and wiser, no harm, no foul. We all did, Luis, and we're more or less contributing members of society. James got into our dad's sipping whiskey when he was six. He graduated first in his class and is a CPA. Trent maintained a 4.0 as an undergrad."

"I can't sing in French, though," Trent said. "Might scare my womenfolk if I tried to."

Luis looked from one man to the next, his gaze eventually settling on Mac. He took another sip of water before he spoke, and Mac saw the bottle shaking slightly in the boy's hand.

"I'm no drunk," Luis said, his accent all but gone. "I could have been, easy, but you drink, you don't care about anything else. All my mother's boyfriends were into drinking and doping. I tried it all. They thought it was fun to get me high, get me drunk. I thought it was fun too, for a while."

"And then?"

Luis shook his head.

James took to studying the water draining from the old trough. "My mom drank. She was grieving, and she drank. Too much, too often."

The tension went out of Luis's shoulders; he took another swallow of water then handed the bottle to James.

"What are we going to tell Sidonie?" Trent, the only married man present, asked the question.

"I'll apologize," Luis said. "I know better, and Sid's stupid crazy about irresponsible drinking."

"Why?" James asked. "She seems normal enough otherwise, except for liking Mac."

"Drunk driver killed her mother," Luis said. "And her brother. Different accidents, different ways. She's got her reasons." His gaze slid away as the last of the water dribbled from the trough into the grass.

Trent passed Luis a clean, dry shirt. "Some diplomatic discretion might be in order."

"What's that mean?" Luis pulled the shirt over his head.

"It means we cover your skinny ass," Mac said. "Just this once, and only insofar as what Sid doesn't ask about, we don't discuss with her. We don't lie, and we don't tattle. You tell in your own good time, if you tell her."

"I can tell her if I want to?"

"You can," Mac said. "I'm not sure I'd advise it."

"It's like this," Trent said. "All morning, we've been busy, with Sid working mostly in the house and the backyard, while you've been with the crew at the hog house. If one of the guys calls DSS and reports underage drinking, then Sid can honestly say she knew nothing about it. If she knew, and she didn't report it, that's worse than if she just lost track of you and you sneaked a few hits from the keg."

"It doesn't feel good to keep something from her," James said, "but what is the benefit *to Sid* of confessing to her while her license is already in jeopardy?"

"She'll feel guilty," Mac pointed out. "She'll worry, she'll blame herself, and she'll doubt her ability to parent you. If it will make you feel better, I'll tan your backside for you, but remorse is often punishment enough."

They gave Luis a moment to consider.

"I feel sick all over again."

"First sign of a full recovery," Trent said, patting Luis's shoulder. "Now, who's going to be our decoy so Luis can get upstairs in peace?"

"I will," James said. "There are pretty ladies and home-made desserts involved. I'm your man." He smacked Luis gently on the back of the head and walked off.

"He really graduated first in his class?" Luis asked.

"And don't cut loose around him in French," Mac said. "His is better than mine."

"I'm going to round up my daughters," Trent said. "Hannah was muttering about sunscreen, which I'm sure has worn off by now."

Mac let Trent disappear around the corner of the barn before surveying a damp, sobering-up Luis.

"I feel like a fuckup," Luis said, sitting on the lip of the trough. "I am a fuckup."

Mac sat beside him. "Everybody, every-God's-blessed-body on this earth fucks up, Weese. I've had some spectacular fuckups, so has Trent, so has James. Ask Trent about his first marriage. Ask James about his entire adolescence—which lasted until this very spring. You do what you can to make it right, learn whatever lessons you can from it, forgive yourself, and move on."

Luis kicked the dirt at his feet. "That's what my mother says."

"Is that what this is about? Your mom's in jail, so you're a fuckup too?"

"Nah…maybe, a little bit. We got more water?"

"Mother's Day is coming up," Mac said. "You making a trip to Jessup?"

"Sid asked the same thing, but my mother will ask about my sisters, and I don't want to tell her I haven't seen them in months. She'll cry, I'll want to hit something, but I won't. Their foster parents already think I'm the big, bad, hoodlum older brother. I might corrupt my own little sisters, or some shit."

"You're an honor-roll student with no juvenile record," Mac countered. "You'll want to bring up the sibling visits with your lawyer so he can get them court ordered."

"My lawyer—whoever the hell that is." Luis finished his water and crushed the bottle in his hand.

———

"I cannot believe a building stood right here just this morning." Sid toed the dirt, which had been graded to a smooth, level surface. "It's like the fairies came through and disappeared it."

"Damned loud batch of fairies," Mac said. "They put the hurt to some steak too."

"But it's done." She beamed a smile at the guy who'd authored this bit of rural magic. "I didn't think it could be as simple as you said it would be, but it's done, and I have a check in my hot little hand. Just like that."

"Sometimes things do work out the way they're supposed to."

Not often, in Sid's experience.

Mac stood a few feet away, but he wasn't entirely present. Was this when he told her she couldn't go attacking him in broad daylight? For hours, she'd

KISS ME HELLO 171

watched him moving around the property, once or twice catching him with his shirt off.

And, merciful God, it had been hard not to stare. His brothers were good-looking men, fit and well proportioned, but MacKenzie Knightley was beautiful. He had a kind of competence in his movements, a confidence that made a train wreck of Sid's higher brain functions now that she knew the feel of his mouth on hers.

His body next to hers.

James had done a much better job of flirting with her—with Hannah, and with the two women who had worked on the demolition crew. Mac hadn't said a word, not even when James had stood, one arm around Hannah, the other around Sid, and complained about a man having to do without his dessert entirely too often for entirely too long.

"MacKenzie?"

He glanced her way.

"Don't let me keep you if there's somewhere else you need to be." Trent and Hannah had taken off a couple of hours after lunch, and James had left by five. Luis was zonked, which sometimes happened on weekends, though he'd lasted at least until lunch.

"There's nowhere else I need to be," Mac said. "Nowhere else I want to be. Have you seen the pond?"

Nowhere else Sid wanted to be, either. "I've seen it."

"Moon will be up in an hour or so, and you should monitor the water level in the pond."

The water level in the pond? And yet, Mac was so dear when he was managing the universe. "Why?"

"The pond is one barometer of your water table, albeit only a rough one. The well here has never gone dry that I know of, but the development farther up the valley puts a greater demand on the aquifer."

"We'll go visit the pond." Because he'd more or less been asking her to, right?

Mac started off toward the pasture, then stopped. "We need a blanket."

"We do?" To check the water level?

"Wait here." He loped off toward his truck and reappeared carrying some sort of camping blanket. "This'll do."

He slung it over his shoulder and took off again, and this time Sid fisted her hands on her hips and advanced on him.

"It will not *do*. You kissed the daylights out me a few days ago, MacKenzie. Now I'm getting the silent treatment? You trying to get your it's-not-you-it's-me speech together?"

"My what?"

"The speech where you tell me you're still involved with your ex, or your hairdresser, or you're one of those guys who needs a lot of freedom, but if I ever want to hook up, you'll work me in, so to speak."

"I don't have a hairdresser. I go to a barber."

"Good to know. Makes all the difference." She stalked past him, or tried to. A large, warm hand on her arm prevented her progress.

"Sidonie?" Mac's tone was gentle, laced with regret, or consternation, or some damned thing that suggested she'd just made a fool of herself. *Again*.

"What?"

"We're in view of the house, and it isn't dark yet. Luis might wake up and take a sandwich to the porch, or check to make sure we brought his mares in. He has enough on his plate without serving as your duenna."

"*Oh.*"

Mac leaned closer. "When we get over the lip of that hill, I know for a fact that he can't spy on us from the house, and I have been waiting all damned day to get my hands on you." He let her arm go. "You kiss the daylights out of a man, then leave him to wonder, while you carry on with his wayward baby brother. Brothers, plural, because Trent is only marginally better than James. My influence on the both of them was limited."

Mac kissed her nose and sauntered off.

Well.

Sid enjoyed the view from a few paces behind him for a half-dozen steps, then caught up to him and slipped her arm through his. He patted her hand where it rested on his forearm, readjusted the blanket on his shoulder, and matched his steps to hers.

MacKenzie Knightley was a good communicator, but he didn't limit himself to words, or necessarily do his best communicating with words.

And he was a gentleman.

"I should have considered Luis's feelings," she said. "I haven't dated anybody since I got my foster care license. Sometimes after a shoot, some of the guys from the crew and I would go out, but that was a work thing. Not that we're dating."

"No, we're not. We have things to discuss before we're dating."

"Rules?" She didn't like the sound of that, not unless her rules figured into the discussion. Prominently.

"Understandings. James would say we need a meeting of the minds, a contract of sorts."

Was that Mac-speak for a meeting of the gonads? "James would say that?"

"Business law comes naturally to him. Goes with being a CPA."

"Suppose it would. What are these understandings, MacKenzie? I won't be dictated to by anybody, not for any reason."

"Who said anything about dictating?"

Sid walked along beside him, trying to fathom his mood. He still seemed preoccupied to her, lost in thought.

"This is a nice spot," he said. "The horses will loaf here in the hotter months because the trees make for good shade, but the canopy isn't quite done leafing out yet, so we'll be able to see the moon come over the ridge." He spread the blanket on a patch of grass up the slope from the pond.

Sid settled on the blanket, running her hand over what felt like soft flannel, while Mac lowered himself beside her.

"Give me your foot." Mac didn't wait for her to comply. He took Sid by the foot, and drew her running shoe off. "Other one."

He peeled her socks down and tucked them into her shoes, then unlaced his boots and set them beside the blanket, stuffing a sock in each one. "Moonrise is always best appreciated barefoot."

The sentiment was poetical; the words were not. "Is that a rule?"

"Suppose it is." He took off his jacket, balled it up,

and lay back to rest his head on it. "Come here and let me hold you, Sidonie. I haven't watched the moon come up with a lovely woman in my arms for years."

She settled against him, resting her head on the slope of his shoulder. "We're going to talk about rules like this?" *He thought she was lovely.*

"We'll come to some understandings." His arm came around her shoulders, and his hand stroked over her hair. "I'll undo this braid while we're at it."

"Don't lose my elastic."

His fingers were soon winnowing through her hair, drawing the length of it over her shoulder.

"How am I supposed to think about rules when you're touching me like this, MacKenzie?"

"You don't need to think. You just tell me what's true for you."

"True about what?"

He went quiet again, while Sid repositioned herself against him. She could hear his heart beat, feel the slow, steady thud of his life's blood beneath her cheek.

"What do you want from me, Sidonie Lindstrom? What do you need?"

"Nobody has asked me that before." She considered her answer, while Mac's hand drifted through her hair, across her back, down her arm. "I want a friend, I guess. You've been a friend to me, and I wasn't expecting to find that here."

"Is that all you want? I can be a good friend. My brothers would vouch for me in that regard."

Sid could not tell from Mac's voice if he was disappointed with her answer, or pleased. "No, that isn't all I want, but I'll settle for it, and be grateful if that's where you want to draw the line. A friend, a real friend, is nothing to scoff at. Tony was my friend."

Another silence, while Mac got his hand on her nape and started massaging the tension there. His idea of friendship would soon leave Sid witless and boneless.

"I can't expect you to put yourself out there without showing I'm willing to do likewise: I want you." Mac's voice was quiet in the gathering darkness. "I want you at least for a friend, an intimate friend, Sidonie, but I don't share something that precious. If you allow me the privileges of a lover, then I will expect that for whatever time I enjoy that status, those privileges are exclusively mine. You will agree to this, or our friendship keeps its clothes on."

Sid shivered, though the night wasn't uncomfortably cool, and Mac gave off heat like a woodstove. He was so serious about this, when they could have shared a casual romp in the moonlight.

She would have settled for that—and settling would have been a mistake.

With Mac, where Sid was now in life, a hookup would have been wrong.

She traced his facial features. Beyond serious, he was solemn, as if these understandings he sought could be the foundation for something even greater than friendship.

"If you agree to my terms," he said, his hand slowing in her hair, "you agree because it's what you want too, not because I need to hear the words and you have a private agenda that's different from what you'll say to me."

He was asking for honesty, the most basic tenet of a real friendship. Friends were kind to each other, considerate, patient, reliable, but above all, a friend was somebody who told the truth.

"I don't have much practice with relationships, MacKenzie. Tony was protective of me, and I never went looking. I'm not a party girl now. I haven't looked at a man in months, possibly years. Then Tony got sick, and there was no question, no possibility."

"You were grieving. You're still grieving." He rolled slowly, like the earth heaving up, until Sid was on her back with Mac blanketing her. "There's more to say." He rested his forehead against hers. "A lot more, but right now, Sidonie, I have to kiss you. Have to."

He'd thought about this. Sid could tell from his kiss that this conversation was what he'd been preoccupied with. These understandings and this very kiss.

He brushed his mouth over hers, slowly back and forth. "Open."

She parted her lips, the better to sigh out her pleasure. His weight wasn't on her, but she craved it and wrapped her legs around his flanks to pull him closer.

"Touch me, Sidonie." He brushed her mouth again, then brushed his lips over her brows, along her hairline, down her jaw. The sensation was warm and ticklish and special. "Put your hands on me, anywhere. Everywhere."

Sid didn't need the whispered invitation, but hearing it sent arousal arrowing down to the secret places in her body. She tugged Mac's shirt free and skimmed her hands over the warm plane of his naked back.

"Feels good," he murmured. "Makes me hot. Hotter."

Mac settled his mouth over hers on those incendiary words, and Sid groaned with the pleasure of it. He would torture her, she was sure of it. She'd caught him unaware the other night on the porch, ambushed him, and now in his own much more studied fashion, he was ambushing her.

"MacKenzie, I want it fast." She spoke against his mouth, felt him chuckle, or maybe groan. She tried to get her hands under his belt to clutch at the muscles of his backside, but he took his mouth from her and rested his cheek against hers.

"You want my clothes off, Sidonie?"

"*Need* them off." She ran her fingers through his hair. She'd been longing to get her hands on his hair, longing to feel the silk and softness of it. "Every stitch. Be pagan with me, MacKenzie."

He sighed against her cheek, which was no damned answer at all. She started undoing the buttons of his shirt while he made up his infernal male mind.

"We're burning moonlight, Knightley." She pushed his shirt off his shoulders and opened her mouth on his chest. He even tasted of cinnamon and cloves. "Ah, God. MacKenzie."

He let Sid tease at his nipples with her tongue, and nuzzle and lick and explore for long moments, until she was squirming her hips against him.

"You are driving me bonkers," she said, "and you're barely moving."

"I'm half-undressed, which is more than we can say for you."

Sid digested that sorry reasoning for about one second. "Get off me."

He was gone in a single, lithe move. His weight and warmth surrounded her one instant; he was flat on his back beside her the next.

"The jeans have to go." She worked at his belt buckle, some tricky arrangement intended to serve the misguided cause of adult male chastity. "Damn you.

No more belts when we're getting lucky. Understand? That's a rule."

He stilled her hands with his own and got the thing undone. "Better?"

"Marginally. Shuck 'em, MacKenzie, or I'll chew through your jeans in the next five minutes."

"Your enthusiasm is wonderfully reassuring," he said, lifting his hips and losing the jeans. "If a little violent."

And there he was, six feet plus of naked, beautiful male, laid out before Sid in the fading light.

"Oh…my." She drew a single finger along the considerable length of his erection. "My, my, my. Why on earth would you need reassuring about anything, ever, MacKenzie Knightley?" She stroked him again, once, twice. "I want to get my mouth on you."

"Sidonie?"

She stopped mid-lean, her hair spilling onto his stomach and glared at him. "Another rule: no intense discussions when I'm about to indulge myself with your tender and willing body."

"Two things." Mac threaded his hand into her hair, which prevented her from taking him into her mouth. "First, fair is fair. Let me take your clothes off, Sidonie."

That was fair, also probably a good idea. Once she focused on the bounty before her, stopping to undress would destroy Sid's momentum, and even aroused as she was, a niggle of disbelief refused to leave her. She pulled her T-shirt over her head and fussed the straps to her bra, only to find Mac's fingers closing over hers.

"Let me do it."

"You want to undress me?" She tried to read his expression, but his features were damnably composed.

"I've thought about it." He drew a single finger slowly down her arm. "Thought about it a fair amount, in fact."

Just like that, Sid's bravado collapsed into self-consciousness.

Into shyness.

"You'll take too long," she said, drawing in a breath.

"There is no such thing as taking too long when a man and a woman are about to be intimate for the first time."

Maybe not in his book. "You said there were two things. What's the second?"

He leaned up and kissed her, slowly, lingeringly, and then he hovered near on the strength of his abs and put his lips close to her ear.

"I haven't permitted myself to share this with anybody in about ten years. I. Will. *Not*. Be. Rushed."

Chapter 10

I AM IN SUCH TROUBLE. ABRUPTLY, SID COULDN'T GET her breath. "Ten years?"

"No intense discussions allowed." He levered up to his elbows. "Not now."

"But *ten years*, MacKenzie?" She subsided onto her back, the enormity of their actions crashing over her. This *meant* something to Mac, meant a lot. For him to be here with her, naked and aroused in the moonlight *mattered*.

"Why me, MacKenzie? You're a beautiful man, inside and out. Why me?"

"Hush." He leaned over and kissed her belly. Sid's hand settled in his hair, wanting to hold him there. "We'll talk. We'll talk as long as you like, but not just now. Now we love."

His breath fanned against her abdomen, and all the wanting in Sid shifted. She went from needing to *have* satisfaction, to needing to *give* it. Arousal subsided into a vast, aching tenderness, one that accepted what loneliness, grief, and emotional exhaustion had to do with the path each of them had taken to that moment.

"Take your time, MacKenzie. Take all the time you need."

He quieted against her, his cheek pillowed on her stomach, and instinct urged Sid to take the moment to learn him in a different way. She petted him, stroked her hands over every inch of his back, his shoulders, his face. Ran her hands through his hair over and over again, cradled him against her belly, and focused on him.

On the shape and feel of him.

The texture.

The scent.

The rhythm of his breathing, the sigh of his exhalations. She brushed her fingers over the soft down secreted in his armpits, traced the shape of his ears, drew her palms across the span and muscle of his shoulders.

To luxuriate in touching Mac this way soothed her—fed a need that had been building forever—and it aroused. Raw, sexual hunger built low down and radiated out, until Sid felt desire literally in her hands.

As if he read her mind, MacKenzie braced on his hands and hung over her for a long moment before slowly lowering himself so only their mouths touched.

This kiss was different, more tender, more intimate. He didn't tease with his tongue, he tasted; he invited Sid to taste him. He drew on her tongue, offered his own for the same pleasure, built an entire language of give and take without saying a word.

Sid's fingers wrapped around his wrists, and longing threatened to consume her. "MacKenzie, I need you."

"Trust me."

He undressed her slowly, like the sun in spring steadily, relentlessly brings life back to places too long left in cold and darkness. His mouth was everywhere, his hands as well. Mac knew how to use his body to reassure and torment, pressing into Sid as he kissed her, taking his warmth and presence away for a progression of instants, then giving them back somewhere different.

And always, he moved slowly. Reverently. His kisses were slow; his hands were slow.

Sid whimpered her need into the solid muscle of his shoulder. "I can't take—"

He kissed her into silence, his hand moving down her body. After an eternity of stroking her neck and shoulders, tracing her collarbones, and gliding his thumb around the base of her throat, he folded his fingers gently around her breast.

Sid moaned, closing her own hand over his to hold him there. "Please, MacKenzie. *Please*."

She was on fire, her breasts heavy with want, her nipples peaked and aching before he moved his hand lower, stroking over her abdomen.

"You'll come for me," he whispered, combing his fingers through her damp curls. She couldn't respond, her wits deserting her as he passed a single finger up the crease of her sex. "You're wet, Sidonie, wet and hot. Ready."

He didn't even need his mouth—she could not have *endured* his mouth—he found the seat of her desire with his fingers, and set up a slow, massaging rhythm. Just as Sid approached a point of no return, his hand would still, and he'd soothe her with lazy kisses, then gently torment her again.

"MacKenzie, you precious, precocious bastard. You have to let me—"

He leaned close, his erection pressing against her hip. He kissed the place where her neck and shoulder joined, then whispered in her ear.

"*Now*."

A firmer pressure where he'd only teased before,

and in two passes of his fingers, Sid came apart. From a great, brilliant distance, she heard somebody moaning, long and low, while her body seized up in the ecstasy of need fulfilled. She couldn't breathe; she could only cling and shake, and cling more tightly still.

Mac laid her back on the blanket, smoothing one warm hand gently over her hair. She wrestled him over her with the last of her strength, needing his body to secure her in her own.

Now, we love.

She bowed up into the warmth and strength of him and cried. She wept for all the nights when there had been no loving, nobody to love her, nobody for her to love. She wept out her fear and loss and soul weariness, her bewilderment at the place life had taken her.

She cried out brokenheartedness and rage and simple wretched grief, and she cried in gratitude for the beauty of what had just been given to her.

And all the while, MacKenzie held her.

When she heaved her last sigh and drew in a breath that didn't shudder, Mac rested his cheek against her temple, but he didn't say anything.

He didn't need to. His body told her he was ready to listen if she needed to talk.

Sid kissed his throat. *I'll be all right*.

He snuggled her closer. *You sure?*

"MacKenzie." She needed to say his name.

"Sidonie. My Sidonie."

Exactly what she needed to hear.

"Close your eyes," he said, kissing her eyelids. "Rest."

———

Life had started denying MacKenzie Knightley perfect moments more than twelve years ago. The death of his father, then his mother, had contributed to this sorry lack, but not caused it. He'd told himself perfect moments were for youth, for the idealism and innocence of a soul unfamiliar with heartbreak.

Tonight, life had proven him wrong.

To lie down on this blanket with Sidonie Lindstrom had taken all of his courage. They hadn't known each other long, and tough discussions lay ahead; but she'd knocked him on his figurative ass with her grit and her tenacity, then flattened him emotionally with her tenderness.

She loved fiercely, and she would hold up to fierce loving too.

The moments when she'd held Mac and given herself permission to truly learn him, to touch him, had been perfect. The moments when she'd surrendered to pleasure in his arms had been sublime.

Now she dozed in his embrace, another precious gift.

"MacKenzie?"

He kissed her temple. "Right here."

"I want to plant a garden."

She was half-asleep, her voice drowsy. She cuddled into his side, stretched, then hiked a leg over his thighs.

What had she said? "Where the hog house was?"

"Is that a good idea? A dumb idea? I think it would be good dirt, because the pigs were there long ago. It's level, and already dug up and smoothed."

"Graded, and, yes, it's a good idea. What will you plant?" He'd have to build her a fence to keep the rabbits and deer out.

Mac thought she'd fallen back asleep, and this funny

little exchange was something she wouldn't recall when she was dressed and bossing Luis around in her kitchen.

"I want to plant food. That's what you do when you live in the country, isn't it? You plant food?"

An image of Sidonie planting a package of nachos and ordering it to sprout into a nacho bush assailed him.

"Vegetables," he said, "as opposed to flowers."

"I want flowers too, but around the house. The house wants flowers, and maybe the barn does too. Did you bury the raccoon? I went back to give it a funeral, and I couldn't find it."

Not half-asleep, but still sweet and drowsy, and this version of pillow talk suited Mac just fine.

"I buried him. I showed Luis where, in case he ever has to do something similar."

"I want to plant some flowers there too." Her hand drifted over his stomach, sending tendrils of lust south.

"The place used to have lots of flowers. Nobody has separated the irises. Nobody has given the bulbs their bonemeal. You can do that, Sid. Make the flowers bloom again."

"Good." She closed her hand around his half-subsided erection. "I think it's time for something else to bloom again too, MacKenzie Knightley."

He let her play while he considered her declaration. Simply to bring her pleasure, to share that with her, had been an entire feast to a starving man. They still needed to get some things out in the open—she'd take umbrage at his profession, but Sid was reasonable too. A criminal defense attorney was not an ambulance chaser; she'd admit that.

First they had more important ground to cover,

because Mac had yet to hear from her the words that assured him their dealings would be exclusive.

"Have I rendered you speechless?" she asked, cupping him gently. "You damned near render me speechless. Witless."

Mac's cell phone went off before he could answer. At first, he couldn't place the low rhythmic vibrating, but the phone was in the pocket of his jeans, humming against the folding knife he usually carried when he wasn't in the office.

"Your phone." Sid reached over him and fished in his clothes. Her breasts pressed snugly right against his scrotum, and Mac understood why a man's eyes might cross involuntarily. "Here you go."

"Maybe I was going to let it ring through." But by the phone's light, he could see Trent was calling, and the only calls Mac invariably took were the calls from family.

"Mac here."

"Glad I caught you. Can you come stay with the girls for a bit?"

Now? His brother wanted him to damned babysit right now? For every perfect moment, there were progressions of imperfect moments on either side of it. Long progressions.

"Everything OK?" Mac managed.

"Not quite. James has found an intruder on Vera's property, and he's asking Hannah and me to get over there as his backup. I'm thinking it might get ugly."

Vera wouldn't call the cops, because this was apparently a family problem, while James would not intervene in any manner that trespassed on Vera's wishes.

"Don't let it get ugly, Trent. That woman is James's best, last hope."

"We'll tell her that. Can you be here in fifteen?"

"Twenty." Mac ended the call.

The moon had edged over the horizon, and the temperature had dropped. The peepers were singing bravely against the chill, while Mac wanted to howl.

Sid yanked her T-shirt over her head. "You have to go?"

"Family calls. I am so sorry."

She passed him his clothes. "Family comes first, MacKenzie. That's a rule that goes on the whiteboard."

"We never did finish that discussion," he said, stuffing his legs into his jeans. He paused when he should have been buttoning his cuffs, and leaned over to push Sid's T-shirt up and get his mouth over one tight, rosy nipple. "A reminder of things we still need to address."

Her expression was a little puzzled.

"I didn't let myself do that before." He patted her breast and tugged her shirt down. "Didn't think I could keep to my plans if I did."

"You and your plans, mister." She crawled across the blanket to get her jeans, giving Mac a lovely view of her naked backside. He shut his eyes and buttoned his shirt by feel.

"What about my plans, lady?"

"I will get even. You reduce me to a quivering mass of gelatinous protoplasm and then ride off into the night."

"Are you complaining, Sidonie?" He'd intended the question to be teasing, but her answer mattered.

"Bitterly." She passed him his boots, and her smile was wicked. "You are doomed, MacKenzie. A marked man. Your virtue is in jeopardy."

"A comforting thought, because I'm off to watch princess videos and make Uncle Mac's signature taco popcorn. Trent said James has a situation on his hands, and I got the short straw."

Except it wasn't the short straw, not really. James and Trent would straighten out whatever was going on at Vera's, aided and abetted by Hannah, who was a whiz-bang negotiator and mediator. Mac would have the little girls to himself for a change.

"Your socks, sweetie." Sid stuffed them into his hand. "I'd volunteer to go with you, but I don't like leaving Luis alone when he might be coming down with something."

"He's coming down with a growth spurt, most likely." Mac stopped between pulling on one boot and the next. "Sid, I didn't think before I set up that keg this morning. That had to be a temptation to a kid like Luis."

"What do you mean, 'like Luis'?" Her tone held a hint of defensiveness as she wiggled into her jeans. "He's a good kid. The best kid."

"He's a typical kid, whatever that means. He'll be sixteen in a couple weeks, and beer and boys have a natural affinity for each other."

Sid stared at her bare feet. "He was probably tippling. My mom was killed by a drunk driver, so I tell myself I have to chill, you know? To not overreact. Luis will experiment, and the safest place for him to do that is right here, surrounded by people who will keep an eye on him. But it's hard. Being a parent is so hard."

Her words triggered a memory Mac had tucked away earlier in the day: Luis had said both Sid's mother *and* her brother had been killed by drunk drivers. Maybe Sid had had more than one brother and had lost them both— God help her—or maybe Luis had been too tipsy to get his facts straight.

"He's a good kid," Mac said, doing up his belt. "He'll use common sense most of the time, and we'll ride herd on him the rest of the time. Kiss me."

He didn't wait for her to acquiesce. He pushed her flat onto the blanket and took her mouth in a long, wet, branding kiss that had his jeans fitting too snugly.

"I'll call you." Mac rose and pulled Sid to her feet. "I am not just saying that, so don't start tormenting yourself with second thoughts and rationalizations, and all the mental anguish of taking a little risk." He folded up the blanket as he lectured, then took her elastic off his wrist. "Turn around."

"You'll be late for your babysitting shift," she said, giving him her back.

"They won't leave until the cavalry thunders up the driveway, and Trent's place is all of two miles away." He drew her hair over her shoulders, divided it into three thick skeins, and plaited it loosely in a single braid.

She fingered her braid. "You are a frighteningly competent man."

"And you are just plain frightening." He pulled her back against his chest. "The evening wasn't supposed to end this way, Sidonie. I apologize." He kissed the side of her neck, putting ten years of longing, frustration, and gratitude into it.

"I can deal with a little anticipation." She folded her hands over his. "A little time to plan your seduction."

"Right," he said, forcing himself to step away. "I'm doomed, thank God." He couldn't stop himself from taking her hand, but held his peace as they walked across the pasture, lest something really stupid come out of his idiot, doomed mouth.

—◆—

"What's all this?" Luis scrubbed a hand over his eyes and gestured with his elbow at the printouts Sid had spread on the kitchen table.

"Stuff I found on the Internet about vegetable gardening. I made a quiche. It's probably still hot."

"You made quiche for breakfast?"

"Weese, it's nearly ten in the morning on a beautiful Sunday in spring. I'm keeping country hours now."

"Let a woman knock over one little hog house, and she's singing the theme to *Green Acres*." The mention of quiche had him looking more awake. "What kind of quiche?"

"Swiss cheese, spinach, some mushrooms, a little bacon."

"Be still my heart." He opened the oven, sending a waft of heat and good food aromas through the kitchen. "What kind of vegetables will you grow?"

Luis was mighty parsimonious with plural pronouns. *We* might have quiche for breakfast, but *we* weren't planting a garden.

"Don't know. You have any favorites?"

"My grandmother always grew tomatoes in pots on her fire escape. They were good. Better than anything from the store." He dished himself out about a quarter of the quiche. "I wonder if you could make a tomato quiche."

"May I ask you something?"

He put the pan of quiche back in the oven and brought his plate to the table. "This sounds serious."

"Did you hit the keg yesterday?"

Luis blinked once at his quiche. "Yes."

"Thought so. Learn anything?"

He used his fork to slice off a bite of quiche but left

the food sitting on his plate, steaming fragrantly. "I learned nothing much gets by you."

"You were zonked all afternoon, Weese. I was worried about you."

"Geez, Sid, don't start, OK? I had a few beers. I caught up on my sleep. This is good quiche."

He'd slept right through dinner, and she and Mac had brought the horses in.

"I turned the mares out this morning. Mac showed me what to do last night."

"Thanks."

"I was hoping you'd show me how to groom them some time."

He started on his breakfast. "I can do that. Mac can brush them standing on the ground. I have to stand on a damned bucket to reach their butts."

"I learned something today, Weese."

"What's that?" The quiche was disappearing from his plate at a steady, no-nonsense pace. If he were truly hungover, he wouldn't be shoveling it in like that, would he?

"I learned I can trust you to tell me the truth, even when it doesn't flatter you. I'm proud of you."

He nodded. Just that, only a nod. No boyish grin, no snappy reply.

Her little man was growing up. Did she dare ask Luis what he'd have done if she'd forbidden him the keg? Would his honesty go that far?

Her cell phone rang, making the question moot. "Sid Lindstrom."

"I'm in princess-video withdrawal," Mac said. "Good morning."

"Poor baby. We're having quiche on the veranda."

"That house doesn't have a veranda."

"Not yet. How are you?"

Sid heard Mac discarding various replies in the small silence that ensued. "I'm doing my laundry."

Two honest men in her life, then. "Is that your idea of what do with a pretty Sunday morning?"

Another silence, which frustrated her. If they'd been sitting at the same table, she would have been able to read worlds into the way Mac quirked his eyebrow, the line of his mouth, the things he did with his hands, his posture.

"This is part of my routine, actually. Monday through Friday I work for the paying clients. The first Saturday of the month, I take my nieces out to give their parents a break, the second and fourth Saturdays, I tend to Adelia's horses. Sunday is for the domestic chores and solitude."

"That leaves you with one Saturday a month to paint the town red?" Good heavens, couldn't he answer a simple question?

"Tell me about your schedule, Sid. I know Luis probably has a lesson at Adelia's today, because he wasn't up there yesterday."

"He was sleeping off a drunk." She wanted to tousle Luis's hair but let him finish his breakfast in peace. "Naughty boy. If Social Services finds out about it, and finds out I was here at the time, they'll likely snatch him right back to a group home."

She saw from Luis's reaction that this outcome hadn't occurred to him. He stood abruptly and darted up the stairs.

"A drunk?"

"Some tippling, at any rate. He was honest about it, and I don't think he'll do it again."

"Then no harm done, and maybe he learned something. What will you do with yourself today, Sid?"

"I'm planning my garden." She waxed eloquent about squash, beans, and tomatoes, all the while aware of what they weren't discussing.

Invite me over for dinner tonight. Invite us. Ask me if I can meet you for pizza on Tuesday. Come help me lay out my garden. Tell me, please, please, please tell me you're missing me, because I am damned sure missing you.

Nowhere in his litany of chores and obligations had MacKenzie Knightley mentioned having fun. He hadn't mentioned hobbies, a social group, a pastime.

"MacKenzie, where do you live?"

"In a house about two miles from you, as the crow flies. James is closer to you than I am, Trent not quite as near."

"Tell me about your house."

Come on, Knightley. Tilt at my quintain. The conversation was obviously an effort for him, but he was trying, and heroic efforts should be rewarded.

"You should come by sometime," he said, slowly, as if the words surprised him. "Bring Luis, and I'll throw together a meal."

"Pick a day."

"Today." For once, his reply came without hesitation. "Come on by after Luis's lesson. We'll eat while it's still light."

Thought you would never ask. "What can I bring?"

"Bring the salad, and don't bother with anything fancy."

"I'm going to be a vegetable tycoon. Salad's easy." She

got directions from him and hung up, feeling a silly, giddy feeling she hadn't had to deal with since high school.

Middle school, rather. She hadn't been exactly honest with Mac last night. There hadn't been many relationships, true, but there had been guys.

Many guys. She had sneaked out regularly when Tony had first taken her in, and then college had been more of the same but without the thrill of thwarting authority.

And then her own body had called a halt to her foolishness—and that's all it had been. Pure, undiluted foolishness. A foolish way to cope with being alone in the world, except for a well-meaning half brother who'd treated her more like a housemate than a sister.

Young people were not well known for their wisdom.

"Luis!"

He appeared at the top of the stairs, his expression wary.

"I won't turn you in to DSS, so stop fretting. Get your homework done, do whatever chores you do in the barn, and then we're supposed to have dinner with Mac after your riding lesson."

"That's it? You'll let me get away with drinking?"

"You disappointed me by drinking. You redeemed yourself by being honest about it. I have a garden to plan."

Sid hoped it was that simple. Hoped and prayed.

—⁓—

Mac hadn't been entirely honest with Sid about several things. He'd told her Sundays were for domestic chores, for example. He hadn't admitted Sundays were also his one day to dream.

In solitude, he'd cruise the Internet for interesting

places to travel. Some were places a man might go with
his family; others were more for couples. He browsed
his library, reading the poetry of the romantics and
the occasional Shakespeare sonnet, memorizing his
favorites. He cooked recreationally, trying this and that
recipe, wondering if children would find a particular
dish appealing.

Monday morning, he put away his imagination's
toys, and went back to work. Mondays purely sucked,
but Sundays made the whole week bearable.

So Mac hadn't much to fret over, at the prospect of
having company for dinner. James and Trent made the
effort to show up for holiday meals, mostly because all
three of them—James, Trent, and Mac—had felt the
need to create family gatherings for Merle's sake.

That would likely change now that Trent had his
own family.

Mac knew exactly what food he'd prepare, which
tablecloth he'd put on the table, what music he'd have
playing when Sid and Luis walked in his door.

Though classical piano might be a little too much like
a date. Luis would feel awkward.

Mac would feel awkward.

And there weren't any roses blooming yet, so he'd
have to rethink his centerpiece.

Everyday or silver?

"Holy Ned on a pogo stick."

Crystal? A pepper grinder on the table or a pair
of shakers?

Which pepper grinder—he had three.

He got out his cell phone, stared at it for a full minute,
then hit James's number.

———∿∿∿———

"What's the best date you've ever been on?" Mac demanded.

James held the phone away from his ear, tempted to pitch the damned thing into the wall, except Mac's voice held urgency—and Mac was about as urgent as a glacier most days.

"I'm on my best date ever right now, if you must know."

"This is serious, James. I'm having company for dinner, and it isn't family."

Not serious—miraculous. "What are you asking me?"

James stroked a hand over Vera's naked back, marveling at the smooth, silky feel of her skin. And the muscle. Of course a concert pianist would have beautifully defined back muscles and shoulders and arms and—

"James, you there?"

"The connection got fuzzy. What was the question?"

"Describe the best date you've ever been on."

"Can I think about it and call you back in, say, twenty minutes?"

"Not one second more. I've planned an early dinner."

"It's not even noon yet, Mac, but OK. Not one second more."

An hour passed before Mac's phone rang.

———∿∿∿———

"I don't suppose you had a chance to talk with Luis about representing him?" Mac put the question to Trent over a meal in the courthouse café. A burger and fries for Trent, a grilled chicken salad for Mac.

"He didn't strike me as being in the best frame of

mind to discuss his case on Saturday. Will you leave me any fries?"

"A few, though they're my one indulgence." What Mac had done with Sid on that blanket on Saturday had gone far, far beyond an indulgence. "James didn't get in until ten this morning."

Trent plucked a fry from Mac's plate. "Noticed that, did you?"

"The managing partner pays attention to the details. I'm thinking this is a good thing. The guy works too hard. I'm also wondering when you'll tell me what went on at Vera's on Saturday night."

"It's really for James to tell you, because I was there in my capacity as Vera's counsel." Trent picked up his pickle just when Mac would have snitched it, then grinned at his older brother. "Beat ya."

"Too much salt isn't good for your blood pressure, and Vera's divorce was final last year. You went because James called you, and you were free to go because *I* held the fort with Grace and Merle, so stop stalling."

Trent considered his pickle. "Suffice it to say, I think James and Vera are talking again."

"Am I getting my tux out of mothballs?" Mac didn't let his relief show, because to do so would have implied he'd doubted James could see the situation with Vera through. Mac hadn't doubted, not for a minute.

He'd worried, though, constantly.

"I hope they're not going the formal wedding route," Trent said, "because that means I'll have to dust off my tux as well, though Hannah might like to see me in it."

"Or get you out of it." Mac took a sip of Trent's cola.

"MacKenzie Knightley, for shame."

"Have to watch my caffeine. You ordering dessert?"

"No, because you'd steal it. I liked your Sidonie, and Hannah did too."

"She's not…" Well, she *was* his Sidonie. "I'm glad you like her, because I like her too."

"Profound, MacKenzie. A sure sign the sap is rising when your nimble brain spouts inanities. Does the lady like you?"

"She seems to."

"You haven't gotten into her knickers yet. What are you waiting for?"

Too many witnesses to put Brother Dearest into a half nelson, and most of those witnesses lawyers.

"Mind your own business, Trenton Edwards."

"No can do." Trent settled back in his chair and aimed a blue-eyed stare at his brother. "James and I played racquetball yesterday afternoon, and we decided we're done letting you wander around in the outer darkness without the occasional encouraging word from your younger brothers."

"I thought you were walking a little funny today." Mac took another sip of Trent's drink. "James has the gene for the physical stuff. You're good too, but he's five years younger, and he's James."

"And you're MacKenzie," Trent said, crunching the pickle into oblivion. "I'm thinking of passing on Luis's case."

Mac set Trent's drink down with a little thud. "Why?"

"Because I can see it getting sticky. His mother's rights were terminated on the two sisters, so they're slated for adoption. Luis wasn't placed with his sisters, and he's never been in a pre-adopt home before his stint with Sid—nobody kept him the requisite six months. She wants to adopt, and his mom still has her parental rights where he's concerned. If Luis were placed with his sisters, the complexion of the case would change."

Sid would support that, if that was what Luis wanted, even if it killed her.

Which it damned near would.

"Luis might change his mind," Mac said, "and ask that family to adopt him when he won't ask Sid. He told me that family doesn't want him."

Or had Luis merely implied that he was unwanted in his sisters' foster family?

Trent munched a fry lengthwise, the same way his daughters did. "OK, but what if, as his counsel, Luis tells me he's tired of being a grieving woman's surrogate brother? What if he wants to be moved? I can live with Sid not forgiving me, but what if she won't forgive you?"

Sid could probably hold one hell of a grudge, that's what. Mac dreaded telling her what he did for a living besides shoe horses.

"You have a point," he said. "Your scenario is farfetched but not impossible. I still don't think Sid would hold me responsible for the position Luis took in court regarding his future."

"She lost her brother less than a year ago, Mac. James says grieving women are trouble."

"James is *talking again* with a woman who's herself both widowed and divorced." Though Vera's circumstances were very different from Sid's. Mac knew it, and Trent knew it.

What was Mac doing, swilling Trent's jitter juice,

when caffeine was something any sane person avoided after breakfast?

"James and I don't want to see you put in the middle," Trent said, "much less castigated for how Luis's case is handled."

Which meant Trent and James had discussed Mac's situation. Mac didn't know whether to be pissed or pleased.

"I don't want to see Luis's case handled by some overworked Legal Assistance attorney with less than two years experience in family law," Mac said. "You don't have a conflict of interest, Trent. Sid's not a party to the case, I'm not a party, and for all you know, the boy will ask you to get the Termination of Parental Rights filed so Sid can adopt him."

"He might." Trent's eyes were guarded, his tone conciliatory.

Mac felt not like a fry-snitching older brother, but like a legal client who wasn't hearing anything he liked at his free consultation.

"What?" Mac balled up his napkin and tossed it on the tray. "Just say it, Trent. If we need to have a knock-down-drag-out, here is probably better than the office, because I can't beat your sorry ass for sassing me."

Trent cracked a smile. "As if."

"Say what's on your mind. I have an evidentiary hearing over a pair of damned magical traveling felony pants in twenty minutes."

"James has pointed out that you haven't dated since before I married Merle's mother. If Sid Lindstrom got you out of hibernation, then I don't want anything—not some foster kid's whim, not a judge's bad decision, not even the fate of the practice—to come between you and her. You're dying on the vine, Mac. You're so much less flamboyant about it than James that I hardly noticed it. Hannah's worried about you."

The burdens of a family-owned law practice were without number. Mac took the last gulp of Trent's cola. "Back to that?"

"Hannah's right: We should be worried about you. You're a great guy. You deserve somebody to appreciate you. Some lady, not those sharks from the prosecutor's office who are always hitting on you."

Trent picked up his drink, scowled at the ice, then fished his corporate credit card out of his wallet.

"*Those* are your encouraging words?" Mac said, more touched than he wanted to admit. *Hannah* was worried about him?

"Yes, damn it, those are my encouraging words."

"OK."

"That's all you're going to say? I tell you to get a life, and you say OK?"

"OK, thanks." Mac snitched one more fry, rose, and went to his hearing.

Chapter 11

"YOU'RE STARING AT THAT PHONE LIKE IT'S ABOUT TO give birth." Luis hiked himself up on the counter. "What's the big deal?"

"No big deal." Sid forced her gaze back to the sketch she was making of her garden plot. "How was school?"

Luis toed off his sneakers, which had become sizable items of footwear sometime in the last year. "A riveting, action-packed, fun-filled, rollicking adventure for the whole family. We had the AP test in history. It went pretty well."

"That's three college credits we won't have to pay for, then. Pat yourself on the back. Do you like beets?" *And please, God, could Luis stay with her until college was a reality, not merely a dream?*

"I've never had beets. The color's not boring. Do we have any of Mac's bread left?

"If you looked in the fridge, you'd see I left a quarter of the loaf for you. It would make really good cheese toast. What about snow peas? Do you like those?"

"I've only ever had them in stir-fry, but they're OK. When will you make that salad again you made for Mac?"

Mac, Mac, Mac. The boy was a broken record.

"You liked it? It's easy to make: equal parts shredded jack cheese, chopped celery, chopped mushrooms, and some Italian dressing. I can get the ingredients if you'd like to make it yourself."

"Put it on the list." Luis shoved off the counter. "I'm off to tend to my girls. Tell Mac I said hi."

And damn the little twerp if the phone didn't start to ring just as he yanked on his Timberlands and sauntered out the door.

"Hello, Lindstrom's."

"Hello, Mrs. Lindstrom, this is Amy Snyder. How are you?"

Not Mac. Not anybody Sid wanted to talk to. "I'm fine, and you?"

"I'm fine. I'm calling to let you know that my supervisor and I met to discuss that outbuilding on your property, and I'm sorry to say he was of the opinion we need to start the licensure revocation process. I'll come out to meet with Luis in the next few days to discuss his next placement with him. You'll be given a copy of the notice, and have some time to effect a cure before the decision can no longer be appealed."

You bitch. "That won't be necessary, Amy."

"I beg your pardon?"

"You'll see when you come for your next visit that there is no more outbuilding, no outdoor plumbing, nothing that would require a revocation of my foster care license."

"But how…? That's not… The paperwork has already been submitted, though I don't have final signatures on it yet."

"Then it can easily be withdrawn, can't it? Luis was just telling me how well he's doing in school here, and it really would not be in his best interests to have to move again so close to the end of the school year, would it?"

"I'll have to look up the regulations, because Luis

was on that property when it was out of code. I'm not sure how you got approval to move there without somebody looking it over carefully first."

"I guess the Baltimore courts were relying on the Department on this end to do just what you did: make sure it's suitable for foster care. Which it is. When shall I tell Luis to expect you?"

Sid heard the sound of a keyboard clicking as Miss I'm-fine-how-are-you-but-I'm-taking-your-kid-away-over-a-formality Amy Snyder made her contact note in the file.

"I'll be out later this week, possibly next week."

That certainly narrows it down. "Do we have a hearing date yet?"

"It will be on a Tuesday, probably in a few weeks."

Sid gave the phone the finger, because the worker's response provided exactly no new information, and not even the cats were around to see her bad behavior.

"Luis wondered who his attorney will be."

"Legal Assistance has the contract in this county. I'm sure they'll call once the hearing notices are sent out."

Don't bestir yourself to part with a name, much less a phone number, Almira Gulch. "Thank you, Amy. We'll look forward to your next visit."

Sid hung the phone up and forced herself to unclench her jaw, her fists, her heart.

That woman had been cheerfully planning to "remove" Luis to some shelter, probably right back down in Baltimore, and then pop him into a group home, or better still, transfer his whole case right back to Baltimore too.

If Mac hadn't been willing to call on his brothers; if

those contractors hadn't been willing to drop everything to work on a Saturday; if weathered barn lumber hadn't been in demand…

A child's life shouldn't be like this. It bloody damned shouldn't be like this, so a worker's whim and narrow-minded interpretation of the regulations resulted in a boy's whole world being turned around. Damned social workers, as bad as the damned attorneys who did their dirty work for them.

The phone rang again. Probably the idiot supervisor calling to snort and paw and wave the rule book around.

"Sid Lindstrom."

"What's put you in such a temper?"

"MacKenzie…" *Thank you, God.* "I just got off the phone with Luis's caseworker. The little twit has already put in paperwork to revoke my license because of the hog house."

"What hog house?"

"Right, and I told her that, but she's flown away on her broomstick to check her regulations. Mac, if she moves Luis over this, I will not answer for the consequences."

"She won't." The conviction he could put into two words was reassuring. "Keep your dire threats to yourself, Sid. Don't mutter and mumble them around the kid, don't mention them to the worker, and don't, for God's sake, put them in writing to the supervisor."

Which was exactly what she would have done. "I wasn't planning to. How are you?"

"Not so fast. Where did you leave it with the worker?"

MacKenzie could do this. He could interrogate like a truant officer, and from him, Sid tolerated it. Mac would take in all the data, spot the issues, make sense of the situation, and find a course of action while Sid was still trying to breathe her way through a tantrum.

Or a panic attack. To think that idiot-twit-bitch had almost moved Luis over a vintage two-seater people would pay good money for on eBay. A wave of weakness came over Sid as the near miss sank in.

"Ms. Snyder said Luis was on the property when it was out of code, but she also said she might not get out here until next week. Mac, she was going to move him. She was about to pluck Luis up from his life and move him, and over an outhouse, like he was some t-two-year-old with no sense. Like I'd let him—"

"She won't do that, Sidonie. Are you sitting down?"

She slid down the wall. "I am now. I hate this. Why would she be such an ass, Mac? The rules are just rules. They aren't the Ten Commandments."

"Look, I have to be somewhere in a few minutes, and I'm sure this merits more discussion, but I wanted to ask if you'll be home tonight."

"Sure."

"Then I'd like to bring you over some dahlias. I always have more than I need, and mine did particularly well last year."

He could be bringing her a used muck fork and she'd be glad to see him. "What are dahlias?"

"Big, showy flowers that grow on tubers. You lift them in the fall and separate them when you plant them each spring. I can pick up some pizza too."

"Pizza sounds good." Seeing him sounded even better. Tubers—whatever they were—were another matter. "What time?"

They negotiated time and dessert, and by the time Luis was back from his barn chores, Sid's panic was subsiding.

"Mac's bringing pizza over for dinner," she said. "We're making dessert."

Luis put the kettle on, then let the hot water keep running. "Are *we* making anything in particular?"

"I was thinking a French blueberry pie. Mac's big on healthy eating. Blueberries are good for you."

He gave her a look over his shoulder as he washed his hands. "You like this guy, don't you, Sid?"

She jammed her hands into the back pockets of her jeans. "I like Mac a lot."

"So do I, so don't take it the wrong way when I ask how a man who shoes horses for a living can afford that big old house with all the trimmings? It must take a herd of gardeners to keep his back lawn in order."

This casual observation was made while Luis took down two mugs, his back to Sid.

"Mac does all that himself, the gardening, anyway. He hires the mowing out."

"Right. Like shoeing horses pays well enough to hire mowers and shit? I counted four bathrooms, Sid. This house only has three and a half. He's got a circular driveway. Only rich people have circular driveways."

"You've rubbed elbows with how many rich people, that you'd know one when you saw him?"

Luis set a stick of butter on the counter, then got out a package of cream cheese. "He has a *nice* house, Sid. Really nice. You could eat off his garage floor, and his pool table probably cost more than your college education. The dessert dishes were Waterford crystal."

"Now you're a connoisseur of pool tables and fine

crystal?" Sid roused herself to scare up the flour to make the piecrust. "What is your point, Weese? Mac is a good man, and he's becoming a good friend. I don't need to know his net worth to know that much."

"If that's where you want to leave it, that's fine with me, Sid, but you're a woman. Why not marry the guy? Didn't your grandmother ever tell you it's as easy to fall in love with somebody who has money as somebody who doesn't?"

Sid had never met her grandmothers. "Luis Martineau, you don't pick out a prospective husband because he has four bathrooms."

"If you're holding out for five, you'll have a long wait in Damson County. Five-bathroom guys don't grow on trees. Where's the mixer?"

"Over the fridge. This is a ridiculous conversation."

"Not noticing the man's driving two brand-new trucks is ridiculous. How much do you think those things go for, tricked out like that? You're putting cinnamon in this?" He waved a half-pint container of heavy cream in the general direction of the spice rack.

"Whip it nearly to butter first," Sid instructed, "then add a dash when you whip in the confectioner's sugar and cream cheese. Mac's house and his trucks and his pool table might be either mortgaged to the hilt, which is not good, or bought with family money, which means it's gone and can't be spent again."

She passed Luis the confectioner's sugar and stared at her rolling pin. "The Knightleys sold this farm not that long ago. Ten, maybe twelve years ago. This property would have been worth a pretty penny even then, even split three ways."

Luis fitted the beaters to the hand mixer. "Rich, I'm telling you. He's got nice toys—you did see the plasma TV?—a nice crib, nice threads hanging in his closet, nice everything. Marry him, Sid. You won't have to dick around with knocking down hog houses or peddling vegetables."

Sid glared at him, prepared to tell him exactly what she thought of such a mercenary approach to matrimony, but Luis turned on the electric mixer, effectively giving himself the last word.

"Brat."

He grinned at her and stuck his finger into the cream.

Sid busied herself rolling out the piecrust, then fluting the edges. Luis had a point—not about marrying MacKenzie Knightley—but about Sid missing obvious clues to who MacKenzie Knightley was.

Horseshoeing, even five days a week for upscale clients, couldn't possibly subsidize the lovely Tudor home Mac lived in. He'd said the place was built in the 1920s by some wealthy Philadelphians who wanted a summer home away from the Chester County country-club set.

Most of the common rooms had twelve-foot ceilings. The floors were gleaming hardwood parquet, the windows on the facade were mullioned, and the gardens…

Maybe the time of year was ideal, maybe the place always looked like that, but if Sid's backyard had that many dogwoods and azaleas, that many redbud trees and flowering crab apples, she'd spend all her spring days on the flagstoned back terrace.

Mac's backyard was a magical expanse that went on for acres. He'd said the daffodils were done for the year, but the tulips and grape hyacinths were still going strong, the pansies were gorgeous, and the lilacs and lilies of the valley intoxicating.

Gardens like that, much like the plasma TV, took money. They took time and energy and forethought and follow-through, but undeniably, they took money too.

Lots of money.

"What are you doing here?" Mac aimed the question at James, who was lounging in the back of Courtroom Three.

"Watching the scourge of the state's attorney's office in action. I forget how good you are, MacKenzie. If you ever leave the practice of law, the judges around here will have to work a lot harder on the criminal dockets, and the prosecutors will be singing in the streets."

Mac slid manila files, one by one, into a fat black leather briefcase. "Might be a better use of their limited talents. Meaning no disrespect. Did Trent send you to spy on me?"

"No, he did not. If you're done here, let's go for a walk."

Courtrooms had ears. The clerks tidying up at the end of the hearing, the bailiff gossiping with the sheriff's deputy, opposing counsel, they all worked with Mac day in and day out and were as prone to talk as the next group of people.

If not more.

"Pretty day," James said as they left the courthouse. "I thought spring wouldn't make it this year."

Small talk, and when James had specifically hunted Mac down outside the office. Mac denied himself a glance at his watch and marshaled his patience.

"You were nursing a broken heart, which you've apparently mended. When were you going to tell me, James?"

"Trent has for once kept his mouth shut?"

"Hannah left me enough hints that I know you and Vera are keeping company again, and it's about damned time."

The sidewalks in this older part of town were uneven, and James was studying them as if he might accidentally step on a crack and lose his train of thought.

"Vera and I cleared up a lot of old business."

They walked along in silence for a few minutes, while Mac tried not to envy his brother this newfound happiness. Vera was a peach, her daughter Twyla was a terrific kid, and they would make a wonderful family.

Mac had always believed his brothers would eventually find domestic bliss, and as for the family average, two out of three qualified for the major leagues.

"I wanted to discuss something else with you," James said.

Now there's a surprise. "I'm going to be an uncle again?" Mac asked. "I'm a big boy. I can deal with nasty dipes. I changed enough of yours."

The breeze lifted, and a shower of white blossoms fell onto the sidewalk. The air bore a hint of sweetness, and Mac abruptly missed the sturdy baby boy James had been.

"Hannah has the look," James said, "but it's not my place to say."

"I've come to the same conclusion. She has that happy, broodmare smugness in her eye, but I was talking about you and Vera."

"You call Hannah a broodmare in her hearing, and she'll come out swinging, MacKenzie."

"Yeah, yeah, and Trent will hold my arms behind my back for her, while you sell tickets to the children. What's on your mind, James?" James did not deny he and Vera might be considering building onto their family immediately.

"I'm in discussions with Hiram Inskip about a business venture."

"Businesses are your thing. You've been bored with ours for a while, and it's time you branched out." What a relief to say that and not risk getting his face rearranged.

"I want to specialize, Mac."

"In?"

"Agribusiness."

Mac almost said: *Why didn't I think of that?* "Farming, you mean. You'll farm with Hiram?"

"I'll buy him out over the next five years. With my land, his, and Vera's, we have a sizable piece of contiguous property. Vera's land corners with the home place, and Hiram has been farming some of that since we sold it. I'd like to talk to Sid about making some changes in the way Hiram's been doing things."

They were several blocks from the courthouse, and it was time to turn around, though Mac didn't want to.

"This is right for you," Mac said. "We'll manage in the office. You keep us in fresh dairy and eggs, we'll manage."

"That's all you'd want? Eggs and milk?"

"I'd want my baby brother happy for a damned change." From the corner of his eye, Mac also saw his baby brother swallowing a couple times and blinking.

Spring breezes. Allergies, maybe.

"I wouldn't leave the practice," James said. "Both my

new hires are crack shots, and between them, they can manage what's there now. I want to court the real money in this county, Mac. I want to go after the family farms. Those guys and gals are sitting on more wealth than the entire rest of the community has combined, and they just climb on their tractors and fret about how much rain we're getting. They don't see the big picture."

James had been stewing about this, and when James stewed about something, it got stewed to damned death.

"You do see a big picture?"

"Hell, yeah. I know how to get them the grants, the subsidies, the tax shelters, the competitive loans. I know how to set up their businesses so they'll still be around when the grandkids get sick of playing in the city. I know how to diversify, how to develop specialty markets, and then there's the growing demand for organic—"

Mac thumped him on the back. "Go forth and be happy. Whatever your plans, they'll make us money. You'll do good while doing well, every ethical lawyer's goal. I was proud of you before. Now I'm proud of you and happy for you."

James let out a sigh, sounding about thirteen years old. "Vera said I was fretting over nothing. Said you and Trent would be my biggest supporters, after her and Twy."

"We were your biggest supporters before her and Twy, and in this family, a guy can have an unlimited number of biggest supporters. We should knock out the wall on the far side of the mail room. Give you a separate entrance, tone down the visible security, get some copies of Progressive Farmer for your lobby, that sort of thing. I'm sure one of Inskip's daughters can handle your front desk."

For improvisation, that was a good list, good enough to have James looking thoughtful. "Makes sense, but we should probably run it by Trent."

"Next partners' meeting."

Another few strides, while Mac tried to sort out what he was feeling, besides relief that his brother was back on track with Vera. Without Vera's hand on the tiller—so to speak—James would soon have run himself aground.

"I wanted to tell you something else," James said. "About the home place?"

"You'll farm it. I got that much, James. Just for God's sake be careful."

"I doubt I'll be on the tractor much, but I will be careful. Very careful. Did you know the property has no mortgage?"

"Every farm has a mortgage."

"None. I looked up the land records, thinking I could maybe find the interim owners and get some idea who left Daisy and Buttercup in the pasture or returned them there, but I also wanted to know how leveraged the land was before I sank a lot of money into farming it. Farming it *again*. Tony Lindstrom bought the place free and clear, except for honoring the land-use leases that conveyed with the title. Sid inherited in fee simple absolute."

A load off Mac's mind, for sure, but he hadn't wanted to snoop into the land records himself.

"Then I'd say she needs a good agribusiness lawyer. Approach her carefully. The estate is taking its good old time settling, and Sid has no use for lawyers generally."

Flat hated them, which could be a small problem.

Or a huge one.

"Then I won't approach her as a lawyer. I'll approach her as a neighbor with some business expertise and an eye for profit."

"Approach her soon. She's broke, and you can't raise a kid on dreams and good intentions."

"There's something else, MacKenzie."

MacKenzie. Whatever it was, James was serious about it, and he'd taken to within fifty yards of the court-house to work up to it.

"Spill. I'm supposed to be at Sid's for dinner tonight, and as pleasant as this constitutional is, defending the downtrodden today has built up an appetite."

"Vera and I are getting married."

"One concluded this."

That got him a smile, though Mac knew what was coming next: Would he stand up with his brother? Of course he would. No question he would. Though the saying about always being a bridesmaid trailed through Mac's mind.

"One concluded this, did he? Yeah, well, Carnac the Amazing, did one also conclude his prospective sister-in-law would ask him to be her maid of honor?"

It was Mac's turn to smile. A sweet, pleased grin he didn't bother hiding.

"Just don't make me wear pink, and no ruffles on the hem of my dress. I look like hell in pink, and ruffles make my ass look fat."

"I'm discovering I like dirt."

Sid made this pronouncement while she tried not to watch MacKenzie Knightley consume a modest slice of blueberry pie with cream cheese filling in a flaky home-made piecrust. The man was a sybarite, savoring each bite, sliding his fork slowly, slowly out of his mouth.

He studied each forkful before he closed his lips around it, a silent moment of gratitude maybe, then he shut his eyes as if to catalog the flavors and textures hitting his tongue.

Sid knew things about that tongue, wonderful, scary, intimate things.

"What's not to like about dirt?" Mac asked between bites.

"What's to like about dirt?" Luis countered. He was putting away the vanilla ice cream, a fat scoop of which sat melting on a slab of pie that was bigger than Sid's piece and Mac's combined. "You're forever washing my duds, scrubbing the floor, cleaning the windows, like dirt's Public Enemy Number One."

He brought his bowl back to the table and took a chair.

"Not that kind of dirt," Sid said. "Soil, earth. I never knew there were different kinds, and that different kinds of plants like different kinds of dirt. I never thought about it. Some plants like a lot of sun. Some don't want as much. Some want a lot of watering. Some will drown if you water them too much. Plants and soil are like people: they have personalities, likes and dislikes, strengths and weaknesses."

"You going to be a dirt psychologist?" Luis asked.

"Elbow, Weese." That from Mac, who was study-ing another bite of pie. Luis lifted the elbow he'd propped beside his bowl, but disgruntlement flittered over his features.

"I'm going to be a gardener," Sid said. "I'll start with

the easy stuff, like tomatoes, squash, and beans, but we have lots of good dirt and lots of free fertilizer."

"That you do," Mac said. "The old muck pit out behind the barn should have some of the best topsoil in the valley. We had cows, horses, and sheep here for most of the years we farmed, and the muck pit was full up when we sold the place. I don't think anybody ever thought to dig it out and spread the contents on the fields, so it's thoroughly composted topsoil at this point. First-rate stuff."

Clearly, Mac liked dirt too. "Will people pay money for it?" Sid asked.

Mac set his spoon down into his empty bowl. No clatter, just the smallest "plink!"

"They will, and this is the time of year to sell it. You can put a sign at the end of the lane, run one of those quickie ads, and you'll have a regular parade of trucks here come the weekend."

They discussed what to charge, and whether to sell some of the soil bagged, while Luis silently finished his dessert. Sid barely noticed when he took his bowl to the sink and slipped up the stairs, so fascinated was she by the idea of selling her dirt.

Topsoil, rather. Her thoroughly composted, first-rate topsoil.

"You up for a walk, Sidonie?" Mac asked as he set the last bowl into the drain rack to dry. His voice was casual, but heat leaped in Sid's middle at his question.

"Are we taking a blanket to the pond, MacKenzie?"

She would have given a great deal to see his eyes, but he was watching the dishwater swirl down the drain.

"We can take the blanket, but we never finished the discussion we started there last time."

Discussion? She cast her mind back, leapfrogging over thank-God-I'm-a-country-girl pleasure, over physical and emotional intimacy every bit as alluring as the pleasure itself, over his cell phone going off at the worst, worst moment.

"I'm happy to continue that discussion, MacKenzie."

He wrung out the dishrag to within an inch of its life, and folded it exactly in half over the spigot.

"Tell Luis we're going for a walk. I'll fetch the blanket."

There was no hurry to him, no display of eagerness, no winking, leering suggestion they were about to get naked under the moonlight again. The questions Luis had raised earlier popped into Sid's head: How did a farrier afford the house Mac lived in by himself? Two late-model trucks? The landscaping, the plasma TV, the pool table?

Mac was on the porch when Sid left the house, the blanket slung over his shoulder.

"You were quiet at dinner," Sid said, taking his hand. His fingers closed around hers, and she was feeling sufficiently insecure that even such a small contact was reassuring.

"I was enjoying you and Luis getting after each other. He seems a little testy to me. School going OK?"

Testy. A good word to describe a cranky teenager.

"Big exam in trig today, and he did seem sullen. He says he likes you, though. I try not to micromanage his moods, and appreciate that he doesn't micromanage mine."

They walked along in silence for a while, Sid listening to the peepers chirping in trees. The air was milder than it had been even a week ago, and when she scanned the hills to the east, she could see exactly where the moon was about to break over the horizon.

"Lovely night," Sid said.

Mac stopped walking and slid the blanket from his shoulder. He settled his hands on Sid's biceps, a gentle, implacable grip, then lowered his mouth to hers.

His dinner conversation might not be his greatest strength, but, oh, the man could *kiss*. His mouth plied her lips delicately, languorously, until Sid thought if he took his hands off her arms, she'd melt into a heap at his feet.

"Now, it's a lovely night. Do you know what a distraction you've become for me, Sidonie?" He rested his forehead against hers, and just like that, Sid's world became again a cheery, hopeful place, where many good things were possible, and not every challenge had to be faced alone.

"Is that what you wanted to discuss, MacKenzie? Because if it is, I will listen very patiently while you regale me with the details of your tribulation."

"Witch." An endearment, coming from him. He picked up the blanket, tucked his arm across her shoulders, and started them walking again. "I can't be distracted when I work. I'm being well paid to keep my mind on the job."

"You mean the horses might kick or stomp you if you blink?"

"That too. Tell me again what the social worker said when she called."

Even Eden boasted the occasional serpent. Sid recounted the conversation again, as close to word for word as she could. That Mac would listen so attentively, that he would care enough to listen, to ask again, helped another increment of Sid's anxiety for Luis abate.

"You do love that kid," Mac said as they spread the blanket under the trees. "I suspect he loves you too."

"I don't say the words to him, because I don't want him to feel obligated to say them back."

"Say them anyway. Love is the furthest thing from obligation."

Sid tried to see Mac's expression in the darkness, but the moonrise still wasn't quite visible. She liked the sentiment though, understood it. Nothing about raising Luis or dealing with all the convolutions and challenges of his foster care situation was an obligation.

"Sit with me." Mac thumped the blanket beside him, leaving Sid to wonder how, exactly, she could get around to relieving him of his clothes and getting his hands and his mouth *and his mind* on her again.

She settled on the blanket and took off her shoes while Mac slid off his boots.

"Come here, Sidonie." He hauled her into his arms, to sit between his upraised knees, then gathered her against his chest and rested his chin on her crown. Maybe having his hands on her like this—slow and warm and knowing—was enough. As Sid cuddled into the solid muscle of his chest, he started rubbing her back.

"You seem preoccupied, MacKenzie. Is work going OK?"

He was quiet for a moment, maybe deliberating on an answer, or maybe, like Sid, trying to spare a corner of his brain for making conversation, when his entire mind wanted to focus on the pleasure of touching and being touched.

Do you know what a distraction you've become for me? To Sid, Mac's question had been sweet, made even nicer by the note of genuine bewilderment in his voice when he'd asked it.

"James is getting married," Mac said.

Ah. That would preoccupy MacKenzie Knightley. "Do you approve of his choice?"

"I do, and she wants me to stand up with her." He sounded perplexed now, in a pleased way. "I thought maybe Trent would get tapped, or maybe James has asked Trent, but it doesn't matter. I wouldn't miss this ceremony for the world."

"You ever been married, Mac?" Sid didn't know what prompted her to ask the question. Maybe it was Luis pointing out to her that Mac was well-heeled. Mac was also intelligent, damned good-looking, blessed with a wonderful family, and good with cranky teenagers. Some enterprising female should have snatched him up—assuming he was interested in being snatched.

"I have never been married."

"Were you ever engaged?" She was wrapped up against his chest, his arms around her, his knees and thighs tucked right along her body. Her question produced a brief, subtle tension.

"Close to engaged. Engaged very briefly once, and turned down another time."

"Two near misses?"

"Once in undergrad, once after that, both a long time ago."

She levered up, pushing against his chest to peer at him in the gloom. "You've been on the shelf for a long time too, MacKenzie. Is there a story here?"

"Not a very interesting one."

That meant he didn't want to be cajoled into further disclosures, but Sid had to ask one more question. "Who broke it off the first time?"

"She did."

"The woman was a fool. Both of them were hopeless nincompoops. If they didn't appreciate what a treasure you are, to hell with 'em." His gleaming teeth told her she'd provoked him into smiling. She cuddled back down against him, willing to leave the subject right there.

"Honestly, MacKenzie, young women are idiots. They don't know what's important in this life. Are you going to kiss me, or will I have to flirt you into it?"

Chapter 12

"YOU ALREADY HAVE," MAC SAID, SHIFTING SID SO SHE leaned back against one of his knees, all the better to kiss the hell out of her.

He lowered his mouth to hers, his hand cradling Sid's cheek in the darkness, not so much so he could find her, but so he could enjoy the feel of her lady-soft skin against his palm.

Though a question intruded on the sense of homecoming he felt as their arms went around each other: Was he kissing her to distract her from the miserable topic of his two failed engagements, or was he kissing her for the sheer, sumptuous pleasure of it?

Or was he kissing her because he was helpless not to?

Sidonie Lindstrom wasn't a shy kisser. She made little sounds in her throat of pleasure, longing, and satisfaction. Her body participated in the kiss; her breasts pressed against him; her hands took a firm grasp of his hair. She moved against him, communicating urgency and desire more clearly than words could have.

And God above, it pleased Mac to be kissed back like that.

Healed a hurt in his soul.

His mind whipped out a memory from the previous winter, the office Christmas party, where as the managing partner, he was the informal master of ceremonies.

Trent and Hannah had arrived together, Trent cutting a fine figure in his tux, Hannah looking both demure and sexy in a black silk dress.

Simply by watching Hannah and his brother, Mac had known they'd been intimate. Hannah had had a glow, and Trent's gaze was both protective and possessive when he'd watched Hannah waltzing with James.

Mac had wanted to be near that glow, wanted it so badly, when the band had started up a slow dance, he'd simply taken Hannah by the wrist and led her onto the floor. Trent hadn't objected, but he hadn't taken his eyes off them either.

For a few minutes, Mac had allowed himself the pleasure of holding a woman's softness and scent close. He'd felt the silky warmth of her hair against his cheek, held the lithesome, graceful heat of her in his arms.

The pleasure hadn't been the least bit erotic, but a purely human, sensory sweetness. People weren't meant to live life in complete isolation from one another. Mac's body knew it; his mind knew it; his heart and soul knew it.

He'd led Hannah back to her chosen mate and smiled cordially while experiencing a new level of despair, and the despair had only worsened in the intervening months. Then he'd found Sidonie Lindstrom literally in his own—albeit former—backyard, waving her broom at two tons of indifferent equines.

Now, Sid was climbing Mac, twisting into him, and kissing him onto his back, pushing bad memories and cold winters far, far away. Mac ended up with Sid straddling him as he lay on his back, the moon rising beautifully over her shoulder.

"Better," she said, her fingers going to the buttons of his shirt. "We have unfinished business, you and I."

Unfinished discussions too.

Mac stilled her fingers by enclosing them with his own. "I told you we'd keep our clothes on if you were unwilling to accept certain terms from me."

If you allow me the privileges of a lover, then I will expect that for whatever time I enjoy that status, those privileges are exclusively mine. He willed her to recall the words, even as desire rose as luminously as that moon.

She climbed off him and sat with her back to him.

"I need to tell you a few things, MacKenzie. Things that will make it brutally clear I'm not—I'm not a player." She sent him a peevish look over her shoulder. "You'd better not be a player either."

The sense of her words was reassuring. The tension in her spine and the truculence in her tone was not.

Mac finished unbuttoning his shirt, and for the sake of his comfort, unbuckled his belt as well. He also got up off his back, for the sake of his ability to concentrate, and shifted so his legs were on either side of her.

"Tell me these things, Sidonie."

"The topic is uncomfortable."

He went to work unraveling her braid. "Take your time, then. We have all night. Or don't tell me if you'd rather not." Except he wanted her confidences. Craved them the way he craved her kisses and the exact, perfect weight of her breasts in his hands.

"I enjoyed an active social life in college."

Mac waited, his fingers teasing her hair free from its plait.

"I was with some guys."

When he had her braid undone, he finger-combed her hair from her shoulders to her waist, the contact soothing him even as he hurt for her.

"I was a tramp."

Mac slipped his arms around Sid's waist. "You were not a tramp. You probably slept with half as many guys as the guys did women, and you were not a tramp."

"I was easy, and once you get that reputation, the guys make it easy to be easy, you know?"

Yes, he did know. Knew exactly how tempting it was to believe sexual congress meant something to his partners, to believe *he* meant something to them because they'd shared some fleeting physical encounters.

"We all have regrets, Sid. Maybe you'd do it differently if you had it to do over, but who wouldn't?"

"Oh, MacKenzie." She sounded so lost, so utterly without hope. He pulled her back against his chest.

"You were young, Sid. You were coping as best you could, and I've been every bit as much at a loss."

"We pay a price for coping like that." She rested her cheek against his arm, and Mac felt a world of sorrow in one small female.

"Tell me, Sid. I don't care who you were with five or ten years ago. I don't care how many people you were with. I don't care about your past at all except insofar as it shadows your future and weighs on your heart."

She turned, so she was again in his embrace, leaning on him. "Have you ever wondered why I'm doing foster care?"

"Because it's what you're supposed to do. Some people are supposed to teach therapeutic riding, and some people are supposed to be foster parents. It's a calling."

"Bless you, MacKenzie Knightley." She rested on him more heavily, and again he waited. Whatever troubled her, to her it was real and powerful, and she was about to share it with him. He felt Sid gathering her courage, so he kept his caresses on her back slow and easy, willing her to lean on his emotional strength even as she leaned on him physically.

"I'm a city girl, but growing up, I always knew I'd end up in the country. It's a better place to raise kids, and if I knew anything about myself, it was that I wanted kids. I used to draw pictures in my imagination of me on a big porch swing with a half-dozen kids around me. We'd read children's stories, the kind where everything turns out all right in the end."

The wistfulness of her words lingered in the night air as the moon rose higher and the tree frogs sang their love songs.

"Pity me, MacKenzie. I am that most pathetic of creatures, the foster parent who cannot have her own children."

Sid's voice was so quiet, a whisper in the darkness, but Mac heard her. By God, he heard her, and the sense of her words slammed through him like a gale-force wind.

"*Not pathetic.*" He gathered her up, held her close, his words coming out in a fierce growl. "You are *not* pathetic because of an accident of nature. You are courageous and beautiful, and a goddamned saint to be reaching out to other people's children when you deserve to have your own. If anybody should be having children, lots and lots of them, it's you. You mother the hell out of the one cub you've got, and for all you know, Luis is just on loan. Jesus, *God*."

Sid wasn't saying anything, and this drove Mac crazy.

"Argue with me, Sid. Kiss me, smack me, tell me you understand what I'm saying, don't just—Sidonie, for God's sake, please don't cry."

"I'm not—it's not that kind of crying. I'm done with that kind of crying."

Mac had to bend his head to catch her words. Her hands were fisted in his hair, though, holding him desperately close, and her cheek was damp against his chest.

"It's some goddamned kind of crying." He brushed her tears away with his thumbs, his chest aching. He should have seen this, should have seen it in the way she watched Luis, the way the social worker's stupid games got to her.

"Men don't get it." Sid rubbed her cheek on Mac's chest. He eased back so she was sprawled over him, the better for him to get his hands everywhere they needed to be. Her face, her back, her hair, her arms, her shoulders, her everything.

"What don't we get?"

"The emptiness, the sorrow, the *ache*. It never goes away, that ache. You have a period every month, just as if your body had the same reproductive ability every other female body does. You have the PMS, the bloating, the cramps, all of the messy, undignified burden, but you never get the reward. You get failure. You get nothing. Then you feel like nothing."

"You're not nothing to Luis." *Or to me.*

"He won't let me adopt him, Mac, and I tell myself that's fine. He shouldn't have to un-choose his mom to choose me. I can love him anyway."

"Have you ever asked him what his reservations are?"

"He's a teenaged boy. He probably doesn't know what his reservations are, and couldn't put them into words even if he did. It comes down to him not wanting to be legally mine, and if I love him, I have to accept that. The legalities aren't what matter anyway."

The lawyer part of Mac's brain wasn't so sure, but family law wasn't his area. The situation was worth discussing with Trent though. Some other time. Some other time, when Sidonie Lindstrom had told him the full extent of her sorrow.

"Why can't you have kids, Sidonie?"

"Indirectly, it's my own damned fault."

"No, it is not." Mac was utterly certain of that.

"I was the hookup queen of my class, Mac, before hooking up was as popular as it is now. I was stupid and I took risks and my body put an end to it. You know what endometriosis is?"

"I do."

"Well, I didn't. I generally comported myself like a shameless hussy on a perpetual spring break, until I was with a guy in the fall of my sophomore year, and for the first time ever, it hurt. Not a big, dramatic pain, just a twinge. When it happened again, I went in to get checked out, and the doc listed endometriosis along with a lot of other it-could-bes. I didn't think anything of it, because the sex wasn't important."

More sorrow, because sex *should* be important. Mac's belief in that regard probably qualified him as a caveman.

"You're important, Sid."

She kissed his heart. "I'm honest enough to admit my sleeping around was one long, protracted mistake.

I settled down, applied myself academically, and found—wonder of wonders—a lot more than I liked sleeping around, I liked learning things, liked excelling in my studies."

"Of course you would. You're smart as a whip." Sid went silent, and Mac mentally kicked himself, because all those good grades hadn't left her *feeling* smart as a whip. "Something happened, didn't it?"

He kissed her temple, hoping to reassure her back into speaking.

"In grad school, I met a guy. We hit it off. We got engaged." She took a deep breath, her chest expanding against Mac's. "We got married because we wanted to have kids."

Mac knew, knew as if he'd written the script himself, what came next.

"We got divorced a couple years later because I couldn't have kids." Her voice caught. "I can't have kids."

"Breathe, Sid. Don't fight it."

She let out her breath on a gusty, miserable sigh. "My husband was a decent guy, and I think if it had just been my infertility, he would have coped. But I couldn't cope. I felt guilty and ashamed and angry, and pushed him away, and clung, and pushed him away. I don't blame him for giving up. He remarried. They're happy."

While Sid was broke, heart-broke, grieving on top of grieving, and pretending nothing was wrong.

"If you tell me they have two adorable kids, which your charming ex has the temerity to send you a picture of with his damned Christmas card, I will know where to dump your first load of top-quality horseshit."

She lifted her head, the tracks of her tears glimmering by the light of the low-hanging moon. "They're all over his social networking pages too. The cutest damned little rug rats you ever did see."

"Two loads, then. One on each of their birthdays."

Sid folded down against him, and if she hadn't been sprawled over him, Mac would have hunted down the sorry bastard and wrapped his nuts around his neck.

"So that was it? He dumped you, and you and your faulty plumbing started doing foster care?"

"You make it sound like I'm a utility sink, but my uterus is fine. My fallopian tubes seem to be the problem, though I still have all my equipment, and my yearly checkups suggest I've dodged the bullet for now."

Mac shifted, because Sid's weight was pressing on parts of his body that had no sense of timing, no respect for a woman's distress. Those parts of him only knew Sid was warm and soft and female, and under other circumstances, probably willing.

"You let yourself have any rebound relationships?"

"Yes, MacKenzie. I got back on the horse, but it wasn't much of a ride. Then Tony was diagnosed, or let me know he was diagnosed, and that was that."

That was a tragedy wrapped in a misery tied up with a sorrow. Mac could feel the gears whizzing in Sid's female brain, maybe thinking up questions he wasn't ready to answer.

"Are you scared to have sex with me, MacKenzie?"

Or questions from so far out in left field, Mac didn't even have sense enough to see them coming.

"Why would I be scared?"

"You should be. I've been a mess most of my adult life."

"Phi Beta Kappa?" Mac asked.

"Well, yeah."

"Mensa?"

"I qualified. I didn't join."

"Dean's list?"

"I missed out freshman year by a whisker."

"And you ran your brother's production company, managed his hospice care, kept an eye on Luis, pulled up stakes and moved out here when that was best for the kid. You're a rolling wreck, all right."

She nuzzled a spot below his ear that was damned near ticklish. "You've changed the subject."

"Not really. Will you respect my request for an exclusive arrangement with you, Sidonie? We're all carrying baggage, and yours is not as unique as you think."

"What about you?" She sat up to survey him, which meant she was again parked on the evidence of his inconvenient arousal. This felt wonderful physically, which made him feel lousy otherwise.

"What about me?"

"You going to tell me about those near misses someday, Mr. Knightley?"

"Yes, I am." If he'd been thinking up ways to dodge that conversation earlier, he knew now he couldn't put it off forever. "This might not be the best time."

"Because you're aroused?" Sid scooted back, her hands going to the fly of his jeans. Before Mac could protest, she had him unzipped. "If I recall, there's a guy in here whose acquaintance I'd like to make, or make again."

"Sid, you don't have to do this. Let me hold you."

"You've been holding me, and we've talked, and, yes, I will guaran-ass-damned-tee you an exclusive, you idiot."

"I'm an idiot?"

"A horny idiot, thank God. Do you think I'd want to share *you*, for pity's sake? I want all of you, all to myself, because I am not an idiot." She extracted him from his clothing, her hands cool and careful on him in a sexy contrast to her brusque tone of voice.

"Sidonie, just because I have the beginnings of an erection doesn't mean you have to humor me." He was as hard as a muck fork handle—before she ran her finger around the tip of his shaft.

"Lose the jeans, MacKenzie." She climbed off him and started unbuttoning her shirt. Her breasts, those glorious, soft, peachy-perfect breasts emerged into the moonlight when her bra came off a moment later.

"I don't take advantage of women when they're emotionally distraught." Mac's voice shook. He hoped Sid didn't hear it, but she grinned up at him, which shot that theory all to hell.

"I will take advantage of you, though, MacKenzie. It isn't polite to argue with a lady, and it's plain silly when you're nakey-nakey and rarin' to go." Her jeans came off, which effectively obliterated Mac's ability to argue.

He wanted those sturdy, feminine legs wrapped around him, wanted to bury his face in that soft thatch of curly reddish-blond hair, wanted to consume her with his every sense. Naked in the moonlight, Sid folded their clothing at the foot of the blanket, and Mac understood that this wasn't about her feminine confidence.

She was a confident woman, or he wouldn't have noticed her.

This was to reassure Sid he *saw her* as confident, he saw her as desirable.

And he did. More than ever, Mac absolutely did. He might possibly desire her more than he could show her, but that wouldn't stop him from trying.

"I'm calling the shots here, Knightley, lest you get some fool manly notion about who's in charge of this round. On your back, please."

She pushed him on the chest and down he went. He was a big guy; women and even men seemed to defer to him naturally in most situations—except, of course, his little brothers and their womenfolk and offspring. Being bossed around by a naked woman, though... Mac could get used to it.

Might take a lot of practice, but he was willing to make the investment. Mac made this vow to himself because he suspected it hadn't been like this for Sid with all those little college boys.

Her freshman year—the single year of her big, wicked sex spree—she would have been eighteen years old. She hadn't been bossing anybody then. Eighteen was still a child, in many ways. Legally, an adult; emotionally, the barest approximation thereof.

"Get comfortable, MacKenzie. This could take a while."

He expected Sid to swing a leg over him and kiss the daylights out of him. Her hair brushed his stomach an instant before her lips settled on the end of his cock.

Between thank-God-I-showered-after-work and complete ecstatic oblivion, Mac had one coherent thought:

he needed this. His first impulse was to protest, to lever up and gently put Sid on her back, while he explained to her that certain intimacies could be reserved for when he'd earned them.

The lecture died a silent death, swallowed up in the vast sea of Mac's gratitude.

He needed this. Needed the reassurance that a worthy woman desired him this way, wanted to give to him this intimately. He needed the trust, the pleasure, the sharing of his arousal, the courage on both their parts.

He needed her.

He settled his hand in Sid's hair, wanting to be connected to her as she drove him beyond reason. Her tongue was a psychological weapon designed to part a man from his wits; her hands were maddeningly gentle as they cupped and stroked him.

Sid paused and shifted her body so she was straddling Mac's leg, her hair drifting over his belly, and her hands sleeving his shaft. He was wet; she'd licked him wet and moved her hands down his shaft, one after the other, as she drew on him. Her mouth tugged one way, her hands the other, and Mac nearly flew apart.

"Slow down, Sidonie. For the love of… You can't… I'm going to…*Jesus.*"

She raised her head to peer at him, teasing her fingers through the down at the base of his shaft. "Am I doing this right, MacKenzie?"

"*Yes.*" That tortured whisper was his voice, telling her the God's honest truth. "Exactly right."

"Good." She arched up and cradled his erect cock between her breasts, getting her tongue on the end of him as she moved her body to caress his length. "Wouldn't want to think I've worn you out already."

Mac knew a vulgar term for what she was doing, but it felt sublime. Her moving on him, her breasts and her mouth, her heat, her tongue…

He tried to think of Supreme Court opinions he'd memorized. Tried to recite the Gettysburg Address, but he made the mistake of opening his eyes as Sid shifted again to rub her cheek over the end of his engorged cock. She looked enraptured, a pagan goddess come to earth to indulge herself with him.

"Sid, I can't hold out much longer. My wallet's…"

"Hush." She licked him delicately, like a cat. "No wallet. We didn't use your wallet the last time we were on this blanket, and turnabout is fair play."

She was going to kill him, and Mac would be grateful. He felt for her hair, palming the back of her head in hopes he might be able to control her if he couldn't control himself. She got her mouth on that spot under the tip of his cock, scraped her teeth over it, and sent lightning bolts through his self-restraint.

"Sidonie, I'm close."

She closed her mouth over him and drew on him firmly, rhythmically, relentlessly. Within five seconds, Mac's mind shut down as pleasure rocketed through him. He barely had time to roll over and wedge himself against the edge of the blanket before he was coming in great, wracking spasms of glory. His body trembled and jerked with it; behind his closed eyes, fireworks exploded in brilliant colors. His lungs heaved like a colt who'd set the new record for the Derby, while his entire being was suffused with pleasure.

He might have passed out, so thoroughly had Sidonie satisfied him.

When Mac could think again, Sid was what he first became aware of. She'd hiked her leg over his hips and cuddled close. Her arm banded his chest, and her body was spooned around him to the extent a woman almost a foot shorter than he could spoon with him.

In the welter of emotions following these physical sensations, he spotted the temptation to cry, which would not do. The urge to laugh wasn't quite right either, so he kept sorting, even as Sid's hand stroked over his chest.

Mac moved to his back and took her in his arms, putting her head on his shoulder.

She sighed the kind of smug, dreamy sigh he associated with women who'd found their pleasure, though he knew she hadn't. She laid her palm to his jaw and turned his head, stretching up to kiss him lingeringly on the lips, then subsided to his shoulder again.

God in heaven, he needed to say something, to *think* something.

Or maybe he didn't. Maybe Sid had just said it for both of them.

They lay in the moonlight, Sid's leg over Mac's thighs, her head on his shoulder, their hands joined over his heart.

She'd given him the exclusive he'd wanted, tossed it at him as if, in Sid's view, any damned fool would know enough to sign up for it, and then she'd blown his mind until he'd felt the earth, moon, sun, and stars moving.

And they were moving still...

Mac tried to place the dull echo of concussion that radiated up from the ground. There had been earthquakes in the area in his lifetime, little bitty geological twitches that barely made the next day's news.

But this was faint, steady, rhythmic…

"Sid?" He shook her gently. "Sidonie, honey, wake up."

Her eyes opened, and she started to smile at him, but something in his face must have clued her in.

"Sweetie, we need to get dressed and move it. I think the horses are loose."

———✧———

The urgency in Mac's tone cut through the fog of lassitude and contentment in Sid's brain. She had been so happy, drifting in his embrace, so at peace.

She reached for her clothes and passed him his.

Mac raised his head like a prairie dog on a windy day. "That's them. Hear it?"

Sid paused in the middle of shrugging into her shirt—to hell with the bra—and cocked her head. Yes, she felt as much as she heard dull, thudding hoofbeats, one-two, one-two, from over toward the house. What caught her attention was MacKenzie Knightley, kneeling up on the blanket like he was ready to sprint off buck nekkid.

What a glorious sight that would be.

"When the dew is falling, sound travels more easily." He snatched up his jeans, tossed them away, and pulled on his socks instead. "The latch on the stall is securely bolted to the beam. I checked it myself last weekend." He pulled on his jeans while Sid fumbled with her shirt buttons.

"If they get to the road, there will be hell to pay." Mac jerked at his belt as he nattered on. "Old man Wyandt keeps a little Arab stud about a mile that way." He pointed with his chin. "If the mares are in season, they'll head to him, and the shortest route is right along the road."

He stood and looked down at her. From where Sid sat on the blanket, Mac looked about nine feet tall.

Then he was beside her again, kissing her on the mouth, hard.

"Bring the blanket when you're decent. Try not to move up on them so you push them toward the road."

He loped off, making not a sound as he ran.

"Wham, bam," Sid muttered, shoving a foot into her jeans. "Maybe have horse burgers for breakfast."

What had happened between her and Mac on that blanket had been beyond words. Profound. Special didn't begin to start to think about covering it. Mac had surrendered to her, surrendered his body, his mind, his trust...

But like an icy deluge, the thought washed through her mind: What if Social Services got wind the horses were loose on the road—a public nuisance, a safety hazard, an irresponsibly dangerous situation? *What if somebody hits one of them, and I have to pay for all the damage?*

Sid stuffed her bra in her pocket, pulled the rest of her clothes on, folded up the blanket, and hustled back toward the house as quietly as she could. The sight that greeted her would have been comical but for the anxiety pushing up her heart rate.

The horses were on the lane, halfway down to the road, and Mac was between the horses and the road. He was trying to herd the mares to the barn, but they were alternately munching on the grass beside the lane and frisking around Mac as if he were playing with them.

Two horses and one man made herding a difficult proposition. He'd get one horse moved a few steps in the right direction, only for the second horse to trot around behind him, looking for a game of tag.

This situation was like when Luis was too busy playing on the Internet to come down to do his weekend chores. He was simply too distracted to give Sid's agenda the time of day. She ducked into the barn and retrieved what she needed.

"Oh, ladies! Laaadies! Come see what Sid has for you!" Both horses' heads came up, and they stood still, ears pricked in the moonlight. "Come to mama, you bad girls. Painting the town red can work up an appetite, and I've got just what you need." Sid shook the feed bucket loudly, and one of the horses—Buttercup, the one with the blaze—took a tentative step in Sid's direction.

"Smart girl, Buttercup. I bet you'll get a lot more of this than that silly Daisy. She's too busy flirting with MacKenzie, and there won't be any left for her." Sid shook the bucket again, and both horses started moving toward her.

"You're brilliant," MacKenzie said, walking slowly behind the horses. "Start backing toward the barn. They'll follow once they get a whiff of the grain."

"Of course they will," Sid said, doing as he suggested. "My girls are too smart to get into any real trouble, especially not for some little old runty stallion with a funny nose, aren't you, ladies? You need your beauty sleep too. You've fallen prey to the full moon and the spring air and an excess of high spirits. Am I right?"

The horses' heads were down as they followed Sid to the barn, almost as if they realized their adventure was over and it was time for bed. She kept talking to them, just as she might read a bedtime story to a tired child.

"Walk right into their run-in stall," Mac said. "Put a little of the grain in each of their dishes then come on out."

"How much is a little? These are the biggest horses God ever made."

"A handful. They're efficient, and all they need is enough to reward them for following you back to civilization."

Sid complied, but part of her wanted to stay with the horses, to keep talking to them until she was sure they were content for the night.

"Good job." Mac kissed her when she was standing beside him outside the horses' stall. Kissing seemed to be his way of saying a lot of things.

"This hasn't happened before," Sid said. "Is it a regular part of keeping animals, because if it is I'm not sure—"

He settled an arm across her shoulders. "It happens, but those mares didn't leave their own stall door wide open, Sid."

The implications sank in, and the anxiety that had been ebbing from Sid's mind rose back up.

"You're saying Weese did this? He loves these horses. He wouldn't do anything to put them at risk."

"Not on purpose, but we're all human. I've done the same thing, or worse, left the feed-room door open, the feed unsecured, and the stall door unlatched."

"Good heavens. When was that?"

"After my dad died. I was older than Luis, but it was an unexpected death. I went overnight from being Dad's treasured firstborn to the man of the house. I'd find myself driving somewhere, and forget where I was going and why I was going there."

Sid kissed his cheek and smoothed down his hair, because the memory still bothered him.

"I've done that. It's like you keep waking up in some stranger's life, except the stranger is you," she said. The horses, meanwhile, had already scarfed up their bedtime snacks.

"Stress, I suppose," Mac said. "Losing a loved one is stressful as hell."

"Losing these horses would be stressful for Luis." Sid turned, so she was nearly in MacKenzie's embrace. "If DSS was ready to shut me down over a hog house, what do you think they'd do if Daisy or Buttercup caused an accident on the highway? People who can't look after horses shouldn't be looking after children."

She could hear Amy Snyder saying those very words as she tapped away at the SmartPad of doom.

Mac's fingers paused midway around the curve of Sid's ear. "When is Luis's hearing?"

"Damn it to hell, MacKenzie. You've hit it on the head. The last time we faced a hearing, Luis would go to school without his backpack, put laundry right into the dryer without washing it, put the teakettle in the refrigerator and the milk in the cupboard. He never said a word, just silently fell apart."

"Court is stressful for most people. Luis still needs to know his girls went off on a toot, or it's more likely to happen again."

"Do I have to tell him now?"

"Yes." Mac's tone held a touch of humor.

Sid let herself burrow closer for one long moment, then stepped back.

"Come along, then. If we're lucky, we can sweeten the lecture with a reprise of that blueberry pie."

"I like it when you're bossy, Sidonie."

Sidonie. The name Mac used for her when the message was intimate. He fell in step beside her, but Sid resisted the urge to take his hand. What to say to Weese, and how to say it?

They reached the kitchen to find Luis was already making inroads on the remains of the pie.

"I left you some," he said from his seat at the table. "It wasn't a big pie to begin with."

"Getting smaller all the time." Sid set a glass at Luis's elbow and retrieved the milk from the fridge.

"We had some excitement in the barnyard," Mac said, putting a plate on the counter. "The mares got out and were halfway to the road before we caught up with them. No pie for me, Sid, but you should have some."

Sid poured the milk. *The mares got out. No pie for me.* Simple, effective, and yet Luis was on his feet, headed for the door, pie forgotten.

"Your mom got them back to the barn with a bucket of feed," Mac went on. "They're safe, and the stall door is latched up tight."

Luis stopped short of the door. "They're OK? You're sure?"

"Better than OK, because they had a little exercise. Finish that pie, son, or I might have to see to it myself. No harm, no foul."

Man and boy stared at each other, exchanging some silent set of signals Sid couldn't decipher, then Luis moved back to the table. She poured his milk and put the jug back in the fridge.

"I must have left their door open." Luis stared at his half-eaten pie. "I can't remember. I think I closed it, but I can't be sure."

Mac lounged back against the counter. "You probably did close it, but you didn't latch it, and they get to bumping on the door, and it moves a little, so they get their noses into the act, and lips that are damned near prehensile, and soon enough, two loose horses. I used to tie some baling twine around the stall doors at night with a bowknot so I wouldn't forget, like tying a string around my finger. Sid, you want some tea?"

He pushed away from the counter and took the teakettle off the stove.

"Peppermint," she said. "Something to settle my stomach after all the night's excitement." Mac held the teakettle under the spigot, his expression…bashful.

Good.

Lest Sid stare at Mr. Bashful until her indecent thoughts were visible on her face, she got down a couple of mugs and the honey. "What about you, MacKenzie? What kind of tea will you have?"

"Same."

"I'm going out to tie some string around the stall door." Luis got right back up again. "I shouldn't have forgotten. Adelia and Neils will kill me if I do something like this at the stable."

"I'll come with you," Mac said. Sid was about to suggest they make a trio of it, when she caught Mac's eye and the slightest shake of his head. "Might as well finish that piece of pie, Sid. Your boy seems determined to abandon it."

Mac followed Luis out the door, leaving Sid alone with a messy, half-eaten piece of very good pie.

Which should not be allowed to go to waste.

Chapter 13

"YOU HAVE A HEARING COMING UP." MAC WAITED until he and Luis were halfway to the barn to drop that bomb.

Luis stopped walking and turned a belligerent expression on Mac. "What of it?"

"You have a hearing coming up, the social worker has already threatened to move you once, and kids get moved at hearings all the time, particularly if DSS wants to move you from foster care to some therapeutic group home."

"What do you know of it?" Luis resumed his march toward the barn, his thin shoulders hunched as if the night were cold.

"More than you think. Hannah was raised in foster care."

"Who? Oh, her. She was nice."

"She's lovely. Luis, everybody makes mistakes. Get that through your thick, adolescent head."

"I don't just make mistakes, I fuck up." He stopped outside the barn, his expression bleak. "Sid deserves better than me."

"She doesn't agree with you, and letting a pair of horses wander around in the front yard for fifteen minutes doesn't make you the eighth biblical plague."

The kid's expression turned hopeless and lost.

"What aren't you telling her?" Mac, veteran of

uncomfortable discussions with many delinquent teens, let the question hang.

"Sometimes you do more harm by telling, right?" Luis replied. "Like when I got into the beer? James asked me what the benefit would be to Sid of telling the truth, and there wasn't any."

"Except you told her the truth in your own time anyway, because there is a benefit to treating the people you love with respect. Truth is usually part of that respect."

"So is keeping a few things to yourself," Luis said. "I know the social worker called today. I was out on the porch when she did, but Sid thinks I was doing my chores. I should have been doing them."

If they didn't move this conversation into the barn, Sid would soon be out on that same porch.

"God almighty, Weese. How many things are you going to beat yourself up for at once? What did the social worker say?"

"I got the impression she was still trying to jerk Sid's license, but Sid got around her."

Mac looked up at the moon, at the cool, remote beauty of it in contrast to all the tension and misery he felt in the boy.

"She won't jerk Sid's license. Teenagers are hard to place, boys handle moves worse than girls, and your lawyer will get you a hearing in a heartbeat if DSS tries to move you."

"My lawyer can't get a hearing if DSS is only moving me from one foster home to the next. It has to be from here to a more restrictive placement, like a therapeutic group home, before I'm entitled to a hearing."

"Ever think of becoming a lawyer?" Mac asked, moving off toward the barn.

"Sid would kill me."

At least the idea put a hint of a smile on Luis's face, but surely the kid was indulging in adolescent hyperbole?

"Well, you're close to right. If you're being moved to a more restrictive placement, then they must give you a hearing, but you can ask for a hearing at any time for a good cause. This is a good cause."

Luis flipped the switch to the right of the barn door, and dim lights came on in the aisle. "None of my lawyers told me that."

Or they'd told him and he'd been too stressed out to absorb it. "What kid wants extra hearings?"

"I do, if they're trying to move me. I don't want to leave here. Not the horses, not Sid, not—I don't want to leave here."

"Then let Sid adopt you."

Luis stalked away. "I'll tie some baling twine around the stall door. The horses won't get out again."

Mac watched him go, wondering what in the hopeless hell the boy was keeping to himself in the name of protecting Sid.

———

"You'd think nobody ever had topsoil for sale around here before," James muttered as he maneuvered Trent's farm pickup so Luis could dump a cubic yard of rich, dark earth into the bed.

"You want more?" Luis yelled. "Sid'll cut you a deal, maybe."

"Fill half the bed," James said, craning his neck to eye the truck's rear tires. The kid was running around with the loader like he'd been born doing it, which

boded well if he expected to spend the summer doing
farm work.

The truck shuddered as the additional dirt was spilled
into the bed, and James moved his vehicle so the next
customer could be served. He parked in the shade near
the house and found Sid on the porch, shaking hands
with Elroy Wyandt.

"You'll do business with just about anybody, won't
you, Sid?" James asked as he ambled up the steps.

"She must," Wyandt said, sticking out a hand to
James. "Somebody let you back on the property,
didn't they? Hear you and old Inskip are getting in bed
together, Knightley."

Old Inskip was probably ten years Elroy's junior, a
good foot taller, and possessed of twice the number of
natural teeth, but the proprieties had to be observed.

"If you heard that, then Louella must have made
you get some decent hearing aids," James said, letting the old man squeeze his hand hard. "I've got
you a new customer too, if you have some wood for
sale, Elroy."

"The pee-anna lady. Heard something about that too."

"You can interrogate him at your leisure about
the piano lady or anything else," Sid chimed in, "but
James has to get out his wallet if he's going to stand
here all day."

She jammed her hands into her back pockets, which
thrust her breasts out against the fabric of her flannel
shirt. Elroy's gaze dropped down over that unwitting
display, then darted out to the pasture.

"I'll be moseying," Elroy said, swallowing. "You tell
me how much wood you want, missus, and I'll have

it stacked for you come September. Knightley, best of luck with Inskip's operation."

He scampered down the steps, a wizened little gnome as spry as a man one-third his age.

"You got him lending you his loader and giving you wood?" James asked.

"He took a look at the quality of that topsoil, set aside three loads for himself, and started talking to me about heating with wood."

In the barnyard, two more pickups lined up behind the one Luis was filling with vintage horse manure.

"I have a woodstove," James said. "It gives off a nice heat, and you have enough deadfall in your woods to make heating with wood a cheap proposition. You heard Elroy mention I'm going into a joint venture with Hiram Inskip?"

"I heard him giving you a hard time about something to that effect."

Elroy had barely been getting started when Sid had run him off.

"Inskip and I are in a partnership," James said, "which I will come to control over the next five years. I'd like to talk to you about it, because working your land figures prominently into our plans."

Sid's smile faded; her hands came out of those back pockets. "Put the kettle on. I'll tell Weese to collect the money while I'm listening to what you have to say." She gave him a visual once-over, as if she could predict what he'd say by studying him, then hustled off.

Not a pushover, Miss Sidonie, and James liked her for it. Good looks and charm in abundance meant James seldom had to work to win a woman's approval, but he was about to work to win hers.

Which, considering MacKenzie approved of *her*, was probably fitting.

The kettle was whistling in earnest when Sid came back in through the kitchen door. "When does it get nice and hot around here, for God's sake?"

"Same time it does in Baltimore, I'm guessing." James opened cupboards, one, two, three, finding mugs behind door number three, same place his mom had stored her everyday mugs. "You notice the weather more out here, you notice the sky, you notice the breezes, or the lack of them, and you surely do notice the smells."

To James, they were good smells, even the sharp scent of that dark topsoil wafting across the barnyard.

"What kind of tea are we having?" he asked.

"Hannah gave me some green tea with jasmine as a housewarming present. Will that do?"

"It's her favorite, and I like it. The nights aren't as cold lately, and the sun's gaining strength. We'll be planting corn in the next few weeks and taking off the first cutting of hay right after that if the weather runs true to form." James was looking forward to both, same as he had as a kid on the farm.

"I know the frost date for this zone is May first, but don't you sometimes get frost after that?"

And with one question, Sid had him going. Frost dates, early hybrid strains of corn, the trade-off between the stress of the heat and drought of midsummer versus the cold nights of late spring, the potential for planting two crops in one year if the winter wheat came off early for wet wrapping and the corn went in late.

James had finished off most of a pot of tea before he realized he hadn't even approached his intended purpose for meeting with Sid, but to sit in this kitchen and talk crops and weather and possibilities had felt comfortable.

Surprisingly comfortable.

"How does a CPA know so much about all this agricultural stuff?" Sid asked, peering into the only orange ceramic teapot James had ever seen.

The question caught him off guard. Most people thought of him as a lawyer, because he purposely didn't lead with his accounting credentials. Lawyering was sexier than accounting, right? And yet Mac had cautioned him not to approach Sid from a legal angle.

"I grew up on this farm," James said. "I watched my parents live and die here, and I considered buying the place both times it came back on the market. Every farmer has to be a competent businessman, but few businessmen understand farming."

Sid topped up her mug from the teapot, fragrant steam curling upward. "You watched your parents die here? Both of them?"

Too late, James realized his error. This was old ground, ground that did not need to be plowed up again.

"I was speaking figuratively."

Sid set the pot down and peered at him, a slow, green-eyed perusal that had probably inspired Luis into admitting all manner of uncomfortable truths.

"I do not abide untruths, James Knightley. Mac told me your mother died in the bedroom where Luis sleeps now. You were speaking literally. How did your father die?"

He stood, taking his mug to the sink to buy time. He washed it out, set it in the drain rack, and tried to figure out why he was stalling.

"Dad died in a farming accident. Tractor rolled; he didn't suffer long. Best we can figure, he had a heart attack doing what he loved." James very purposely did not close his eyes as he spoke, because he knew exactly which memories and which images would crowd into his mind if he did.

They crowded anyway, but he focused on folding a dish towel over the handle of the oven.

"How long has it been, James?"

"Seventeen, eighteen years since Dad died."

"It's still hard to talk about, isn't it?" She stayed at the table, as if she understood James needed space to keep breathing. This wasn't on his agenda. This topic was never on his agenda.

"The accident was my fault, at least partly."

She regarded him steadily, and all James could detect in her eyes was concern.

"It couldn't have been your fault. You were a kid. My brother died of AIDS—that is my least favorite sentence in any language, by the way—but I still blame myself. Tony was an adult who made his own choices, but I blame myself."

She was still blaming herself, from the sadness in her voice. James shifted to stand at the window, where he could see Luis filling the bed of yet another pickup with vintage horse poop.

"You're right, in a sense, Sid. I didn't push the tractor over on him, didn't give him a bad ticker, but as the youngest, it was my job to take Dad his lunch if he didn't come in for it. I got to making a hay fort in the mow, lost track of the time, and all the while, he was under that stupid tractor."

"But even if you'd found him earlier, James, could you have lifted the tractor off him? Fixed his heart? Pulled a medevac chopper out of your pocket, if they even had them around here that long ago? No, you could not. It was his turn."

"This isn't what I came to talk about."

"You don't ever want to think about it, either. I do apologize for prying. Tell me some more about why I should sign a five-year agreement to let you work my land."

To launch into the cost-benefit analyses, the figures and percentages, the risk assessments, was a relief, and all the while, Sid followed the discussion. She asked the right questions, comprehended the answers, and spared James having to break things down as he might have for a less savvy audience.

"Does Mac know you're so smart, Sid?"

"I'm not smart, James, I'm educated."

"MBA?"

She nodded, but it hadn't been much of a guess.

"From?"

"Wharton. My primary emphasis was human resources management, but they don't let you through that gauntlet without getting a thorough grasp of numbers. How about you?"

"I'm Maryland educated. Maryland and the school of hard knocks. You want some time to think this over?"

"No, I do not. I'll read this carefully." She tapped a folded document with her index finger. "If it says what you've represented it to say, I'll sign it."

"You won't have somebody look it over for you? I wouldn't be offended."

"If a Wharton MBA can't read a land-use agreement, then Wharton needs to lower its tuition. The last purpose I'll put my money to is paying off some lawyer's sailboat. You hungry?"

Her animosity wasn't the garden-variety lawyer bashing, which suggested retreat was prudent.

"I told Twyla I'd have some dirt for us to make flower beds with this afternoon, so I'd better get moving. My thanks for the tea and the conversation."

"Who's Twyla?"

"My fiancée's daughter. She's eight and believes a deal's a deal. I disappoint her at my peril."

"I believe a deal's a deal too, James Knightley." Sid stuck out her hand, and James shook it, then held her hand a moment longer.

"Mac likes you."

"I like him too."

"He likes you a lot. I can see why."

He brought her knuckles to his lips in an old-fashioned gesture of gentlemanly respect, and left her in her kitchen, her expression perplexed.

Why hadn't Mac disclosed that his father died on my farm? Of course, any parent's death would be hard to discuss, but should it be a secret?

Sid made herself another cup of tea—James had pretty much downed the entire last pot—and took it back out to the porch. The spring sun was beaming through a greening canopy of leaves, and over the grind and growl of the loader, birds sang.

Such a pretty place Tony had bought for them, but

what she wouldn't give to have her brother to share it with. To have somebody to share it with besides a teenager bound to leave for college in a couple of years, if she got to provide a home for him even that long.

Why didn't Mac ever talk about his clients, their horses, or their farms? Why didn't he bring up work when he and Sid shared a meal? If he lived with them here on this farm, would those confidences and commonplaces be shared between them?

What was she doing, letting her curiosity wander off in that ridiculous direction? The last place Mac would want to live would be the scene of his parents' respective demises.

"Yo, Sid!" Luis waved from his perch on the loader. He hadn't been off the thing all morning, apparently enjoying a masculine delight in powerful, noisy equipment.

"Coming!" She set her tea aside and walked across the yard. "You ready for a lunch break? We're enjoying a momentary lull, it seems."

"Get up here. I'll show you how to run this." He beamed a brilliant, open smile at her, a man-boy happy to share his new toy. "It's really cool."

"I dunno, Weese. It's really big."

"It's a glorified skid loader. Stop being a girl and let me show you."

Squeezing into the cab next to her foster son was a little awkward, but he was right—operating the loader wasn't that hard, and manipulating the bucket and the vehicle itself developed a rhythm that was almost fun. The noise of the treads and the engine became a kind of music, the rearrangement of the remaining topsoil a sculpture.

"So you take care of that guy coming up the drive," Luis said, "and I get a pee break."

"See that you don't strand me out here, Weese."

He didn't, but he sat on the porch with a sandwich and a bag of nachos, wolfing his lunch while Sid took care of the next three customers, two pickup loads and a three-bagger.

Luis gestured with what remained of the bag of chips. "You going to let me back on?"

"Not if you'll get orange crumbs all over." Sid climbed out, oddly disoriented without the vibration of the loader under her butt.

"I counted up the money between sandwiches, Sid."

"How are we doing?"

He named a figure.

"You're shitting me, Weese. That is not nice, not when money is so tight."

"I shit thee not, Sid. Anybody ever tell you to work on your trust issues?"

"Shut up and scoop the poop. I'm going to recount the money."

—ᴡ—

On Sunday morning, Sid took a break from reading the help-wanted ads to count the money yet again, amazed once more at what a certain kind of dirt was worth. She'd just set the jar aside when Mac pulled up in his horseshoer's truck.

"Hey." Mac's version of a greeting rose considerably in Sid's estimation when he followed it up by drawing her to her feet and kissing her lingeringly on the mouth.

"Hey, yourself, cowboy. I'm rich."

He settled back against the porch railing, crossing his arms. "Did the estate settle?"

"Hardly. I'm the topsoil tycoon of this valley. We made a small fortune, Mac, and I met most of my neighbors. What have you been up to while I was raking in coin of the realm and cleaning out the muck pit?" Half cleaning it out—in one weekend.

"Shoed a few horses, and yesterday was my standing date with my nieces. We took Twyla with us, and it's the first time I've been outnumbered that badly."

"You look a little tired. Come on in. I made raisin bread this morning, and Weese hasn't been around to scarf it all up." Sid took Mac by the wrist and tugged him into the kitchen, which still sported a wonderful yeasty aroma. "Your brother James came by to get some topsoil yesterday and stayed to talk business."

"He's good at talking business. The topsoil was because he's landscaping Vera's place before she and Twy move to his farm." Mac leaned back against the sink, looking marvelous in his jeans and denim shirt.

"What will Vera do with her property?"

"They're renting the house to her ex and his kids so the ex can sell his own place. James will farm the land with Inskip. We washing the bread down with tea or milk?"

"What kind of woman rents her house to her ex?" Sid cut off a couple of slabs of raisin bread from a loaf that was still warm in the center. She passed Mac a fat slice, enjoying bustling around her kitchen while a hungry man looked on.

"Thanks." He saluted with the bread. "Vera's a nice woman. Her former stepson will work for James and Hiram this summer, so the location will be convenient.

Vera's practical, and she loves her kids. Her ex is not a
bad guy, though he's got his share of faults."

"You want butter on your bread?"

"Of course."

"Mac, how did your father die?"

He paused with his bread partway to his mouth.
"Would I like butter, how did my father die? What kind
of segue is that, Sid?"

"Death is on my mind a lot. I know your mom died in
this house of an aggressive cancer."

Sid got the butter dish out of the fridge, purposely
turning her back on Mac to give him a measure of privacy. The question had come out of her mouth without
forethought or planning, and now she wished it hadn't.

Mac stared at his piece of raisin bread. "Dad had a
heart attack as best we can figure. He was on the tractor
when it happened. Why do you ask?"

"James sort of brought it up." Or she'd sort of pried
it out of James.

"James was just a kid, and it was bad. Dad was con-
scious when we found him, but Dad understood the situation. Mom and James did not. I'm not sure about Trent."

And in all the intervening years, Mac and Trent had
never discussed this?

Sid slid an arm around Mac's waist. "You were all
with him when he died?" Along the length of her body,
he felt as unyielding as one of the centuries-old oaks in
her yard, so she laid her head on his shoulder.

"We were. Dad understood that as soon as the tractor
was moved, he'd bleed out. He told me to get the horses,
when I wanted to call for the medics. I got the horses,
and he said his good-byes while I hitched them up."

"Tell me, MacKenzie."

"James kept assuring him help was coming and everything would be fine. Mom sat beside him, holding his hand, crying. Trent cursed a lot, and pulled Dad free when the horses got the tractor up. I knew, and Dad knew. He said he'd always been proud of his family, and that he loved us very much, and then he was gone."

Sid held on to him, mentally raging at herself for the casual cruelty of her stupid, curious question. This was why Mac avoided mention of the past: because his father's death had been terrible beyond imagining. A memory of horror and helplessness and loss that likely abated little with the years.

"I'm so sorry, MacKenzie. Sorry I asked, sorry you had to live through that."

A big sigh eased out of him, and some of the rigidity left his shoulders.

"I thought James would never stop crying. He was the baby, Dad's little buddy. Of the three of us, James was the one most likely to be at Dad's side. Trent and I were older, thinking in terms of life beyond the farm. Not James."

Mac had apparently only seen this with the perfect torment of hindsight.

"James is a successful man, and he seems happy," Sid said.

"You should have seen him a year ago. I've always wondered why I went and got those horses just because Dad told me to. I was an adult, technically. I knew the consequences, I knew there was a choice, but I ran to get those horses."

"Are you *blaming* yourself?"

"Not blaming, exactly. Second-guessing. There's a trauma center out here in Western Maryland. Dad was in good health otherwise, and he wouldn't have been on that tractor if I'd been more conscientious about the farm work."

Good God, worse and worse. Sid fed Mac a bite of raisin bread, wanting to give him something, anything.

"What the hell does that mean, MacKenzie? I cannot imagine you shirking a responsibility for love nor money."

"Someday I'll walk the north pasture with you. We always kept that parcel in pasture, and for good reason, because it's littered with granite outcroppings. You can't plow it safely with a tractor. Dad's death proved what should have been obvious."

Obvious *in hindsight*. "He had an accident, very likely because he had a heart attack, not the other way around. Don't be an idiot."

He brushed a crumb from her lip, a hummingbird wing-beat of a caress. "You're saying the heart attack caused the accident? I guess we'll never know, but I do know I told him I'd turn up that ground with the horses, and then I didn't see to it. You have to plant when it's planting time, and I wasn't getting to it."

Sid endured an abrupt certainty that even the departed Mrs. Knightley had blamed herself for her husband's death.

"So your dad didn't remind you? His only choice was to hop on that tractor and start taking risks? He couldn't have used the horses?"

Another stare, this one downright perplexed. "With horses, you farm ahead of yourself," Mac said. "You can see the ground as it meets your plow or your rake.

With a tractor, you're always farming behind yourself. You drive the tractor over the ground before you till it, or plow it with whatever you're dragging along behind you. I've never enjoyed that, but it didn't bother Dad. He was an engine guy, like James."

Whatever that had to do with the price of horse poop. Sid took a bite of raisin bread lest she start shouting.

A long moment later, she tried for reason, despite the emotional nature of the conversation. "You can't blame yourself for your dad's death, Mac. He made choices, and he's the one who took the risks that led to the accident."

Mac set the rest of the raisin bread on the counter. Slowly, his arms came around her. "Where's Luis, Sid? Inskip said the boy's a natural on the loader."

The subject was officially, if gently, changed. "He's working at the riding stable until he has a lesson this afternoon. Left to his own devices, I think he'd live there."

"And leave his girls?"

"Leave me, in any case. You should eat the rest of your raisin bread." Sid slipped away from Mac before the lump in her throat overcame her composure, and why the hell was that?

"You have a hearing date for Luis yet?" Mac asked as he finished off the raisin bread.

"Soon." Sid set the butter dish on the counter beside him. "I'm hoping it will be the same old, same old. We get more and more tense as the day approaches, and then it's five minutes of nothing in the courtroom. His case plan remains return home or relative placement, and nothing changes."

Mac slapped a fat dab of butter onto another slice of raisin bread. "How long has he been in foster care?"

"Better than two years." Nearly three.

"His plan ought to be changing to adoption, Sid, or independent living."

For a horseshoer, Mac knew a lot of what had been covered in foster parent training, but then, his sister-in-law was a former foster kid.

"Luis would go for independent living," Sid said, "not for adoption. I've asked and asked until it feels like I'm torturing him."

"He's torturing you by saying no." Mac held the bread out for her to take a bite. "You ever considered therapy with him?"

Good stuff, raisin bread, especially with butter. "No, because family therapy presupposes you're both holding your own in individual therapy, or that you could. Luis hates talking about his situation."

"It's killing you that he won't talk about it."

The lump in her throat was becoming an obstruction, making it hard to breathe. "I mind more that he won't tell me *why* he doesn't want to be a family with me. But if I love him, then I respect his silences. He's a kid doing the best he can."

"Come here, Sidonie."

She stopped wandering around the kitchen and tried to assess Mac's mood, but as usual, he gave away little he didn't want to give away.

"Why?"

"Just come here, stop thinking and fretting, doing whatever females do when you can't clean or cook or fuss a problem into oblivion. Louie has a few things to work through. Give him time. He'll come around."

She took a step toward Mac, toward the low, soothing

reason in his voice. She liked the way he Frenchified Luis's name. Luis would like it too.

"Guys can be slow," Mac went on, holding out his arm. "Be patient with us."

Sid let his arms settle around her again. This embrace was different, more personal.

"James said you put him through his paces." Mac's hand began to move on her back in a caress already both dear and familiar. "He was bragging on you. Said you're a damned Wharton MBA."

"La-di-flippin'-damn-da."

"You should be proud of yourself, Sid. We don't see too many of those out this way." His nose traced the curve of her ear, which tickled in odd places.

"Take me to bed, MacKenzie."

"You're saying that because you're out of sorts, we have the house to ourselves, and you want comfort."

She pulled back enough to glare up at him. "None of which outweighs the fact that I want *you*."

"Ah, Sidonie." He didn't answer her in words, but started in kissing her. His mouth was a slow-moving force of nature over hers, warming her up from the inside, sending her blood singing through her veins, and bringing her to life in places low and lonely.

"Is that a yes? I'm in the mood for a yes, MacKenzie Knightley. A yes from you right this instant would be nice."

"You don't have to invite me into your bed twice. Just tell me you're sure about this, Sid." His lips brushed along her neck, pausing so a warm current of his breath caressed her throat.

"I'm damned sure, MacKenzie."

He switched sides. "We need to talk."

"Not here," she said, pressing close. "Upstairs. My bed. Now. And economy of words is one of your best features, MacKenzie."

He smiled slightly as she led him by the hand up the steps, and as they reached Sid's bedroom, the first gusting patter of raindrops hit the roof.

"Perfect." She bounced down on the bed, intent on shucking out of her socks. "I love a rainy day spent lazing in bed."

"You think I'll let you *laze* in bed with me, Sidonie?" His question held both humor and threat.

She liked the threat better. "You'll need to catch your breath if we're in this bed together for any length of time, buster. Pride goeth, and all that." She stood to get out of her yoga pants and tried to think up something that would taunt him into a retort.

In the next instant, he was *on* her, and Sid was flat on her back across the bed, nearly six and a half feet of MacKenzie Knightley blanketing her body.

"I love it when you spout biblical allusions while you're getting naked for me," Mac growled.

He didn't give her a chance to speak, but sealed his mouth to hers and kissed her breathless. Witless, mindless, breathless.

Kiss me hello, why dontcha?

"Don't make promises you can't keep, MacKenzie," she managed when he let her up for air. "I want you."

"You'll have me." But the damned man climbed off her, and Sid wanted to wail with the ache of his absence. She lay on the bed and watched as he undressed as if they had all the time in the world.

As if a woman wasn't nigh panting with desire for him just a few feet away.

A woman who by rights ought to be getting naked herself.

Chapter 14

MAC UNDID HIS CUFFS AND PULLED HIS SHIRT OVER HIS head. Worn denim this time, going frayed at the elbows and around the collar, but it fit him wonderfully. A T-shirt that looked so white it proved that, already, Mac Knightley had spent time outdoors shirtless in the sun. That belt of his, the one with the trick buckle, came off next. He piled his clothes on the chair at Sid's desk. Hung the shirt over the chair back, then the T-shirt, then the belt.

"Like what you see, Sidonie?"

Loved what she saw. "Show me some more, and I'll let you know."

He sat on the bed next to her, and his running shoes hit the floor, then a pause. She expected him to stand and lose the jeans, but found him regarding her instead.

"Time to unwrap my present." He put a hand on her belly. She felt the heat of his touch through the loose cotton top she'd put on first thing in the day, and with just that one hand, he held her motionless.

A small panic beat against her insides, right under that hand. This time there'd be no cell phones ringing, no horses getting loose, no interruptions—no escape. This time, Mac would be inside her, where she needed him to be.

This time, no hiding and no turning back.

"Last chance, Sidonie. Tell me you're sure."

He brushed his palm up over her ribs, pushing the fabric aside to expose her vulnerable belly—over the womb that would not conceive. Sid watched his face, mapped the intensity of his focus and saw utter commitment to his purpose.

"I'm sure, MacKenzie." She covered his hand with her own, and when she let him go, Mac straightened, and the jeans joined the clothes on her chair.

His endowments were in proportion to the rest of him, something Sid hadn't noticed before quite the way she noticed it now.

"We'll go slowly," he said, putting a knee back on the bed. "Until we can't go slowly anymore."

Another threat, a wonderful threat, and a promise of more pleasure than Sid could withstand. Mac hooked his hands under her arms and hefted her back a couple of feet so she lay across the middle of the bed. When Sid didn't move, but merely watched him to see what he'd do next, he smiled a slow, sweet, piratical smile and straddled her middle.

His erection was in her immediate line of sight, the washboard of his abs and the sinewy thickness of his thighs the backdrop. Surely the time to start back in with the kissing had arrived.

Mac scooted a few inches lower and grasped Sid's wrists, spreading her arms to either side. She closed her eyes, the better to revel in his heat and weight, and his voice very near her ear.

"Will you be bossy now, Sidonie?"

She lifted her middle up to push into him.

"I'll take that for a maybe." Mac's voice held a smile, and the idea that he was amused helped Sid find her courage. She arched up and found his mouth with her own.

She'd surprised him. He was still for an instant before he kissed her back, and when she wanted to pillage and plunder, he kept the pace slow. His grip on her wrists was as gentle as it was implacable, and his kisses held the same qualities: sweet, savoring, tender, but with more than a hint of command in them.

Sid turned her head to breathe, to admire the look of Mac's clothes draped over her chair.

"Why should you get to be the boss, MacKenzie? There are two of us here in this bed."

He shifted. He was so damned much bigger than Sid was that he could hold her wrists against the mattress and still curl down to get his teeth on her shirt. He nudged it up, inch by inch, using his mouth.

The fabric slid up her rib cage, then over the swell of her breasts. She'd owned the shirt for years—the next thing to a comfortable old rag—but it had never felt naughty against her skin before. He paused when another nudge and slide would have exposed her left nipple.

"I'm asking you to *let me* be the boss now, Sidonie, because you trust me to do this properly."

He'd said the one right thing, the words that made all the difference. She *allowed* him to call the shots, and he knew it, and he made sure she knew he knew it. Mac didn't want to get this wrong, in other words, and needed permission to find his way to *their way*.

"I do trust you," Sid said, "and you will, do it properly that is."

"Every. Time." He let her hands go and slid her shirt up those last two inches, exposing both breasts, then sat back and simply stared. "You are so damned pretty. I'm intoxicated looking at you, Sidonie."

Not drunk, *intoxicated*. Oh, yes, he was going about loving her properly.

A touch of anxiety laced through Sid's anticipation. *Properly* was a heady proposition for a lady who'd lectured herself for years about life on the shelf not being all that bad.

Mac folded down and rested his cheek on the slope of her breast. "The scent of you, Sidonie…" He inhaled through his nose and exhaled a moment later, a warm, sighing-out breath.

Had any other man taken the time to savor the scent of her? Sid brought her hands up, abruptly near tears, and buried her fingers in Mac's hair. She held him like that, his cheek against her breast, feeling protective and vulnerable and aroused all at once.

He crouched up and caged her with his body. "Stay with me, Sidonie. There are two of us here in this bed, you know."

She slid her arms around him. "Kiss me, MacKenzie. Please."

She thought maybe he'd tease and argue with her, but he only studied her for a moment before slipping one hand around to cradle her head in his palm.

By virtue of his hand, his long limbs, and his weight, he held her still, but Sid was kept busy focusing on his kisses, on the delicate invitation of his tongue, on how he welcomed her into his mouth, into his loving. He moved away, but only far enough to run his nose up the column of her throat, then return to join their lips.

And gradually, Mac's lack of hurry, his due and

deliberate pace, communicated itself to Sid. She'd braced herself to be ravished—and she had every confidence she would be, thoroughly—but she had no defenses whatsoever against being *cherished*.

—⁓—

Mac was the starving man at a banquet, and this time, the place of honor had been reserved for him.

The whole banquet was his, in fact, which made him only that much more determined to lay everything he had, everything he was, at Sidonie's feet. He could come simply from kissing her, and briefly considered letting himself do that—to take off a little of the pressure, or maybe take it off, only to increase it all the more.

Sid was moving against him, arching into him in a slow, seeking rhythm he doubted she was even aware of.

Mac was aware of it, by God. Aware that the only thing between the woman beneath him and one glorious, joining thrust was the soft material of her yoga pants and his own self-discipline.

"MacKenzie." She cradled his jaw against her palm and hid her face against his throat. "You're scaring me. Stop thinking."

Mac was respectful of the challenge ahead of them, but scared wasn't on the agenda. He rolled them, so Sid was on top. "Better?"

"Not that kind of scared." She straddled him, intimately, no hesitation about matching up the parts that wanted to match up most. In her gaze he saw uncertainty, but he prayed there was no real trepidation.

"Tell me what kind of scared, Sidonie. We have all

day." He let his fingers run along the undersides of her breasts, couldn't stop himself from touching her.

"I'll… You'll… This isn't just a hookup."

"Of course it isn't. You deserve more than that, and you know it now." He closed a thumb and forefinger around one nipple, and her eyelids went to half-mast. "You have more than that to give."

She would give it to him. He tugged on her breast gently; her eyes closed, and her shoulders dropped.

"Do that again, please."

He did, both breasts, and spent long, happy minutes pleasuring her with only his hands on her breasts. A light touch of the fingers, a caress with his palm, a delicate brush over the ruched flesh of her nipples, and she was swaying into his hands, her body humming with what he could give her.

Whatever else Sid was, she was not scared. Not scared anymore. Her body knew better, and as for her heart, Mac could hardly blame her. He slid his hands lower, down rib by rib, to play around her navel, then to trace the bones at the crests of her hips.

"Eyes closed, Sidonie. See with your body." The way he was seeing with his hands. The feel of her skin was incredible. Soft, warm, pliant, and alive. She had freckles sprinkled across her chest and down her arms, but not on her breasts, not on her flat belly. He untied the drawstring of her pants, the line about packages tied up with string flitting through his mind.

A favorite thing, indeed.

He watched her face as he stroked his thumbs over the fabric where reddish-blond curls hid. She arched forward, her expression that of a woman listening intently to a faint, sweet melody on a soft, warm breeze.

"Relax, Sidonie. I'm not even touching you."

Ah, but Mac was moving her. He could tell that from the tension in her neck, the lift of her chin that had her hair falling down her back to brush his thighs.

He'd walked into her yard this morning, aware only of the need to be with her, to assure himself she was hale and happy. He hadn't called—what if she'd said it wasn't a good time for him to come by?

But she'd been waiting on the same porch where he'd shelled endless gallons of peas, shucked bushels of sweet corn, snipped acres of beans, and read entire libraries of police procedurals.

Her hair had been loose for once, no bra, just two pieces of black cotton fabric covering her on a cool, overcast Sunday morning.

She'd looked adorable, sitting on her swing, money jar at her elbow, the classifieds spread in her lap. Sidonie in her own element was sweet, dear, and precious, but also, to Mac's starved body and lonely eye, *hot*.

Through the cotton of her yoga pants, he used his thumb to start a slow, rhythmic pressure against the seat of her pleasure.

"MacKenzie." A little surprise in her voice, some relief too. She kept her eyes closed, but grabbed his free hand and placed it over her breast. He didn't oblige her immediately, but instead enjoyed the weight and heft of one rosy, perfect breast against his palm.

"Damn you." She covered his hand with her own, and closed his fingers around her nipple.

"Greedy, Sidonie. I like it when you're greedy." He gave her a small pressure, and her hips rolled forward against his thumb. Greedy and hungry, both.

He made a study of her, increasing pace and pressure, only to back off and urge her within kissing range with a hand at her nape. When she was kissing him back enthusiastically, he'd drift his mouth down to close it over a tight nipple, all the while aware of her rocking herself against his touch.

She was growing damp and her breathing was deeper. Mac was damned near throbbing with a want he fully intended to satisfy, but not until he'd taken the best care of his lady that discipline, imagination, and manual dexterity allowed.

He eased his hand away from her breast, and again intensified both the pressure and the speed of his thumb.

"This time, you let go for me, Sidonie. For both of us."

She made a sound of want and wonder, rocking harder against his hand.

"Mac...Ken...zie..."

She was close. Close enough that when Mac got his mouth over one nipple and drew in synchrony with the rhythm of his thumb, she went over the edge.

Sid was silent, her head thrown back, her body grinding against him, her pleasure drawing her up so strongly he could feel the pulse of it wracking her through the pad of his thumb. He watched shamelessly while she surrendered to long moments of glorious feminine satisfaction.

When the storm passed, she hung over him, her hair falling forward to curtain them both as she braced herself on his chest.

"Come here." He urged her against him, needing to hold her more than he'd needed to bring her pleasure. That she'd trusted him this far was almost gift enough.

Almost.

"MacKenzie Knightley."

May Sidonie please have many occasions to speak his name in that very wondering, wistful, pleased tone.

"I'm here." He matched his breathing to hers, and organized her hair, drawing it back over her shoulders and twisting it into a single rope.

"MacKenzie, you have undone me."

"Good. I'll undo you more before we leave this bed."

She kissed his throat. "I believe you mean that, and if I could locate my common sense, I'd be mildly alarmed by it."

"It's all right to be alarmed." He squeezed her backside, and she sighed into his ear, so he lingered, massaging and kneading and generally getting to know another wonderful part of her.

"That should not feel so good." While she contemplated this injustice—or whatever her female brain was up to—she took his earlobe in her mouth and sucked gently.

"Everything about you feels good to me, Sidonie. Why shouldn't it feel good to you?"

He made words for her and fashioned them into sentences, because he understood about pacing, about giving her time to find her balance, so she could enjoy losing it again. Though this time, in fairness to the arousal straining its leash harder, moment by moment, Mac would lose his balance as well.

"I want you on top." Sid punctuated this pronouncement by brushing her thumb over his nipple, then resting her hand on the side of his ribs. He understood the implied threat.

He was fair game now. Thank a generous God.

"Then you will have me on top, though it might

be more comfortable for you in some other position," Mac said.

She brushed his hair off his forehead. "I have no intention of remaining comfortable, MacKenzie."

"I'm careful, Sid. I won't hurt you, but there are positions that make it easier for me to behave, so to speak."

"For God's sake, MacKenzie. You don't be careful with me, all right? You be passionate."

Sid was bossing him—always a good sign—but her touch on his face as she stroked his hair back again was so gentle, and the look in her eyes was one of concern.

Of tenderness.

If Mac hadn't known it before, he knew it in that moment: he was in trouble. He was in deep, deep trouble.

"Stop fretting." Sid pushed Mac's hair off his forehead in a caress he seemed to enjoy, but then, she hadn't found one he didn't enjoy. He liked her hands on him, plain and simple. He practically purred when she touched him, anywhere, anyhow. Her body against his, her mouth on his, her hands on him in any location, they all provoked him to move in the subtle ways that invited her to keep touching him, to stay near.

Exactly where Sid wanted to be.

She climbed off him and lay on her back, taking Mac's hand in hers.

"I tell myself I've forgotten what a pleasure it is to share intimacies with a man, but, MacKenzie, it was never like this. You're with me in ways most guys don't know how to be, or don't care enough to be. With you, I have nowhere to hide."

He rolled up on his side, perusing her with a frown. "If you need to hide, then what are you doing naked in bed with another person?"

The question was sincere, perplexed almost.

"You really don't understand casual sex, do you?"

He stared at her for a long moment, his expression unfathomable but solemn. Then he climbed over her, which was exactly where she wanted *him*...almost.

Sid patted his butt. "I want to be naked, mister."

He was off her in an instant, kneeling beside her while she scooted out of her pants.

"I could devour you." He traced a finger down her middle when she lay before him naked, his touch gentle and at stark variance with the harsh rasp of his voice. He cupped her sex, a caress as arousing as it was comforting.

"Do you know, MacKenzie, being with you like this has shown me something a little hard to deal with." Sid lay on her back, his hand resting on her mons, while she wanted him over her, inside her, all around her.

He brushed his fingers through her curls, a slow, mesmerizing touch. "What has it shown you?"

"I've had heartache in my life because I can't have children, but it was never specific. The pain was simple—no children for me, so sorry. But I suffer an extra sense of loss to know I will never have children *with you*. I shouldn't say that—we're not technically even lovers yet, are we?—and yet with you, I think it might be all right to say such things."

Sid hoped so, hoped she hadn't just descended into a female exercise in Blowing It with a man who wasn't interested in commitment, even if he did talk about exclusives.

Mac pushed her knees apart, so she was exposed to him, then kept his hand on her knee.

"You say I don't understand casual sex, and you're right. There's a reason for that."

Sid didn't move. Didn't deny him the most intimate sight of her, because she had a looming sense she was about to be given an intimate glimpse of *him* as well.

"A reason, MacKenzie?"

He kissed her knee, his expression sad and self-mocking. "You are not the only person in this bed who cannot be a parent, Sidonie Lindstrom."

Cannot be a parent? What did that mean to a man who had never married? Her puzzlement must have shown on her face.

"You are barren, a difficult, indelicate word, but I am sterile, which is somehow an even more unfortunate appellation, imbued with not even backhanded compassion."

He closed his eyes, a token of surrender against the sadness vibrating through him. Sid had felt its echo time and again, watching other people's children playing in the park. Seeing other people's children tagging along in the grocery store. Hearing other people's children laugh at the zoo. Watching other people's children grow into adults capable of renewing life in their turn, while Sid merely grew older and more resigned.

More sad and brittle and dried-up and *barren*.

"Love me." Sid drew Mac down into the cradle of her body. When he pulled away and his gaze strayed to the pile of clothes on her chair, she read his mind.

"What would be the point of that kind of protection, MacKenzie? We've both been abstinent for years. I get tested regularly. I'm assuming you've been tested as well, and we don't have to worry." *Worry*, as if either one of them would worry did they conceive a child. "We don't have to worry about consequences. Please, just love me. Let me love you."

He smiled that sweet, piratical smile. "I did not want to presume."

"Love me," she said again, trying to make it more of a plea, less of a command. "Please, love me now."

After all of his careful, assiduous foreplay, the lovemaking was gratifyingly straightforward. He eased himself inside Sid, slowly, gradually, and Sid felt the sun rise in her body. The more of him she took, the greater her pleasure and sense of rightness.

"We're doing OK?" Mac braced himself above her, a slight tremor in his arms.

"We're wonderful, MacKenzie, soon to be even more so." Sid kissed him, borrowing his tactic, while she caressed his back in long, slow strokes. She was close to coming without either of them moving, though she assured herself that novelty was a result of years of abstinence.

And of being with him, her conscience added. Mac's honesty was more of an aphrodisiac than all his studied moves or even his considerable endowments.

Sid undulated beneath him, loving the sensations welling up from her center. "I'm close, MacKenzie. Where are you?"

"Right…here." He moved with her, their rhythm languid. Sid had never given in to the temptation to have unprotected sex before. She'd never trusted her partners enough to even consider it. She trusted MacKenzie, and if ever two people deserved the pleasure of unfettered intimacy, it was she and MacKenzie Knightley.

"I'm going to come," she whispered in his ear. "I am…" Her body drew up, ecstatically, while Mac kept moving slowly. The combination of his rhythm and her hunger made for a protracted, intense experience of both pleasure and intimacy.

"I wanted to keep my eyes open," Sid said, sighing her contentment. "I wanted to see you while I came. At least I could feel you."

"So come again," Mac said. "This time, you can see and feel me both." He hitched his hips, shifting the angle slightly, and Sid gave up any semblance of control. She might be sore—she might be *lame*—but she let him rock her from one peak to the next until she didn't know where one orgasm ended and the slow, lovely build toward the next one began.

"MacKenzie?"

"Love?"

"This time, you too."

He said nothing, not until he slipped a hand down under her backside, anchoring himself against her.

"Kiss me, Sidonie."

Oh, God, the things the man's tongue could say without uttering a word. Everything amplified: the cadence of his hips and the thrust of his tongue, all slower, more powerful than ever, until Sid was exploding once more into pleasure upon pleasure. She keened against his shoulder, unable to keep silent as he drove into her.

She was coasting down, her mouth still pressed to his shoulder, when Mac tucked even closer.

"Hold me, Sidonie. Hold me tight."

She had to remember to breathe as he moved inside her. This was lovemaking, not simply sex. Not lust, but ardor, passion, and holy bejeezus, *intimacy*. Mac's breathing became harsher, and his grip on her grew more secure.

Sid felt a spreading warmth inside as Mac began to shudder in her arms.

"Jesus…God…Sidonie…" His voice was low, a rasping whisper in her ear as he pushed into her hard and spent himself against her womb.

She held him tight, tears pricking her eyes, and closed herself around him, inside and out.

This was how it was supposed to be. This intensity and sharing, this closeness. Sid knew a glancing sorrow for the younger woman she'd been, a woman willing to settle for so very much less on too many occasions.

As Sid stroked her hand down Mac's back and pressed his head to her shoulder, she knew profound sorrow for MacKenzie as well.

—⁓—

Sid was at least giving him time to literally catch his breath before she started asking questions. Mac was grateful for that, but he also wasn't dreading the questions as much as he'd feared he might.

She kissed his cheek.

"Is that a nice way of saying I'm too heavy?" He took more weight on his forearms but didn't want to leave her. To be joined this way, no latex, no gooey contraceptives or Popsicle fruit scents—it was fortunate he'd had no previous experiences with unprotected sex, because he liked it.

With Sidonie, he liked it a lot.

Who would have thought infertility had any fringe benefits?

"You're not too heavy." She kissed his throat, her tongue swiping up his neck toward his ear. "I simply feel like kissing."

"Like devouring me?" What a lovely idea.

"Maybe over the course of several servings, but, yes, like devouring you. I'll walk funny for the next week, MacKenzie, but people will be too distracted by my idiot grin to notice."

"So you're OK?" And, yes, he worried. He'd gotten carried away, wonderfully so.

"I am blissful, physically, but scoot off me and get on your back."

How he loved the way she patted his butt, as if it were her very favorite butt in the whole entire world. He heaved off her and did as she told him, loving the unself-conscious way Sid crossed to the bathroom.

Displaying *his* very favorite butt in the whole entire world.

She came back to the bed, carrying a washcloth, but more than that, Mac noticed the rosy flush on her chest.

She propped a hip on the edge of the bed and lifted his softening cock away from his body.

"The mighty sword does wilt." The washcloth was warm, and her touch gentle. "One wondered if it could."

"It can unwilt," Mac said, closing his eyes lest he be caught ogling the sway of her breasts as she handled him. This meant he became more aware of the sensation of her moving the warm washcloth over him. He opened his eyes and stared resolutely at the ceiling.

"Promises, promises." Sid tossed the washcloth onto her dresser, some kind of heavy dark antique with a slab of marble across the top.

Mac patted the mattress. "Get in here. You've earned your rest."

"Now you say I can laze about. Generous of you, MacKenzie." Her smile was wicked as she climbed in beside him, but she hiked herself up on the pillows, wrapped her arms around him, and wrestled him to lie along her side with his cheek resting on her breast.

Sidonie Lindstrom was protective of those she cared about, and in her choice of embrace, Mac concluded he fell into that privileged category. He nuzzled her breast and settled in to be, for the first time in his long and sometimes lonely life…cuddled.

"Those two engagements, MacKenzie. Why did they fail?"

Cuddled and interrogated, an interesting combination, but it felt to Mac as if by holding him so close, Sid was trying to protect him from the pain of answering truthfully.

"They failed, as you put it, because I could not give my prospective wives children."

"Idiots, the both of them. How did they know?"

Such contempt in her voice. He wanted to make her say it again. Idiots, idiots, *idiots*.

"The first one was a pre-law major, and she wanted a pre-nup agreement spelling out that we would have not more than two children, unless they were the same gender, in which case we could try for a third, but not more than three. Then it occurred to her she'd best ensure we could have any, and I flunked the test."

"You flunked?"

"Medically sterile, as measured in both motility and count."

"You had no explanation for this state of affairs?"

"Yes, there was an explanation. The doctor who did the test for me said I'd smoked too much pot, and if I knocked it off, there was some possibility I'd regain my ability to reproduce."

"You did not hit him, did you? Did not report him to the AMA, did not sue the idiot."

"No, I did not." He nuzzled her again for her perceptivity. As if he'd had time, funds, or the inclination to use recreational drugs when he was working two part-time jobs, carrying a full class load, and keeping an eye on the rest of his family.

"And idiot number two? You disclosed your situation to her, didn't you, and she flounced off to go have a litter of Barbie and Ken dolls with some other idiot?"

"I did tell her, but infertility was just the straw that broke the camel's back. I'd started dating her in part because she'd said she didn't want kids, but when it came down to it, she decided she wanted the freedom to change her mind, so, yes, off she went."

"And here you are, mine for the devouring. Their loss."

Mac waited for the rest of Sid's questions, resisting the urge to taste her nipple, until he realized Sid's breathing had become suspiciously regular.

He'd worn her out, poor thing. Carefully, he extricated himself from her embrace, and arranged himself to curve around behind her. His John Henry fit very comfortably in the curve of her backside; her breast nicely filled his hand.

The rain pattered down on the tin roof, the clock said it wasn't even noon, and by God, at long, long last all was right with MacKenzie Knightley's world.

Sid slept for nearly an hour in her lover's arms, a sweet, trusting sleep that left her at peace and pleased with life.

Her lover. She'd never had a lover before. She'd had hookups, a fiancé, a husband, but never a man who cared enough to inflict such overwhelming pleasure on her. MacKenzie's lovemaking had no selfishness to it, none. Even when he allowed himself pleasure, Sid had the sense his loss of control, his trust in her, was yet another gift laid at her feet.

Mac hadn't rushed off when they'd eventually left the bed. He'd helped her dress, and let her provide him the same assistance. How intimate that was, standing still for him to pull a sweater over her head, sitting so he could put socks on her feet.

He'd taken the time to show her how his belt buckle worked, another small intimacy, one Sid particularly treasured.

They'd shared a cup of tea, and she'd known what he was doing. He was explaining to her how to knit what had happened in her bed into the rest of her day—their day, their lives. He'd insisted, by making her a cup of tea, by scolding her for going without socks, that lovemaking would be normal and right between them.

When they'd sat in the kitchen listening to the rain, he hadn't withdrawn, but his touches became the mundane interactions any two people in any kitchen might share. A brush of hands, of bodies, a pat on the shoulder. *His* hand, *his* body, *his* shoulder, and to Sid, no aspect of Mac Knightley would ever qualify as mundane.

When he took his leave, he'd held her, not for very

long, but with a perfect, possessive snugness, one that said every inch of his body was open to her. A younger woman might have clung to him, might have looked for ways to prolong the encounter, would almost certainly have led him back upstairs.

By leaving her in peace, though, Mac was assuring her he'd be back, and Sidonie appreciated the solitude he'd given her before she had to fetch Luis from the stables.

Time to savor the day, and even savor the future.

That future needed to include gainful employment. Sid shuffled her stack of help wanted ads, so the one she'd found last night sat on top.

This one wasn't for the blue- and pink-collar work typical for the area. Hartman and Whitney, described as a "midsized family-owned professional services firm" was looking for someone to head their Human Resources Department. The ad emphasized that general business management education was sought, as well as applicable experience.

Sid had the education, she had the experience, and the place was nearby in the county seat. The job could not be more convenient, and as long as the benefits were decent, it really didn't matter much about the salary. She needed to pay the bills for a few months until the estate settled, no more, so off her application and résumé did go to the email listed in the ad.

The odd thing was, when she searched on the firm name, nothing came up. No website, no mentions in the press, nothing but a white pages listing. But then, Damson County was hardly a hotbed of commercial enterprise, and a website might still be seen by a conservative organization as unnecessary.

She wasn't due at the stable for another hour, so she had time to check email, which included a short just-checking-on-you email from Thor, and a reply from Hartman and Whitney.

Sid opened the second message, expecting to find an auto-reply. She was dumbfounded to read that a Gail Russo—apparently open for business on a Sunday—was offering her one of three interview slots…the very next day.

"What to wear?" Bojangles was no help, and when Sid fetched Luis home from the stables, he was no help either.

"You look good in your baggy jeans and old T-shirts," he said over a dinner of quinoa-feta salad and grilled chicken. "You have this one, Sid. I can feel it. My grandmother had the sight, you know."

"And she grew tomatoes on the fire escape, a sure sign of prescience. I don't know how dressy to be out here. In Baltimore, I'd know exactly how to play it, and an online search of any professional services firm in the city would yield something."

"Maybe they do top secret work for the feds. Camp David isn't that far."

Not a bad guess for a kid who was inhaling his dinner. "Maybe, or they're some kind of government contractor, but I saw no requirement to have security clearances."

"You could call Mac. He grew up around here, and he might know."

He *would* know. He grew up around here, and he paid attention. "I don't want to tell him I'm interviewing. If he does know these people, he might put in a word for me."

"This would be a bad thing? The man you intend to marry puts in a word for you?"

"Luis Martineau, you are jeopardizing your dessert."

"Four bathrooms, Sid. You won't listen to me."

She took a bite of a very good salad. "What are we doing for your birthday?"

"Taking my driver's test?"

"You haven't had your permit quite long enough. We can go out for dinner, for starters, or maybe you'd like to step out with a young lady?"

Though step out where? To the pizza joint up past the feed store?

The change in topic at least got Luis off the man-she-was-marrying riff, but yielded nothing in the way of plans for his sixteenth birthday. Maybe Mac would have some ideas.

Sid fell asleep, a little nervous about tomorrow's interview, but mostly pleased as hell with her day.

She had MacKenzie Knightley for her lover, a gorgeous, considerate, sexy man who seemed to like the very things in Sid others had objected to: her independence, her bluntness, her demanding nature. He understood about not being able to have children. Better than even that, she had an exclusive with him from the beginning, because he was a man who insisted on honesty and integrity.

Maybe Luis wasn't so far off the mark after all.

Chapter 15

"WHAT THE HELL DO YOU MEAN, YOU'RE GIVING notice?"

Trent's voice wasn't raised, but the tone was incredulous. Papa Bear was rattled because he hadn't seen this coming. Across the conference table, Mac exchanged a look with James that confirmed they'd have to handle this discussion.

"My arrangement here is the same as any other associate," Gail Russo said. "I'm an at-will employee. You can let me go at any time, and I can quit at any time. I'm not jumping ship, though. I'll stick around until I've trained a replacement who will take as good care of my people as I tried to."

"As you did." That from James, who watched Gail with the considering expression of a man who'd watched more than his share of women. "You won't entertain a counteroffer, Gail?"

The question would soothe and flatter, which gave Mac time to think through his own reaction to Gail's announcement. She'd been with them since they'd incorporated, she was their first hire, and she'd done a good job.

Not a great job, a good job. As good a job as an administrative assistant could do when company growth beached her in the position of head of human resources.

"I'm not leaving for another job."

"You're off to teach Zumba," Trent said, his tone more bewildered than teasing. "Dammit, that's three employees in three years, abandoning a perfectly respectable career in law for what? A room full of sweaty people dancing around and calling it exercise."

"I'm going to graduate school," Gail said, chin tipping up. "And I'll get in some traveling, and I'll wear sweats and slides, and sleep in on nice days, and I'll equip myself with some useful credentials before I look for another job."

"You have expertise, Gail. You have experience; you've worn as many hats here as anybody, and worn them well." James smoothed his fingers over the back of Gail's hand. A caress, not a pat. "We'll miss you."

She looked relieved to have his support, but guilt and defensiveness lurked in her eyes. "There's more."

"You talk Debbie into going to grad school, and I will hunt you down and drag you back here," Trent said. "I can't lose you and my best paralegal at the same time."

"Debbie will be happy here as long as Gino is happy here." Gail studied her nails, which were painted neon watermelon—something only James might have picked up on as a warning sign of impending change. "I've set up the interviews today, because none of you have court. This is considered a department head position, so you all have to meet the candidates."

"How many are there?" Mac asked while he mentally rearranged his schedule. If Gail was leaving—and she was—then a replacement was imperative. Human resources was an aspect of the company that should remain largely invisible, like paying the bills. Nobody thought much about it, but if it wasn't adequately tended to, all hell could break loose.

"I started with a half-dozen candidates, each scheduled for thirty minutes. Do you want to see the résumés?"

"Let's not," James suggested. "We can study the résumés later. The candidate's first impression will carry the most weight with me, because you would not ask us to spend time with anyone who isn't qualified on paper."

"Not a bad idea," Trent said. "Was there anything we could have done, Gail? I wasn't teasing all those times I offered to send you to law school."

The expressions crossing her face were hard to decipher, but regret was among them. Somebody had carried a torch for Trent, a quiet torch.

"I should have taken you up on that," Gail said. "DC has good law schools with strong evening programs, and I can see where the practice of law fits well with a human resources background, but if I did that—"

"You'd be stuck here for life," Mac interrupted, feeling some of Trent's consternation. What was so bad about being stuck here for life?

Gail tidied up a stack of papers, the résumés probably. One was pink, several were cream stationery.

"Someday, I want a family, and the practice of law…" Ah.

"If you two will leave us," Mac said, "Gail and I will negotiate terms of severance."

Trent's expression shuttered; James looked relieved. Trent shook Gail's hand; James kissed her cheek. They both wished her luck, and thank God, left Mac alone with his soon-to-be-former head of HR.

"You're sitting there, thinking you're letting us down," Mac said.

"I am, but it isn't only that." Gail didn't look exactly middle-aged—she wasn't much past thirty—but she bore the signs of a woman whom life had overwhelmed. "I'm in a rut here, Mac. I do a good job, but anybody would do a good job for you three. I'm not—this isn't as much of a relief as I thought it would be."

Mac got out the corporate checkbook, more so Gail would think he was only half listening, when in fact, she had his whole attention.

"I'm not happy, and it's my own fault. I'm lonely, and I want a family, and the good ones here are taken, with the exception of present company."

"Now you'll tell me I've always been your favorite?" He slid a folded check across the table at her and offered a smile to leaven the moment.

"You were always the guy who could solve the hardest problems," she said, taking the check. "You were the guy I'd want in a foxhole with me, but you were the guy I worried about the most too. Still do."

That surprised him, but he wasn't about to unpack her comment, lest he find she—who wanted a family— had been carrying a torch for him too. All the ladies carried torches for James, making a perfect hat trick of emotional land mines upon which Mac would not step.

"Stay in touch, Gail. You helped us get off the ground, and we don't forget who our friends are. You ever need a reference, you have three of them."

She was about to tear up, so Mac took a leaf from James's book, and kissed her cheek in parting. A few weeks ago, he might have simply shook hands, or even left without any parting gesture, but Gail was a lady in difficulties, and a little gallantry wasn't too much to ask.

Though why on earth would she have worried about him?

———⁓⁓⁓———

Sid was relieved to conclude that Hartman and Whitney was a first-class operation. The grounds of the low-rise building housing the firm were landscaped with walking paths and with big trees, azaleas not yet blooming, and cheery beds of red and yellow tulips. A mailbox stood outside the main door, allowing Sid to send James a signed version of his land-use agreement.

The place had plenty of parking—city girls were big on free, well-lit parking—the windows were spanking clean, and the carpet in the lobby plush and spotless. The armchairs had none of the frayed seams and nubby upholstery of furniture left too long in public use, and the people coming and going were energetic, if not always smiling.

More to the point, Sid wasn't left to cool her heels in the lobby with six other interviewees. Somebody knew what they were doing and cared enough to do it well.

A door opened behind the receptionist's desk, and a smiling brunette emerged. "I'm Gail Russo, whom you'll be replacing if you get the position. You must be Ms. Sidonie Lindstrom?"

The lady was well put together, dressed in a pale blue suit, and wearing makeup Sid considered "trying a little too hard." Maybe Gail was a local gal, or maybe Sid shouldn't have let her subscription to *Cosmo* lapse.

"Sidonie Lindstrom, pleased to meet you."

Gail swiped a badge down a security reader, proving that whatever Hartman and Whitney did, they were willing to spend a little on keeping it confidential.

"You're probably used to interviewing with HR first, Sidonie, or do you go by Sid?"

"Either is fine, and in truth, I haven't interviewed in quite a while. I held my last position for more than five years, and had only a couple of other jobs before that."

"We don't have high turnover here." Gail led Sid past a secretarial station and down a quiet hallway. "It's a family-owned firm, and the partners try to make it a good place to work."

"May I ask why you're leaving?" And what did this family-owned firm *do*?

The smile Gail gave her was a little sad, but honest — not an HR smile.

"Time to move on. I'm going back to school, because most people in my position have a master's, or at least some certifications. I don't mind telling you that your credentials were the most impressive in the short stack."

"Good to know."

Sid was also glad to know the firm didn't put a lot of money into window dressing, only to stuff its employees into rickety cubbyholes with no privacy and less visual appeal. The offices Sid glimpsed had touches of originality — a live ficus, pictures of the hubby and kids — and yet the whole place had a tidy, businesslike feel.

This could work. She let open-mindedness blossom into hope, and determined to make as positive an impression as she could. Damson Valley was not where she'd hoped to grow old and gray, but the reasons to stay were piling up.

"The partners have not seen your résumé," Gail was saying. "They don't want to prejudice their first impression by what's on paper. The clients and employees will be dealing with you, not your résumé."

"Interesting approach. How many partners are there?"

"Three, and they're all good guys, great guys. They're waiting for you in the conference room down the hall. I'm happy to make the introductions, though we're not particularly formal here at Hartman and Whitney."

A test: Did the candidate have the self-confidence to walk into a room full of strangers and introduce herself?

Hell, yeah.

Sid paused outside the door to make sure she had extra copies of her résumé, then pasted a smile on her face, rapped twice on the door, strode into the room, and froze.

What the hell?

The Knightley brothers were getting to their feet, but not any version of the Knightley brothers Sid had seen before. They were in three-piece suits, cuff links and tie tacks gleaming, hair perfectly combed. James looked delicious in a pale green suit and cream shirt, while Trent made gray pinstripes look handsome. A whiff of clove and cinnamon told Sid who she'd see if she turned her head a fraction of an inch.

Mac was even more impressive than his brothers, in a dark blue ensemble that had to have been hand-tailored for him.

They were battle ready. Sharp in a professional way, and not at all like the nice fellows who had helped Sid knock down her hog house. These guys were savvy and confident. Everything, from their dress to their posture

to the way they casually dominated the cushy conference room, screamed corporate competence.

As Sid absorbed that shock, she came to several other
conclusions, none of them happy. She set her shoulder
bag on the table with a thud and put her hands on her hips.

Despite the sense of dread roiling in her gut, Sid kept
her voice level.

"Where are the horses, MacKenzie? You *told* me you
were a horseshoer."

―――・^^^・―――

"Sidonie." James, God bless him, went toward Sid with
a hand outstretched in welcome. Mac could read her
though, and knew James would be lucky to keep that hand
attached to his arm. "A pleasure to see you, and I have to
assume you're the first candidate for the HR job."

She let him take her hand and steer her to the seat
at the head of the conference table―Mac's usual
post―but she threw Mac a look over her shoulder
that boded ill.

It boded bloody damned disaster for a guy who'd put
off a dozen times having the I'm-a-lawyer discussion
with her. Also the my-brothers-are-lawyers-too conversation, and the we-own-a-law-firm chat.

"I'm not sure I am here to interview for the job,"
she said, visually measuring each man as he took a seat
around the table. "I thought MacKenzie was a farrier,
and clearly he is not."

"He is." Trent jumped in, treating Sid to his best I'm-
your-lawyer-you-can-trust-me smile, probably the worst
move he could make. "He's also the managing partner
here at Hartman and Whitney."

"Which he owns with you two." Her expression said, *You two shyster-meisters*. "So what kind of business is this? You don't have a website, the ad was very general, and I got nothing specific when I googled you."

Sid was too astute not to see the looks Mac's brothers were tossing him. They were tap-dancing as fast as they could, but it was time to end this.

"We own a law firm, Sid," Mac said. "James is in charge of corporate clients, Trent heads up domestic, and I have the criminal defense department. We recently put Hannah in charge of alternative dispute resolution and collaborative law. I also shoe horses, and James is a CPA."

Sidonie studied her hands, hands that had touched Mac so sweetly, hands he wanted to reach for right now. When she looked up, the disappointment in her gaze was probably invisible to his brothers, but Mac saw it plainly.

Not even anger, which he might have known how to deal with, but disappointment.

Sid rose and snatched up her shoulder bag. "Gentlemen, I wish you all a good day. I'm sorry. As much as I need this job, I'm not what you're looking for. Good-bye."

She'd looked Mac square in the eye as she'd spoken the last word, two little syllables that sent Mac's world straight to the bottom of the muck pit.

"Hire any-damned-body you please," he said to his brothers as he followed Sid out. He caught up to her in the lobby, and when he laid a hand on her arm, she whirled on him.

"Shame on you, MacKenzie Knightley." She kept

her voice down, her tone civil. "You led me to believe you were a horseshoer. An aw-shucks farm boy who looked good with his shirt off and knew how to use his hands. You let me—" She looked away, tears glinting in her eyes.

Goddamned tears, because her husband had dumped her, Tony had died, Luis could be snatched away at any moment, and the guy who'd taken her to bed apparently couldn't be trusted either.

"I don't like lawyers," she went on. "Lawyers have authored more misery for me and my family than all the biblical plagues combined. And while I could never hate you, I've grown to positively loathe surprises. This is not a nice surprise, MacKenzie."

She could have called it a betrayal and not been far wrong, and yet, Mac had to state his case.

"Given how you're reacting, when was I supposed to tell you this truth?" He kept his voice down too, but he wanted to shout, to plead, to shake her so she'd see reason.

Was his profession the only part of him that mattered to her?

"You had a hundred opportunities to tell me, and I don't even care so much that you're a damned lawyer. In fact, I'm sure you're a very good lawyer—also an ethical lawyer. I care that you weren't honest with me. At the very least I need time to sort out how I feel about your...dissembling."

Dissembling wasn't quite lying. Mac took small comfort from that distinction as they emerged into the sunshine of a pleasant spring day.

"I wanted to tell you, but the moment was never right."

Sid's expression went from disappointed to sad, and that chilled Mac right down to his Johnston and Murphy's.

"What else can you say? Of course you *wanted* to tell me." She turned her back on him, as if Bradford pears past their prime and rows of parked cars were more interesting than he was. "It might be a good idea if you looked for another place to keep those horses, MacKenzie."

"That will take a while." Forever, if he could manage it. Sid hadn't insisted, she'd only suggested, and she was a woman who could insist with the best of them when she needed to.

"Then you'd better start on it immediately, hadn't you?"

The words "I'm sorry" welled up in Mac's conscience, the words that might build on the punches she'd pulled, the crumbs of understanding she'd thrown him. He *had* lied by omission, and he'd dodged this confrontation.

He, a highly skilled courtroom attorney, and he'd dodged the confrontation. Sid wasn't a judge, and yet, he needed to present her with a Motion to Reconsider.

"Sidonie—"

"Not now, MacKenzie. Not here." Her tone said, *maybe not ever*. She walked away, her posture militarily erect as she crossed the parking lot and climbed into her little red Mustang.

She made the turn onto the road at a decorous speed, and quite possibly, drove out of Mac's life.

——◆◆◆——

"Get back in here." James took Mac by the arm and tugged him down the hallway toward the conference room. "That could have been worse."

"James, I love you like the precious baby brother you

are, but if you don't get your damned *frigging* hand off me, I'll wipe the floor with you."

"You're welcome to try. I'm sure Trent would referee, and Hannah and Vera would patch you up when I was done with you." James did not take his hand off Mac's arm until Mac was in the conference room, the door closed behind him, both his brothers watching him like a defendant who'd been under secure transport from the psych eval unit—the locked one, where the nurses of both genders looked like Russian weight lifters.

Trent broke a tense silence. "I told Gail not to send us any more interviewees until I call her. Sit down, MacKenzie, and answer a few questions."

The expressions both Trent and James wore sent Mac to his customary seat at the head of the table. They were worried about him. They *looked* pissed, and they'd probably *sound* pissed, but they were worried.

So was he.

"I take it Sidonie did not know how you make your living?" The question came from James, who obligingly poured Mac a cup of water from the pitcher on the credenza—as if Mac were on the witness stand, and opposing counsel was warming up for some grueling cross-examination.

"She assumed I'm a farrier, which I am. I did not volunteer that I belong—that we each belong—to a profession she loathes."

"You were planning to get around to it?" Trent conjectured.

"Of course he was." James leaned a hip on the table and studied Mac for a moment. "The way I see it, associating with us has done nothing but benefit Sid. She still has her foster care license because we scraped her hog house."

"At a profit to her," Trent added.

"The terms of the land deal I put before her are beneficial to her," James went on. "You're providing her income through Daisy's and Buttercup's board, and you arranged the free loan of Inskip's loader so she could sell her topsoil. Then there's the fact that Trent will represent Luis. I don't see how us being lawyers has worked to her detriment. Sid's sensible, and she'll figure that out."

"Sid's also lonely, emotionally wrung out, and proud as hell," Mac said. "She as much as said the greater wrong wasn't practicing law, it was not telling her we practice law."

"Like her entire life is an open book to you?" Trent groused as he flopped into the chair on Mac's right. "You haven't known each other that long."

"What I do for a living is not a detail. I can't see Sid forgiving and forgetting." Not anytime soon.

"She's stubborn," James said. "But what's the issue with lawyers? Everybody tells the occasional lawyer joke, but this is personal. What's behind it?"

"I don't know." Mac stared at his hands, hands that were aching at that very moment to caress Sid's hair, her face, her arms, her anything. "I know somebody who might be able to help me find out."

––⁂––

"Sid's upset over something." Luis scratched Thomas right on the midline of the pony's substantial belly. Thomas craned his neck, making Luis smile despite the seriousness of the topic.

Luis liked all the therapy ponies—some of them were big enough to qualify as horses—but Thomas was special. The horse's big dark eyes held compassion for fellow creatures to whom life wasn't always easy or kind.

"She doesn't say anything, she's eating junk, and she's jittery," Luis went on. "What is it with women, you know? Mac hasn't called all week, and I'm thinking maybe that's the trouble. I could call him." Luis moved his hand up under Thomas's shaggy mane. "Maybe it's just PMS, though. Sid takes all that stuff too seriously. But then, what do I know?"

Luis fell silent as he heard the sound of the stall door being unlatched.

"Could be the caffeine's giving her fits."

MacKenzie Knightley stood there in his usual jeans, boots, and faded denim shirt. The cuffs of his shirt were rolled back to reveal sinewy forearms, and the dirt on his hands suggested Mac had been working on a horse.

"Mac. You here to do Tom's feet?"

"No, I am here to ask a favor. Walk the fence with me?"

Luis did not want to be asked for any favors. People who moved on every few months weren't the best ones to rely on for favors, but Mac had done Luis some favors. A lot of favors, really. Big ones. This looked like an immediate kind of favor, which was good, because there was no telling where Luis would be next week.

"Let me top off Tom's water first."

Mac stepped out of the stall and waited silently while Luis tended to the horse. Mac was good at being silent, being quiet. Luis wanted to emulate that quality, though if being more than six feet tall was part of the trick, that might take some doing.

"Where to?" Luis asked when the horse's bucket was full.

"South mares' pasture. I want to see how Luna's doing."

He would. The guy had caretaker written all over him, and if Luna liked anybody, it was MacKenzie. Luis tried remaining quiet for about two minutes, before he decided silence wasn't accomplishing much.

"What's this favor?"

"Sid's pissed at me."

Luis risked a glance at Mac as they walked along. Mac wasn't hustling, but Luis still had to work some to keep up with him. Mac's expression was hard to read—a different kind of silence—and his body gave off tension.

"I wouldn't call it pissed," Luis said. "More disappointed. Disappointed is worse."

"That's for damned sure. Why does she hate lawyers?"

Was this the favor? Some family history, such as family applied to two people living in the same temporary household? Luis cast back, trying to recall what Sid had told him over the months of their acquaintance.

"When her mom died, the lawyers wanted to pop her into foster care. They were calling Social Services before they even asked Sid if she had anybody she could stay with. She was sixteen and very independent, had her own car and a job. She'd probably been taking care of herself by then for years anyhow. Then when Tony died—"

Maybe this was the favor, because it was harder to tell this part. Why was he sharing this information with MacKenzie?

"Don't violate confidences for me, Weese. Just tell me what you can."

"Why do you want to know?"

They'd reached the fence along the closest boundary of the south pasture. Most of the mares were nose down in the grass, a tail occasionally flicking at the few flies out this early in the season. Luna lay flat out in the sun, so still that if Luis hadn't seen her resting like that many times before, he'd have thought she was dead.

"Sid is upset with me." Mac propped a foot on the lowest fence board, his relaxed posture belying the tight misery in his words.

"Usually when Sid is upset, everybody for a hundred yards on either side knows about it, and then she's over it. She's gone quiet, Mac. I thought it was her"—he waved a hand over his middle—"female stuff."

"You know she can't have kids?" A sidewise glance accompanied this, suggesting Mac hoped he wasn't betraying a confidence himself.

"She told me, kind of made a joke about it early on. 'I can have kids, but only if the stork has hung up his wings for a social worker's license,' or something like that."

"I'm a lawyer."

"Yeah, so?"

"You knew?"

"I was at your house, dude. I saw the books in your study: William Blackstone, Black's Law Dictionary, biographies of Supreme Court Justices, the Maryland Bar Journal. A bunch of books that weigh more than I do and have titles longer than my arm. You have money coming out your ears. Of course you're a lawyer."

Luis had apparently stumped the great Perry Mason of Damson Valley.

"You didn't say anything?" Mac asked.

"No harm, no foul. Except now I guess there is harm. Sid doesn't like you lawyering?"

"If I'd told her right up front, she might have reconciled herself to it, or she's assured herself she would have. She doesn't like that I didn't disclose this, or that my brothers are also lawyers."

"All three of you? Not good, bro. How'd she find out?"

This was odd, Mac talking to Luis as if he were an adult. Odd, a little uncomfortable, and a little nice too. To think he had some help to offer MacKenzie Knightley, who likely never needed anybody for anything.

"How she found out was bad. She tossed her hat in the ring for the position of head of human resources for us, and came to interview at the law office without knowing exactly what the midsized, family-owned professional services firm did for its coin."

Luis climbed up on the fence, though sitting on fence boards was a short-term undertaking.

"You screwed up?" he asked.

"I am in shit up to my eyeballs with that woman, and my brothers are none too impressed with me either."

"Welcome to my world."

"What's that supposed to mean?"

"Everything turns to shit, and you can hardly figure out how before it's turning to shit again." Court hearings could turn things to composted, top-quality shit in about five minutes flat.

"Life isn't supposed to be like that, Luis, and you never told me exactly what happened when Tony died. I know the estate lawyers aren't exactly breaking land-speed records to get the estate settled, but Sid wouldn't let me do anything about that."

"Those guys. They're enough to make anybody hate lawyers. You know Tony had life insurance money go into a trust for me, and Sid's the trustee, but she hasn't even been given a copy of the trust document?"

"Life insurance proceeds don't normally pass through the estate."

"Like I understand what that means?"

"It means the estate being settled should have nothing to do with your trust getting off the ground. Sid should be free to make disbursements from that trust right damned now, unless the terms of the trust forbid it."

Like one more instance of lawyers holding things up would endear Mac to Sid?

"Tony told me the terms," Luis said. "Sid can spend that money any way she thinks will benefit me. Not just for college or grad school or clothes. It's up to her. Tony wanted it that way."

Mac's expression wasn't puzzled, exactly, but very focused. "You and Tony talked about this?"

"Tony left me pretty much alone, because the whole gay thing meant he had to be extra careful."

Mac scraped his boot against the bottom board, and Luna's ear twitched. "Careful how? Gays don't molest children any more than anybody else does. Trent does enough child abuse work that I know that much."

"Yeah, well, tell it to the newspapers, would you? We talked some. Tony was a good guy."

The look Mac gave him then was enough to make anybody squirm, so Luis focused on Luna, focused on trying to mentally communicate with the horse to get up and come see her visitors.

Not even an ear twitch.

"You were telling me what happened when Tony died that made Sid's dislike for lawyers even worse, though trying to throw her in foster care probably did enough damage for a lifetime."

Mac was a man swamped with misery and trying not to show it, like a kid new to foster care tried not to admit he missed his mom's rotten, stinking dump in public housing because it was *home*. Didn't even admit it to himself, if he was smart.

"They tried to say Tony committed suicide," Luis said, "so the insurance company wouldn't have to pay the death benefit, which is a lot of money."

"Then they would have failed. I don't think there's a judge in the country who would say contracting AIDS is a method of committing suicide."

"Not the AIDS, the slamming his car into a bridge abutment at sixty miles an hour. There was another car involved, but that driver died too, and it was hard to figure out what happened."

"Accident reconstruction is not an exact science, but I gather Tony's death wasn't ruled a suicide?"

"It was not, but Sid's limited patience with lawyers and their stupid games has been exhausted. Then too, the foster care hearings don't always go the way Sid thinks they should, and that just gets her muttering about the damned lawyers all over again."

"So what do I do?" Mac asked quietly, as if he put the question to himself—or to the universe. "I haven't simply screwed up, I've made about the worst mistake I could have, given Sid's history."

"Hell if I know. I was rooting for you, but you weren't

straight with Sid. I'd cut another pony out of the herd if
I were you."

Mac scrubbed a hand over his face, then stared hard
at the small white horse lying in the sun. "Get up, girl.
It's a pretty day for a little walk, and your friends have
come to see you."

The horse could not possibly have heard him. He'd
kept his voice down, just above a whisper, and the
breeze was blowing toward them.

She got up and walked right to them. Slowly—she
had her dignity, after all—but she came right to Mac's
outstretched hand. Luis figured that was a good thing,
because a guy needed all the friends he could get.

Chapter 16

TWO WEEKS WENT BY WHILE SID DUTIFULLY SENT OUT résumés, took Luis for a steak dinner to celebrate his sixteenth birthday, and planted her garden. She tended seedlings in the big south-facing kitchen window, and she dug up old flower beds around the house. She bought a weed whacker and barely learned how to use it before Luis stole her new toy and headed around the side of the house, goggles on, head down, shredded plants in his wake.

Luis was around less and less, spending more time at the stables, making a few friends at the local high school, and starting after-school shifts on the Inskip farm. He was making money, that much Sid knew, and she also knew he was determined to earn his keep, because Sid had failed so miserably in her job search.

Her heart wasn't in it. What was the point in getting into a work routine when in a few months, they'd be moving again?

She sat back on her heels, surveying the tomato seedlings she'd transplanted. The book said to use a string to ensure the rows were straight, but as far as Sid was concerned, Mother Nature would grow the plants whether they were in a perfectly straight line or an almost straight line.

Even dirt was more capable of generating new life than she was.

The board check for the horses had shown up the previous week—thank God—with a terse note that Mac wasn't having any luck finding a place that could accommodate the mares.

That he'd write so little hurt. A man who would lie about his profession would lie about many things. Sid hadn't had the first inkling Mac might be sidestepping issues on her, even though Luis had tried to point out to her evidence that hadn't added up.

She felt stupid and ashamed and angry and even more painful emotions that had no names. The ache hurt worse than being rejected by a husband over something Sid couldn't change and couldn't accept. It hurt worse than the remnants of her grief over Tony's passing; it hurt worse than anything.

She'd kept Mac's damned note, sniffed at it hoping for a faint whiff of cinnamon and clove. Pathetic.

Wheels on the driveway had Sid glancing up, even as she told herself it wouldn't be Mac. Not his truck, but the black SUV looked familiar.

Luis and another kid got out, followed by a pretty dark-haired woman Sid put at about her own age.

"You Sidonie Lindstrom?"

"I am." Sid struggled to her feet as Luis and the other kid hustled off to the barn.

"I'm Vera, James Knightley's fiancée. How do you do?"

Sid tossed off her gloves and shook hands. "You're the one who gave MacKenzie the brownie recipe?"

The lady's face split into a grin. "You didn't say, 'You're the pianist.' We'll get along just fine. I'll happily share the recipe with you, but I heard Luis rhapsodizing about your pies. Care to trade kitchen secrets?"

"Cream cheese filling, and use fresh fruit if you can get it," Sid said, grudgingly charmed. "Look, if Mac sent you to plead his case, then I don't mean to be rude, but it won't work."

Though Sid's attempts at being righteous and stand-offish weren't making things any better either.

Vera swung her gaze to the barn, where Luis and the other kid were emerging with halters and lead ropes in hand.

"I *wish* Mac had sent me to plead his case," Vera said. "My stepson will be working off a debt to me at Inskip's farm this summer, and I gather he and Luis have hit it off. Darren wanted to see Luis's famous horses, so I gave Luis a ride home. How are you settling in?"

What did that mean, Vera *wished* she'd been sent to plead Mac's case?

"Settling in is a slow process. I need to find work, though there doesn't seem to be much call around here for what I do."

"I heard about your interview at the office. MacKenzie is the last person I'd suspect of deceptiveness, but he picked a disastrous time to start keeping secrets. I hope he at least apologized?"

"He tried to." Would he try again?

Vera walked over to the garden, and now that some-body else was viewing Sid's garden, she wished she'd bothered with the string.

"What are you planting? James is putting in a vege-table garden for me, though how he expects me to learn to can and freeze this late in life, I do not know. These are tomatoes, aren't they?"

Sid walked Vera around the garden, surprised to find

how enthusiastic a person could get about four different kinds of beans and three different varieties of tomatoes.

"What are the marigolds for?" Vera asked.

"To keep the bugs down, and for eye appeal. They're cheerful and heat tolerant."

"If Mac asks me, is there anything you want me to say, Sidonie?" The question was meant as kind, the tone could not have been more sympathetic, but Sid felt the words like hammer blows.

"Tell him…" She walked off a few paces, her gaze landing on the mares as Luis and Darren led them in from the paddock. Their coats were glossy, their manes and tails were clean and combed out, and they followed the boys happily.

"Tell him his girls are doing fine."

Vera got down on her knees to sniff a marigold, which was silly. Nobody sniffed marigolds.

"Mac won't even come by to check on the horses? Is he not welcome?"

Oh, to see him again…

"I honestly don't care one way or another if he wants to visit his horses. Luis might like to see him, but Mac knows how to look Luis up at the stables."

"Those are the largest equines I have laid eyes on. Magnificent, if you don't mind feeling like a midget. Would you introduce me?"

As Sid's guests gushed over the horses, and Sid met Darren MacKaye, she concluded Vera Waltham—Vera Winston to her adoring fans—was a person imbued with an innate sense of calm. Vera had brought Mac up without pleading his case, and without concealing her sympathy for him either. And yet Sid didn't feel put on the defensive.

Though why should she feel defensive? She hadn't repeatedly failed to disclose her livelihood.

"Have you ever considered doing day care?" Vera asked as they walked back to the porch. "You have a wonderful property, you're set plenty far back from the road, the house is enormous, and James says you're good with Luis."

"Day care?"

"Yeah, you know, rug rats climbing your porch railing, sitting on the steps and seeing how far they can spit watermelon seeds, chasing the cats up trees. Day care?"

An odd sensation skittered up Sid's spine, hot and cold at the same time, but Vera wasn't done speaking.

"You've probably done the CPR and first aid classes already as part of your foster care license, and if you can handle a teenager, you can probably handle anything."

"I like children," Sid said, "but it wouldn't be fair to them. They'd just get settled in here, and Luis and I would be moving on."

"So open up shop for the summer." Vera knelt by the garden again, and pinched off some dead marigold blossoms. Her hands would smell like marigold until she washed them now. "I am still wracking my brain for how I'm supposed to get my practicing done when Twyla isn't in school for hours every day. Hannah's in the same boat. She could send Grace to her usual day care over the summer, but that place doesn't have room for another kid, which means Grace would go one place, and Merle another."

In Damson Valley, those places could be miles apart. "I've met Grace and Merle. They'd build a cat palace in the tree the minute my back was turned."

Vera rose. "Then you'll consider it?"

"No, I will not." Though Sid was sorely, terribly tempted. Little girls would love baking cookies, not simply come by and snitch the batter, as Luis did. "If I watched those girls over the summer, I'd give Mac's brothers the perfect opportunity to convince me I've wronged him, and the last thing I want is a bunch of lawyers turning loose all their arguments on me."

Though she did want to talk to Mac, most days. Most nights.

Sid sat on the front porch steps and wondered how far she could spit a watermelon seed.

"Hannah and I would not allow the guys to badger you," Vera said. "Think about it."

The boys emerged from the barn, shoving at each other as normal young guys did.

"Hannah's a lawyer too, isn't she?" Sid asked.

"Sort of. She's admitted to the bar, and she can snort and paw with the best of them, but she detests the posturing and procedural baloney. She's in charge of keeping cases out of court, the way I understand it. She mediates and negotiates, and takes cases where the parties agree not to litigate."

The porch smelled good, of petunias and impatiens. Little girls could help look after the flowers too.

Sid gave in to the curiosity Vera's description aroused. "How do Hannah and Trent manage that? She doesn't like what he does, and he probably never considered doing what she does."

Vera fished her keys out of a bright orange and fuchsia shoulder bag. A gold quarter note dangling from the chain winked in the afternoon sunlight.

"I'm marrying a guy who sat for the CPA exam," Vera said, "then decided to try law school, but has now concluded he was meant to farm and work for farmers. I don't think the Knightley family is particularly rigid about how anybody pursues happiness. Give me your email address, and I'll send along the brownie recipe."

Sid complied—no reason not to—and walked Vera and her stepson to the car. At the very least, Luis seemed to have found a friend, though it would be a friend connected with the Knightleys.

"So what's for dinner, oh foster mom?" Luis didn't even wait until Vera's SUV had disappeared to ask.

The *foster* part hurt a bit; the mom part comforted. "Dunno, foster son. You have a suggestion?"

"Yeah, I do. I think we should have company for dinner. I think you should call up MacKenzie Knightley, tell him you're missing him like crazy, and get him over here before sundown. Maybe take a walk with the guy and hear what he has to say."

"Traitor." She had to look up a little to call him that, suggesting country sunshine and farm work agreed with his adolescent growth spurts.

"I've watched you for two weeks, Sid. You're going through the motions, just like you did when Tony died. Don't do this to yourself. No guy in his right mind would look forward to delivering unpleasant news to you. Mac might have been slow with the deets, but he's not stupid or crooked."

"He's an idiot," Sid said, hating the whine in her voice. "He treated me as if I were stupid, Weese."

"So he *was* stupid. You crucify every man who's ever stupid, and the race will die out in a hurry." He patted her shoulder—Luis's version of a hug—and loped off into the house.

If it were up to Sid and Mac, the race would die out. About that, uncomfortable as it had to have been for him, Mac had been honest.

"She hasn't answered my calls, and I've pumped Luis about as much as I can stand to." Mac hated admitting that much, but this was his brother, and Trent's family law practice meant nothing that transpired between adults, consenting or otherwise, would surprise him.

Trent leaned against the front of his desk in what Hannah referred to as his corporate conqueror pose.

"What do you mean, as much as you can stand to?"

"Luis is keeping something from Sid, something he thinks will hurt her. I don't know what it is, but it has to do with how Tony died. Maybe Tony made a pass at the kid, or introduced Luis to some chicken hawk—to something a teenage boy would be uncomfortable sharing with his foster mom."

Or a foster mom would be furious to learn. Mac touched the soil in the pot that held a very healthy rhododendron, though the plant never bloomed.

"Something that could cost her a foster care license?" Trent asked.

"I do not know."

Which was killing Mac. Vera had passed along that he was allowed to go visit his horses, but had Sid meant something else by saying, "Tell him his girls are doing fine"?

Had she meant she was still his girl? Could she possibly have meant that, even subconsciously?

Mac picked up the water pitcher that sat near the rhodie on the windowsill, wondering if Sid might also have meant "Tell him we're fine *without him*."

She'd probably meant exactly that.

"MacKenzie, you zone out like that in court, and you'll be post-convicted for ineffective assistance of counsel," Trent said.

"I've never been post-convicted." Except by Sidonie Lindstrom. Mac gave the plant a small drink, though the soil was still moist.

"Not once?"

"Not one damned time, but that's neither here nor there. If this interrogation is over, I'm leaving for the day." He set the pitcher down and headed for the door.

"Go then, but two phone calls that might have been swallowed up in voice mail isn't much of a campaign. Sid got you out of mothballs, though maybe you're too comfortable being the family spinster to fight for your lady."

Mac turned to face his brother, wanting to belt him in the chops or laugh. Maybe both. "The family *spinster*?"

"You dote on your nieces, you tend your garden, you fuss over cholesterol, and you watch the retirement investments as if we're all about to pick out our rocking chairs. You're several years shy of forty, and your life is over."

Mac did not coldcock his brother, because this was simply what came after the Hannah-is-worried-about-you speech.

"Is Hannah expecting?" he asked.

"Jesus Rockefeller H. Christ on a damned pogo stick, you're as bad as James."

"Well, is she?"

Trent came around the desk and mumbled something as he rummaged in a drawer.

"Didn't catch that, Trent."

"I said I don't know, but she could be. There are indications. She hasn't said anything. It's more—"

"A look in the eye," Mac said, smiling despite the envy piercing his soul. "A glow, a luster. James and I agree with you. She looks like she's on the nest."

Trent stopped pretending to fish for something—his sense of equilibrium, maybe?—in the desk drawers.

"It's too soon," he said.

"What, seven years parenting experience apiece isn't enough? Wait much longer, and it will be too late. You'll be fine." Though what did Mac know about parenting? What would he ever know?

Trent flipped his tie, a navy-blue silk with unicorns charging around on it. "If she's pregnant."

"Get me a nephew, would you? The numbers in this family have abruptly tilted in favor of the opposing team."

"I'll do what I can, but, Mac?"

Mac waited, hand on the doorknob, knowing whatever misbegotten sentiments came out of Trent's mouth, his brother meant well.

"You can't let Sid slip over the horizon. You have to take a risk."

"I took a risk, Trent. Risked what I thought was the biggest gesture of trust I could make toward a woman, any woman, and she didn't let me down over it. She instead let me down over something so insubstantial I'm tempted to think she would have found a pretext sooner or later to dump me."

Though to Sid, it hadn't been insubstantial at all. That

Mac was a lawyer had been a reminder of every trauma and loss she'd suffered. Could she see that? Could she see that connection if Mac brought it up?

"If practicing law is insubstantial, and I would argue that conclusion on behalf of every defendant you've ever seen acquitted, then why not give it up?"

Mac's grip on the doorknob slipped. "*What?*"

"If Sid doesn't like you being a lawyer, but she's necessary for your happiness, then quit. You don't need the money. We can manage without a criminal department. Every other defense lawyer in town will rejoice, as well as the state's attorney's office. Quit."

"I can't…" *But he could.* He could give it up in a heartbeat. The whiny clients, the scared clients, the arrogant clients, even the nice clients, the ones who went meekly to their fate. They got Mac's best efforts, each and every one of them, but what did he get?

A fatter portfolio?

"I haven't told you this for a while, Trenton Edwards, but I have the best brothers in the world, mostly because I raised you that way."

Trent smiled, a smug grin with a hint of relief in it. "James said you'd threaten to punch me out for suggesting it."

"In which case, you'd tell me it was James's idea?"

"I'm thinking it was Vera's, and you're not rejecting it out of hand, are you?"

"No, I am not."

Another Sunday morning home alone, and Sid's nerves were stretched thin. Her damned useless period was late,

playing games with her at a time when she needed her
body to treat her decently. Luis was off at the stable,
though he'd continued to needle her, to hint and wheedle
that she should call MacKenzie Knightley and give him
a fair hearing.

She'd given Mac her body, her trust, her affection...

Wheels splashing up the lane, a big engine with a
particular knocking rhythm.

Mac. Maybe he'd go right out to the barn, see his
girls, whom Luis hadn't turned out because of the rain.

Maybe he'd come to apologize.

Maybe it wasn't even him.

"May I come in?"

He stood outside the screen door to the kitchen, a
bouquet of flowers in his hand. Seeing him hurt and
filled Sid with gladness—and pissed her off.

She let him in, because pissed off was reassuring.
"Those are for me?"

"They're only yard flowers, but yes."

Yard flowers meant lily of the valley, lilacs, tulips,
a fat blue hyacinth, some kind of narcissus that smelled
heavenly, and a blossomy white flower on woody stems
that smelled even better.

"Why are you here, MacKenzie?" Sid set two mugs
on the counter, hoping he'd stand his ground long
enough to share a cup of tea with her.

"As soon as I understood how you feel about lawyers,
I should have told you I'm a criminal defense attorney.
I apologize for that. I didn't try to deceive you, but I
avoided the confrontation much too long. I regret that
more than I can say."

Sid took the flowers without touching Mac's hands.

The regret was sincere, that much she could read in his eyes, but the apology was grudging.

"You like being a lawyer." She fished a green glass vase out from under the sink. "It galls you to have to apologize for what you are."

"I do like being a lawyer, and I'm sorry you can't respect the profession. I'd like to hear your reasons, though I'd clarify one point: I practice law, it's what I do, it isn't what I am, or not the biggest part of what I am."

Oh, he was trying so hard, looking so solemn.

"This isn't about your profession, MacKenzie. It's about not being honest when you knew it was important to me." Though it was about his profession too. Why couldn't he have been a mortician? A trash collector? Anything but a lawyer?

"Would it make a difference if I weren't a lawyer anymore, Sid?"

She was glad her back was turned to him, lest he see the shock his question gave her. That he would offer to give up his livelihood meant more than it should—and he was offering. This wasn't a negotiating ploy. Mac was being honest.

Damn him.

"Yes, it would make a difference," she said, turning to face him. "It would make you resent me, but it wouldn't fix what's wrong between us."

His eyes went blank, his expression utterly calm.

She'd hurt him, and that wasn't any help either. "We'll torment each other if we pile words on top of deeds. I'm sorry, Mac. I like you. I do respect you..." She stopped herself before she could say she desired him, but heaven help her, she did. Just keeping her hands off him, just keeping enough distance that his scent didn't invade her brain was killing her.

"Don't say it." He crossed the kitchen and pulled her gently into his arms. "Whatever brush-off you're about to give me, Sidonie, don't say it. I will keep coming around, bringing you flowers, begging you on my knees if that's—"

"Oh, hush." She put her hand over his mouth, but he turned his head and kissed her palm. "MacKenzie, we mustn't—"

"You're not eating," he said, running his hand over her hips. "It's Mother's Day, Sid, and you're sitting here, alone, still in your nightie, when you should be—"

Double damn him for being able to read a calendar.

Bless him too. Sid kissed him to shut him up, mostly. To shut him up and to satisfy the hunger aroused by the simple sight of him. He felt so good against her body, his kisses tasted so clean and sweet, and the scent of him fed a need Sid had tried to ignore.

"Mac, we can't *do* this."

"I'll stop when you do." He hoisted her up on the counter, so she could wrap her legs around his flanks, get her hands on his belt buckle. That took some doing when she couldn't tear her mouth from his, but she got his jeans undone, and delved into his clothing with her hands.

"Want you, MacKenzie..." Though she shouldn't, she shouldn't, she absolutely *should not*.

"Honey, I know."

Honey. Had he ever called her *honey* before? "This doesn't change anything."

"Touch me, Sid. Touch me, love me, let me love you." Her breasts were exquisitely sensitive when he brushed his thumbs over her nipples through the thin cotton of her summer-length nightie. The hem was above her knees, but to Sid, that was still too much clothing.

She would regret this, and Mac ought to hate her for that. She fused her mouth to his anyway.

Mac was the perfect height for having sex with a woman sitting on the kitchen counter, but they weren't having sex. Mac touched her with a combination of tenderness and ferocity, kissed her like he'd been starving for the taste of her, ran his fingers over her sex with delicate insistence.

Sid did not mistake this for a hookup. This wasn't a quickie, wasn't anything casual at all. This *mistake* was MacKenzie Knightley making love to a woman he cared for very much. Sid groaned at the first touch of him near the entrance to her body, wiggled her hips closer, and then went still.

The moment of joining, of penetration beyond that first glancing nudge, stood out for her as so right, so pleasurable, so *inevitable*, she laid her cheek against his shoulder and let him move into her. She bit his shirt to keep from crying, because they were joined bodily, and Mac would feel the shudders moving through her.

He kissed her eyelids, her cheeks, her brow, her mouth, not denying her tears, but offering what comfort he could. Oh, how she'd missed him, how she was going to miss him if she couldn't get over her mad.

Over her fears.

Mac had missed her too. He communicated that in every kiss and sigh, every undulation of his hips and caress of his hands. Pleasure came over Sid, the building heat of a summer morning, pushing against the pain, absorbing it, consuming it, and turning it back on her in satisfaction that blurred her awareness of MacKenzie as a separate being. He was inside her, around her, *with her*, and she never wanted the moment to end.

But it did. The sense of union faded like the last notes of sweet music, leaving Sid panting against Mac's shoulder while his hand stroked her hair. The tears were spent; the passion was subdued for the present.

In its wake lay a bitter, bottomless ache despite the fact that Mac was still hilted inside her. Grief, disappointment, and anxiety tangled up with whatever Sid felt for Mac, and made her reckless.

"I can't do this again, MacKenzie. Not until I've sorted this out. Have your pleasure of me, and go." The voice of a despairing old woman, Sid barely recognized it as her own.

Mac held her for a moment longer, his hand moving over her hair slowly, and then he withdrew. The absence of him made everything hurt worse, but she understood the gesture: he'd denied himself what pleasure he could have had, contenting himself with the pleasure she'd taken from him.

"That was unnecessary," she said, plucking her nightgown off the counter and dropping it over her head. When had she lost it?

He finished tucking himself back into his clothes and gave her a level look.

"I needed to be with you. I didn't need to be selfish about it. Cut line, Sid. We're both miserable without each other, and we can work through this if you'd give me a chance."

"I gave you the first chance I've given any man in

years. Luis tried to tell me horseshoers don't live in four-bathroom estate homes, but I was so needy, so imprudent, I didn't heed the signs. I'm eighteen again, grieving, adrift, and clinging to any spar. A relationship can't work when I'm in this shape."

Sid hadn't understood that dynamic until she'd said the words out loud. She wiggled off the counter and past Mac, though that meant she'd brushed against him momentarily.

And he hadn't budged. "It was working fine a minute ago, and let me remind you I gave you the first chance I've given any woman in years. We belong together, Sidonie, and you're too scared to admit it."

She ignored the plea in his voice and focused on the words, on the traction they gave her.

"Thank you for sharing, MacKenzie. You've just repeated my own conclusions: I'm scared because I let things move too fast with you. I'm rattled as hell because Luis is facing another hearing. I'm anxious over money, though on paper, I'm supposed to be wealthy. I'm not happy that you lied by omission about your profession. I'm *upset*, MacKenzie, and tired of being upset, and it's damned Mother's Day. Brilliant closing argument, but this isn't a courtroom."

So upset, she was about to throw herself back into his arms, and that would be a horrendously mixed message to a guy who wasn't the villain of the piece.

"I love you, Sidonie. I'm in love with you. I want to spend the rest of my life with you. But if you can't understand that, if you don't want that, then just *please forgive me*."

She turned away, as if his words were more than

verbal threats to her fragile composure. As if they could hurt her physically, steal her resources, addle her feeble wits, and break her already broken heart.

"MacKenzie, I absolutely do forgive you. That's the easy part, but as for the rest of what I want—"

She wanted her brother alive and in good health. She wanted Luis to be legally hers and for him to have a real relationship with his little sisters again. She wanted Mac and she wanted her mother and she wanted to *be* a mother.

"Mac, I'm sorry, I can't do this now." Sid pelted up the steps, bare feet slapping on the risers, half hoping he'd chase her and make her listen again to those terrible, awful, unbelievable words.

But as she threw herself on her bed, all Sid heard was the kitchen door banging closed, then silence.

Complete, hopeless silence.

The most neglected tactic of all the tactics used on cross-examination was silence. In theory, the witness should not say anything other than to answer questions put to him or her by counsel. In practice, opposing counsel was allowed to ask leading questions, and this could be exploited to create the fiction of a dialogue.

Mac exploited that fiction shamelessly. In the days following his most recent encounter with Sidonie, his courtroom technique graduated from flawless to brilliant. His clients were offered sweet plea-bargain deals; his cases were settling left and right.

Because he was in love, but his lady wasn't in love with him.

Or was she?

Sid had wanted him desperately, clung to him, wrung herself out, poured her soul into that interlude in the kitchen, and then she'd gathered up her anger, fear, and exhaustion like so much dirty laundry, and left Mac standing alone, his balls aching, his heart in tatters.

"Come with me." Trent swept past Mac and headed for a witness interview room, the closest thing to privacy the Damson County Courthouse had to offer.

"What's on your mind?" Mac asked when the door was closed.

"*I told you so* is on my mind. Look at this." Trent passed Mac a document eight or ten pages thick. Mac recognized it as the report a social worker would complete in anticipation of a hearing on a foster care case.

Luis's case.

"Read the recommendations."

Mac flipped back to the last page and scanned the document. "This will kill Sid, to say nothing of what it will do to Luis. What the hell do they have up their sleeves?"

"I'm not sure," Trent said. "But the recommendation to transfer Luis's case back to Baltimore will be easy for the court to approve. Moving the case gets a teenager out of Damson County's hair, one who has no ties to speak of to the community."

Trent's tone was detached, while Mac wanted to start throwing chairs.

"For God's sake, Trent. Luis has two jobs here, friends, his foster mom, a physician, and a dentist, and he's enrolled full-time in merit and advanced placement classes at the local high school. What kind of ties does DSS want?"

Trent snatched the document back and jammed it in a briefcase. "DSS wants to see *family*. Luis's sisters are in Baltimore County, his mother is locked up over near the city, and he might have some cousins over there. His case history is there."

"Right, but the Baltimore County courts tossed him up here to keep him with the same foster mom. The kid is thriving. Something else is going on."

Something rotten, and Sid had had enough rotten lately.

"I can ask," Trent said, "but I've left two messages for Ms. Snyder between cases this morning. I get voice mail."

"Call her supervisor, and if that doesn't work, the supervisor's supervisor. Call the damned head of the agency. This isn't right, Trent."

Trent snapped his briefcase shut, both locks in the same instant. "What if moving back to Baltimore is what Luis told the worker he wanted in those private tête-à-têtes they're supposed to have with each kid?"

Trent playing devil's advocate would result in something close to fratricide.

"Luis told *me* he wants to stay with Sid," Mac said. "They're a family, regardless of the legal labels, and that kid is thriving in Sid's care. He hasn't changed his mind about this, Trent. I know that kid."

Knew him and loved him.

"I need to meet with him," Trent said. "Get my marching orders. The hearing is next Tuesday, and I don't think anybody will let Sid know what the Department is recommending, unless Luis tells her."

"If Luis even knows. I'll tell her. She won't like it, but she'll listen to me. What aren't you telling me, Trent?"

Trent set his briefcase on the table and busied himself fussing his cuff links—gold unicorns.

"MacKenzie, when we enter our appearance counsel

for the client, we enter as a firm, not only as an individual attorney. You could represent Luis."

No, he could not. In this situation, for Mac to be a lawyer would be no help to anybody and a conflict of interest even if the strict letter of the law didn't see it that way.

"If I lose, Trent, and Luis is sent back down the road, where does that leave me? Sid's holding on by a thread and has been for too long." Which even she admitted, an aspect of the situation that gave Mac hope.

Why in the name of all that was stupid had he tried to confront her on Mother's Day?

"This isn't a divorce, Mac. When it comes to contested litigation, you're a better litigation strategist than I am. We won't lose."

Not true, also not worth arguing over. "With those recommendations, somebody has to lose."

Mac hoped the somebody wasn't Luis, or Sid—or *him*.

Chapter 17

"LAND, KATIE SCARLETT," SID MUTTERED, TAKING A swig of lemonade.

Gardening was good for her soul. She'd realized this when she was making her fourth trip to the Farmers' Co-op, buying yet another flat of impatiens for the beds she'd dug in the shade of her oaks. Between the flowers, the vegetable garden, the weed whacking, and the occasional can of paint, her property was looking more and more like a home, and feeling more like one too.

Which didn't make sense. When the money came through, she and Luis would probably pull up stakes and find somewhere near some good colleges.

Except DC and Baltimore both had excellent colleges in abundance. Hood was in Frederick County, along with Mount St. Mary's. Frostburg had a campus over in Hagerstown.

And Mac was in Damson County.

Mac, from whom she'd run in a teary swivet.

Sid sat back on her heels and swiped her hair from her eyes with a gloved hand. Instead of hanging baskets on her front porch, she'd settled for big pots of petunias on the steps, purple ones, while the beds she labored over were full of red, white, and pink. The fragrance soothed, the colors cheered, and the sense of having planted something of her own to grow and beautify the house—

Wheels. *His* wheels, and because Luis wasn't home from school yet, Sid made a silent vow not to go inside the house with Mac. Though they'd certainly been intimate out-of-doors too. She stood, pulled off her gloves, and tossed them in her tool basket.

"MacKenzie."

His expression was more unreadable than ever, and the fact that he was still in his lawyer togs reassured Sid not one bit.

"We need to talk, Sid, preferably where Luis can't overhear us."

Foreboding congealed into outright dread. "We can talk here, and we can talk now."

"On the porch."

A compromise. Sid sat on the swing, surprised and perversely pleased when Mac sat beside her. He did not reach for her hand, and she did not reach for his.

"Luis's hearing has been scheduled, and Trent has been assigned to represent him."

Relief washed over her. "I appreciate your telling me. I'm pretty sure Luis will ask for sibling visits, because he hasn't seen his sisters in months." That Mac would bring this news to her in person boded well.

Mac's hand twitched, as if he might have reached for Sid, or for her hand, then thought better of it.

"You will not appreciate this: the Department is recommending that Luis's case be transferred back to Baltimore, Sid. Trent's digging, and he'll fight it if that's what Luis wants, but we can't figure out where this is coming from."

So much for going home to Tara. "You mean, did I ask for it? No, I did not."

Sid resisted the urge to turn her face into Mac's shoulder and scream. Barely. Luis, uprooted again, probably for the last time before he simply beat feet and told the foster care system where to shove it. She tried to focus on what Mac was saying, on the unhurried cadence of his voice.

"I never thought you'd ask for him to be moved. Did you get anything in writing about your license being in good standing?"

"I never got anything in writing that it wasn't or that it was."

Sid sorted through the possibilities: that Luis had asked for this, that his sisters' social worker had asked for this, that his sisters' foster family wanted to adopt Luis.

That family had had months to make overtures, and they'd been as possessive about the girls and as selfish and close-minded toward Luis as possible.

"Amy Snyder does not like me," Sid said slowly. "That sounds petty, but she's one of those by-the-book, clueless social workers. Luis was lucky in Baltimore, his worker was a gem, and she never gave up on finding him a placement that was a good fit, never blamed him, never took the dips and twists in his case personally."

Mac did take her hand, and Sid let him, closing her fingers around his. "We can't all be gems, Sidonie."

They sat in silence while Sid's awareness split, as it often had immediately after Tony's death. In one part of her mind, she considered all of the roots Luis had put down in the past few weeks.

All of the roots *she'd* put down, despite intentions to the contrary. The other part of her brain purely and

selfishly savored the pleasure of holding Mac's hand
while her world tried to reel off its axis.

She hadn't comported herself like a gem where he
was concerned. Amid the fragrance of petunias, and
with the breeze blowing softly through the oaks, she
could admit that to herself.

And try to admit it to him. "I'm scared, Mac. Scared
about this too." The words were out before she could
swallow them back. "If Luis wants to go, I'll live with it,
but if they're jerking him around to gratify some bureau-
cratic agenda, I will not stand for it."

"Nor will I, nor will Trent. James has dated a few of
the ladies at DSS, he's collecting what information he
can, and Trent is papering the hell out of the file."

In a game of rock, paper, scissors, paper often lost.
"What does that mean?"

Mac gave the swing a push with his toe. "Trent's
requesting in writing the Department's reasons for
moving Luis again when the kid's barely getting settled
here in Damson County. He's inquiring into why sibling
visits have not been maintained per the Baltimore court
order. He's requesting discovery—demanding to see
documents, reports, letters associated with the case—
though the Department won't have time to comply."

The rhythm of the swing was soothing, and so was
Mac's voice, despite the circumstances.

"You're telling me that Trent's lawyering up."
Thank God.

"With a vengeance," Mac assured her. "He'll meet
Luis at school, and if Luis doesn't want to move back to
a Baltimore placement, then Trent will stop at nothing
to keep him here."

"Luis won't fight it. The fight went out of that kid about four placements ago." The "kid" was now as tall as his foster mother.

"Then we'll fight for him."

Mac spoke calmly, with utter conviction. When he gently pushed Sid's head to his shoulder, she resisted, peering around to see his eyes.

More conviction.

She rested her head on his shoulder and wished like hell she'd done a better job of accepting Mac's apology when she'd had the chance.

Trent Knightley closed the door to the world's plainest conference room, and set his briefcase on the floor.

"It's like this, Luis. The Department is in charge of licensing foster homes. They can move you from one to the other without so much as waving at the judge, but when they move you to a more restrictive placement— treatment foster care, a residential treatment facility— then they have to get the judge involved."

Luis gave the guy credit for holding eye contact when he delivered bad news. Terrible news, really. Sid wouldn't like this one bit.

"Mac told me that," Luis said, folding into a bright orange plastic school chair that was probably sized for a fifth grader. "Isn't moving me out of county something a judge needs to do?"

Trent took one of the other chairs—blue, which went with his shark suit. "A judge has to be the one to order your case transferred. Do you know when your last permanency planning hearing was?"

Plans, plans, plans. Luis's last social worker had explained to him that the feds got tired of paying for kids to grow up in foster care, so the local jurisdictions had to do a creditable job of moving kids to some final destination, as if a kid's life was a game of Chutes and Ladders.

The state had to come up with a plan to situate a kid somewhere permanently, and then had to get a judge to sign off on the plan at a hearing. Across the room, etched in red on a square whiteboard were the words: "I have a dream."

"I was fourteen the last time the permanency planning came up at court," Luis said. Sid had dreams. "Why?" The hearing had lasted a whole five minutes longer than usual too.

"The Department isn't recommending any change to your permanency plan. In fact, DSS isn't even putting your plan before the judge to consider. They're treating this as a routine case review, when you're way overdue for a change of plan to adoption or even independent living, which they call Another Planned Permanent Living Arrangement, or APPLA. You can read their recommendations on the last page of this document."

Trent slid the usual ration of crap across the table, though at each hearing, the social worker's update was a few pages longer.

When had the Department's damned plans ever done Luis a bit of good? "So what will happen?" Luis would read Amy Snyder's immortal prose later.

"First, tell me what you want to have happen."

As a lawyer, Trent Knightley was different from his predecessors. He'd scheduled this meeting at school, during gym class no less, and he hadn't let the guidance

counselors leave them in the guidance suite's waiting
area to meet. Trent had insisted on privacy.

So Luis studied a Rorschach butterfly-shaped stain
on the industrial tan carpet and chose his words.

"I want to stay with Sid."

"You're positive about that? I work for you. My job
is to make sure the judge knows what you want, and to
advocate for that if it's reasonable. If you want to be
placed with your sisters…?"

Sid had been babbling, apparently. The stain also
looked like pelvic bones, sorta.

"Don't insult me, Trent. Ozzie and Harriet would no
more take me in than you'd leave your kids alone with
a starving wolf." A starving, rabid wolf with deviant
sexual tendencies and bad body odor.

"If they'd take you in, would you go?"

"No, I would not. They'll take good care of the girls.
My sisters look more Anglo than I do."

Meeting Trent's eyes when that truth saw the light of
day was hard, but not impossible. The guy knew better
than to let his pity show.

"You want to stay with Sid. Anything else? You want
regularly scheduled visits with your mom? Visits with
your sisters?" Trent wasn't taking notes, he was *listening*.
Grown-ups who listened were a damned pain in the ass.

Grown-ups who didn't were worse.

"Visit with my sisters, yes, though that won't happen.
Mom—I write to her."

"She might be at the hearing."

Huh? "They never transported her to my hearings
before, not after the first couple. I thought that meant
she didn't want to come."

Trent withdrew a business card from a gold case with a rearing horse on it, and tossed the card in Luis's direction. The white rectangle settled immediately before him, as if that toss had been one of the skills taught along with evidence, divorce law, and how to look sharp in a three-piece suit.

"Sometimes," Trent said as Luis picked up the card, "failure to transport an incarcerated parent means nobody gets the writ for transportation submitted in time, or the Division of Corrections loses it, or their van is in the shop, or there's traffic on the interstate. If she's there, you have to ask permission to hug her, though talking to her is usually OK, as long as nobody gets upset."

Luis would deal with Mama if she was there; he'd deal with it if she wasn't. "We're going to lose, aren't we?"

"Why do you say that?"

"Because the Department has legal and physical custody of me. It's their ball and their bat." A Louisville Slugger, aimed at Sid's happiness.

Trent's smile was reassuring and not at all nice. "But not their rule book. The gold standard for making decisions in these cases is the best interests of the child, and your interests are in no way served by moving you out of county." Trent took the card and wrote on the back—even this guy's pen was gold. "This is my number, my cell's on the back. If I'm in court, I can't pick up, but I answer all messages usually within the same business day. You think of anything, you call me, and, Luis?"

Luis stood and picked up the eraser at the bottom of the whiteboard. "I know: No screwing up the night before court. No shoplifting. No putting my hands on some girl. No getting into a pushy-shovey with Sid. No hooking school. No getting high or partying. No AWOLing. No nothing. I'm not stupid."

"You're human," Trent said, rising. "If you're tempted to misbehave, just think of how much fun you'll have when DSS bounce-passes you to juvie. Lotsa smart guys have ended up in juvie. Don't you be one of them."

"I won't."

Trent smiled at him, a brief flash of teeth that reminded Luis of Mac, and of that wolf he'd mentioned earlier. Not a guy to mess with, this one. The image of Luis on his knees before a bucket popped into his head.

"You saw me drunk."

"I did."

Luis tossed the eraser just high enough to kiss the drop-ceiling tile but not leave an imprint.

"Why would you go to bat for me when you know I don't deserve to stay with Sid?"

Trent flipped his tie, some abstract design in blue and white. "If you think one tipsy morning makes you worthless, you need to reexamine your priorities. Everybody stumbles—me, Mac, Sid, everybody. The difference is that some of us acknowledge our mistakes and try to do better, and others pretend they never screw up. Mac is meeting with Sid to go over the Department's recommendations—informally, of course, because a foster parent has no standing in the court case."

Trent extended a hand. "I'm trying to get hold of your worker, and James is checking his traplines for random intelligence. We'll meet with Hannah before court, because she has foster care expertise that goes beyond the courtroom. Your job is to not screw up between now and court."

Trent had a good handshake. Nothing pansy or reluctant about it.

"I can do that."

With four lawyers circling the wagons on Luis's behalf, screwing up wasn't an option, no matter how badly he might be tempted. Trent left, and Luis followed him out, but took a minute first to erase Dr. King's inspiring words from the whiteboard.

⁓⁓⁓

Luis reported to Sid that Miss Amy Snyder had met with him at school—he'd missed lunch to hear her out—and she'd patiently explained to him that being nearer his sisters was in his best interests, even if the girls' foster family treated him like dirt and thumbed their noses at court-ordered visits.

She'd further explained—Miss Amy was apparently fond of the sound of her own explanations—that Luis's attorney, whose name had escaped her, would advocate for his interests before the judge. Luis was not to worry. His attorney would be certain to be present the day of court.

"Sometimes," Miss Amy had said, "the Department's hands are tied, and the regulations leave us no options."

Then she'd taken his damned picture, switched off her SmartPad, and left.

She wasn't even nice. Most of Luis's workers had been at least superficially nice, many of them more than that. They tried their best to make a complicated, unwieldy system do handsprings, and it wasn't their fault the results were disappointing.

"You made brownies for a legal meeting?" Luis asked Sid as she took the pan out of the oven.

"Double batch, considering who's coming over. Anything you want to say to me before they arrive?"

I love you. Except admitting that smarmy crap now would just make Sid cry, and that would make Luis crazy.

She was smart, Sid was. She didn't turn and spear him with her mama-eyed lightsaber, she kept puttering in the big kitchen, making a racket with the bowl and spoons she'd used to put together the brownie batter.

"I don't want to leave here. I don't want to leave you."

She did turn then, draped a dish towel over her shoulder, and crossed her arms as she leaned back against the counter.

"You know I love you, Weese?"

"I know that. You should be more careful who you love, but I know you love me." And leaving Sid would ruin him *and* his chances for a decent future. Luis knew that too. Sid talked about college like that was just the next thing on the list.

"If you want to go to damned Baltimore," she said, "I'll drive you there. I'll pack your stuff and call DSS myself, if it's what you want."

Damn her and her mama-bear bravery. "I don't want to go to Baltimore." Luis hadn't meant to raise his voice.

She folded the towel over her shoulder, as if it were some kind of fashion accessory.

"OK, so you want to stay with me, but you don't want me to adopt you. One measly little adoption, my friend, and they couldn't do this to you anymore."

"I know that too. Just lay off, would you? I'm going to check on the horses."

Luis left the kitchen at a near run, letting the screen door slam, though he knew it drove Sid nuts. He was already in tears by the time he buried his face against Buttercup's coarse, stinky mane.

———∿∿∿———

"The Department isn't wrong," Trenton Knightley said.

If his tone were any more reasonable, Sid would have to choke him. The kitchen bore the lovely scent of fresh-baked brownies, some fool bird was chirping madly out in the oak tree, and Sid was contemplating lawyer-cide.

Not for the first time.

"Viewed from one perspective," Trent went on, "if Luis were placed closer to his sisters, that would be less restrictive. The Baltimore court would have considered that before they sent Luis out here with Sid, though, and the Baltimore judge decided continuity of placement was more important than visits Luis wasn't even getting."

"Sid would haul him to those visits if DSS set them up, I'm sure." The comment came from James, who sat on one side of Sid at the kitchen table. Hannah sat on the other, which meant Sid was across from Mac, Luis, and Trent. Vera, may the woman be canonized, had volunteered to look after Grace and Merle.

"I got Luis to every visit that was scheduled," Sid said. "When Luis and his sisters were in the same juris-diction, their respective workers could coordinate visits, though the other foster parents had endless excuses. This week it was a cold, the next week it was a dress rehearsal for the first-grade play. Always something."

While Luis had stopped asking if he could even call his sisters. Both girls apparently took the world's longest showers, then went immediately to sleep. Every single night.

"I can hammer on the fact that the visits haven't been set up since Luis got here," Trent said, choosing a brownie from the stack on the plate in the center of the table. "I can make the point that the local Department has dropped that ball miserably."

"And you'll lose," Mac retorted. "The Department will apologize heartily, and point out that you've made their case for them. The visits were easier to schedule when Luis was in the same jurisdiction as his sisters. Brian Patlack isn't stupid."

"Who's he?" Luis asked around a mouthful of brownie.

"The attorney for DSS," Trent said. "If he knows he has a contested case on his hands, he'll sometimes try to reason with his client until a compromise can be hammered out, but he's out of town all week at some golf tournament. I'm striking out with Ms. Snyder's supervisor, as well, because he's at an off-site training."

Worse and worse. The half mug of milk Sid had managed wasn't agreeing with her at all.

"If it's any comfort," James said, "nobody at DSS likes Amy Snyder. My contacts there are reasonably professional, but some of them go back a few years, and every single one of them gets that pissy, oh-her tone of voice when I mention Amy's name. She's not a team player, won't take the hard cases, and seems to have her supervisor wrapped around her finger. One of the ladies hinted Amy's uncle is close to the governor."

The *governor*. Sid could not bear to meet Luis's eyes when James had shared that cheering tidbit.

"Did you get the sense she cuts corners, James?" Hannah asked.

"I can answer that," Luis said, balling up his napkin and lobbing it into the trash. "Amy Snyder loves the rules, and they are more important to her than what's right. She wins if the rules are obeyed, and if the rules are contradictory, like the best interests of the child, meaning I'd stay, while some other rule means I'd go, she gets mad. She hates it."

Hatred, a fine quality in a child welfare worker.

"I agree with Luis," Sid said. "He's pegged her accurately. Amy isn't confused or bewildered by conflicting guidance, she's *pissed*. Insulted, peeved, affronted that she should have to deal with untidiness. Luis and I are square pegs to her, and the right outcome is for Baltimore to solve the problem that Baltimore created."

James pushed the plate of brownies at her—a considerably less full plate of brownies than it had been at the start of the meeting.

"Why are you square pegs?" he asked.

When had they ever been anything else? "Because Luis doesn't want to be adopted, he doesn't have relatives who can take him in, and he isn't clamoring to be emancipated."

"That's an option," Mac said. "The judge can spring him, turn him loose by court order, make him an underage adult, and then Luis is free to do whatever he wants."

Trent dipped his brownie in a glass of milk and took a considering nibble. "Judge Stevens won't spring a sixteen-year-old new to the area who has no money in the bank, no family around here, no place to stay outside a licensed foster home, no plan for how he'll complete his education."

"I have a trust fund," Luis said. "That might count for something."

The four—count 'em!—attorneys at the table exchanged glances. Four of them, and still they'd be unlikely to convince a judge to set aside the Department's plan.

"You haven't seen a nickel of that trust," Mac said. He'd not touched the brownies. "But the fund is another reason to leave you with Sid, because she's the trustee. Much easier for her to disburse the funds to you if you're living under her roof."

Excellent notion, though still probably not excellent enough.

They batted ideas around until the brownies were nearly gone and Luis was discreetly yawning behind his hand.

"I'm going to turn out the girls for the night." Luis said.

James got to his feet. "I'll go with you. Moon should be coming up soon, and it's a pretty night. Sid, try not to worry. If the judge wants to know where Luis will stay when he's emancipated, he can stay with us. Be convenient to his summer job, and Twyla would adore him."

"He could stay with us too," Hannah said. "Grace has asked me more than once for a big brother."

"Or there's my place," Mac said, staring at the few remaining brownies. "Kid could put that pool table to some use."

"You'd take him in, just like that?" Sid asked.

"Why not?" Trent replied. "You did."

Sid sat back, swallowing hard, saying not one word

as Trent and Mac left the kitchen behind James. Hannah patted her shoulder and rose, taking the brownie plate to the counter.

"Something puzzles me," Hannah said.

While Sid was tied completely in knots. "That would be?"

"Where is your foster care worker in all this? And where's your plastic wrap?"

"You mean Amy? She's all too apparently running the damned show. The plastic wrap is in the drawer beside the sink."

"No, *your* worker. Every licensed home has a worker whose job is to look after the foster families, not the foster kids. They handle the things that relate to licensure, they stay in touch with the families as a kind of support chain, and they visit from time to time regardless of which children you're fostering."

While Hannah covered the brownies, Sid cast back, recalling a few such visits from pleasant, harried ladies, and the occasional guy. They had a fancy name—service home foster care liaison, something like that.

"Maybe I haven't been assigned one yet." Now, when the brownies had been put away, Sid abruptly craved one—and more milk.

Hannah stashed the plastic wrap, which was running low, back in the drawer. "If Amy cast doubt on your license, then your worker should have been immediately involved."

"Amy said she didn't have all the signatures on the paperwork. Maybe my worker is on vacation, or is the reason Amy's plans didn't bear fruit."

Hannah wrung out a rag and began wiping the

table. "I'll mention it to Trent. Good brownies. Is it Vera's recipe?"

"It is. I cannot believe I'm sitting on my backside while you clean up in my kitchen." Sid got up, intent on putting the milk jug back in the fridge.

"I'm buttering you up," Hannah said. "Now isn't the time to ask, but school will be out soon, and there's no good time: Will you watch my daughters this summer? They love it here, and you're a child care professional."

Ambushed. Sid set the milk jug—also considerably lightened—on the counter. "You hardly know me, and I'm not a licensed day care mom."

"You have time to get a license, and Mac vouches for you. Vera will ask you to keep Twy as well, so get your acceptance speech ready."

Sid added milk and plastic wrap to the grocery list she kept on a pad by the kitchen phone.

"What about my you-do-me-great-honor speech?" she asked. "I've always steered clear of the little kids, or I did after the first year."

"Why?"

Beneath the last items on the grocery list, Sid scrawled the word "miracle." They might have a spare one of those at the feed store, right?

"The big kids need the love more," Sid said. "The little guys can cute their way right into anybody's heart, but the big kids are special. I genuinely like them, and they seem to appreciate it."

Hannah hugged her, a good solid, comforting hug that had tears pricking the backs of Sid's eyes.

"You're the foster mom I should have had," Hannah

said. "Don't worry about Luis. If anybody can keep that kid under your roof, it's Mac, Trent, and James."

From whom Sid had scorned to accept a job.

Hannah gave Sid's hand a pat, and called out to her husband, who'd taken Mac—or been dragged by Mac—out to the porch.

Sid found James and Trent sitting on the swing when she and Hannah left the kitchen.

"Mac's visiting his girls," James said. "Probably giving Luis a pep talk."

"While you two do what?" Hannah asked, wedging herself between them.

"We're reminiscing." Trent looped an arm around his wife's shoulders. "It's good to see the place looking cared for again. Our mom used to have good luck with geraniums around the porch, but the petunias smell better."

"Mom had a green thumb." James rose from the swing and propped a hip on the porch railing.

Trent didn't answer, leaving Sid to wonder what it would be like to have family like this. Family that shared memories both sweet and sad, who came together to support each other, who comforted one another through life's worst hurts and difficulties.

Across the yard, Mac and Luis emerged from the barn, walking side by side. Mac was talking, Luis was listening, nodding, then Mac stopped with a hand on Luis's shoulder.

Luis shook his head emphatically, the night breezes carrying the words away. Mac pulled Luis in for a hug, probably intending a brief, backslapping man-hug, but Luis lashed his arms around Mac's waist and dropped his forehead to Mac's shoulder.

"Let's go inside." James kept his voice down and held the door for Sid, while Trent brought up the rear.

"We weren't supposed to see that," Sid said. "I'm glad Luis is willing to lean on somebody." He'd never hugged Sid like that, though.

Trent tousled her hair. "You might give it a try yourself sometime." His tone was teasing, but Sid felt chastised and un-huggable.

"If having the four of you collaborate on Luis's case doesn't constitute leaning, I don't know what would."

James's arm settled on her shoulders. "Give it some thought. You're a bright lady. Some good ideas about this leaning business might come to you. They've finally arrived to MacKenzie's stubborn way of thinking, so there has to be hope for you."

He bussed her cheek, which from him was endearing. He smelled good, a little cedary with undertones of smoke and spice, though Mac's cinnamon-and-clove fragrance had more appeal.

Mac, who was out in the moonlight comforting the kid Sid would not be allowed to adopt.

Much less raise.

———

"I wonder if he's able to sleep, when tomorrow might be the last night he spends under this roof?"

Sid's voice held such an aching load of misery, Mac took the risk of putting an arm around her. She'd been quiet all evening, and watchful, focused mostly on Luis.

"He'll finish out the school year here at least, Sid. Judge Stevens is big on education and good grades."

How much comfort would that be? That for the

next two weeks, Sid and Luis could anticipate leaving each other?

She gave the swing a desultory push with her toe. "If not knowing what will happen the day after tomorrow drives me half-batty, how can Luis possibly cope?"

"He's a survivor, Sid. He's moved on any number of times, and if he has to weather this, he'll make the best of it." Mac had given Luis the same speech about Sid not fifteen minutes ago.

She cuddled closer. "I hate you. You're right, you're spouting common sense, but I have to hate you for it."

"Weese asked me to look after you." Had made Mac promise to look after her. "He said this would be harder on you than it was on him."

"Oh, God. That boy…"

Mac fished for his hankie and passed it to her. Sid was quiet and relaxed against him, her scent teasing him even while she blotted her eyes. He could feel her thinking, feel the gears turning in her mind, though physically she seemed wrung out.

"I owe you my thanks, MacKenzie. Your family has been wonderful. They wouldn't be doing this if you asked them not to."

"Trent does a good job for all his clients. We all do."

As did the great majority of lawyers. In the interests of remaining on the swing with Sid, Mac let that sleeping dog snore a while longer.

"That's not what I meant. To pick Hannah's brains, to offer Luis your homes was not lawyering. I think what hurts Luis the most is the separation from his sisters. He sees letting me adopt him as a betrayal of them."

They were talking, not about their relationship, but

they were talking, and that—despite the circumstances—
was wonderful.

"I have my own theory about Luis's motivations, Sid."

She lifted her head to peer at him. "Will you share
this theory?"

"Will you stomp off into the night if you don't like it?"

Sid blew out a breath while Mac held his.

"That was fair," she said. "Given the way I've treated
you, given some of my reactions, that question was fair.
I will not stomp off into the night."

Progress. Significant progress. "Luis doesn't feel
worthy of your love, and he punishes himself by denying
himself adoption. He's trying to protect you somehow."

"Protect *me*?"

Must she sound so incredulous about a guy's honorable efforts to keep her safe and happy?

"Just a theory."

"I want to say you're full of baloney," Sid muttered.
"I like my theory better."

"But?"

"But I will think about what you've said. It's late, and
I've kept you here long enough. Tomorrow is a workday
for you, and I have yet to thank you."

"I don't need thanks."

She was silent for long minutes, while Mac savored
the feel of her next to him, her head on his shoulder.
Maybe this was a weak moment on her part; maybe he
was a port in a storm. He'd enjoy the time spent with
Sid, nonetheless, and build on them as best he could.

"I castigated you for not telling me you're a lawyer,
MacKenzie. Now lawyers are all that stand between my
foster son and disaster."

He'd trusted her to come to this realization; he loved her for owning up to it.

"You castigated me for not being truthful. I understand that, Sid." He also understood she was tired and fretful, and now was not the time to rehash his transgressions. "Let me make you a cup of tea."

"Oh, MacKenzie."

Oh, MacKenzie, what?

Mac led Sid into the kitchen, brewed her a cup of chamomile tea, sweetened it with agave nectar, and took his leave before he was offering to tuck her in—and before she was telling him what he could do with that offer, and any others like it.

Chapter 18

"ALL RISE! THE CIRCUIT COURT FOR DAMSON COUNTY is now in session, the Honorable Paul Stevens presiding. You may be seated."

Sid's stomach jumped at the bailiff's call to order. She'd made a few calls to DSS yesterday, posed as somebody curious about becoming licensed as a foster parent. She'd been told the worker responsible for handling those calls was out on medical leave, but somebody would get back to her.

Another dead end, and a perfectly reasonable explanation for why Hannah's "support chain" hadn't materialized.

Luis sat beside Trent at a table in the front of the room. Beside Sid in the first row of the gallery was Mac, on her other side Hannah, then James. A show of support, for her and Luis, though by rights they probably weren't supposed to be in the courtroom, even though they were lawyers.

"Call your case, Mr. Patlack." Judge Stevens's voice was crisp with a hint of irritation. The docketed time for the case had passed forty-five minutes ago, an earlier case having run over.

"Your Honor, the Department calls the case of Luis M., A Child in Need of Assistance." Patlack, a fast talker in a blue seersucker suit, rattled off the case number and explained the case had been transferred from Baltimore to allow the child to remain with the same foster parent.

"Though as Your Honor will see, the Department's recommendations are for the child to return to his prior jurisdiction at the close of the school year."

The judge glanced over the documents Patlack had passed to the clerk, and the clerk had passed to the judge.

"The boy just got here, Mr. Patlack. Did the Department scare up some long-lost relatives at the last minute?"

"No, Your Honor, we did not, but neither did Baltimore do a very thorough investigation of the foster parent's circumstances. Then too, the child's siblings are stably placed in the prior jurisdiction, and the least restrictive placement would be closer to them."

Bullshit, lies, and weasel words. Sid knew better than to utter a peep.

Stevens peered over his glasses at Trent. "Mr. Knightley, what's your client's position?"

Trent rose. "We're of the opinion, Your Honor, that two Departments dropping the ball doesn't make for good case management. We believe Luis's best interests are served by remaining exactly where he is, which is also what he emphatically wants."

Stevens scowled as he flipped through the social worker's recommendations. "Mr. Patlack, call your first witness."

"The Department calls Ms. Amy Snyder."

Amy had worn one of her damned jumpers to court. A navy-blue sailor suit this time, complete with white stockings and red patent leather flats. She also carried her SmartPad right up to the witness stand.

Sid wanted to bean her with the damned thing.

When the swearing of the witness was concluded,

Patlack sat back in his chair and started the litany Sid
had heard many times before.

"Ma'am, are you the worker assigned to the case of
Luis Martineau?"

"I am."

"How long have you been so assigned?"

"Not long." She simpered at the judge. "Baltimore
sprung him on us just a few months ago."

Bad Baltimore, in other words. *Bitch*. And to refer to
Luis in the third person when he sat twelve feet away
qualified as *demon-bitch* behavior.

"During your tenure on the case, did you formulate
recommendations regarding what's in the child's best
interest?" Patlack asked.

"I did." Another smirking preen for the judge's benefit.

"Are those the recommendations you've put
forth today?"

"Of course."

"Can you explain to His Honor how you came to the
conclusion that Luis's best interests are served by sending him back to Baltimore? The boy has only recently
arrived here, if I'm not mistaken?"

Oh, the condescension in Patlack's voice. The sweet
reason and civility. Sid wanted to kick him in the balls.

"Our thought was that Baltimore had been hasty
with Luis's situation. Because we'll have to move
him anyway, we thought placing him closer to his two
younger sisters would be less restrictive, more consis-
tent with his needs and with his permanency plan."

"What is that plan?"

"Return home, though relative placement hasn't been
ruled out."

"Are any relatives willing to take him in?" The worthless sack of manure managed to sound hopeful as he posed the question.

"Baltimore would know more about that, because they had the case for nearly three years. From what I've seen of the file, no. No relatives."

She shot an apologetic glance at Luis—whom she hadn't bothered to ask about relatives—and whose countenance made the Easter Island statues look sentimental. Beside Luis, Trent made notes on a yellow legal pad, his expression also unreadable.

This is what it looks like; this is what it feels like to lose my son. All the procedural window-dressing in the world was only so much anesthetic for the people taking Luis from her. Sid would know very well that the surgeon in the black robe at the front of the room had cut her heart out, regardless of the sterile procedure or the legal protections intended to ensure she survived the proceedings.

Patlack was far from finished, apparently. "Is Luis having contact with his siblings now that he's moved out here to western Maryland, Ms. Snyder?"

"None at all." Alas, poor Luis. Ms. Snyder conveyed such sympathy for the boy, obliterating the fact that arranging the visits was exclusively her job.

"Just a few more questions, ma'am. You said Luis would be moved anyway. Why is that?"

Ms. Snyder cradled her SmartPad to her chest, as if what came next pained her. Just watching her performance curdled the caramel mocha breakfast latte Sid had snatched from a drive-through on the way to court.

"Baltimore didn't do a very thorough job of investigating what Luis's situation would be with his current foster parent when he moved out here. They knew the family's arrangements in Baltimore, of course, and I'm sure those complied with the regulations, but out here, it's a different story."

"You're saying the foster home isn't compliant with the state's requirements?"

"I'm afraid not." A glance at the judge conveying regret. The stage had lost a real talent when Amy Snyder went after her social worker's license.

"Then I have no further questions."

Which made no sense. Sid's home was in compliance. They'd literally had to move earth to do it, but she'd gotten rid of the infernal two-seater, though Ms. Snyder had yet to come to the property to verify that. Sid gripped Mac's hand more tightly, then wondered when she'd taken it in hers.

Or had he been the one to join their hands?

The judge tapped a pencil against his lips. "Your witness, Mr. Knightley, though we don't have all morning."

"Thank you, Your Honor. Ms. Snyder, how long has Luis been in care?" His voice was casual, merely curious.

"I'd have to consult my notes. The case didn't originate in Damson County."

Yeah, you made sure we knew that, at least three times over.

"Take all the time you need," Trent said.

This time when Ms. Snyder visually flirted with the judge, her glance was timid.

"It's, um…" She scrolled through her smarty-pants notes. "Three years this month."

"When was the last permanency plan hearing?"

"Objection." Patlack was on his feet. "This is beyond

the scope of direct examination of the witness and not relevant. Today's hearing is a routine review of the case only, and quite frankly, I do not think the Court has the time—given the rest of today's docket—for Mr. Knightley's detours and fishing expeditions."

The foul excrescence sounded convinced of his own rhetoric, and Sid's latte threatened to make a reappearance.

"Mr. Knightley?" the judge asked mildly.

"The worker is responsible for managing the case, Your Honor. If we're not reviewing that case management, what is the point of the proceeding? Luis is long overdue for a permanency planning hearing, he has been denied the permanence any foster child in the system for three years is entitled to, and his case—with eight moves in the three years—is exactly the situation where the Court should prohibit further shuffling around of the child unless it's absolutely necessary. Rather than toss this child over the transom *yet again*, Ms. Snyder ought to be exploring adoptive resources for the child in county."

Eight moves. Trent's spiel put information in front of the judge that the worker wouldn't give up willingly— though Patlack looked unimpressed.

Sid's belly settled marginally.

"Objection overruled," the judge said. "The witness may answer the question."

Ms. Snyder smoothed a hand down her hair. "I forget the question."

'Cause you're a lot dumber—and meaner—than you look.

"When was the last permanency planning hearing in this case?" Trent said.

"I'd have to consult my notes."

Trent said nothing, and the bitch idiot lying witch Kewpie doll conniving excuse for a low-down scheming she-snake put a worried look on her face.

"Um, I think it has been quite some time."

"The witness's answer is nonresponsive to the question," Trent said, looking directly at the judge.

"Find us a date, if you can, Ms. Snyder." And praise be to heaven, the judge sounded more pissed than avuncular.

She fussed and scrolled and fussed some more, then recited a date nearly two years in the past.

"You don't think Luis deserves any permanency planning?" Trent asked, his tone still mild.

"Oh, of course he does. That's why we're moving him. His sisters are in a pre-adopt household, and we're hopeful that things will work out for Luis too."

A commotion at the door stopped the proceedings. A slender, dark-haired woman was led into the courtroom by uniformed guards, her handcuffs and ankle bracelets jangling. She wore jeans and a modest cream blouse, her hair was swept back in a tidy bun, and her gaze, her entire being, was focused on Luis.

The judge glanced at the court reporter. "Let the record reflect we've been joined by the boy's mother. Ma'am, please state your name for the record."

"Phillippa Martineau, Your Honor." A beautiful voice, her words spoken as the deputies unlocked her ankle bracelets.

"Have a seat, Ms. Martineau. Was it your intention to appear here without representation?"

"Yes, Your Honor."

"Then, Mr. Knightley, you may proceed."

"Ms. Snyder, you were telling us that Luis's sisters are to be adopted, but you don't intend to place him in the same foster home, do you?"

"That would be up to Baltimore."

"Who in Baltimore?"

"His worker."

"Who will that be?"

"Baltimore will assign the worker when the case is transferred."

"Do you mean to tell me, Ms. Snyder, you have no idea where Luis will be placed, not the first clue, but somehow you think it's better for him to be a few miles closer to his sisters, even though it means removing him from the pre-adopt family where he's thrived for nearly the past year?"

"Mr. Knightley, the home he's in isn't properly licensed. I'm sorry, but if his foster parent truly cared about Luis, she would not have allowed her qualifications to lapse."

No string of expletives was adequate for the rage that comment ignited in Sid. Three varieties of green beans were growing where the damned two-seater had been.

"We'll get to the licensing issues," Trent said. "How many times have you called Baltimore to coordinate with them regarding this transfer?"

"Well, I haven't called them yet. They haven't assigned a worker."

"Right. Because you haven't told them you want to transfer the case."

"Objection." Patlack didn't bother to rise this time. "Counsel may not testify."

"Sustained," the judge muttered.

"My apologies." Trent sounded anything but apologetic. "Now why is the foster parent's license in jeopardy?"

"She's out of compliance."

"Can you be more specific, Ms. Snyder?"

"She lives on a farm, and there were difficulties with the physical home."

"Such as?"

"Well..." Ms. Snyder gave the judge an awkward smile. "Outdoor plumbing is unacceptable in a licensed foster home."

Trent jumped in with the next question. "You're implying Baltimore sent a child out here to a home without indoor plumbing? How many bathrooms does Luis's foster home have inside the farmhouse?"

"I'd have to check my notes."

Trent merely crossed his arms.

"It looks like...three and a half."

"So the outdoor plumbing wasn't in use, was it?"

"The family said not. I have no way of knowing, really."

Mac's fingers closed more snugly around Sid's, which was all that kept her from bellowing obscenities at the state's witness.

"The building housing the outdoor plumbing has been razed, hasn't it?" Trent asked.

"That's what the foster parent claims."

"You haven't verified her claim? Or is the presence or absence of a building difficult to assess?"

Go, Trent.

"Really, I haven't had the case that long, and the issue of the outdoor plumbing isn't the greatest problem."

"Why is that?"

"The household income is the problem. We pay our foster parents a stipend to meet the needs of the foster children in their homes, but the family has to have independent income. Often, if there's a divorce, or the breadwinner dies unexpectedly, the foster care license has to be given up."

Sid didn't hear the rest of the woman's tripe. Income was the problem? *Income?* She needed an air-sickness bag, and duct tape for Amy Snyder's mouth.

Mac patted Sid's knuckles, his expression willing her to remain quiet and seated. Sid had no steady income; that was the damned, ugly truth. Mac's board money wasn't employment. Her land would make her money come fall, and she'd tucked away a little from selling the hog house lumber and her topsoil, but that was incidental income.

The estate that would give her investment income might not settle for months.

Sid was really, truly going to lose her son. What little hope she'd harbored died, and if it wouldn't have been abandoning Luis, she would have quit the courtroom that instant.

"When did you inform the foster parent that income was an issue of sufficient stature to cost her her license?" Trent asked.

"I told her several weeks ago that I'd submitted the license revocation paperwork, and in that time, I'd think she would have told me if she'd found a job. Luis has found work." She beamed approval of her client for that bit of initiative.

"So has the foster parent's license been revoked?"

"Not as of today, or we'd have to shelter Luis in

another home. We're trying to have him finish out the school year without moving."

Trying so hard.

"When did you inquire as to the foster parent's income?" Trent said.

"Income information is on the forms that came up with the case from Baltimore."

"So it would not surprise you to learn that this foster parent has a net worth in seven figures?"

Ms. Snyder blinked rapidly, twice. "That's not income."

"You were aware of her net worth?"

"Net worth isn't on the paperwork."

Patlack tipped his chair back to have a whispered conversation with a supervisor, then got to his feet.

"Your Honor, I'm going to object to this line of questioning. It is exclusively in the Department's purview which foster home we place which child in. We can move the boy tonight to another foster home, and it's quite frankly none of Mr. Knightley's business. We're trying to keep the child with his current placement through the end of the school year. You'd think counsel would appreciate that consideration, not criticize it."

Patlack cast a disparaging glance at Trent, who didn't bat an eye.

"Your Honor, to the child, one foster home is *not* as good as another," Trent said. "If called upon to testify, my client would assure the Court he is thriving in the current home, he wants to stay in the current home, and that like most Maryland foster homes, this home is licensed for adoption as well as foster care. The

Department is elevating form over substance, and to the child's detriment."

Damn straight they were.

"I can't ignore a revoked license, Mr. Knightley," the judge said, frowning at the Department's recommendation.

"The license hasn't been revoked, nor have I completed my case."

Rather than piss the judge off, Trent's statement seemed to amuse him. "By all means, Mr. Knightley, please proceed."

"Ms. Snyder, if you were to learn that the foster parent had acquired substantial household income since arriving to our county, you'd have to stop the license revocation procedure, wouldn't you?"

"I suppose so."

"Wouldn't you, Ms. Snyder?"

"Yes."

"Just a few more questions then. When have you scheduled Luis's permanency planning hearing?"

"I haven't. Because his case is being transferred, that means Baltimore will have to schedule—"

Trent held up a hand. "Correct me if I'm wrong, Ms. Snyder, but I was under the impression *His Honor* has yet to decide what to do with this case. If *His Honor*'s input is no longer considered germane by the Department, this is news to me. Wouldn't it be better management of the case to have scheduled the permanency planning hearing as soon as you noticed that Luis's file was *out of compliance with the regulations*?"

Sweet—if too little too late.

That blow to Ms. Snyder's ability to enforce the

regulations rattled her composure. Her expression turned ugly for an instant, while she stared at her SmartPad.

"It's not my fault somebody in Baltimore forgot to schedule a hearing."

"Not your fault, but it was your job to bring the case into compliance, and you decided to pass the wet baby instead, didn't you?"

Patlack rifled through *his* notes, though his worker was glaring at him.

"Ma'am, if you'd answer the question?" Trent's tone was patient.

"Could you ask it again?"

"Was it, or was it not, just as much your job to bring Luis's permanency planning into compliance as it was to hound his wealthy foster parent because, in a difficult economy, she didn't find a paying job as soon as she moved her household to Damson County?"

Now Ms. Snyder's expression was positively venomous. "I am responsible for both aspects of the case, as was Baltimore, and it isn't my fault if Baltimore didn't do its job."

"No further questions, Your Honor." Trent's tone, dismissive and almost disappointed, stated his opinion of the witness and her testimony.

"Any questions for this witness, Ms. Martineau? Any redirect, Mr. Patlack?" the judge asked.

Luis's mother declined to question the witness.

"Not at this time, Your Honor," Patlack said, "though I may call Ms. Snyder in rebuttal, depending on how much longer Mr. Knightley wants to delay the inevitable."

This sniping also seemed to amuse the judge, while Sid wondered if Luis would ever laugh again.

"I'll delay the inevitable," the judge said, pushing out of his high-backed chair. "We'll take a short recess before I hear closing arguments."

"All rise!"

The room got to its collective feet, the judge left, and Mac's arms came around Sid.

"We're good, Sidonie," he whispered fiercely in her ear. "If you'll trust me, we've got this. Luis isn't going anywhere."

She didn't comprehend his words, but his tone—confident, emphatic, *battle ready*—got through to her.

"What do you have up your sleeve, MacKenzie?"

"Do you trust me?"

He could ask her that, after the way she'd treated him? "Yes, I trust you with my life and with my son. I've been meaning to apologize, but, MacKenzie—"

He kissed her into silence. "I have to talk to Trent. The judge could come back on the bench at any moment."

Trent did not look confident. He was talking quietly with Luis and Luis's mother, his expression grave. Mac interrupted, pulled Trent aside, and started talking. James joined them, his expression as serious as Sid had ever seen it, and then Mac motioned for Hannah to join them.

Sid greeted Luis's mother and tried to exchange pleasantries, but that was like trying to ignore the proverbial pink elephant—a lame, bleeding pink elephant.

She moved down the table and hunkered across from Luis. "How you holding up?"

"I was worried."

"And now you've given up?"

"Nope. Now those four are smiling, and it's Ms. Snyder who'd better be worried." Luis gestured to Mac,

Trent, James, and Hannah, and damned if the boy wasn't right: all four lawyers were smiling.

What the hell could that mean? What the hell could that possibly mean?

———∿∿∿———

"Gentlemen, you will make your arguments brief in the interests of judicial economy." The judge cast a meaningful glance at the clock, but Trent was on his feet.

"My apologies, Your Honor, but I have at least one more witness, possibly two before the conclusion of my case. I'd call MacKenzie Knightley as my next witness."

Before the judge could grumble, Mac was sworn in, his expression calm as he took the seat in the witness box.

Sid tried to muster some confidence—Mac had said to trust him, and she did. Despite misunderstandings, despite cold feet, despite the odds, despite the sheer impossibility of the situation, she trusted MacKenzie Knightley.

No, she thought, her throat constricting with unshed tears. She *loved* MacKenzie Knightley. Loved how he didn't waste words, loved how he touched her. She loved his commitment to his clients, even as she wished he had a different calling. She loved how he dealt with Luis, straightforward but caring. She loved how he looked after his brothers, and how they did the same for him.

She loved—oh, God, did she ever love—how he made love to her, with her, his whole heart and soul in every touch.

On the witness stand, Mac was relaxed, at ease, and somehow in command of the room despite the judge sitting two feet higher to his right.

"Mr. Knightley, how do you know Luis Martineau?" Trent's question was brisk and impersonal.

"I board two horses on the farm where Luis lives. Luis has their regular care, and he does a d—darned fine job with them."

"Are you acquainted with his foster mother?"

"I am well acquainted with Ms. Sidonie Lindstrom."

"Were you present when Ms. Snyder made her initial visit to the premises?"

"I was."

"Did you hear Ms. Snyder indicate that the reason the foster care license was in jeopardy had to do with outdoor plumbing? I'm simply asking what you heard, Mr. Knightley."

"Plumbing was the *only* factor Ms. Snyder mentioned. She did not mention income in any way, shape, or form, which was unfortunate. I could have easily cleared up her misunderstanding. Her *mistake*."

Patlack tossed down his pen and leaned back to whisper again with the supervisor. Did those people feel a tenth of the anxiety Luis did when the case tilted away from their preferred outcome?

"What response have you observed to the criticism regarding outdoor plumbing?" Trent asked.

"I explained to Ms. Snyder that I was raised in the immediate area, and the, uh, facility at the back of the hog house had not been used in my lifetime. She ignored that information, but I've been to the farm many times since that discussion. The hog house has been razed in its entirety. A vegetable garden has been put in on the same site, and the tomatoes are coming along nicely."

Stevens's lips twitched, but his voice was stern.

"Counsel for the child will note that a vegetable garden is not a paying job."

Mac turned to face the judge, his expression diabolically angelic. "Ms. Lindstrom can have one of those too, Your Honor."

"Explain, Mr. Knightley."

"As Your Honor no doubt knows, I am the managing partner at the Hartman and Whitney law firm, and as such, I can testify to the fact that we've offered Ms. Lindstrom a job as our head of human resources. She has a Wharton MBA, plenty of applicable experience, and she interviewed well. The position takes somebody who can stand up to a passel of lawyers who are sometimes obstreperous. She did that exceedingly well. I have a copy of the offer letter with me, if you'd like to enter it in the record."

Sid nearly bellowed her incredulity. She didn't want the damned job, but she *did* want to leap the railing and kiss MacKenzie long and hard, until she heard the next words out of his mouth.

"I doubt she'll take the job, though."

The judge's lips thinned. "Why would she turn down the job that allows her to keep Mr. Martineau where counsel would have me believe Mr. Martineau belongs?"

"Because she's getting a better offer, though she could in theory accept both."

"I'll drop the other shoe, Mr. Knightley: What is this better offer?" the judge asked.

"If Ms. Lindstrom accepts this offer, the result will be the addition of an immediate, substantial income to her household, but Ms. Snyder never inquired into household finances at all, or she'd have to have interviewed me as well."

What on earth was Mac up to? Luis's future hung in the balance, Sid's *heart* hung in the balance, and MacKenzie was playing courtroom games.

"Stop being coy, Mr. Knightley. A boy's happiness is at stake."

Damned right, Your Honor.

Mac shifted his gaze from the judge, to Trent, to Luis, and finally to Sidonie herself. Sid heard him over a faint roaring in her ears, though it sounded as if Mac spoke to her alone. The intensity of his gaze suggested he saw only her.

"My happiness is at stake as well, Your Honor. I am asking Sidonie Lindstrom to be my wife. I am asking her to live with me, to raise with me such children as God or the foster care system might give us, to let me provide for her and for our family, to make my family hers, and to share our joys and sorrows for the rest of our lives. I am promising her my love, my fidelity, all my worldly goods, if she'll just say yes. And, Sid? If you want me to quit the damned job, I'll do it happily. Trent and James are big boys now, they don't need me riding herd on them quite as much, and they said I could."

He beamed at her, a big, happy, thoroughly un-MacKenzie-like smile that lit up the whole room. The judge smiled, Luis and his mom were smiling, the deputies, the clerk, the court reporter—even Patlack was trying to stifle a grin.

While Amy Snyder tapped furiously on her SmartPad.

The judge banged his gavel. "In light of Mr. Knightley's testimony, I'm continuing this matter for thirty days until such time as the Department is prepared for the court to hear the issue of permanency. Luis, you

stay right where you are, and keep an eye on the love-
birds. I'll expect a full recounting of the nuptials at the
next hearing."

"All rise!" the bailiff barked. "Circuit Court for
Damson County is now in recess."

Around Sid, two-dozen people got to their feet and
gathered up their effects. Luis pounded Trent on the
back and high-fived James. Mrs. Martineau admonished
Luis gently in French, while the DSS supervisor hissed
an admonition to Amy Snyder to be prepared to staff the
case immediately after lunch.

A few minutes later, Mac lowered himself beside Sid.

He had so many different silences. Tender, considering, thunderous, amused. He could say more without
speaking than anybody Sid knew, but he had spoken up
for her today, for her and Luis.

"Thank you." She shredded a tissue in her lap. Where
had it come from? "Thank you for everything. Did you
mean it?"

"The part about quitting the practice of law?"

"Not that. I've told you, I know you're a good
lawyer." A lawyer who'd hold hands with her right in
front of the judge. "The other part."

Mac settled against the hard bench, resting his arm
along the back. "The part about making a very comfortable income?"

Sid needed another tissue, and she needed that air-
sickness bag, so great was her internal upheaval. "Not that.
The 'same household' stuff, the raising kids, that part."

"The part about will you marry me? Be my best
friend, my lover, my wife, my partner in all things?
That part?"

Worry played a role in the chaos of Sid's emotions, as did towering relief and a fat helping of sheer disbelief. Beneath all of those feelings, though, a seed of hope had sprouted. Stubborn, vigorous, joyous hope.

"MacKenzie, you had better not have been lying under oath."

"I was telling the truth, the whole truth, and nothing but the truth. Sidonie Lindstrom, will you marry me?"

Two thoughts collided in Sid's tired brain. The first was that a proposal in a courtroom, under oath, was a fitting irony. The second had her turning loose of Mac's hand.

"I'm going to be sick." She bolted to her feet and dashed to the door.

Chapter 19

"I KNOW IT'S AWKWARD HAVING TO CHASE THEM."
James hauled Mac off the bench by the arm. "But
we're supposed to enjoy chasing our women all over
creation. It's the caveman thing. What are you waiting
for? You just proposed to the woman, and she took off
on you."

"I love you, James," Mac said, "but Sid is not you.
She doesn't scamper off to make me chase her. She
needs a minute to gather her composure. She won't go
far, because Luis is here with us."

"You think I do that? Run off to get you to follow
after?" James's frown became a scowl.

"I think you *did* that, until Vera outsmarted you. I want
to introduce myself to Luis's mother before the guards
finish putting her jewelry back on and whisk her away."

And Mac wanted to hear Sidonie accept his proposal,
but the fool woman had probably been hitting the caffeine again.

Mac brushed past his baby brother, hoping he'd
correctly read Sid's abrupt departure. He hadn't
come to court today intending to propose in front
of his entire adult family, Luis, God, the Honorable
Paul Stevens, half the Department of Social Services,
and the courtroom staff, but he'd trusted the prodding
of instinct.

Sid deserved a public declaration, particularly a

declaration under oath, that he'd quit practicing law, because she'd believe words he spoke under oath.

Or would she?

Mac waited—in vain—for Sid to come back into the courtroom while Luis introduced him to Mrs. Martineau.

"You will tell her?" Mrs. Martineau was asking. She shot a glare at her son, then turned pleading eyes on Mac.

"I beg your pardon?"

"You will tell Miss Sidonie to adopt this stubborn, proud boy who is getting so tall I cannot spank sense into him anymore?"

Another fierce woman, also honorable where her children were concerned. "You want Sid to adopt Luis?" Mac asked.

"Of course I want this. She loves my son, I cannot be the mother Luis needs now, and we will make agreements about visits and so forth. Sidonie brings Luis to see me whenever he asks. But Luis does not come to see me because I scold him."

The look she gave Luis held more love and frustration than Mac was comfortable observing.

"You are so stubborn, Luis. I will always be your mother, and I will always love you. The girls know I am their mother too. You cannot change what has happened to them by being difficult now. Better you let Sidonie and Mr. Knightley adopt you."

The guards gave Mac an apologetic glance, signaling that their time was up.

"I love you, Mama." Luis brushed a kiss to his mother's cheek without embracing her. "I will write to you."

"Thank you, Mr. Knightley, for what you did for my son." She stepped away and held still while the guards fastened her ankle bracelets. "And, Luis, you eat your vegetables. You're still growing, and the chips will only make you fat."

"Yes, Mama."

Head held high, she let the guards each take her by an arm and lead her away.

"That is quite a woman," Mac said.

Luis's lips quirked into a sad smile. "That was quite a proposal. Did Sid accept?"

"She will." Wherever she was. "I hope."

"Better buck up," Hannah said from the bench beside Sid. "Mac's spotted you, and you are doomed."

He came striding up the courthouse corridor as confidently as a shark cut through tropical waters.

While Sid felt wobbly as hell. Time to swear off caffeine for all eternity. "I'm not doomed, but Mac and I have things to talk about."

Hannah kissed her cheek and stood. "Welcome to the family. Resistance is futile."

Sidonie certainly hoped so. She got to her feet and hefted her bag. "Hannah, my thanks for the tissues and the moral support and everything. If you'll excuse me, I have a foster son to collect and tomatoes to weed and résumés to send out and—"

Mac walked right up to her. "And a proposal to accept."

Hannah pushed Sid's hair back over her shoulder. "Three flower girls and their mamas will be upset with you if you don't accept. So will two handsome maids of honor."

Hannah strolled off, taking her husband by the hand

as he emerged from the courtroom, leaving Sid nose to nose with the man she…needed to talk to.

"One of my brothers will give you away if Luis won't," Mac said, slipping his arms around Sid. "The other will stand up with me. Something tells me you want to talk this over first."

"Mac, you don't have to do this." Not what Sid had meant to say.

"Hush. We deserve more privacy than the hallowed halls of the world's busiest gossip mill." He led her outside the building to a day Sid could now appreciate as one of the best western Maryland could offer. Spring spreading her peacock feathers, in the profusion of blooming red and white tulips in the courtyard, the flowering cherries that scented a soft breeze, the gentle strength of the sunshine.

Mac escorted her to a bench in dappled shade, then sat beside her, keeping their hands joined.

Sid tried to memorize the moment. The strength and warmth of Mac at her side, the shadows dancing over the pavement, the breeze teasing the blossoming trees. Such a beautiful day. Such an important moment.

"MacKenzie, as much as I might want to, I cannot accept a proposal made simply to prevent Luis from being sent to Baltimore." Sid was proud of her level tone, proud of her honesty.

So proud she'd start bawling any moment.

"Sid, I wouldn't want you to accept an expedient proposal. Luis is a good kid and deserves a loving family, but I would not expect you to marry just any guy whose income would allow you to keep your license. You deserve more than that. Better than that."

"Explain yourself." She hadn't meant to sound annoyed, but she knew how Mac's mind worked, and he'd make his point in his own good time. "Explain yourself, please."

"I did not have to propose to you in that courtroom, Sid." He brought her knuckles to his lips and kissed them. So fractured was Sid's focus, it was as if he kissed some other woman's hand. "The job offer from Hartman and Whitney was enough to back DSS off."

"I don't think the Department was the enemy. I think it was Amy Snyder, breaking rules and misrepresenting the case to her superiors."

"Interesting we should reach the very same conclusion, but off topic."

Sid thought about retrieving her hand, but Mac kept stroking his fingers over her knuckles, and his touch was…good. Soothing.

"What is the topic, MacKenzie?" What day was it, for that matter?

"The topic is why I proposed, Sidonie Lindstrom." He did drop her hand, and Sid felt a stab of grief to lose even that small connection with him. Then he slid an arm around her shoulders.

"It is not enough that I can make you legally mine for Luis's sake," Mac said. "You are the woman I love, the woman I can't see spending the rest of my life without. I have to know you're mine in every sense, Sid. Mine and mine alone when it comes to a few important things. That was a proposal of marriage, not an offer to live together until you adopt Luis. That was my heart talking, not my law degree. That farm is the place where I can dream again, but I want us to share that dream, one that includes Luis, a pair of rings, and forever. Now you say yes."

Mac made the rest of his argument tenderly, his kiss offering comfort with a hint of seduction. He stroked Sid's jaw until he settled a hand around the back of her head, a warning and a solace.

Gently at first, he offered his kisses. *Hello, this is MacKenzie. Your MacKenzie.* Then Sid was opening her mouth for him and moaning softly against his lips.

"Now, Sidonie, you say yes."

She drew away half an inch. "I wronged you."

"And I wronged you, and we've both apologized. Maybe you overreacted, but I predict it won't be the first time we have to step back, regroup, and talk things through. Marriage isn't about legalities, Sidonie, it's about hearts. It's about love and commitment and years and years to keep polishing a relationship based on those good things."

"You'd adopt Luis?"

"This isn't about Luis, but yes. Of course I'd adopt him."

Mac was quiet. He'd made his closing argument, and it was unbeatable. *You are the woman I love, the woman I can't see spending the rest of my life without...*

Sid wanted to say yes, yes, and yes. "I can't have children, MacKenzie. I'll want to adopt."

He kissed her temple. "I took the foster parenting classes over in Wicks County last year without saying a word to my brothers. Had the house inspected, did the physical, the fingerprinting, everything. I didn't follow through. Children who've lost their families should have a mom and a dad if at all possible."

Oh, how she loved him. Loved his courage, his heart, *him*.

"You're wrong, you know." Now Sid held Mac's hand tightly. "The legalities matter, and sometimes in a good way. If Luis would let us..." She stumbled over the simple little word. *Us*. Two letters could hold a universe of dreams. "If Luis would let us adopt him, it would mean something."

"If you marry me, that will mean something too. If you want to live in sin, I'm willing to do that, but, Sidonie, I will hound you and harass you and wear you down until you marry me simply to keep the peace."

And Mac could hound with the best of them.

"I love you, MacKenzie, and, yes, I will marry you and share dreams with you and do all that other stuff you said. I will marry you gladly. I'm tired." She rested her head on his shoulder and closed her eyes, the beauty and peace of the day washing over her as she dozed off, right there beside the man she loved.

"Shouldn't we have a family meeting?"

Sid followed up her question by worrying a fingernail, so Mac gently extricated her finger from her teeth and kissed her palm.

"I won't lawyer something this important, Sid. Luis is out in the barn grooming Luna, and that's a good place to have a tough discussion. Court is next week, and we've run out of time."

Sid was still worried. Mac loved her for worrying, and yet he hated the worry itself. "Come along, Wife."

She looked sheepishly pleased, as she did every time he called her that.

"I don't know what to say to him." Sid slipped her hand into Mac's, something else that seemed to please her.

"I think it's more a matter of listening than talking."

He hoped so, but it wasn't as if they'd stop loving Luis if he refused to let them adopt him. Still, this mattered to Sid, who had more lawyering tendencies than she wanted to admit, so it mattered to Mac.

"How are my favorite mares?" Mac had to tug Sid up the barn aisle as he put the question to Luis.

"Time to put them on night turnout, I think." Luis pushed his hair out of his eyes. God in heaven, the boy was shooting up. "They stand in the shade for most of the afternoon anymore, and it's getting hot."

"We want to adopt you, Luis." Mac kept his voice quiet and reached out to Luna, who had decided of all humans, MacKenzie Knightly belonged to her. The therapeutic riding school had been happy to surrender her into Mac's care, and the draft mares seemed to like her too.

"I can't let you adopt me," Luis said, misery in every line of his body. He led the pony to her stall, slowly, because Luna was still none too spry.

"Suppose you tell us why that is," Mac said, "because I heard your mother badgering you in two languages to get yourself adopted by Sid."

Luis shook his head and ducked into the draft mare's stall, so Mac plowed onward. "This has to do with Tony, doesn't it?"

The kid froze as if he'd taken an arrow in the back.

"You might as well tell us, Luis," Sid said. "Tony is

dead, and nothing you say can hurt him. Nothing you say will make us love you any less, either."

Luis stayed in the stall, which was dimly lit. "You can't love me."

"We do." Sid's voice was firm. "We always will, and there's nothing you can do about it."

"You should hate me."

Buttercup nudged at the boy's back pocket.

"Why, Luis?" Mac asked.

"Tony might still be alive—shit." Luis leaned against Buttercup's thick neck. "Tony was drinking the day he died. He said some crazy things."

Sid's expression was startled, not disbelieving. "Crazy things, Luis, like he was going to kill himself? End it before things got too bad? Those crazy things?"

Luis looked at her without lifting his head from the horse's neck. "Things exactly like that."

"He said the same crazy things to me, regularly." Sid dropped Mac's hand and moved to the open stall door. "He would tell me his suicide plans, get them off the Internet, and trade them with his friends like dessert recipes. It was ghoulish and unworthy of him."

"He said the *same things* to you?"

"Sometimes, but I'd yell at him, pull the guilt card, and he'd settle down. I think he was mostly looking for reassurance that I still wanted him around. Besides, his death wasn't ruled a suicide."

Sid said that as if she was simply stating fact, not rehashing a painful chapter of her past.

"But he was drinking," Luis protested. "He came around after school, before you got home, and I could smell the beer on him. He was drinking, and really down, and I could have taken his k-keys..." Luis squeezed his eyes shut and leaned hard into the horse. "But I didn't. I didn't take his keys. I didn't call you or Thor. I told him to take care and try to lighten up."

The boy started to cry soundlessly, his shoulders shaking, his thin body bowed into the horse's bulk, a corporeal study in anguish. This was worse than if Tony had made a pass at the kid, or let one of his friends proposition Luis. Worse, and entirely unnecessary.

"Luis, you didn't kill Tony." Mac emphasized each word and spoke slowly. "The pathology reports from the accident would have revealed if he were drinking, and he was not." Sid gave a quick nod of affirmation. "I've done enough DUIs and DWIs that I know this. Trust me."

"He's right." Sid put a hand on Luis's shoulder and kept it there. "Tony couldn't drink, because it screwed up his meds. He was starting to black out, though. Thor didn't tell me that until after the funeral, because Thor wouldn't take Tony's keys either. He knew I would have if I'd known."

"Tony was blacking out?" Luis sounded pathetically hopeful. He straightened and stroked a hand down Buttercup's shoulder.

"The meds he was on did screwy things to his blood pressure, and he wasn't always careful about what he took when." Sid slid an arm around Luis's shoulders. "The beer would have been nonalcoholic, Luis. He and Thor had agreed to that much. Mac is right. As much as the insurance company was trying to prove Tony killed himself, they would have leaped on any trace of alcohol in his veins."

Luis folded away from the horse to wrap his arms around Sid. He dropped his head to her shoulder and cried openly, bringing tears to Mac's eyes as well.

"You had nothing to do with Tony's death," Sid said. "Tony was sick. Very sick, and not going to get better. In all the times he hinted about suicide, he never once said he'd drive himself to death. It wasn't your fault, Luis. It was not your fault."

"So he's willing to be adopted?" Trent sat beside Sid on the porch swing, pushing them in a lazy summer rhythm with one foot.

"He is, thank God."

"Then congratulations are in order. If it's all right with you, Hannah would like to handle the pleadings."

Hannah? Fitting somehow, because each of the brothers had taken on an adoption for a sibling already, though adopting Vera's daughter would take James some time.

"I would be very pleased to have Hannah do this for us," Sid said.

They fell silent, but Trent's quiet wasn't as restful to Sid as Mac's, or as easy to translate. He brought the swing to a halt and rose.

"Is Mac around somewhere?" he asked.

"Out in the barn. It's like he can't take his eyes off Luis for fear the kid will disappear before we can get through the legalities."

"Maybe. Maybe he wants Luis to know his parents won't disappear." Trent scratched an itch between his shoulder blades on one of the porch posts, the same way Daisy and

Buttercup scratched themselves on obliging tree trunks. "James said he talked to you about the day our father died."

Sid kept her seat, not familiar enough yet with her brother-in-law to read his expression. "He did, and so has Mac. I cannot imagine a harder day for your family."

"Or for me."

"Why do you say that?"

He turned his back to her. Across the barnyard, Bojangles pounced on something in the weeds near the fence.

"I was supposed to put the damned roll bars back on that tractor. I wanted to paint them the same red as the tractor, though. They were sitting in the carriage house, still a rusty white when Dad died."

This again? "Your dad, who'd farmed his entire life, couldn't have bolted those roll bars on the tractor himself, had no other tractors on the property, and didn't know better than to plow rocky ground on a vintage tractor without its roll bars?"

Trent studied her for a few minutes but said nothing, so Sid got up and stood beside him.

"Blaming ourselves is a way to stay connected to someone who's gone. I know that now. It's a way to get into that nice, cozy coffin with the deceased and shut out the world. I had to figure this out before I could marry your brother. I ranted about Mac's reticence regarding his profession, I fretted over Luis's situation, but part of what nailed my emotional feet to the floor was simply a lack of courage. Shoving grief aside takes as much courage as enduring it does."

Before she could say more, James's black SUV came bumping up the lane.

Twyla, Vera's daughter, hopped out, barreling across the yard, followed by Vera and James.

"I asked James to come by and join Mac and me on a walk," Trent said. "I'm not sure why he brought reinforcements."

"They come bearing brownies," Sid said. "Don't complain. Hullo, Twy."

"Hi, Aunt Sid. We made brownies!" As if making brownies didn't happen at James and Vera's as often as doing a load of whites. "Dad wants to take a walk with the uncs."

School had been out for more than a week, and Sid kept all three nieces for most of each weekday. She still lit up inside every time she laid eyes on her nieces, and Luis's resumption of the role of big brother had been wonderful to watch.

Wonderful and sad.

"Let's find some milk to wash down our brownies," Sid said. "James, greetings. Vera, the party is in the kitchen today."

"We had lunch in the tree house last week," Twyla reported, taking Sid and Vera each by a hand. "There were bugs, though. Uncle Mac said next time we should wait until it snows to have lunch outside."

"That's because Uncle Mac had to figure out how to get the cooler up the tree," Sid said. "Trent and James, Mac is in the barn. Enjoy your walk."

She let Vera and Twy take the brownies inside, but waited on the porch until she saw all three brothers walking slowly, side by side, in the direction of the north pasture.

When Sid joined the ladies in the kitchen, Twyla

turned a curious gaze on her. "Mom wants to know when you're going to tell Uncle Mac about the baby."

--- ∿ ---

"Did you enjoy your walk?" Sid positively cuddled against Mac, in a way she hadn't before they'd married.

"Enjoy isn't quite the right word. I appreciated it. I appreciate my brothers." Mac propped his chin on her crown. "That walk was overdue."

Overdue. He'd used the word advisedly, hoping his new wife would confide in him. He understood completely why she wouldn't: she was afraid to hope, just as she'd been afraid to trust. But not, by God, afraid to love.

"Sidonie?" He kissed the side of her neck, which had her snuggling yet closer in the broad light of day right in the middle of the kitchen, such were the blessings of holy matrimony. "I can count to twenty-eight."

"Hmm?" She lipped his ear lobe as her hands slipped down around his backside.

"I said, I can count to twenty-eight, my love. Married men develop the knack. Isn't there something you want to tell me, but haven't, because you're trying to protect me from being disappointed if you can't carry to term?"

She went from twining herself around him like a randy vine of ivy to clutching at him in shock.

"How did you know?" Sid planted her forehead on Mac's chest, which meant he could not see her eyes. But then, he didn't need to.

"I caught you crying yesterday when the mares played tag with Luis. Then too, Trent and James have been nudging each other each time they see you."

"Hold me."

He held her, he waited, and he thanked God for the miracles that had recently deluged his life. "You scared, honey?"

She nodded.

"You'll make a wonderful mother, and the baby will be fine."

She relaxed. "This wasn't supposed to be possible."

"Maybe one or both of us healed what was ailing us." The phone rang, cutting off his litany of comfort. He reached for it over Sid's shoulder.

"Knightleys'."

The call was from Social Services—perfect timing, as usual—but Mac listened in silence and had to revise his opinion.

"I think you want to speak with my wife." He handed her the phone and stepped away. They could celebrate in private at length—they had *so much* to celebrate— later. Mac fished out his car keys, mentally mapping a shopping route.

He would love having a pregnant wife, except Sid was shaking her head as she held the phone to her ear. By degrees, her expression clouded, which wasn't at all what Mac had expected.

"I'll have to ask you to hold. I need a minute."

She covered the mouthpiece with her hand. "This is awful. This is just—do you know why they're calling?"

"I got the gist of it, yes."

"You left it to me to tell them we can't take Luis's sisters? I can't—this is just—those poor girls. Luis will never forgive us if we tell the Department no. To think, their foster parents are divorcing when the girls were expecting adoption. And then to toss a pair of perfectly adorable little girls back into the system as if they were—I cannot deal with this."

Mac threw his keys into the air and caught them. "Can too. When you're done with your phone call, we have places to go."

Sid's eyes filled with tears—she would be a weepy sort of pregnant wife, apparently. Mac mentally added tissues to their shopping list.

"I am very disappointed in you, MacKenzie. They aren't puppies, they're children, and if you think it's easy for me to turn my back on them just because we might have a child—"

He plucked the phone from Sid's hand. "You will have to excuse us now. My wife and I are going shopping. We'll be picking up twin beds, a doll house, at least two ponies, possibly a dog, tissues, an aquarium, an entire library of horse books, a sturdy piano, probably a bunny or two before my brothers try to pull that maneuver, an entire nursery set for a child of either gender, and a hammock for parents only. We'll figure out the rest when you get those girls where they should have been all along."

He hung up the phone, soundly kissed the mother of his children, and bellowed for Luis over Sid's squeals of happiness. And later—not too much later—they did, indeed, celebrate their good fortune at great and glorious length.

Read on for an excerpt from *A Kiss for Luck*, a Sweetest Kisses novella

SIZE IS NOT IMPORTANT.

Sadie Delacourt knew better than to put stock in breed prejudices, though the canine panting at her from across the breezeway was a mastiff/rottweiler cross, as homely as it was substantial.

"Know any Baskervilles?" she asked the dog, shifting a bag of groceries to dig for her keys. "I bet you get that a lot."

The dog was jet-black, had a fine set of teeth, and was not smiling that Sadie could tell.

"I see you have a collar and tags," Sadie went on in her best nice-poochie tones. "That suggests you also have an irresponsible owner, who's probably worried sick that his little friend has gone for a romp to devour helpless single women too stupid to find their keys."

The dog cocked its head, a disarmingly human gesture.

"Move to Damson Valley, they said," Sadie muttered as she groped around in the bottom of her purse. "Everybody's friendly in Damson Valley. Great schools, not much crime. You probably eat anybody dumb enough to be on the streets after sundown, don't you?"

The sharp edge of an apartment key greeted Sadie's index finger.

The dog rose from its haunches, and fear dripped acid

into Sadie's veins as she extracted her keys from amid wallet, hairbrush, unpaid bills, mints, pens, toothbrush, water bottle, vegan granola bar (she could resist those most easily), and notebooks.

"Too late to ignore you," Sadie said, because that was the safety protocol with a stray dog. Look away, stay cool, drop what you're holding in case the dog is attracted to it.

"You're not attracted to high-quality toilet paper, are you? Orange and spice tea? Organic whole milk?"

The key did not want to go into the lock, and the dog's toenails clicking on the concrete told Sadie the Baskerville's missing pup was the curious sort.

Screaming might alarm the dog, and Sadie doubted she could have mustered a scream in any case. Just as a cold, whiskery, nose-kiss hit the back of Sadie's knee, the key slipped into the tumblers. She wedged purse and groceries aside, twisted the lock, and was about to push open the door to her new apartment when a male voice stopped her.

"Baby, what the devil do you think you're doing? Stop right there, or you'll be sorry."

───◆───

Moving was second only to death of a loved one in terms of creating stress, apparently for dogs as well as humans.

"You come here right now, young lady," Gideon went on, using his stern-papa impersonation. "You know better, and I'm ashamed of you."

The petite redhead with the groceries froze, probably terrified out of her wits by a two-hundred-pound canine Welcome Wagon.

"You're addressing your dog?" she asked, hiking her groceries onto her hip.

"My naughty dog," Gideon said, keeping his tone disapproving, because Baby knew how to work those big brown eyes. She'd gone butt-down onto the concrete, aiming her doggie version of the "please don't let him take my squeaky toy" look at the woman.

"Could you possibly ask your naughty dog to sit somewhere else?"

The lady's voice shook, suggesting Baby was about to get her owner sued.

"Baby, come."

Up she did get, across the breezeway she did amble, head down, as if reluctant to part from her new friend. Damned beast should have been in pictures.

"Park it, dog."

Baby sat with an air of martyred resignation and turned her gaze on the woman, whose arms had to be tired by now from lugging those groceries.

"May I help you with those?" Gideon offered. "I'm Gideon Granville, and I'll be moving in here at the end of the week. Baby has never hurt a soul, unless you count the affronts to dignity suffered by my partner's cat. The cat gets even, though."

The lady passed over a heavy bag of groceries and slumped against the brick wall beside her door.

"Once, when I was kid," she said, "I was playing at the park, and I went to the water fountain, same as I had a hundred times before. A golden retriever didn't like me getting a drink before him. I ended up with thirty-seven stitches and a phobia about big dogs."

She had bright red hair—none of that titian, auburn,

strawberry-blond equivocation—so her version of pale
made the freckles across the bridge of her nose stand
out. She was five-two or five-three, fine boned, and no
match for a big, territorial dog. Her shoulder bag was an
artful rendering of an English saddle, and she gripped
the strap as if it held her sanity together.

"I'm so sorry," Gideon said. "You're absolutely safe,
I promise you, but you look a tad rattled. Should we
get you out of this heat?" For western Maryland was
enjoying a late, ferocious St. Martin's summer.

The woman shot a glance at Baby, who was panting
across the breezeway and could probably do with a bowl
of water.

Though the dog had been known to drink good
English ale too.

"I'm Sadie Delacourt," the lady said, passing Gideon
her keys. "And when I'm scared, I shake. If you'd do
the honors?"

The private investigator in Gideon wanted to scold
her for allowing a strange bloke into her apartment,
particularly when she was off-kilter and maybe about
to faint.

The guy who'd spent half his life in Damson Valley
unlocked her door and waited for her to precede him
into the cool space within. That same guy—thirty-two
years old, single, and in excellent health—noted that
Miss Sadie Delacourt's figure did sweet things for her
Hawaiian-print board shorts and raspberry scrub top.

"You can't leave Baby out here," Miss Delacourt
said. "I doubt property management wants her tied to
the stair rails."

"Property management is how she got loose," Gideon

said, following Miss Delacourt inside. "I stopped by to pick up a key, and the building manager didn't close the door all the way. Baby, come."

The dog sprang to her feet, two hundred pounds of hairy, panting, tongue-lolling good cheer.

"She's well trained," Miss Delacourt observed as Baby joined them inside.

"I can only take credit for some of that," Gideon said, carrying the groceries into the galley kitchen. "She was found running loose at the truck stop, wearing a spike collar with the name Baby on it. People don't adopt big dogs, old dogs, or black dogs—it's called Black Dog Syndrome—so when I decided to get a dog, I went for the biggest, blackest, mature canine at the pound."

"I don't think I could do that," Miss Delacourt said, opening the fridge. "I couldn't leave all the other dogs behind. Would you like something to drink? I have cold water, lemonade, or iced mint tea."

Miss Delacourt had manners, also a lot of unpacking to do. Her apartment was a mirror image of the space Gideon had rented, a beige-carpeted rectangle chopped into a combined living room and dining room, galley kitchen, bathroom, a small bedroom, and a human-sized bedroom with attached second bathroom.

Both the living room and the larger bedroom would have tree-shaded balconies, and the complex backed up to the farmland bordering the town of Damson Valley. The last cutting of hay had come off in recent weeks, but some of the late corn remained, giving the valley a bucolic checkerboard beauty that reminded Gideon of Surrey.

"Lemonade would be delightful," Gideon said. "May I offer Baby some water?"

"If I can find something large enough for her to drink out of. I set up my studio first, and the rest of the place…"

Taped, labeled boxes sat on the floor, sofa, and on the dining-room table; ferns occupied the odd level surface—all of them healthy—and a mobile of stained-glass hummingbirds hung crookedly from a curtain rod, two of the birds entangled.

"The rest of the place will be there when you get to it," Gideon said. "Are you an artist?"

One box read "acrylics" and another "pastels," suggesting she was, but a competent private investigator should be as good at small talk as he was at observation and recall.

Miss Delacourt handed him a serving of lemonade in a mason jar and went back to stuffing salad fixings into her refrigerator.

"I test and design video games," she said, "but I also dabble in the studio arts. What about you?"

"I have a law degree," Gideon replied, which was true. Maybe because his dog had scared Miss Delacourt, but more likely because Gideon despised misrepresentation of any kind, he gave her the rest of the truth. "I abhor the whole suit-and-tie drill though. Did it for three years. 'Yes, Your Honor. No, Your Honor. May it please the court…' Courtroom attire, bar lunches… that's not what I do best. I'm litigation support now, fact-checking, investigating, document analysis. Longer hours, but my own hours."

More interesting hours too, and every bit as lucrative.

Miss Delacourt wrinkled a nose nobody would call cute, though Gideon liked the character in that nose.

He liked her green eyes too, liked the hint of caution in them, and the shadows that said despite her cordial manners, she valued her privacy.

"So much education only begins when the schooling is over." She produced a saucepan from inside her oven. "Baby can drink out of this."

While Miss Delacourt poured herself lemonade, Gideon filled the pan from the tap.

"Probably best if Baby drinks out on the porch. She's not the tidiest pup."

Baby rotated her floppy, silky ears at his mention of her name. She'd taken up residence directly under an AC vent, her expression relaxed and alert.

"Shall we join her?" Miss Delacourt asked. "I've been running around all day, and I chose this place in part for the big trees. Might as well enjoy them while the weather holds."

Making conversation with complete strangers was part of Gideon's job, and he was good at it. That he could enjoy a glass of lemonade on a pleasant fall afternoon with a pretty neighbor was a treat though, one he wouldn't have encountered were he staining floor boards in his summer kitchen.

So he settled with his lemonade on the concrete a few judicious feet away from the slurping dog, while Miss Delacourt took a seat on a bentwood rocker that had seen better days. The breeze in the nearby oaks had that dry, leaf-snatching autumnal quality, while the afternoon sun spread a benevolent warmth, and a wind chime tinkled on the next floor down.

Miss Delacourt took a sip of her lemonade, apparently inclined to enjoy a moment of quiet. Her toenails were painted in a Hawaiian palette—lime green, magenta, cyan.

Inside Gideon's back pocket, his phone buzzed. He should dump messages, review his email, and check in with Finn, because his partner was the fretful sort.

Instead, he took a sip of sweet, tart, cold lemonade, and for the first time in a long time, prepared to spend time with a woman for the sheer pleasure of her company.

~~~

Gideon Granville's speaking voice was as saturated with beauty as Sadie's shorts were saturated with color. And yet, like an element of a sketch deliberately off center, that Oxford purr made her look at him twice.

Faded blue jeans, a black T-shirt molded to a trim torso, and scuffed running shoes struck her as a failed attempt at camouflage. Gideon was a couple of inches over six feet—tall enough to catch a woman's eye across a crowded bar, not too tall to kiss.

What the hell, Delacourt. Too much country air?

"Are you from Maryland?" he asked, patting the concrete beside him.

"I'm most recently from Washington, DC," Sadie replied, because Damson Valley was a friendly place, and the question was reasonable from a prospective neighbor. "I'll have to commute into Adams Morgan from time to time, but my job can be done pretty much wherever I have my computers. What about you?"

The dog left off parting the Red Sea in the bottom of Sadie's double boiler and padded over to her owner. She flopped onto the concrete and put her damp chin on Gideon's thigh with an air of weary surrender.

"I was born in Surrey," he said, "which is very pretty, much like here. Green and kind to trees. My mum came over with my stepdad when I was sixteen, and this has been my home since."

Too bad for Surrey. Gideon was a handsome addition to the scenery, despite his nondescript clothing. Tousled dark hair; blue, blue eyes; and enough breadth of shoulder to suggest he worked out conscientiously.

And could move boxes.

"You didn't like the lawyer shtick?" Sadie's feeling about lawyers were mixed. Jay-Jay's lawyers she had liked, despite their exorbitant wages. Hollister's lawyers should have been disbarred and feathered.

"I liked lawyering fine when everything went according to plan, and the obvious scoundrel went to jail while the blameless victim was compensated for his troubles. That happened about once a year."

He pet his great hound with a slow, stroking caress to her shoulder, and while the dog's gusty sigh suggested she enjoyed it, Gideon seemed soothed by the contact too.

"And those few cases that followed the TV script took an entire year," Sadie added. "The wheels of justice grind slowly and often with a lot of squeaking."

"You're divorced, then?"

A reasonable conclusion, also a tad nosy, though if Gideon had checked out her left hand, Sadie hadn't caught him at it. He, however, *had* mentioned a partner.

"Never one time," Sadie said. "You?"

Still he stroked the dog's shoulder, much like Sam twitched at his favorite blankie as he fell asleep.

"Never found the lady who'd have me for the long term. This is very good lemonade."

Oh, right. If he'd zipped his jeans when Sadie walked into the men's bathroom by mistake, his evasion could not have been less subtle.

Which was fine with Sadie. A friendly neighbor she could use, a distraction, *not*.

"Squeezed the lemons this morning," she said, "before I went on my whirlwind tour of Damson Valley's lone grocery establishment. I didn't find the liquor store, though."

"Next to the post. Vineyard Street, opposite the college."

Which was on the northwest side of town, maybe. "Handy for the students. So what brings you to Damson Valley Apartments?"

"Renovations," Gideon said, sloshing the ice in his glass. "My farmhouse is at least 150 years old, and that takes a toll on a building. When I discovered some of the wiring was still wrapped in paper, I decided there's no time like the present to come up to code. That was in May."

"Renovations are like a medical diagnosis. A simple bellyache turns into six weeks in the hospital, the end of your life savings, and possibly the end of your job."

His rhythmic petting of the dog slowed. "You speak from experience?"

"Not direct experience. I take it winter's coming on, and your contractor hasn't given you a firm completion date?"

Sadie knew all about firm completion dates. Several of them had eluded her in the past year. That was another motivation for moving to Damson Valley— without distractions, she'd make faster progress toward her project goals.

"I also have rather a penchant for clean laundry and properly prepared food," Gideon replied. "Hard to come by those without proper wiring. Now I wonder if I should have found some obliging farmer to foster Baby over the winter. She needs her exercise."

"Get a doggie treadmill," Sadie suggested.

A small silence erupted, because Sadie had *done it again*, had solved a problem nobody had asked her solve. Jay-Jay had an entire lecture on Overfunctioning Is a Coping Skill.

Jay-Jay, whom Sadie should call.

"Hadn't thought of a doggie treadmill. Suppose it could work. I'd hate to part with my best girl for even a few months."

The shameless beast lifted her head from Gideon's thigh and licked his hand.

"I can see why," Sadie said, finishing her lemonade. Hollister would have liked Baby, until she had her first accident or splashed a single drop of her drinking water onto his Italian loafers.

"I noticed you bought salad ingredients," Gideon said, rising in one lithe movement. "I'm firing up the grill tomorrow night for the guys helping me move in. A salad would make the meal healthier, and a lady's presence would ensure Trenton Knightley's daughter had some company besides Baby."

Damson Valley had the reputation for being small-town affordable, rural-pretty, and bedroom-community convenient. In short, an ideal solution to a lot of Sadie's problems.

One of which had been an increasing sense of isolation in DC.

"How old is this daughter?"

"Merle's so high," Gideon said, holding his hand at about his waist. "The Knightley brothers will help me move. Trent is her dad. Mac and James are her uncles. Good fellows; hard workers too, but I get the sense a little girl is sometimes lost in the male shuffle amongst them."

Why was Gideon extending this invitation? If he was trying to pick Sadie up, he wouldn't ask her to join a testosterone party. Maybe he wanted a babysitter for the kid and the dog? If he was trying to be friendly...

Sadie would not recognize such an overture, no matter how sincere. That's what the last five years of living in the professional penguin rookery of DC had done to her.

"What time?" she asked.

"About five. I'm in 209, around the corner and down a level. Shall I leave you my cell number?"

Gideon had extended his hand to her. Sadie took the space of an awkward moment to realize he was offering to assist her to her feet. As if...

Not as if she were incapable of standing. As if— novel, bewildering concept—he were a gentleman, and she were a lady.

She put her hand in his and rose. "Salad, then, and maybe brownies if I can make enough headway with my unpacking."

Because this Merle kid sounded like she was about Sam's age, because grilled veggies were a treat not to be missed, because everybody could use a muscular neighbor from time to time.

Gideon squeezed her hand gently. "Thanks. See you then."

"Right. Apartment 209. Don't forget your pooch."

Baby had risen to sitting and had become an insistent, gentle pressure against Sadie's right leg. The dog's head just happened to be at ideally pet-able height, so Sadie obliged. Baby's coat was surprisingly soft, plush, and pleasurable to touch.

"She's a leaner," Gideon said. "She's also a lady of particulars. She must like you."

He winked, picked up the nearly empty water pot, and disappeared inside, his dog trailing after him. A moment later, Sadie heard the door close and followed her first guest into the apartment.

As she rinsed out glasses, Sadie was assailed by an emotion she didn't at first recognize. Her middle was not quite settled, her thoughts were hopping around, and yet she felt an inclination to smile.

She'd met a neighbor and through him would soon meet a few more locals, possibly even a friend for Sam.

She'd made small talk as she'd sat sipping lemonade on her porch—when had that *ever* happened before?

Her studio was set up, but she wasn't, for once, holed up with her computers, oblivious to everything except urgent bodily functions.

And Sadie had petted Baby as the dog had leaned against her leg, panting gently. Without even thinking, without worrying, Sadie had petted the biggest dog she could recall meeting.

Surely, surely that was an omen, and relocating to Damson Valley had been a smart move after all, for the emotion crowding against Sadie's ribs and burbling through her veins was none other than...*hope*.

"I hope you're grilling half a cow, Granville," MacKenzie Knightley said as he put down his end of the sofa. "I spent the morning shoeing fractious equines, and this afternoon wrangling your furniture. I'm as hungry as a bear in springtime."

At nearly six foot four, Mac was entitled to his appetites, and Gideon had passed peckish an hour ago.

"Whine, whine, whine," James Knightley sing-songed, following them in with a captain's chair rocker and nudging the door closed with his foot. He was the youngest of the three brothers, the only blond, and the family Don Juan. "Here's your rocking chair, old man. To heck with the cow. I could use a few cold ones."

"Somebody sent you flowers, Granville," Trenton Knightley said, peering out the dining-room window. He was the dad of the bunch, and as such, had an assistant in the task of wiring up Gideon's entertainment center.

"They're pretty," Merle, his daughter, added. She hopped off the desk and ran a zigzag pattern amid Gideon's furniture and boxes to the door. She opened the door before the bell had rung. "Are those for Gideon?"

Baby, not a creature who enjoyed upheaval, took to barking, but didn't leave Gideon's side.

"Stay," he commanded softly, for behind the colorful bouquet of zinnias, daisies, and asters stood a small red-haired woman in jeans, sandals, and a lime green T-shirt.

"I'll get these," Gideon said, taking the flowers and setting them on a speaker. "Please do come in, and perhaps Baby will cease rousing the watch."

"I'm Merle," Trent's daughter said. "Did you bring brownies?"

Baby disobeyed Starfleet orders and ambled over to sniff Sadie's knee, while Gideon put an arm around Sadie's shoulders. Cheeky of him, but his neighbor looked leery of joining the pandemonium that was Gideon's moving day.

"My friends, please welcome to the madhouse Miss Sadie Delacourt, late of 319 one floor up."

"I did bring brownies," she said, "also salad, vegetable shish kebabs, and some lemonade."

Sadie had a reusable green shopping bag looped over her wrist. James relieved her of it, though to Gideon, the point of the exercise was for James to nearly hold hands with Sadie in the process.

"I'm James Knightley. Pleased to meet you."

"My dad is putting together the stuff so I can watch my videos," Merle offered. "Do you like princess videos?"

"I do," Sadie said. "If they aren't violent."

"I'm Trenton Knightley." Unlike his scamp of a younger brother, Trent offered a proper handshake. "Always a pleasure to meet a woman packing brownies."

"Our older brother is MacKenzie Knightley," James said, waving a hand at Mac. "He's shy. I'm friendly."

"I'm hungry," Mac said, "and wondering what the lady will think of you, James, if you're hitting on her within thirty seconds of learning her name."

Quite the older brother, was Mac, though James merely grinned at the rebuke.

"I like lemonade," Merle chirped, "and flowers."

The bouquet was an interesting gesture, also visually out of place in an apartment done in Tidy-Bachelor neutral tones. That bouquet would draw the eye away from the brown leather sofa, the cream rug on the beige carpet, and the cream-and-brown drapes.

"The flowers should have another inch or two of water," Sadie said, "and I'll bet your kitchen isn't set up yet."

"Nothing is set up," Merle volunteered. "Uncle James said bad words when he tried to put the bed together."

"I apologized for the bad words," James chimed in, "but you're right. I didn't finish getting the frame up."

"I'll show you how it's done, Baby Brother." Mac took James by the arm. "I'm sure Merle is perfectly capable of guarding the brownies without your help, and Trent was grilling steak before you learned how to drive."

As Mac dragged his youngest brother down the hall toward the bedrooms, James aimed a smile in Sadie's direction. She was rummaging in her shopping bag, oblivious to James's flirting—or purposely ignoring it.

"You have something else in that bag?" Gideon asked.

"A sketch pad," she said, straightening with a small spiral-bound notebook in her hand. "Merle, you can draw pictures until your dad's done wiring up the equipment. Baby might like her portrait done."

Sadie passed over the sketch pad, a pencil, and an eraser. Merle took them, her expression suggesting she'd been entrusted with the scepter and orb of some princessly realm right in Gideon's very living room.

"Brilliant notion," Gideon observed as Merle took up a cross-legged seat before Baby's bed. "The dog's worn out from policing all the coming and going today, and Trent will make faster progress for having fewer interruptions."

"Where's Baby's water bowl?" Sadie asked.

In a sea of boxes, rolled up rugs, stray electronics, and camera equipment, Gideon saw no shiny silver bowl. Baby would drink from a clean potty if she were desperate, which wasn't much of an excuse for Gideon's oversight.

"Good question. Likely in a kitchen box."

As Sadie put his kitchen to rights—"Yes, you need shelf paper, Gideon, and, no, the bread can't sit out on the counter"—Gideon took a moment to lean on the doorjamb and enjoy a cold glass of lemonade.

"What's that look about?" Sadie asked as she snitched a lettuce leaf from the salad bowl. "Are you missing your farmhouse?"

Down the hall, Mac and James were engaged in an argument that, in the language of brothers, was a form of play. From the porch came the scent of good steak on the grill, and in the living room, both dog and child were content in each other's company.

"My first plan for today was to ask Dunstan Cromarty to help me move. He's another lawyer, a Scot with a work ethic that won't quit. We trade that type of chore, but his back has been bothering him."

"He's a friend?" Sadie asked, passing Gideon an inch-square serving of gooey, dark-chocolate confection.

"Of a sort. We both have funny accents, though his is much harder to understand than mine."

A standing joke between them. Cromarty was one of the most competent and ferocious litigators in Damson County, though Gideon wondered if he weren't also one of the loneliest.

"A comrade, then. You have things in common, but don't pry uninvited. If anybody sees you with that

brownie, Granville, you'll never hear the end of it."
Sadie took the brownie from his hand and held it up to
his mouth.

The scent alone was decadent, particularly on an
empty stomach. Gideon nibbled, then took the whole
brownie into his mouth. Soft, warm, sweet, rich *heaven*
greeted his palate.

"Good," he managed. "Very good. You're not to give
the recipe to anybody but me."

Sadie stood before him, petite and considering, and his words took on a significance he hadn't
intended—consciously.

She stepped back and resumed tossing the salad. "So
the Knightley brothers are your B team?"

"My C team. When I struck out with Dunstan, I asked
my partner, Finn, but he's hot on a case that involves
weekend work. I was at the law library, on the phone
to a moving company, when MacKenzie overheard me.
The Knightleys offered."

"That surprised you," Sadie said, helping herself to
a whole black olive from the salad. "Would you have
helped them?"

"I have. We work together a fair amount, profession-
ally, but I've also done the occasional weekend project
with each of them. For all he impersonates a tramp,
James knows everything about renovating old houses,
and his brothers are handy too."

A tea towel bearing a damp, wrinkled list of Scottish
dialect terms was draped over Sadie's left shoulder. She
looked good in Gideon's little kitchen—comfortable,
competent, and at home.

"One of your parents drank?" she asked.

The sense of her question took a moment to sink in. "I beg your pardon?"

"You're not at ease with garden-variety friendship. You're self-sufficient to a fault, and yet everybody likes you. You have excellent people-radar but are at sea in relationships. You're observant, even hypervigilant, and yet your own emotional landscape is terra incognito to you. Adult Child of an Alcoholic, or ACOA."

Gideon had wanted to like Sadie Delacourt, which realization came as something of a surprise. Yes, he also wanted to shag her, in a stray dog, passing sense—his sex life drifted in a permanent state of benign neglect—but mostly, he'd wanted to like her.

He did not like being reduced to an acronym and a Google search.

"Sorry," she said, tossing the salad as if it had committed a mortal sin. "Didn't mean to armchair-analyze a near stranger. I do best if I stick with my games and graphics. I'll write down the brownie recipe before I leave, and Merle can keep the sketch pad. I don't get out much—though my sister can tolerate my company—and this whole small town, bucolic…I guess I'm more tired than I knew."

The part of Gideon that could skip trace a deadbeat dad through thin air, locate missing heirs two continents away, and catch straying spouses with their pants literally around their ankles tried to keep him pinned to the doorjamb.

The part of him that was homesick for his half-destroyed farmhouse, that had adopted a too-big stray dog, and had been surprised to have help moving, crossed the kitchen and snagged a bite of radicchio.

Sadie had given up flailing at the salad, and yet she

stood before the salad bowl, head down, staring a hole
in a bunch of leafy greens. Gideon studied her earrings,
swirly blue-green malachite and gold dangles. Pretty
and doubtless one of kind.

She arranged the salad tongs against the side of the
wooden bowl, a laying down of culinary arms. This
close, Gideon could catch some summery, flowery
scent from her and *feel* how small she was—also how
badly she wanted to pack up and leave, possibly never
to return.

All that mortification over a question that had been
awkward, but courageous rather than rude.

"Was it your mum or your dad who drank?" Gideon
had kept his voice down—the Brothers Knightley were
all loose on the premises somewhere, to say nothing of
Merle.

Even Sadie's earrings were still.

"Both."

That single word, coupled with the way she braced
herself against the counter, suggested anger, consternation, and possibly even relief to have shared this miserable, defining bit of truth.

Gideon slid an arm across Sadie's shoulders, lest she
resume mauling the lettuce.

"No alcoholics in my family," he said. "My dad had
cancer. Took him seven years, two remissions, and a
whole lot of experimental trials to die. I was six when
he was diagnosed."

A breath went out of her. She sagged against him, as if
she'd dodged a bullet. Maybe Gideon had surprised her.

He'd certainly surprised himself.

The brownies were arranged in a tower of decadent

pleasure on a red serving dish. Gideon found a small one and offered it to his neighbor. Sadie bit off half; he took the remainder, and for the space of a single bite of chocolate, they stayed like that, not quite embracing, but closer than either had planned on being.

Return to You

A Montgomery Brothers Novel

by Samantha Chase

New York Times and *USA Today* Bestselling Author

—∿∿—

She will never forget their past...

He can't stop thinking about their future...

James Montgomery has achieved everything he'd hoped for in life...except marrying the girl of his dreams. After a terrible accident, Selena Ainsley left ten years ago. She took his heart with her, and she's never coming back. But it's becoming harder and harder for him to forget their precious time together, and James can't help but wonder what he would do if they could ever meet again.

—∿∿—

What readers are saying about Samantha Chase:

"Samantha Chase really knows how to tell a story."

"Perfect romance! Love it, love it, love it!"

For more Samantha Chase, visit:

www.sourcebooks.com

One Mad Night

by Julia London

New York Times and *USA Today* Bestselling Author

━━∿∿∿━━

Two Romantic Adventures

One winter's night a blizzard sweeps across the country, demonstrating that fate can change the course of lives in an instant…and fate has a sense of humor.

One Mad Night

Chelsea Crawford and Ian Rafferty are high-profile ad execs in cutthroat competition for a client. When a major winter storm puts New York City on lockdown, the two rivals have to make it through the night together.

The Bridesmaid

When the weather wreaks havoc with transportation systems, Kate Preston and Joe Firretti meet as they are both trying to rent the last car available… As Kate races to her best friend's wedding, and Joe races to a job interview, it looks like together is the only way they'll make it at all.

━━∿∿∿━━

Praise for Julia London:

"London knows how to keep pages turning… winningly fresh and funny." —*Publishers Weekly*

For more Julia London, visit:

www.sourcebooks.com

About the Author

New York Times and *USA Today* bestselling author Grace Burrowes hit the bestseller lists with her debut, *The Heir*, followed by *The Soldier*, *Lady Maggie's Secret Scandal*, *Lady Eve's Indiscretion*, *The Captive*, and *The Traitor*. All of her Regency and Victorian romances have received extensive praise, including several starred reviews from *Publishers Weekly* and *Booklist*. *The Heir* was a *Publishers Weekly* Best Book of 2010, *The Soldier* was a *Publishers Weekly* Best Spring Romance of 2011, and *Lady Sophie's Christmas Wish* won Best Historical Romance of the Year in 2011 from RT Reviewers' Choice Awards. *Lady Louisa's Christmas Knight* was a *Library Journal* Best Book of 2012, and *The Bridegroom Wore Plaid*, the first in her trilogy of Scotland-set Victorian romances, was a *Publishers Weekly* Best Book of 2012. *Darius*, the first in her groundbreaking Regency series The Lonely Lords, was named one of iBooks Store's Best Romances of 2013.

Grace is a practicing family law attorney and lives in rural Maryland. She loves to hear from her readers and can be reached through her website at graceburrowes.com.